NOBODY
KILLED
HER

SABYN JAVERI

SABYN JAVERI

NOBODY KILLED HER

First published in India in 2017 by Fourth Estate
An imprint of HarperCollins *Publishers*

Copyright © Sabyn Javeri 2017

P-ISBN: 978-93-5264-155-0
E-ISBN: 978-93-5264-156-7

2 4 6 8 10 9 7 5 3 1

Sabyn Javeri asserts the moral right
to be identified as the author of this work.

HarperCollins *Publishers*
A-75, Sector 57, Noida, Uttar Pradesh 201301, India
1 London Bridge Street, London, SE1 9GF, United Kingdom
Hazelton Lanes, 55 Avenue Road, Suite 2900, Toronto, Ontario M5R 3L2
and 1995 Markham Road, Scarborough, Ontario M1B 5M8, Canada
25 Ryde Road, Pymble, Sydney, NSW 2073, Australia
195 Broadway, New York, NY 10007, USA

Typeset in 12/16 Adobe Devanagari
by Jojy Philip, New Delhi

Printed and bound at
Thomson Press (India) Ltd.

This book has had an incredible journey. Like the inspiration behind its main characters, the book is unique in its creation. It has had a hard path to publishing and as you hold this in your hands, know that it is you who has made it possible. The book is dedicated to you, its readers.

'The day the power of love, overrules the love of power, the world will know peace.'

– Mahatma Gandhi

'I think you can love a person too much. You put someone up on a pedestal, and all of a sudden, from that perspective, you notice what's wrong – a hair out of place, a run in a stocking, a broken bone. You spend all your time and energy making it right, and all the while, you are falling apart yourself. You don't even realize what you look like, how far you've deteriorated, because you only have eyes for someone else.'

– Jodi Picoult, *Handle With Care*

'Who Killed Her?'

'Death doesn't knock on the door before entering, Your Honour. It comes suddenly, unannounced and uninvited. A bomb blast, a bullet gone astray, a blow in the head and before you know it, boom! The life has gone out of you. Cooked, as we say here in the city. You are smiling, sir? Perhaps you think I didn't try to stop her. I tried to tell her there's danger. Truly, I tried. The General and his men, I said, they will kill you. Why do you think they are letting you do the rally? So they can send you away for good! To a place you can never return from, I added, in case she hadn't understood. Her Urdu was not that good, you see, and my English... well, never mind. So I said to Rani Madam, don't go, it's a set-up. Even told her the story of the spider and the fly. But she just laughed. Laughed that careless laugh of hers, so unafraid, so unaffected. As if death itself was on her payroll...'

'Miss Khan, you must only answer the question asked. Tell the court how you knew the deceased.'

'I knew her the way I know God, Your Honour. I worshipped her, believed in her, yet never knew if she was real or an illusion. Perhaps, I had imagined it all...'

'Miss Khan, you are digressing. Think back, and answer correctly.'

'Think back?'

NEW YORK, 1982

The first time we met, you were wearing borrowed clothes. You sat there in your too big platforms, bell sleeves and a neckline that plunged sharply to the right. Your yellow jumper hung loose over your thin frame. Your head was defiantly uncovered, your frizzy hair as rebellious as your nature, your heart-shaped mouth stubbornly set. Later you told me that your friend Yasmin had lent you the clothes because your mother stopped your monthly allowance. She thought it would make you give up politics.

Your mother didn't know you well.

Looking deceptively sunny in that blinding yellow, you smoked as Yasmin stood behind you, searching through a high bookshelf. I had never seen a girl of your stature smoke. Or sit publicly without a veil.

'Ashtray,' you ordered and Yasmin came running up with one.

To avoid staring, I looked up at the highest shelf, my neck craning as I tilted my head all the way up, then bending as I looked down to the last. I wondered if you had read all those books.

Perhaps it was my head bobbing up and down like a duck in water that caught your attention. Sit, you gestured, and I nervously looked around for a chair to park myself on. I noticed your forehead crease in a frown as you crossed your legs like men do. You leaned back, stretching your hand over your knee and it was then I knew. With downcast eyes, I settled on the floor.

'What's your name?' you asked at the exact moment I opened my mouth to say, 'I want to be in politics.'

You pretended you hadn't heard and I knew from then on not to speak unless spoken to. Nobody can say I wasn't a good learner.

That much, at least, is true.

Yasmin brought tea and as she handed around the cups, you asked me again what my name was.

'Nazneen Khan,' I said. 'But everyone calls me Nazo.'

You smiled and I said, 'Madam, I am working in Aijaz Sahib's dry cleaners. You know Aijaz Sahib from Jackson Heights? He sent me to you. He said you help people fleeing the General's regime. My whole family was murdered in the coup. My father was a doorman at the Parliament. He resisted when they tried to break in. Later the General's men came to our house and killed everyone. I hid under the bed … survived somehow…' I could not carry on talking.

You didn't offer me any condolence. Instead you said, 'Can you type?'

And that was how it all began.

Bailiff: All rise!

Clerk: Judge Muzzamdar will be presiding over this case.

Bailiff: The court is now in session. Please be seated.

Judge: Good Morning. Calling the case of Mr Omar Bin Omar versus Miss Nazneen Khan on the assassination of former Prime Minister Rani Shah. Are both sides ready?

Prosecutor: Ready for the prosecution, Your Honour.

Defending Counsel: Ready for the defence, Your Honour.

Clerk: Your Honour, the plaintiff Mr Omar accuses the defendant of premeditated murder and of espionage against the state. The defendant is represented by the able and veteran lawyer Mr Hamidi while the plaintiff, being a known human rights lawyer, has decided to prosecute the case himself. Given his knowledge of law, and his closeness to the murdered politician, the court requests that his lack of criminal practice be overlooked and Mr Omar be allowed to prosecute.

Judge: Permission granted. Prosecutor Mr Omar and Counsel Mr Hamidi, please present your opening statements.

Prosecutor: Your Honour, Miss Nazneen Khan, commonly known as Nazo, has been accused of conspiring to assassinate the country's first female Prime Minister, Madam Rani Shah. Although the body was charred in the explosion, new evidence has revealed that her death was not due to the suicide bombing as was previously believed, but by a bullet shot at

5

```
    close range. Almost as if by someone seated right
    next to her...

Counsel: Objection!

Judge: Sustained.

Prosecutor: Very well. Let me start by asking a very
    simple and straightforward question. Miss Khan must
    answer why it is that she, who sat right next to
    Madam Shah at the time of the assassination, managed
    to escape unscathed, while Madam Shah lost her life.
    Now, Miss Khan, tell the court who sat where...
```

⚖

The cushion next to your desk became my space. Every day after work I came to your Uptown apartment and positioned myself by your feet. At first Yasmin did all your correspondence but slowly, as my typing speed increased, the typewriter too found its way down to the carpet. Tahtahtahtah, I type like a machine gun, you'd comment from your throne on the sofa. I'd smile, silently collecting any scraps of compliments that came my way. For me, you were the saviour – the Prophetess who would rid us of the General.

I wasn't the only one. Throngs of people came. Every day, the apartment grew, its walls stretched, and sometimes I thought its square shape would bend with the number of people who squeezed inside, each offering whatever service they could. We grew rich in people power. Students pledged support. Immigrants rallied outside the home embassy. Housewives sent us parcels of food, children came with little posters. The pressure in the house spilled out across the seas and into the country we had left behind. Our day grew to eighteen hours as we worked non-stop. And then one day, the Big Brother stepped in.

'Senator Ted Kennedy called!' You burst into the room and although I had no idea who he was, I found myself feeling inexplicably happy. You reached out and hugged me. 'The day is not far,' you said. 'Don't forget.'

I won't, I thought, as I felt the warmth of your bony hands seep into my rough palms. Later I folded my hands into the tiniest of fists and tucked them into the folds of my hijab.

'I won't ever forget,' I said to your receding back.

⚖

'No one can silence us now. No one can take our voice away, now that our words have become the voice of so many.' It was 1983 and you were speaking at a rally in Downtown Manhattan. Afterwards at the flat, you explained that Washington had begun to listen. 'The world is finally looking beyond the communist threat. Now is our chance. We have to get in there.'

'He can't keep us out any longer, Miss Shah,' said a man so thin he could have been a reed. He sidled up to you and started talking in a low, oily voice. 'The General has been exploiting the country. Sending our people to the borders to fight a war that isn't ours. In fact, it's nobody's war. The Americans have exaggerated the threat. What do you think?'

I thought he was standing too close to you.

'The General is cashing in on USA's fears,' you replied, exhaling smoke. 'He's fleecing them.'

The man leaned his thin body in. His drooping moustache towering over your petite frame.

You didn't push him away.

⚖

That night I did not go home. I watched unblinking as you both talked through the night, endless cups of tea your only companions. As the sun rose, you yawned and stretched across the sofa. 'Fetch me a glass of water, won't you, Nazo.'

But I did not want to leave you alone for a second with the Reed. I called out to the young tea boy, an Afghan refugee, who had been hired to help with the increasing number of visitors to the house and their endless demands for steaming cups of chai.

'Refugee,' I called out, my voice echoing in the still silent house. The boy rose from his makeshift bed on the carpet and rubbed his eyes.

'Water for Rani Madam,' I said. 'And make sure the glass is clean.'

When he brought it in, I took the glass from him and wiped off his fingerprints from the frosty surface with the ends of my hijab.

'Here you go,' I said, as you looked curiously at me. After you finished the water, you handed the empty glass back to me and said, 'You can show Mr Riaz out.'

The Reed rose and smiled down at me.

'I'll save your gatekeeper the trouble,' he said, putting on his sunglasses.

The Gatekeeper?

I smiled as I held the door open for him.

'Till tomorrow,' he said from the doorway just as the door slipped from my hand and slammed in his face.

I never did want to be your gatekeeper.

It wasn't long before your hard work began to reap its rewards. The West seemed to like the idea of the woman who had survived the General's coup, this veil-less Muslim woman who threatened the status quo with her unusual Western education and liberal outlook. The Americans called you 'Daughter of Peace'. After all, nobody could resist your charm.

And then, in 1986, the General finally gave in to American pressure and announced elections. That day when I entered the flat, laughter greeted me from all sides. The mood was jubilant and I thought I must be hallucinating, for you were spinning around in circles. Round and round you twirled, like a Sufi dervish, your skirt skimming around your black tights. Yasmin tied a bell-edged tablecloth to her waist and joined in. She shook her thin waist, moving her hips like a slender belly dancer. I clapped.

You both stopped to notice me.

'The door was unlocked,' I said. The silence was thick.

'Sorry,' I began to turn back when I heard you say, 'Where to, Nazo? Join in.'

Smiling, I walked into the circle. 'Dance,' you said, but I couldn't. I had never felt more self-conscious in my life.

Standing next to you and Yasmin, I suddenly found myself thinking about pores. Open pores, I thought, as I saw the Reed coming out of your room. He winked at me and said, 'Perhaps you need some Bollywood music to see her moves.' I wanted to show him a filmy punch instead, but I held myself.

'Will this do?' You put on a tape of Nazia Hassan's.

'Aha!' you said as I smiled. 'Aha!' you said again, as you took my hand and we began twirling around the room.

'Listen to this,' the Reed said, turning off the music.

'What is it?'

He held out the small radio he was holding against his ear just as the BBC signature tune faded out.

'Oh, you missed it, Rani!'

You marched up to him and said, 'Will you just tell us already?'

I saw your forehead crease at his silence. My stomach tensed. This better be good, your scowl seemed to say, as you pressed the rewind button on the tape recorder.

'That jackass General has called elections, but banned all political parties,' he announced.

'What!'

'You heard me,' he said, switching off the tape again.

'Yeah, of course, he has,' Yasmin said. 'Must be unIslamic or too present-century for him. Don't you know, fifteen hundred years ago when Islam was being spread, there were no political parties?'

'And no democracy either,' the Reed added.

'That General,' you said, slamming the radio on the floor. 'That General has definitely lost it.'

'I can't believe people are falling for this,' Yasmin said, untying the cloth around her waist and flinging it on the sofa.

'How can he do this?' you shouted. 'How does he get away with this farce?'

'Hitler said, "the bigger the lie the more it is believable".'

All three of you looked at me as if I had spoken in Russian.

Prosecutor: Madam Shah barely knew you for a month, Miss Khan, before you became her self-appointed personal assistant. Do you think...

Defendant: I think sometimes it just takes a few minutes to get to know someone, Omar Sir, and sometimes – a lifetime is not enough.

⚖

In the days that followed, I found you looking at me differently. It was almost as if you had spotted something that no one else could see. When I next sat down to type, you shouted at Refugee and asked, could no table and chair be found for me? I was so surprised that I could not even thank you.

'It's not like she's playing the piano,' the boy grumbled, as he dragged in a desk from the study and placed it next to the sofa.

Perhaps you didn't hear him, or maybe you chose to ignore him, but I could see that you raised your chin slightly. It was enough for me. I grabbed the chair he was dragging and held his wrist. 'Give your forked tongue a rest, boy. Don't think too much about what I can or cannot do.'

The look you gave me as he left was the longest you would ever look at me.

⚖

Later that afternoon, you called me into your study.

'Here,' you thrust a brown package at me. I unwrapped it

greedily only to discover that it was one of your big fat books. *Crime and Punishment*, the title read.

'You look disappointed.'

I felt myself shiver. A goose must have walked over my grave. *Or mine...*

'You can read, can't you?' you asked, looking curiously at me. 'Tell me, Nazo.'

How could I tell you otherwise? So I said, 'I can read enough to type your memos.'

'I had a feeling you were just copying,' you said, rubbing your chin, disbelief drawn all over your face. Perhaps the image of an illiterate fitted in well with your perception of me. I hung my head low.

Always one to go along.

'I think I know what you are worried about. Here, sit down,' you pulled a chair and sat across from me. 'Look, all that stuff the Jihadists say about education being haraam for women is wrong. Just imagine, the very first word revealed to the Prophet was "Iqra". It means read, Nazo. It literally means to read! So how can it be a sin?'

There have been very few times in life that I've been wrong. This was one such time. Looking at the passion in your eyes, the honesty in your voice, it began to dawn on me. All that I had heard about you: your idealism, your commitment, your sheer belief in what you had set out to do, it was all true. Perhaps the impossible *was* possible. The ten-year rule of the General's *could* be broken after all...

'Nazo, are you even listening?'

I blinked.

'Yes, of course, Madam,' I stammered.

'Good. As I was saying, the very first word of the Quran was "Iqra". Why would God do that if he didn't want us to educate ourselves? Do you understand what I'm saying, Nazo?'

I didn't. But I saw your mad, unshakable faith, your passion, your fire – and I wanted to believe you.

I nodded. 'I do.'

'Here,' you thrust another bunch of books at me. 'Read these.'

I looked down at my hands. *War and Peace, Anna Karenina, Macbeth, Hamlet* ... You didn't know it then, Rani, but you had begun to mould me the way one shapes wet earth.

'Now go and read,' you instructed, in that naturally bossy tone of yours. 'And remember, readers become leaders.'

They certainly do.

Prosecutor: So you admit that you were a trusted member of her personnel, with access to the most confidential of information. You had the Secret Service at your fingertips, yet you did not stop Madam Shah from going to the rally. In fact, you goaded her. You dared her! I was there, I saw it.

Counsel: Objection! Prosecutor is letting his emotions get in the way of reason.

Judge: The court advises Mr Omar to take a more straightforward line of questioning.

Prosecutor: I apologize, Your Honour. My intention was to reveal how the accused gained Madam Shah's trust. But perhaps it is better to begin at the beginning. Please tell the court, Miss Khan, how a barely literate asylum seeker like you rose through the ranks so swiftly?

Humpty Dumpty sat on a wall. Humpty Dumpty had a great fall… Nobody could put Humpty and Dumpty back again…

You laugh, Rani, but you're the one who taught me life is all about improvising. Remember that day when you fell apart? It was me who taught you how to stand up again. It was me who urged you to fight on.

No matter how crushing the defeat…

Your work for women's education, banned under the General's Jihadist regime, gained much publicity in New York. But I guess some things are just not meant to be. All your lipping about women's education came to a grinding halt. Perhaps you had said too much or perhaps you didn't say enough … Whatever the reason, the General put a full stop to it.

The day the news came, I was the first one you called. When I entered the flat, you were sitting with your head in your hands.

'Nazo,' your voice sounded strange, muffled, as if buried under a great bundle of cotton wool.

I found my heart sinking.

You tossed a newspaper towards me. I picked it up haltingly, as if it contained not the printed word but some deadly arson. And lethal it was, the news on that papery thin broadsheet, as piercing as a bullet.

A teenage girl had been shot in the head for going to school. The Jihadists proudly took credit for it.

I crumpled the paper. My hands, I noticed, were trembling.

'The girl took a stand,' you were saying. 'She refused to be cowered. She went to school, Nazo, because I told her to. I encouraged these girls. I told them to stand up for their rights. I'm her killer … This little girl's blood is on my hands.'

You slid off the bed like an ice cube melting under the hot sun. It was a strange sight, watching someone so resolute crumbling so easily, so quickly.

I felt anger pricking my throat.

Soldiers don't leave the battlefield at the first sight of blood…

'Get up,' I whispered.

You were too busy sobbing to hear me.

'Get up,' I shouted.

This time you looked up, red colouring your cheeks bright. I could tell by your frown that even at a time like this, you didn't like being addressed as such.

I took a slow deep breath and said, 'You can let this get you down, Rani Madam. Or you can keep going, unafraid and unashamed.'

I thought I saw you look at me differently. I thought I saw you try.

⚖

Since the coup in which the General executed your father, the Army and the Jihadists had run the country to the ground. It wasn't the most liberal of places to begin with, but now it was a prison; one giant cage for women and children, elderly and disabled, and all those others who weren't men enough or Muslim enough. We were the waste, to be swept under borders of black cloth. My country had been colourful once, now it was a sea of black. Black burqas, black beards, black burnt-down buildings pockmarked with bullets … But amidst all this darkness, you appeared like a white dove, a messenger of peace. Nobody really knew how you had managed to escape the General's prison, but there you were, carrying on your martyred father's mission.

Was I wrong?

Tell me, was *I* wrong to believe that you alone could free us from the Jihadist's clutches. In those dark days in New York, you worked day into night to make it happen. You promised to make it all better.

And maybe I did. You just couldn't see.

⚖

Sometimes clocks don't obey rules. Time slips away unnoticed, days somersault into nights unseen. This was one such time. We worked unaware of the hours. The girl's murder had given you the kick you needed to launch a full-scale human rights operation against the General. Campaigns, slogans and fundraisers drew people in with their tentacles, and it was there we stayed till our eyes could no longer stay open. As soon as we awoke, the cycle began again. At times the exhilaration was unbearable. At other times it felt like being trapped in a nightmare. A kind of fear gripped us all the time, the kind that comes from knowing something too well. We all knew what the General and his men were capable of, if they remained in power. Failure was out of the question.

The time had come for you to challenge him openly. There was no turning back now. You knocked at all the doors and surprisingly many of them opened, sick as they were of turning a blind eye to the General's atrocities. World leaders were beginning to show their support, but back home, people were still afraid. They say time heals all wounds, but for them, they had turned septic. A reminder of the past they were still trapped in.

Before we knew it, another year had passed. It was 1987. You carried on, the image of the schoolgirl's brains blown out pushing you on. 'We have to win,' you chanted night and day. 'We have to defeat them. We have to. We just have to.'

As if we had a choice…

And amidst all this, I worked the hardest. Even I couldn't tell you exactly what I did for you. Perhaps it would be easier to list what I didn't do. All I knew was that I was no longer, 'Nazo, the typist'. Somewhere somehow the lines had blurred. The divide was hazy and I crossed back and forth at will. I was your Woman

Friday, ironing your shirts one minute, keeping your diary the next. Yasmin was only too happy to hand over the bulging organizer, now that she was engaged to an American. It was she who first started teasing me as your new personal assistant. I never could tell when someone was joking.

'Hello, Nazo Khan, Personal Assistant to Leader of the Progressive Party, speaking,' I'd say, exactly the way Yasmin used to, when I answered calls. My face flushed with warm pride at this unabashed self-promotion.

Every now and then, I'd see you look at me in amusement, but you never once corrected me. Until one day, like Ram's Sita, I crossed a boundary.

One that you never knew existed.

⚖

Snow covered New York like a fluffy white blanket that day. Snow, a substance I had never seen back home, a magical, furry smoothness I thought existed only in fairy tales. But perhaps this was a fairy tale and you were a brave princess being chased by the ogre General. And the day wasn't far when you'd slay his ugly bald head. Every day, we were edging closer to our goal. There was anticipation in the air, the central heating in the stuffy Uptown apartment as stifling as the suspense of our mission. It was one such wintry day when the phone call came. A renowned international magazine rang to ask if I could fit in an urgent interview with you that afternoon. They wanted to do a profile of your stance on women's education for their 8 March issue.

'Yes, yes. It will be done,' I replied, crossing out an appointment with the Reed's father.

That afternoon, you called me into the room and asked why.

Surely you knew why, I thought, staring at you and the Reed, sitting side by side, like two birds on a branch. You were here to lobby, not socialize with silly old fogies. But I held my tongue.

'Sorry, Rani Madam, I thought it would be useful to meet the press instead. They wanted to focus on our cause for their Women's Day issue.' I should have stopped there, but I didn't. I couldn't help adding, 'I thought this would be a better use of your time.'

As if on cue, the Reed jumped in, 'I told you she's appointed herself your gatekeeper.'

You looked sideways at me.

'Nazo,' you said, your voice a strange mixture of alarm and anger. 'I'll decide whom to meet or not. You just organize my diary, okay? Don't control it.'

'But Madam, you can't back out now. They'll be here soon.'

'See what I mean?' the Reed snorted.

Once again he called me your gatekeeper and once again you let him. I had been undermined and you, who were supposed to look out for me, had done nothing. But I knew I was more than just a servant to you. Much more. And you were better than the impressionable teenager you were behaving like. You were Leader Rani. That was the name your father had given you. You, and not your younger brother Shanoo, were his legacy. Were you forgetting that? He believed in you. People used to laugh at your father for educating a daughter, but he didn't care. You were the first girl from his town to go abroad for further studies. People taunted him, accused him, judged him, but he didn't care. Your father championed you. They called his faith in you fatherly indulgence. But the day the General killed him, *you* were the one who stood up for him. You, not your younger brother who went into hiding, faced the General. That day you became Madam Shah. And now it was only a privileged few who were allowed to call you by the name your father had chosen for you. I was one of them.

In the mirror behind you, as the Reed laughed at me, his skinny jaw jutting out like a pair of scissors, I whispered your name. 'Leader Rani,' I chanted under my breath, as I consoled myself that he would never know the intimacy of calling you by your chosen name.

His laughter ceased.

⚖

They say tears follow laughter the way night follows day.

And death follows life…

The very next day, news came that your younger brother was dead. Your baby, your Shanoo, limp and lifeless, lying face down on the stony cold floor of a villa in Kabul.

That night when everyone had left, I watched as the Reed held you against his chest, stroking your back as if you were his pet cat.

'She killed him,' you said, your voice cracking as tears soaked your eyelids wet.

'I didn't even know he was married,' I heard him murmur.

'Two Afghan sisters. They were the daughters of the ruling family. Some sort of alliance, I suppose. They offered him refuge from the General. But he had to marry to be allowed to stay.'

'More business than marriage,' he said. I could see approval in his eyes.

'But who would have thought the elder one would kill him? Poison him!'

'Perhaps she wasn't happy with this compromise…'

'But to kill someone?' you flared up and he quickly changed tack.

'Back home, the General's got the papers saying, Shanoo died of drinking...'

'That bastard,' you said the words slowly.

Immediately he pulled you towards him and held you tight. 'It's all right, my darling.' Out of the corner of his eye, he glanced at me.

I looked away.

Earlier that morning, the General had sent a consolatory telegram. Under the customary 'Sad for your loss', it read, 'Alcohol is forbidden in Islam; foolish deaths are just one of the reasons'. Sprinkling salt on raw wounds, I thought, as I angrily tore it into tiny pieces. I turned around to see the Reed standing behind me.

'Aren't you taking this gatekeeper business a bit too seriously?' he asked. Then stubbing out his cigarette, he said, 'Let her decide for herself what she wants to rip up.'

He walked past me, then stopped. 'I'd hide that if I were you. Rani doesn't forgive easy.'

I swallowed the paper in one gulp.

You cried yourself to sleep that day. When you woke up, darkness had enveloped the room. The evening shadows stretched long and dark in your little Uptown apartment. You lay still on the bedroom sofa, your eyes fluttering open, then shutting tightly as you realized your brother was gone forever. Never before had I seen you sleep so long.

Refugee ran to fetch a glass of water when you finally sat up, but you waved it away. I went into the kitchen and brewed a cup of steaming hot chai. Back in the bedroom, I held it out to you and said, 'Night before day, day before tea.'

'Tea before whiskey,' the Reed said, strolling into your room without knocking.

'Hush!' you warned, gesturing towards me. He raised his eyebrows and murmured a sorry. I looked from one to the other. Did they really think I did not know? And what was it they were trying to hide anyway, their drinking or their affair? Did they really think I was that naïve? No, they must think I'm stupid. That's what it was. They thought I was too dumb to figure out what was going on under my nose. Or perhaps, I paused in my train of thought, your innocent pleading eyes staring deep into mine. Perhaps you thought I would judge you. I grinned. Me, who would back you one hundred per cent no matter what, you thought I would judge you? Oh Rani, how could you? For me you were the true leader. You were the only one I knew who had blurred the boundaries of what a woman could do or not do. You had challenged everything that had been hammered into my head. You freed me. It was you, Rani, who taught me that a woman was made, not born. Remember the time when you got out that big fat yellowing book *The Second Sex*, which had nothing about sex in it, disappointingly. You told me that the book said, I wasn't just someone born to bear children, marry, cook, do the whole lot women were expected to do back home as soon as they first bled. How, then, could you even think about hiding anything from me? The very thought made me shiver. The hot tea trembled in my hands and a few scalding drops blistered my skin.

It was time to leave.

'Stop,' you said and I stopped midstep.

'Nazo, no one must know.'

I remained silent.

'You know they are calling my little brother a drunk, a non-believer … They say he drank himself to death. He was poisoned, Nazo, but that bastard General is using him to ban alcohol in the country. He's mad, he's a killer, he killed him, he…'

'Rani Madam,' I interrupted. 'No one will know,' I said, my eyes on the Reed.

Your tense face relaxed. You took the tea from me.

'Thank you, Nazo.'

I stood there waiting, but no more words came my way. As if on cue, the Reed stood up and held the door for me.

'That'll be all.'

There was a full moon that night. I sat outside your door, waiting for you to come out. But you didn't. Nor did he. All around me the room grew darker and darker. The moonlight seeping in through the open windows painted shadows across the door. Every time the shapes shifted, daybreak seemed closer than ever, but never came. Any minute now, I thought, you would step out of your room, tell me to show him out. But not tonight. Tonight it seemed the Reed would be staying over. A wave of nausea rose up my throat. I thought of all the calls that had to be returned, the letters to be written, the pleas to be posted. He was keeping you. And then I could think of nothing else but his chest hair. Wiry black curls that peeked conspicuously from his unbuttoned collar. I hated the thought of those rough black whorls rubbing against your smooth ivory skin. It seemed to me an act of blasphemy. And everyone knows that blasphemy is unforgivable.

The first birds had begun their song by the time I reached for the telephone. My hands were clammy, my fingers as if made of ice. I dialled the number and waited as the bell rang.

Back home, it would be noon.

Promises are made to be broken.

Who'd know that better than you...

The next day, news of Shanoo's death in the papers was overshadowed by the news of your involvement with a certain tall, thin, moustachioed man.

Prosecutor: The person you trust the most often betrays you the worst. Isn't that what happened to Madam's father? Shah Sahib trusted the General and it turned out to be the biggest mistake of his life. As they say, history repeats itself.

Counsel: Get to the point, Mr Omar.

Prosecutor: Miss Khan was meant to be her protector. Madam's safety is said to have been her responsibility.

Counsel: Miss Khan was an assistant, Mr Omar, not a bodyguard.

Prosecutor: The body is not the only thing that needs sheltering. Reputation, privacy, image – those things also need protection. And this is where Miss Khan failed...

⚖

In the morning, I woke up to find a battle brewing between you two. Two wrongs *do* make a right, I thought. I felt strangely content.

'How did this get out?' Your face was red as you walked into the dining room, holding an overseas newspaper.

'What?' the Reed continued to chew his toast like a camel.

You held the newspaper close to his face.

'Smell it. It smells cheap.'

He looked at the photo of you two smiling adoringly at each other on the front page and caressed your cheek with the back of his hand. I sat up in alarm.

'Rani, my darling,' he said in a slick oily voice, 'I've already seen it.'

'Do you have any idea what this means?' You slammed your palm on the table.

'Rani, you are overreacting. So what if they found out? It had to happen sooner or later. In fact,' he glanced sideways at me, 'I think whoever did this actually did us a favour.'

'Don't flatter yourself,' you said in a voice so cutting that I feared you might strike him. 'What you should be saying right now is that it's not true. I don't want the Jihadists slandering my character, accusing me of having premarital affairs so soon after they've accused my brother of being an alcoholic. I want you to deny the whole thing. Outright. Okay?'

'But it's true, Rani.' He placed his hand on yours.

You shook it off. I felt myself applauding.

'I see,' you said.

'I see, what?' the Reed repeated like the parrot he was.

'I see what you are after. Publicity, is that what you want? Is that what this is about for you? Reflected glory, huh?'

'Rani,' he shook his head and smiled. 'Darling Rani, my family is no less. Don't forget my father is a leading industrialist. I don't need your family name.'

'Your father's a crook. A corrupt loan defaulter, one of the General's henchmen, and everyone knows that.'

'Your's was no saint,' he said, the smile disappearing from his face.

'Shut up,' you threw the papers at his face.

'Stop it!' he pounded his fist on the table. Dishes scattered all over the table, the juice trickling steadily onto the carpet. Bits of egg clung to his trouser leg.

I looked expectantly at you, but his outburst seemed to have silenced you. You stood mute, almost in awe of his authority.

This was not the woman I knew.

I hurried forward to clean the carpet.

'The stain will only grow deeper,' I murmured.

You both looked at me as if suddenly realizing my presence. You glanced at the newspaper. I pointed to his trousers.

'Take them off,' I said. 'To wash.'

'But some stains never wash off,' you said, balling up the newspaper like a sullen child who'd been chastised.

The Reed shook his head. I couldn't tell if he was annoyed with me or regretful about his outburst, but all of a sudden, he snapped off his belt and took off his trousers right there in front of me.

'Here, take it. Now can you leave us alone?'

'But the mess...' I started gathering the things. He pulled me up by the shoulder and said, 'Get out.'

I looked at you, but you seemed frozen by this new macho avatar of the Reed. Unsure, I stepped out but left the door wide open. Whatever he was up to, I wanted to know.

Collapsing onto the sofa in his green boxers and brown uneven socks, he crossed his pole-thin legs and said, 'Now, Rani, I want you to calm down. There is no need to panic. Look, darling, I know that for you women, image is everything and everything is image, and I also know that you are worried about what people will think. But darling...'

I watched his oily mouth spew words I couldn't hear at the other end of the flat as I scrubbed out the stain. When it had washed out, I came back in with the damp trousers – just in time to hear him say, 'I am willing to marry you. It's the only way to save your reputation.'

I don't know why but I burst out laughing.

You looked at me, then at him. You smiled.

'Save your reputation!' I said in between the loud guffaws and before I knew it, you had joined in as well.

'I fail to see why that is so funny,' he said coolly.

When we continued laughing, he began to lose his calm again.

'What the hell is so funny?' he shouted, glaring at us as if we had lost our minds.

Watching him pace the room, wearing a tie and blazer, with nothing underneath, I longed to say, 'You, sir'.

You seemed to notice it too, for you began to laugh even harder.

'Look here, Rani, you won't find a man like me.'

'That's true,' you said, as he lifted one hairy leg and scratched.

'For God's sake, Rani, think practically. The truth is, you need me. You think a woman can govern a country full of Jihadists? Far-fetched, my girl. Not in a million years. First of all, it will be decades before democracy is restored back home. And even then it won't change the way people think about women. Years of brainwashing by the General won't get wiped out so quickly. Look, at least if you were married to a decent guy, your husband could lead the party and you'd still have an input backstage. What are your chances of finding a husband like that? Huh? Frankly, who would marry you after you've been accused of sleeping with a man, which by the way, is true.'

You stopped laughing.

He walked up close to you. 'Face it, Rani,' he said in a soft menacing voice. 'Without a husband, the General's men will chew you up and spit you out. My dear girl, you need me.'

You slapped him.

⚖

Later, when you'd flung his trousers out of the window and turned a deaf ear to his threats and rants, you stood in front of your father's photograph.

'I don't need him,' you said to the dead man. 'I don't need any man. It was you, Papa, who told me I can, I must. And I will do it, Papa. I won't let you down. I'll keep my promise to you. I'll be the leader you wanted me to be. I will learn to fight. I will crush the General. You said, I will. You said, I was as good as a son, Papa. You said, I was like you. Remember your last words, Papa…'

You kept talking feverishly till, without any warning, you collapsed onto the floor. Rushing up to you, I held you in my arms as I sprinkled water on your face, the whole act as intimate as baptizing a newborn. And when you came to, it was as if you had been reborn. 'I can,' you whispered, your eyes fluttering open.

'Yes, you can,' I whispered back. 'You can and you will.' I held a glass of water to your lips and said, 'Even without your father, people will vote for you, Rani Madam. His memory is enough. You're his heir.'

It was the second time I saw you cry.

And the last.

In the midst of all this drama, it was I who brought you back to the real needs.

'Rani Madam, this is not the time,' I said, bringing up the tea tray. You frowned as you read the papers, your character assassination taking up the entire front page. Without looking, you reached for a cigarette. I immediately handed you the tea. Your forehead creased further, but you said nothing.

After a tentative sip, you sat up and said, 'You are right. This is not the time to be nursing a broken heart. This is the time to leave it all behind.'

Suddenly you looked up at me and said, 'Nazo, do you think I can do it alone? Do you really believe in me?'

'Of course,' I said. 'More than myself.'

'Then let's do it. It's now or never.'

A decision was made. You were heading back, this time to stay. And so it was…

The beginning of the end.

Prosecutor: What do you have to say about this headline, Miss Khan? Who could have possibly leaked out this information? Who, indeed, was close enough to have known about the 'alleged' affair?

Defendant: Things are not always as they seem.

Prosecutor: I agree, Miss Khan. Things are certainly not how they seem.

Defendant: I meant that the infatuation was one-sided.

Prosecutor: I'm sure you did. Your sentences are laced with double meanings, hidden agendas...

Counsel: Slander!

Prosecutor: Your Honour, I have reason to believe that Miss Khan may have been working undercover. Many believe she was sent to America to break into Rani Shah's inner circle. And to prove this, I would like to call Mr Riaz, a well-known businessman and a good friend of Madam Shah's, to the witness box.

Judge: Proceed.

Prosecutor: Mr Riaz, thank you for flying in from New York. Please take oath.

Witness: I swear on this Holy Book to tell the truth and only the truth.

Prosecutor: So Mr Riaz, in your testimony, you have stated that Miss Khan was a damaging influence on Madam Shah.

Counsel: Objection! Madam Shah was not a child who could be easily manipulated.

Prosecutor: Ah, but Miss Khan has her ways. What do you say, Mr Riaz?

Witness: Yes. I can give you many examples of her persuasion. I wouldn't be surprised if she turned out to be a trained spy.

Prosecutor: Thank you, Mr Riaz. Would you agree that this brainwashing may have been a conspiracy to lure Madam Shah back from self-exile, knowing that it was dangerous for her to return?

Witness: Yes, I firmly believe that Miss Khan had been planning the assassination much before she met us. That is why she wanted me out of the way because I...

Prosecutor: Thank You, Mr Riaz, you may step down.

Counsel: Your Honour, the testimony of a jilted lover is hardly credible. It should be disqualified.

Prosecutor: Mr Riaz's testimony is of immense significance, Your Honour. It is important to see Miss Khan as she was, when she first entered the Shah household.

Judge: Go ahead, Mr Omar.

Prosecutor: Thank you, Your Honour. To support my argument, I present Exhibit A, Miss Khan's application for asylum. If you look closely, she was first offered refuge in the Netherlands as a victim of the General's atrocities in 1980, but she waited another fourteen months to get a US visa. She even agreed to wait in a prison on the outskirts of Arizona till her application was processed. Would an actual terrified asylum seeker be so picky?

It wasn't till I chose to leave New York that I decided to look at it.
From the eyes of a tourist, this very American city seemed unreal
to me, like the set of a film. America, the place I had chosen, if
for no other reason than for the familiar comfort of Hollywood
films where everything always turns out well. I still remember the
heavily snipped black-and-white films broadcast every Friday
night on the state channel. I remember our entire neighbourhood
staying up to watch it at the only house with a TV set. All the
English I knew was thanks to those films.

At first when they offered to send me to some place called
Norway, where they spoke a guttural language and ate sausages,
my heart lurched. I told them I'd rather wait indefinitely in a
brick building from where I was not allowed to go out, so long
as I understood what was being said around me. I never could
stand it when I didn't. Although in the end, I only needed three
words – really, sorry and thank you – to get by in those first few
days there.

Now in my last days in this city, I rode the banana-yellow
taxis, staring at the gleaming skyscrapers that spoke to the sky. I
watched the dolled-up women, the busy-looking men, hurrying
along, unmindful of the cold.

Cold but free.

I loved walking on the sidewalks, craning my neck to look up
at the sky-high buildings, their heads literally in the clouds as
they stood proud and erect. I was especially attracted to the Twin
Towers, the ones the Jihadists called the evil swords of the West.
That last day, too, I felt a shiver run up my back as I stood under
its shadow. This was what hope looked like, I decided. Long,
gleaming and silver. But I couldn't pause for long as the large
crowds of people who seemed to constantly throng the narrow

sidewalks pushed past me, jostling me along, almost as if I was some spare part on the assembly line of a machine. Everyone was going somewhere, scurrying like ants. Here, they did not stand about watching the world go by as they did back home.

I sat down on the steps of Lincoln Centre and watched the hustle of men and women, walking shoulder to shoulder, side by side. And then, amidst the colourful crowds, I saw a figure swathed in black. At first I was gripped with fear, thinking that a Jihadi assassin had somehow gained entry to the US, but then I saw it was a woman in a black burqa, walking alone. I smiled thinking that back home she would not be able to step out unaccompanied, no matter how wrapped up she was. But perhaps all that would change after your return…

A shrill honking broke into my thoughts and I saw a group of youngsters crossing the road mid-traffic. I watched as they made their way up the steps. Thin girls and even thinner boys in black leather or blue denim, their hair dyed various shades of pink, puffed up in spikes, smoke billowing out of their pale, blood-drained lips. Some had their heads shaven, some had their faces pierced, some had entire arms tattooed with blue and purple designs. The purplish tattoo on the arms of one of the girls reminded me of the bruises the Jihadist's lashes left on women who resisted the veil. One pierced and punctured girl sat down next to me.

I remember thinking that here people do this to themselves, deliberately.

⚖

When I got back, I found her waiting at the door. Yasmin, who had quit politics and moved away after getting married, had come back to the apartment one last time at your mother's request.

'Don't go,' she said. 'They won't let you return.'

'Who said anything about coming back?' you replied.

'You can't be serious, Rani. The General's men are everywhere. People say he's more brutal than Saddam, more deadly than Jong-il, more…

'Yasmin!' you laughed.

'But it's true,' she argued. 'His spies will be watching your every move. Even if he doesn't arrest you, Rani, he'll make your life unbearable.'

'He can employ all the spies in the world, but he still won't win the elections. His days are numbered.'

'Well,' she tried a different approach, 'you have to admit he has a following.'

'So did Hitler.'

Yasmin shook her head and sighed.

'For old times' sake,' she said, lighting up a cigarette.

You took it from her and stubbed it out. 'No smoking.'

She looked at you with eyes wide open.

'But you are a chain-smoker, Rani!'

'Things change,' you replied calmly.

'Giving up cigarettes and alcohol or donning a hijab won't make the General and his Jihadists accept you,' Yasmin said. 'You're still a woman to them, a worthless afterthought created from a spare rib. And it's not just the Jihadists, you're fighting an entire team of people. From the top brass of the Army to the foot soldiers of the Secret Service, there's a whole host of men out there who hate you and your family. Not to mention, they find it demeaning that a woman might liberate them from the General.'

'Well, thanks for the news flash. Do you think the three years I spent rotting in custody didn't prepare me for this?'

'For God's sake, Rani, please don't go back there. They'll kill you as soon as you land. It's lawless there.' She grabbed your arm. 'Who is to stop them?'

You paused before answering. 'I have American support. Now that the Soviet threat is over, they want to see a more progressive government in the country. The Jihadists are done, Yasmin. Their role is over. Don't you see, the Americans want a change of regime. This is it. This is my chance.'

Yasmin let out a sound that was halfway between a snort and a laugh. 'You think the Americans can protect you? You think they can undo the monster they've created? The General doesn't play by the rules, Rani, and you know that. He's not going to roll over and play dead just because the Americans tell him to. He'll find something else to string them along with.'

You seemed to deflate slightly at this, but composed yourself quickly enough. 'Look, it's more complicated than that. I know what I'm doing. People back home need me.'

'No, Rani,' she stepped forward and hugged you. 'I won't let you go. I don't want to lose you.'

'The thing is, Yasmin,' you gently pried yourself away, 'I don't belong to you to lose. I don't even belong to myself. I belong to my country and my people. They need me.'

Yasmin's eyes took on a teary glassiness and she took a step back. 'Save the speech, Rani.'

You looked as if you'd been suddenly bitten by your pet dog. 'This is not a speech, Yasmin,' you raised your voice a notch. 'Don't you see? I really believe in it. I believe in myself, why can't you?'

'Because these men are ruthless!'

'I am not afraid.'

Yasmin wasn't impressed. 'Rani,' she said, 'they will destroy you.'

If there was one thing you loved, it was a challenge.

'I'm a fighter, Yasmin. I survived before and I will survive again.'

'But, Rani, at that time, they thought you were just a woman. Now they know you are a force to reckon with.'

She placed a hand on your shoulder. 'Please, my darling, don't go.'

'Yasmin, I have to do this,' your eyes flashed, as you shook yourself free.

Yasmin grabbed your hands again. 'I won't let you go. I won't let them kill you like they killed your father.'

'Yasmin, my dear,' your tone suddenly became weary as if you were addressing a stubborn child. 'Nobody is going to kill me,' you said. But you looked as unconvinced as I felt. Nevertheless, you put on a brave smile and sat her down. 'Look, seven years ago, the General tortured me mentally and physically, put me in a dark cell with rats and roaches, starved me, humiliated me, shamed me for being a woman, especially one who dared to dream. He tried to break me. Not only me, he killed our supporters, shot the protestors, hell, he hung the only legally elected prime minister the country had ever had. He tried every which way to break me. But you know what, Yasmin? He made one big mistake.' You took a deep breath and said, 'He let me go.'

A mistake you shouldn't have made.

⚖

After Yasmin left, I found you by the window, stubbing out a cigarette.

'What's this?' I lifted the tail end of a cigarette from the floor. One amidst many, I noticed later.

'A virgin's kiss, I think they call it. Do you even know what that is, Nazo?' Your look was cruel and I turned away.

'So, Nazo, any boyfriend, any lovers? Or do you only spy on mine? Tell me actually, who sent you here? Did my mother send you? Did the General? Are you spying on me? Is that why you cling to me like a shadow, you fucking bitch.'

'You've been drinking.'

You laughed. 'What are you? A closet Jihadi or something?'

'Alcohol is harmful.'

'A glass. A single glass won't kill me, stupid.'

'But if anyone finds out…'

'But they won't. Will they?' You looked sharply at me. 'Forty lashes. The penalty for a woman found intoxicated. But none for a man. A man can do whatever he wants. Take four wives, divorce them with three words…' you took a swig.

Disgust inched up my throat. 'But, Madam, you were doing so well.'

'I *am* doing so well,' you corrected me.

Your left eye twitched and there were dark hollows under your eyes. You looked burnt out yet you held my gaze. 'Say it, Nazo. I *am* doing so well.'

Still maintaining eye contact, you put another cigarette between your lips. You struck a match, and just as you cupped your hands to light up, I swiftly plucked the cigarette out of your mouth. I stood in shock of my own courage.

'How dare…' you slapped me hard across the cheek, putting me back in my place. 'Get out,' your voice was sharp, cutting me like glass. Yet I felt relief wash over me.

Outside, I leaned against the door, exhaling slow and deep. The half-lit cigarette smouldered in my palm.

⚖

Just before dawn, you opened your door a crack.

'What are you doing here so early?' your voice was shrill with surprise. You looked like a scared little girl in those oversized men's pyjamas, your hair tied clumsily in two knots, your nose running.

'I never left.'

You didn't seem surprised any more. Instead you nodded knowingly. 'Come inside,' you said.

Your room was dark and smelled of stale smoke. It made me feel sad, as if something dear to me was dying.

'Sit,' you said and I sat down at your feet. I was still, so still that I could hear the ticking of the wall clock behind you. You reached for a cigarette, but then seeing my expression freeze, you thought better. Even you had had enough drama for one night, I thought as you withdrew your hand back into your pyjama pocket. We sat like statues for a good five minutes before you finally spoke. 'The thing is, Nazo,' you said in a small voice, 'I'm scared. I'm very scared.'

I opened my mouth, but instead of words, a strange sound came out. A mix between a cough and a cry. It made you smile. 'Nazo, I wish I could show you the fear that grips me all the time. I pretend to be brave, but inside ... I'm shaking.'

No, I wasn't ready to see this vulnerable side of you. I tried to reason. 'This fear is a very strange thing, Rani Madam. My father used to say that if you let fear scare you, it will paralyse you. But if you embrace it, the same fear becomes courage.'

You looked at me curiously.

'Sometimes, Nazo, I find it hard to believe that you've only studied till seventh grade.'

'Life is a better teacher than any school, Rani Madam.'

'So it is,' you said and slid down to the floor beside me.

That night you talked to me like you never had. Amidst the papers and campaign posters scattered on the floor, we sat. You told me about the jails, about the rats the General let loose at night, and how the lights were turned off so you had only the sound of the animals scratching to guard yourself against. You told me how you moved from leg to leg, sleeping standing up so the rats wouldn't bite your face. And then you told me about the infection on your fingertip that spread to your shoulder, and how your brother's contacts finally managed to sneak you out of the country and had you admitted to a hospital.

'The nerves in my right hand were completely dead. I thought it was all over, that I would never use it again. But the doctors here worked a miracle. They operated on me and restored all feeling. It was like being born again. I got a second chance. And that's when I vowed, I wouldn't forget about those who I'd left behind, those who couldn't escape the General's regime. I would go back for them.'

'But when?'

Just then, the clock struck six. You looked guiltily at its outstretched arms as they pointed to opposite ends.

'Tell me, Nazo, why do we only notice time when it's gone?'

Prosecutor: What about the fact that each time Madam
    Shah's life was in danger, Miss Khan was present
    somewhere close by. Your Honour, it should be noted
    that when the first attack on her life took place
    in 1988, Miss Khan was right next to her...

⚖

We chose Metro City as the battleground instead of the Capital.
It was here in this city by the sea that you would first set foot
upon your return. It was here that you would choose to test your
loyalties. Only a handful were allowed to accompany you.

Naturally, I was one of them.

⚖

'The risk is great,' you said to me as I followed you on the plane.
'This flight may take off but never land.'

But it did. And what a landing it was. Local journalists,
foreign media, party workers, supporters – even women came to
receive you. Veiled in black with only their eyes showing through
the slits, they stood behind the men, their voices matching the
men's in strength and in spirit. Everywhere the eye could see, the
ground was filled with people welcoming you. Not an inch was
left uncovered. And only one name lay on everyone's tongue.
'Leader Shah, Rani Shah, Leader!' the crowd chanted madly. 'Our
Leader lives on in you, Rani Shah. Long live our Leader.'

To say that I was overwhelmed would not be a lie.

Before landing, we had estimated a few hundred people might show up to greet you. Less if the General could help it. Stories of torture to stop supporters on their way to receive you were ripe, but people kept pouring in. Their faces sunburnt, clothes torn and feet bare, yet they stood their ground, chanting, 'Long live Rani Shah'. The sight was enough to melt the stoniest of hearts.

Even you looked moved.

And then, you raised your right arm and placed it on your heart, the same way that your father used to. The crowd went wild. But you didn't stop there. You raised your hand further up and touched your black veil. I heard sharp intakes of breath all around, the crowd fell silent. You were about to unveil your face, an act unthinkable under the General's regime. You unclipped your niqab and the black cloth fell away, revealing your beautiful ivory face. You left your hair loosely covered with a thin translucent, white hijab. But it was enough. The point had been made. Change was on its way.

'Rani Shah!' Once again the crowds roared your name and it was as if there were waves of sound drowning us all.

'Rani Shah, Leader Shah, long live!' the chant grew louder as many other women tossed their veils in the air.

Sirens rang through the air. A law had been broken. We realized with alarm that you had just given the General a reason to arrest you. A stampede broke out, with the loyalists chanting your name and the Jihadist supporters beating them down. I saw a man moving towards you with great alacrity. He didn't wear the checkered head-cloth of the Jihadists, but a black turban half hid his face. He was chanting the same slogans as the others, but his eyes were unblinking. His focus was you.

It was a moment of choice. And I chose life.

For you, Rani.

He pushed his way out of the crowd and came towards you. Without another thought, I pressed myself against you.

'Nazo, stop blocking me.' You tried to push me away just as the man lunged towards us. I shielded you with my body.

'*Allah Ho Akbar*!'

I took the sharp twist of the knife in my back.

Later they told me, the crowd fell on him like hungry dogs. Took him apart limb by limb. It was a while before people realized that you were safe. It was I who had taken the hit.

'A servant girl.'

'No, a secretary!'

'All the same, hired help.'

'Thank God, Rani Madam is safe.'

'That's all that matters, our hope is alive.'

The voices around me grew faint, the lights dimmed and I thought this was it. The end. I tried to keep my eyes open, searching the faces nearby. Why did I even think you would be by my side?

And then I heard you say, 'Nazo! Look at me. Nazo, say something. Speak to me.'

Anxious voices muffled yours. 'Let's go,' someone was shouting. 'Rani Madam, come! You must leave. It is not safe here.'

'No,' I heard you say.

'But, Madam, the General's men will open fire anytime.'

'Sirens! Can you hear the sirens?'

'The Jihadists are here.'

'Hurry! They're unleashing tear gas on the crowds. Let's go!'

In the chorus of panicky voices, I heard your reassuring voice one more time. 'But what about Nazo? I can't just leave her here.'

'We will take care of the girl. Don't worry.'

'The best hospital,' I heard you say, as they took you away.

'Yes, yes. Now you must hurry. We have to leave.'

And so you left.

But not before you turned back to say, 'We'll meet again.'

And so we did.

Prosecutor: Your Honour, eyewitnesses say that Miss Khan was holding Rani Madam down, not shielding her as she claims.

Counsel: But my client has already said that she used force only to protect Madam Shah.

Prosecutor: Even if I were to believe Miss Khan saved her life instead of attempting to take it, phone records show that there was no contact from Madam Shah's side after the attack. Why didn't she visit Miss Khan in the hospital? Not even a phone call to someone who saved her life? Surely Madam Shah must have suspected something.

Counsel: Madam Shah was a busy person. And a considerate one. Perhaps she didn't want to disturb Miss Khan in the early days of her recovery. As you can see by the disfigurement scar on my client's face, she suffered further injury by a fall right after her operation. The bottom line is that my client was welcomed back in the Shah household once she recovered fully.

Prosecutor: Or forced her way in?

Counsel: Objection!

Prosecutor: My point, Your Honour, is how did Miss Khan worm her way back in? That, you see, is the puzzle. And solving this puzzle is crucial in assessing her motive for murder...

⚖

The next time we met, you were surrounded by people. And if it wasn't for the intense heat and the blinding sunlight, I would have thought we were back in your Uptown apartment. Laughter, smoke and drinks. So many chattering mouths, so many words flying across the room, it made me wonder where these people, who sat about discussing politics in drawing rooms, got hold of all their thoughts. How did they have so much to say?

But I'm getting ahead of myself. On that hot humid autumn day when even the sea breeze felt warm, I got to your place just after midday. I stood at the gates of Shah House, waiting for the Independence day crowds to thin. People had gathered there from all over the country. They waved their little Party flags and chanted slogans. There was to be a feast afterwards and people thronged to the gates, lunging at the free food. The guards, thinking I was one of them, pushed me roughly to the side.

It was hours before Refugee stepped out for a smoke and saw me.

'Nazo! What are you doing here?'

'Refugee!' I ran up and hugged him. He shrank back with a mix of surprise and shyness.

'Look, Nazo,' he said, extracting himself from my embrace, 'No one calls me Refugee here. I have a status now, you know. I have come back from America after all. I am the cook now. I can cook mutton biryani, chicken korma, lamb chop, beef steak, poached egg...'

'Listen,' I interrupted, 'has Rani Madam asked about me?'

But he was in no mood to be hurried.

'First, you tell me,' he said, 'how are you? Have you recovered fully?'

I decided to try another method. 'What is there to recover

from? My life is for the cause. Aren't you going to offer me a cup of tea even?' I asked, as he reluctantly invited me in.

'So tell me, has Rani Madam been asking about me?' I said, once inside. 'She must know I've been discharged from hospital.'

'The truth is, Nazo,' he averted his eyes, 'I really can't remember. The whole incident seems so long ago and there is so much to do now...'

I got up so suddenly that I knocked back the chair I was sitting on.

'Is it the rumours?' I asked.

'What rumours?' Refugee asked, without meeting my eyes. I knew then that he believed it too.

'Not you as well, Refugee? You're thinking I'm with the Jihadists? That I was holding Rani Madam down so the man could strike her? I saved her life, Refugee! Look! Look at my scars! The General's men murdered my family. Why would I be siding with them? Just look at the cuts, the stitches. I risked my life and you...'

'Oho, why are you getting so worked up?' Refugee scratched his bulging stomach and frowned. 'Anyway, I'm not the one saying it.'

I took a deep breath. 'But Refugee...'

'Enough,' he cut me off, 'stop feeling sorry for yourself, Nazo-ji. It doesn't suit you. Now look, there is so much work to be done. I'm not just a tea boy any more, you know. I am the cook now. I have a whole kitchen to handle! Three people working under me! Now shush. Fifty guests to cater for and you are wasting my time, harassing me with faltoo questions.'

I knew that brisk, abrupt manner of his from our New York days. I used it myself when I wanted to dodge a question. I hovered around till the tea boy, now promoted to full cook status, beckoned me close. Rushed off his feet, he pointed to the stove. 'Now that you are here, you might as well make yourself useful.'

'Fry those,' he said.

'Mix that.'

'Wash this,' and so on, till he distractedly handed me a plate of sizzling hot samosas. 'Serve these.'

I walked into the main hall with the plate, circling the place where you stood surrounded by an adoring crowd of Party workers. The room was grand. A huge chandelier hung in the middle, crystals sparkling along the cut glass, like twinkling stars in a country sky. Long red velvet curtains draped around tall French windows that opened onto a beautiful patio garden. It could have been transplanted out of New York itself. Men and women mingled freely, reminding me of a time before the General took over the country. Women without veils, although modestly dressed, and men without beards raised their glasses to freedom, even if it was behind closed doors only. And in the centre of it all was you, the woman who would bring back freedom. You were wearing a long green dress, and your head was covered with a translucent white hijab that showed an elaborate hairdo. You looked so young, so glamorous. More like a movie star than a struggling politician. In fact, you looked nothing like the girl in the ill-fitting yellow clothes I had met in New York. Only your eyes reflected the passion you still carried deep.

I didn't know, then, that eyes could hide just as much as they revealed. And unlike tongues, there was no danger of the secrets spilling, either.

But you mustn't misunderstand me. I wasn't jealous. Certainly not disillusioned, either. I was, I think, surprised to see this side of you. You looked unreal. Like one of those lifelike dolls that blink. Lifelike but not lifeless. After all, you could have been someone's trophy wife had you not entered politics. But you chose sacrifice. For us. For me. Warmth surged through my body and I could feel an urgency inside. I wanted to know that you were real. I wanted to check you were not a mirage in this dry dusty desert. I wanted, right then, to touch you.

I moved closer.

Hidden behind a tray full of tall glasses, I nearly approached you twice, but shied away at the last moment. As the crowd thinned, I began to wonder if you would even recognize me. It had been six months and I had lost weight. A scar on my face from a fall after the operation had left me disfigured, and sometimes when I saw myself in the mirror, I too jumped back wondering who the stranger in the room was. I ran my fingers along the bumpy edge of my scar, feeling the crude roughness of my skin. After the operation, I had tried to stand up too quickly, such was my hurry to get back to our cause. Still drowsy from the anaesthetic, I had fainted and fallen on the hard floor, cutting open my lip and chin. The doctors at the local hospital had stitched the wound coarsely, leaving an ugly scar that ran lip down to my chin, making me look like a dog that couldn't stop drooling. I wondered now what you would think of me. Ugly, most likely. Ugly but faithful.

As bitches tend to be…

When you finally saw me, you did your best not to notice me. I held back like I always had. It was only when there was no one else left in the room that I approached you. You had your eyes closed and your head back. A cigarette smouldered in your delicate fingers.

'Rani Madam?'

You said nothing.

Something inside me crumbled. Such indifference.

Was it really necessary?

'You are not a bad person, Rani Madam,' I couldn't resist saying. 'But you are trying very hard to be one.'

A smile broke out on your face. Like sunshine on a cloudy day.

'Nazo,' you said, without opening your eyes. You blew rings out of your mouth, perfectly circular puffs of smoke that surrounded you like fluffy white clouds. You looked, at that point, a goddess descending from a misty sky. I sat down at your feet as I used to.

It was a while before you asked, 'When did you leave the hospital?'

'It's been some time. I wrote to you. Telephoned...'

'Good that you came to see me.'

But you didn't.

Aloud, I said, 'Rani Madam, I can understand why you kept away.'

You were quiet as my words sank in. Behind you, the floor-length red curtains gave the illusion of a stage that had been set.

The play began.

You were silent. And your silence made the fire inside me flare higher.

'You ... you don't believe the rumours too, do you?' I felt my voice raising a notch. 'You think I would do such a thing to you? You would think that?' The 'you' came out shrill, high pitched and accusing. Like nails on a blackboard.

You raised an eyebrow.

I covered my face with my hands. My body trembled. 'Please. You must believe me, Madam. I ... saw the knife coming. I wanted to protect you. I ... I could have moved ... I...' my voice broke.

It was then you turned to look at me. I saw the faint look of distaste cross your beautiful features as you quickly looked away. Ugliness always did unsettle you.

I kept staring at the pattern on the sofa, memorizing the fishlike shape of the paisleys, counting the times each one appeared before it was crisscrossed by an upside-down one. I kept looking, kept counting, kept remembering, until finally you spoke.

'Nazo,' you patted the space next to you on the sofa. 'Sit.'

In the entire time I had known you, that was the closest you ever came to saying sorry.

When I finally sat, you said, 'I wanted to visit. You know I did. But I couldn't and I really don't know why. I suppose I haven't really had the time. There was always something more pressing or the other ... But now that I look at you, I feel I should have. Nazo, I'm so...'

'Don't say it,' I placed a finger on your lips.

You shrank back at my touch.

Embarrassed, I smiled and felt the scar stretch along my lip. You turned your head away.

'Ignoring is harder than ignorance, Rani Madam. You have to keep on doing it.'

I had challenged you to look at me. You couldn't back down now. But it was a while before you conquered your demons. You turned to face me. This time your eyes focused in on my scar.

You didn't flinch.

'My father used to say, wear your scars proudly.' You met my eyes and said, 'They are maps to your journey.'

I felt embraced.

'Now, go get me one of those amazing brews you used to make in New York.'

Behind you, a breeze blew and the curtains flapped.

Encore.

⚖

I was smiling as I brewed the tea, the golden-brown liquid boiling to a clear coral as I added the milk. Refugee didn't look too happy to have me back in his kitchen, but I ignored his grumbling. After all, I was back where I belonged. In my rightful place.

With you.

I brought out the tea and sat down at your feet. You turned off the local news in irritation and tuned in to BBC. After a few minutes of static, I heard the broadcaster say, 'This is BBC London', in a grim foreboding voice. We sat in silence till the signature tune came on.

It felt as if someone had turned back time.

Later you talked politics till darkness gave way to light, and sleep was no longer a threat.

'Make yourself at home,' you said, stretching your arms with a wide yawn. 'I need people I can trust around me.'

You always were a bad judge of character.

Prosecutor: I heard a saying once that it is easy to spot a spy. They look just like us.

Counsel: What does this have to do with my client?

Prosecutor: What I'm trying to say, Counsel, is that double agents in real life are less than impressive. They are ordinary people, average, usually working class...

Counsel: I'm afraid, Your Honour, Mr Omar is wasting the court's time with his musings.

Prosecutor: Counsel will see the point when I ask Miss Khan my next question. It's no secret that there was a lot of anxiety not just amidst the politicians but also within the Secret Service, the Army and other smaller pressure groups for the General's rule to end.

Counsel: Can the prosecutor please come to the point?

Prosecutor: Very well, I will. Now, Miss Khan, do you remember the time when you advised Madam Shah to co-operate with the Army to overthrow the Jihadist regime? No? Well, surely you must remember this. Did you or did you not, at that point, suggest that she try to kill the General?

Defendant: One can only try, Omar Sir. The rest is in God's hands.

⚖

I had got what I wanted. Or had I? Why is it that every time we think we have found the one thing that will make us complete, we change shape. The piece no longer fits or if it does, some other part dislodges. Perhaps we can never be whole. Were never meant to be.

And then, just when I least expected it, life took another turn.

The day was not far when you would be sitting in the Parliament. If only the jackass General would call elections. But why would he? Even he knew that not even a cockroach would vote for him. And so he delayed and delayed. Until one day we got tired of waiting. You slammed the telephone into the wall after yet another call about delayed elections. You slapped a party worker reading a paper that blared the headline 'No Polls Ahead'. You knocked off the radio when it announced conditions were too hostile for electioneers. You nearly smashed the TV screen during the General's address in which he told the public that he simply could not put the country's future into the hands of corrupt and power-hungry disbelievers – in other words, politicians. But it was only when the bastard announced that women could neither vote nor contest for office that you broke down.

Enough. I marched up to you and said, 'You have to do something. You've got to stop him. Now.'

You laughed at me. That mad carefree laugh of yours that did nothing to mask how frightened you were.

'What can I do, Nazo?' you said, when the hysterical laughter had subsided. 'Nothing short of death can stop that monster.'

You said it, not me.

For days after that, I could think of nothing else. One day when you were having your favourite curry, I approached you and said, 'Rani Madam, can I speak to you? It's important.'

You didn't look up from your food.

'I have been thinking.'

'Good for you.'

'The General must die.'

You nearly choked on your curry. Later when the coughing was over, you told me never to disturb you during dinner again.

But the thought had been planted. Later, as I was clearing the table, I heard you mutter, 'As if it was that easy to kill him...'

It was all I needed. You had thrown me a bone and the bitch I was, I leapt to fetch.

You played me well.

⚖

After dinner, I brought it up again. 'Madam, it's not difficult at all. There are lots of factions within the General's party. The cracks are beginning to show. In fact, I hear that one breakaway group has already put a price to his head. We can join their mission and then...'

'Stop right there.' Your tone was serious.

I backed down.

'Always remember this, Nazo. Murder is never the answer to a problem.' You leaned in close and said, 'Killing one bad person gives birth to ten more.'

But I didn't remember.

What could I do, my memory isn't what it used to be.

⚖

You met him by chance.

It had taken much persuasion for Major Q to dine at the Shah House. The whole affair had an air of secrecy. The long red curtains were drawn shut, the shimmering crystal chandelier dimmed, and a feast laid out. You planned the menu for ages.

'We have to get this right, Nazo,' you kept repeating. 'He can be our eyes and ears if things go right.'

He turned out to be much more than that, but I'm getting ahead of myself.

That night, after the appetizers had been served, the old Major, who was known for his debauchery before his born-again Jihadist avatar, debated whether to have a drink of whiskey.

'We are all friends here, sir,' you said sweetly.

I placed a glass of whiskey before him. Major Q eyed the icy glass sweating on the table. 'But, my dear, *He* is watching,' he replied wistfully. 'He is omniscient.'

A chill ran through my spine. If even the Major was scared of that dreaded General, then what hope was there of a coup? This meeting was useless.

'*Allah Ho Akbar*,' a soldier standing guard by his side said and it occurred to me that the Mighty One in question was not the General but the Mightiest of all.

'I never miss my prayers,' he said. 'Take it away, girl,' he gestured.

I started as I realized the Major was looking at me.

'You know, Rani Madam,' he said, turning to you, 'alcohol taints the Wazu. Tempting as it is, I will have to bathe before my prayers if I touch even a drop of this forbidden liquid.'

'Then pray before you drink,' I said.

'Brilliant idea!' you clapped your hands and laughed like a little girl.

The Major seemed appalled. 'If the General should ever find out, my dear, he'll have me hanged, or flogged, and that too in public.'

You laid a hand on the Major's shoulder and said, 'Well then, he won't find out. Neither about the drink, nor about our meeting.'

'Yes,' the Major leaned back. His paunch stuck out and a slight leer appeared on his face.

'Say your prayers,' I said.

'What?' the Major looked up, startled.

A rabbit in headlights.

'Forgive us, Major Sahib. Nazo means to say, offer your prayers first and then have your whiskey,' you said, giving me a sideways glance to leave.

I left. But not before handing him a prayer mat.

Three tumblers of whiskey later, the pious Major had to be helped out by his trusted soldiers. As one of the soldiers leaned over to support him, he slipped under the old man's weight. I noticed it was the same man who had been muttering '*Allah Ho Akbar*', trying to ward off evil from the devil himself. As he stood up, something slipped out of his pocket. For some reason, I couldn't be bothered to point it out. Let it be, I thought, turning away. In any case, I would have had to bend between his legs to reach it, and he would have had to put the drunken Major down to take it from me. It was probably nothing, I told myself, as I shut the door firmly after them.

As I returned to the living room to clear away the dishes, I tried to avoid looking at the creased sofa, the cushions scattered all over as if a battle had taken place. Instead, I kept my eyes on the floor, and that's where I saw it. A piece of paper, folded many times over, in precise even squares.

I sighed as I unfolded it and realized the paper I had dismissed as useless was actually a jeweller's receipt. 'As if I didn't have enough on my plate,' I murmured, thinking I would now have to track him down to return it. 'Nothing is easy.'

Or is it? I wondered, as I tucked the square paper safely in my bra, an idea forming in my mind.

The next morning, I decided to visit the jeweller. I stood outside for thirty minutes before I worked up the courage to go in. Once inside, there was no turning back. I handed the young cashier the collection receipt.

'This has been pawned,' he said with a yawn. 'You will have to pay the full sum plus interest to get this back.'

He didn't seem too happy as I asked how much.

'All of Rupees 1550.'

I nodded, sure that whatever it was would be worth much more than that.

He disappeared into the back room and returned with a small green velvet pouch.

'Here you are, exactly the way you left it.'

I snatched it and walked out before he could ask me to sign the return ledger with proof of ID. I broke into a run as he called after me and I didn't stop till I reached your doorstep. Then in the cool dark interior of the servant's bathroom, I opened the pouch. Inside was a box in which lay a gold medal for bravery. Next to it, a chit that read: 'Pawned by Soldier Rahim Khan for the sum of

Rupees 900. To be melted in full if borrowed amount with interest not paid by 24 June'.

I felt sick.

I spent the next few days trying to forget about the medal and how desperate someone must be to pawn a medal of bravery for such a small loan. Every now and then, I would pull out the box and peer inside the lid, only to shut it quickly like the door of an occupied toilet.

And then once again, time sped up. Elections were on. Elections were off. The bloody General was more indecisive than a bride picking out her wedding dress. I wanted to grab his throat and shake his bald head till he said yes to the polls. But security around him was so tight that not even a mosquito could sneak through. Rumour had it that he made the American Ambassador travel with him wherever he went because everyone knew there wasn't a safer hostage, nor a more willing one, to safeguard himself against. The 'will he/won't he' suspense was killing, yet *you* seemed unperturbed, rubbing face cream into your skin as if all was well.

I wondered if you knew something I didn't.

You sat staring adoringly at the jar of La Prairie cream you had sent over from Macy's every few months. It was nearly empty. Scooping up the last of it, you rubbed it into your cheeks. You examined your face from side to side, stretching the skin around your eyes, smoothing non-existent wrinkles and kneading your temples. Then you sighed, 'Only thirty-four.'

'But in politics, it is better to look older than your age.'

You frowned at me in the mirror.

'Or so they say,' I added hurriedly.

You tossed the empty cream jar at me. And missed.

With a wave of your hand, you motioned for the lighter. 'You are right,' you said, as I offered you a light. 'These creams don't work anyway. Waste of money, not to mention all the trouble I go to, asking friends to smuggle them in.'

'Maybe so, Madam, but,' I pointed at the cigarette in your mouth, '*that* is something that actually does do what it says on the pack.'

You looked at the warning on the cigarette packet, then at me. You burst out laughing. 'Really, Nazo, you are too much!'

You have no idea how much, I thought as I bent close to you and placed an ashtray by your side. As I moved away, I scooped up your gold cigarette case and hid it in the folds of my hijab. Nasty habit, I thought. Very nasty, this smoking.

You were still admiring your reflection when I left the room, my own face dull and plain in comparison, almost invisible in the mirror. As a consolation, I pressed the cold hard, metallic surface of the case against my skin.

I wondered if the Soldier smoked.

You never know what will come in handy when dealing with the poor and needy.

Judge: The court will adjourn for ten minutes. When we return, the questioning will continue.

Prosecutor: Your Honour, may I approach?

Judge: Yes, Mr Omar.

Prosecutor: I would like to request one last question before we break. You see, I'd like to produce a witness depending on Miss Khan's answer. The break would then provide us with time to brief the witness on court procedure.

Judge: Permission granted.

Prosecutor: Thank you, Your Honour. Miss Khan, I am aware that you have a very selective memory, but still I would like to ask you to recall your whereabouts on the night of 7 January 1989. Can you tell the court what happened that night?

Defendant: No, sir, I can't.

Prosecutor: You can't or you won't?

⚖

It took much convincing for him to even meet me. Soldier Rahim belonged to that rare breed of servants who stayed loyal to their masters all their life; kicked and punched, left to starve, while their masters dined fine. They reminded me of dogs. But then, I liked dogs. They could be loyal and made good sniffers.

Takes one to know one.

⚖

I should have known that things have a way of falling into place, just as they have a way of falling apart. And so it happened that the next time Major Q came to Shah House, he brought the Soldier along in his protection team. After much asking around, I now knew two things about him. He didn't take bribes and he was poor. Poor *and* needy. Needy being the swinging factor. Suddenly, breaking into the secret world of the Secret Service did not seem so impossible. I watched as the Major prayed piously to his Lord, then fell upon his alcohol like a thirsty man in a desert. Later in his drunken state, he kicked the honest Soldier, thrusting his foot at him and telling him to tie his shoelaces.

'Hurry up, you sister fucker! Who are you waiting for, your mother to undress?' he slurred.

I could see the Soldier turn a beetroot red, yet he remained silent. Something huge must be holding him back, I thought. Whatever it was, it was big enough. Yes, big enough for him to do our bidding.

But if it was a difficult route to the General, getting to his staff was even more challenging. First I had to befriend Major's driver, Shafiq. And Shafiq was no beau to fool. A new recruit to the General's Jihadism, he was as tough as they came. But still, I was tougher.

While the big folk dined inside, I sat out in the driveway with the driver and Refugee. It was funny, I thought, how the distinction between the sexes ended once you crossed over into the very poor or very rich zone. I sat in the company of men, my hijab hardly covering my head, yet no Jihadist came running up to lash me. Perhaps it was because people like me didn't really count. I was, after all, just a nobody.

Anyhow, we sat in the evening breeze till Refugee was called back inside. After plying him with numerous cups of my by-now-famous brew, I managed to get Driver Shafiq to speak. Unrolling his long green turban, he accepted a cigarette and squatted down beside me. The Soldier's full name was Rahim Khan Haqsani, I found out, and he was from Major Q's ancestral village in the northwest Frontier of Haqsan. This was a place where loyalties were fierce, friendships forever and betrayal, almost never.

'Forget it,' Shafiq said, as I watched Rahim do the Major's bidding. I shivered and wrapped my arms around myself. Was I so transparent?

'He won't sleep with you.'

'What?' For a second I wondered if I had heard him right.

'Don't go falling in love with him, Nazo-ji. Now don't deny it, I've seen you staring at him. Us Jihadists are hard to resist, huh?'

All I could do was stare at him, speechless.

'But listen here, he is already married. Has three daughters, a blind sister and a mother dying of cancer.' He winked and said, 'Poor man has an army of nephews and nieces, all dependent on the Major's morsels. And you know what these Major X, Y and Z are like. No mixing between the staffs. As it is they like to keep the choicest bits of meat for themselves. And you know what, Nazo-ji, you look pretty juicy to me.'

He ran a hand over the curve of my waist. '*Arre*, don't be shy now. Everyone needs a release now and then.' His grip tightened as he dug his fingers into my flesh.

I froze. What had I got myself into? Shafiq inched closer and I could see a bulge appearing in his loose trousers. His eyes were fixed on me and I could smell the curry on his breath. I felt myself stiffening.

If you let fear scare you, it paralyses you. But if you embrace it, the same fear becomes courage.

Slowly I told myself that I had survived the General's men, travelled halfway across the world, made the climb from servant to secretary. I wasn't about to be mishandled by some two-bit driver.

Taking a deep breath, I lifted my shaking hands and unbuttoned the top of his shirt. I circled his wiry chest hair. Then wrapping one strand around my finger, I plucked it sharply. He screamed.

Grabbing his collar, I kicked him in the crotch with my knee. 'The hardest thing I've ever had to do,' I said, spitting by his side, 'is resisting a Jihadist.'

The look on his face was priceless.

⚖

'There are two kinds of people in this world,' the Major was telling you when I came back inside with the snack tray, 'Good people and bad people.'

Wrong, I thought as I served you two. There are only clever people and fools. And the roles are not interchangeable. Once a fool, always a fool, I thought as the Major blew his nose ferociously, then thrust the dirty tissue into the honest Soldier's hand. I watched in revulsion as Soldier Rahim folded his palm, not a flicker of disgust on his face.

'So tell me, Major Sahib,' you said, 'does that General of yours ever intend to hold elections or is he just stringing us along?'

The very pious Major knocked back another glass of whiskey before answering.

'Truth is, my dear Rani, that nobody really knows.'

Your face slackened and you suddenly looked like a young schoolgirl whose ice cream had melted in her hand.

'I wouldn't give up hope though,' he added hastily.

Probably he was one of those men who were afraid of a woman's tears, I thought. As if you were the kind to burst out crying. But looking at you just then, I considered the possibility.

Quickly I jumped in, 'But surely he can't be leader of the Jihadists, president of the country and General of the armed forces for much longer. He must decide on one or the other.'

'He is not a fool, my dear Miss,' the Major said, a deep frown lining his already wrinkled forehead. 'He knows that he will never be democratically elected and he also knows that if he appoints another army general, a coup would be inevitable.'

Then, looking you in the eye, the Major said very slowly, 'But, my dear, like any God-fearing man, he, too, fears death.'

Bailiff: All rise.

Judge: The court is back in session.

Prosecuter: Not long now, Miss Nazneen Khan, before the truth is revealed.

Defendant: The truth, Omar Sir, is what you want it to be.

⚖

'No.'

'But Rani Madam...'

'I will not kill a person.'

'It's the only way.'

'Don't be such a fool, Nazo,' you said. 'I am not getting involved in any criminal activities.'

Stifling a laugh, I said, 'Killing a man like him would hardly be a crime.'

'Murder is murder. And there is no other way to put it.'

'But,' I persisted, 'what if it was done quietly? I mean no one needs to know...'

'You think we can just hire some goon to shoot him?' you said, your voice rising again. 'You foolish, obstinate, illiterate girl! The man has the protection of a superpower. Even if we wanted to kill him, it would be impossible.'

'There are ways, Rani Madam,' I said, with a seriousness to my tone that made you cock your head and listen, if only for a second. 'You just have to say yes.'

You looked into my eyes and said, 'No.'

⚖

Later that day, I placed a list of names and numbers of breakaway Jihadist factions, disgruntled army colleagues and political enemies who all had one thing in common. They, too, wanted to see the General dead.

When I came back into the study, I found the list on your desk. In bold red letters was scribbled the word, 'Impossible'.

I read it as 'I'm possible'. I always did say my reading wasn't very good.

Next day there was a great frenzy in the household. I was summoned.

'Call a meeting,' you said, as soon as I stepped in.

Behind you the TV was on, and the General's ugly bald face filled the screen. He thundered in his high-pitched nasal wail that instead of elections, a referendum will be held. 'I will not let the reins of my blessed country fall into the hands of disbelievers,' he raged on the screen. 'I ask you, my countrymen, do you want some *kafir* running our beloved Nation? Do you want someone who drinks alcohol and lives in sin as your guide? Do you want someone who is an agent of the West to be your PM? Tell me, my dear countrymen, do you want to be ruled by a woman? Do you want to put on bangles and mind the kitchen while your wives and daughters go out to earn? If not, then say yes to the referendum. Say yes to the country being run by Shariah laws, the way the Prophet, peace be upon him, intended it to be.'

'The Prophet?' you shouted at the TV. 'How can he drag the Prophet into this?'

Others who had gathered into the room, sensing the rage in your voice, started slinking out discreetly. You turned to me. 'When will that man stop using religion as a ruse?'

'Not as long as he is kicking and living.'

'Alive and kicking,' you snapped.

'This is not the time to be giving English lessons, Madam. This is the time to be planning.'

'Planning what exactly?' you sounded weary, ignoring the cynicism in my tone.

'His assassination, Rani Madam.'

'Not now, please.'

'He doesn't deserve to live.'

'Let God be the judge of that.'

'I don't believe in God.'

'I don't believe in murder, Nazo.'

A thick white, suffocating silence built up as you stared coolly at me. Behind you, the General's face filled the screen.

You reached for a cigarette.

An easy escape.

'Damn.'

The pack was empty.

I tried again. 'Please listen, Rani Madam, the time is right...'

'I could have sworn I had a full pack.'

I wanted right then to shake you. 'Do you think killing him would make you a bad person, Madam?'

'Fetch me a new pack,' you said.

I persisted. 'I know you only ever want to do the right thing, but all your foreign education doesn't apply here. It's survival of the fittest.'

'Why the fuck are you still here?'

'Here a person has to separate their actions from themselves, Madam. *Arre*, doing something bad doesn't make me a bad person.'

'My cigarettes, Nazo...'

I was on thin ice, but it was as if I didn't care any more. I let loose all that was simmering inside. 'Truth is, Madam, if I was getting raped, it'd be better for me to kill my rapist than to go knocking for justice on the door of a society where a raped woman has to provide four eyewitnesses! What of that blind girl who has been jailed by the General because when she was being raped, she was too blind to look for any voyeurs who might be standing around, watching? Tell me, Rani Madam, in a society like this, are you going to wait around for democracy to come to you, or are you going to fight for it?'

'Enough!' Your voice struck me like thunder as you said, 'Do as I say, Nazo. Or do you not consider yourself my servant any more?'

⚖

I don't know what I consider myself, I thought, as I stepped out into the harsh light to buy your cigarettes. Your protector? Well-wisher? Friend? Healer? Schemer? A witch from *Macbeth*, here to make you king ... Or perhaps I was more suited to the role of the evil wife who made him murder.

'Oh to kill for the crown,' I whispered to myself, as I picked up a pack at the little kiosk nearby. I ran my finger over the warning.

'Rupees fifty-five,' the shopkeeper said, interrupting my reverie.

'Giving, giving,' I said. 'I'm not running away with your measly cigarettes,' I shouted at the skinny man sitting cross-legged in the kiosk. 'Actually,' I said, narrowing my eyes at him, 'you are the real murderer in all this.' I stuffed some loose cigarettes in my kurta pockets and tucked the pack into the folds of the long chador I had wrapped over my body.

'Can't take things without paying,' he protested. 'I'm not running a free house, you know.'

'Shut up!' I shouted, more determined than ever not to pay him. 'I'll take what I want. And if you say one more word, I'll scream that you were trying to molest me.'

The man touched the holes in his torn vest.

'Look, sister,' he pleaded, 'I have six hungry mouths to feed.'

'Is that my fault?' I said. 'Why should I pay for your fun?' I helped myself to chewing gum, pan masala and a large egg-shaped chocolate bar.

'*Arre*, why are you making trouble for no reason?' he tried to stop my hand.

'Five lashes,' I hissed, 'for touching a woman in public.'

A few people were beginning to gather.

The poor man cowered in his corner.

'Please pay or … or…'

'How dare you!' I screamed. 'Help, help, someone help me!'

A man dressed in the khaki fatigues of the Moral Police approached. 'Everything all right, sister?' he asked.

I looked at the shopkeeper, his eyes wide with terror, and thought, perhaps not all of the Jihadists' laws were so bad.

Back at home, I found you sitting alone in the dark.

'I thought you were scared of the dark, Madam?' I asked cautiously.

'These days I'm scared of the light.'

I switched on the bedside lamp and a soft golden haze surrounded us.

You exhaled a long slow breath, then said, 'At least darkness is always with you, but light, you never know when it will leave your side.'

As if on cue, the lamp flickered. We were plunged into darkness.

'Power failure,' Refugee shouted from downstairs.

The real power failure was here, I thought.

Aloud I said, 'I'll get some candles.'

I drew open the curtains and a bright yellow filtered in from the streetlights outside.

'Your order, Madam,' I said, giving you the cigarette pack.

You grabbed at it and lit one. You held it dearly, your fist wrapped around the cigarette like an addict relishing his last fix. Your neediness was pitiful.

I couldn't watch.

'Rani Madam,' I hesitated, 'I have something else for you.' I held out the chewing gum and the chocolate bar, with little hope. But you surprised me.

Stubbing out the cigarette, you picked up the chocolate and started to stroke it.

'Papa used to get these for me.'

You tore it open and ate it quickly, almost desperately. And then you did something you had never done before. You reached out and hugged me.

I knew, then, things were worse than they seemed.

Prosecutor: You can remain silent, Miss Khan. But things have a way of coming out no matter how much one tries to hide them. I would like to call my next witness, Soldier Rahim Khan.

Clerk: Sir, the Police regrets to inform prosecution that Soldier Rahim Khan has been seriously injured on the way to court. He is fighting for his life in a hospital bed at this moment.

Prosecutor: That's shocking news. I should have known ... But don't think you are getting away with this that easy, Miss Khan. You may have thought that Soldier Rahim would never talk after his 'accident', but unfortunately for you, we have his testimony right here. Perhaps now you regret not killing him earlier.

Counsel: Objection! Miss Khan was close to Soldier Rahim Khan. Why would she want him killed?

Prosecutor: Perhaps, Your Honour, because she is afraid he would recognize her for what she really is - a pretender.

⚖

When the first streak of orange lit the sky, I left the house. All around me, the call for morning prayers rang out. Each muezzin seemed to be competing with the other as he sang higher, louder and shriller. Their voices shot through the air like blind arrows. I ducked through these invisible strikes and made my way to the jewellery store, the medal tucked safely under my shirt. The jeweller was not an early riser, nor a mosque goer, I realized, after waiting three hours for him to open shop. Finally a thin boy came down the steps and began fiddling with the locks on the shutters.

'Brother,' I said, startling him as I stepped out of the shadows. 'I have a favour to ask.'

He looked at me and then at the medal in my hand. He ran off screaming.

⚖

It turned out that Soldier Rahim had showed up to collect his medal sans a receipt, and when he found out that it had been handed to an unknown woman, he had wrecked the shop in his rage. He even threatened to beat the jeweller to death if the medal was not returned.

'You sold my honour,' he had screamed at them.

Thinking that they had melted it for the gold and were now making excuses, he gave them seven days to retrieve it, or else he would burn down the shop. Rahim being Major Q's bodyguard, the jeweller had taken the threat very seriously. His relief, as I handed the medal back to him, was indescribable.

'These are strange times,' he said. 'Nobody wants to take up against the General's men, and that man, they say he is Major Sahib's Man Friday. How were we to know?'

I nodded.

'It was a mistake,' he continued. 'Anyone can make a mistake. But Allah save us from these Jihadists. They never forgive. Perhaps they are not created from the same dust as us.'

I counted the notes he gave me.

'Well, sister, here is the money you paid us. Thank you for bringing it back. I will make sure my son doesn't mix up people's belongings again.'

I turned to leave just as he said, 'Please, sister, if you don't mind, I want to ask a question.'

I stopped in the doorway, my back towards him.

'What made you bring it back? Don't mind, but honesty is such a rarity these days that one tends to question it.'

I turned to face him.

'I never take what isn't mine.'

But would kill for something that is.

Prosecutor: Please take a look at this, Miss Khan. Recognize it? The forced blankness on your face tells us that you are trying hard not to. Your Honour, I draw your attention to a jeweller's receipt, Exhibit B. It's for the pawn of a medal. Not just any medal, but a gold medal for courage. I ask the court: what kind of woman steals a soldier's recognition of bravery? It reveals her crooked and amoral personality. She would do anything for money.

Counsel: On the contrary, Your Honour, it shows Miss Khan's kind and fair nature. True that she took the medal. But it was a mistake. Mr Omar has conveniently left out that Miss Khan returned the medal to the jeweller despite being handed it incorrectly. I suppose Mr Omar will have an argument against that as well?

Prosecutor: In the larger scheme of things, it probably suited her plan. For *this* woman is a manipulator, an exploiter, a schemer of the worst kind.

⚖

A strategist, perhaps, but not a schemer.

Surely, Rani Madam, you must know that by now. I just like to plan ahead, that's all. When you grow up in one room crammed amidst six much-stronger siblings, you learn to make up for what you lack in strength with what you can in strategy. I've always been clever, though that's not a quality cherished in girls of my background. Unlike you, I didn't have a father who'd send me to school over my less smart brothers. I didn't get praise for doing well; I got a slap for making my brothers look bad. I learnt fast that planning ahead was the rule of the game. Yes, game. You see, I figured out early on that life was a game that had to be played, and for every move that you made, you calculate the ten possible moves of your opponent first.

Impulse, spontaneity, compulsion are all forms of recklessness, I always say.

But then, if you had listened to me, you wouldn't be in this situation in the first place.

Anyhow, that day at the jeweller's, I returned the medal without any quibbling. My only request being that when the Soldier came to collect his medal, I be informed immediately. I told them I wanted to apologize.

Of course I did no such thing. Instead, I made the meeting turn into a fortuitous coincidence, bumping deliberately into him and sending the medal shattering through the air. I then fell on all fours to retrieve it, wrapping my hijab around my neck to unblock his view.

From the floor, I caught his eye as he stared down my cleavage, embarrassing him so that when I handed the medal back to him, it was he who apologized.

'Don't I know you from somewhere?' he asked, as we left the shop.

'I'm only a servant girl.'

'In one way or the other we are all servants,' he touched his ear, 'servants of Allah.'

I glanced sideways at him, marvelling that they still made people like him.

'If there is ever anything I can do for you, let me know,' he said and quickened his step.

'Wait,' I caught up with him.

'What is it, sister?' he said.

I looked around me and spotting a large overweight man looking my way, said, 'That man. He's bothering me. I think he's been following me.'

I expected him to tell me to complain to the Moral Police. I'd then ask for help trying to find one, buying myself some time to get to know him. But the Soldier was more pliable than I imagined.

'That guy?' he asked.

I nodded.

The fat man smiled as the Soldier approached him.

'Don't you have any sisters at home, you swine?'

The man barely had time to blink before the Soldier's fist hit him in the eye.

'Let's go,' I said, taking his hand and dragging him away before the man could speak.

He looked at his hand, then at me. He didn't pull away.

⚖

I took him home and put ice on his hand. Later I made him a cup of tea. He stared into the murky brown liquid with bits of cream floating on top and said, 'Ah, the impossible shade of homemade brew.'

'Do you not go home often?'

A restless look came into his eyes and he took a tentative sip of the scalding tea.

'Not as often as I would like to.'

I nodded.

'And you?'

'I have no one, no place to call my home,' I said, and for the first time, I realized what a blessing that was.

'Must be hard.'

I bit my lip, suppressing a smile. The Soldier took it for tears.

'What happened to your family?'

I told him how they had been slaughtered in front of my eyes by the General's men, and he looked away, uneasy at the thought of being a part of the establishment. He got up abruptly.

'I should go now. Thanks for the tea.'

'Will I see you again?' I asked.

He looked at his feet.

'If Allah wills.'

'*Khuda Hafiz*, Soldier,' I bowed my head and bade him goodbye, stepping towards the door at the exact time as him. As we brushed against each other, I slipped my hand into his pocket and made sure the medal fell out, *accidentally*.

I guess it was inevitable. We would *have* to meet again.

⚖

He came to me again on a stormy night. The soldier's eyes looked terrifying. 'I know you have it.'

It was not the time to play games. Wordlessly, I went to the cupboard and retrieved the medal.

'I didn't have your address.'

It was as if he deflated. His shoulders dropped and his face relaxed.

'Stop,' I said, as he turned to leave, 'let the rain lighten. You will get soaked.'

He looked around at my cramped quarters, at the painfully thin mattress on the ground and at the steel almirah in the corner. Relaxed by my poverty, he settled down on the floor and asked for a cup of tea. I poured some from the kettle on a small kerosene stove I kept burning day and night, the brew as strong as a stiff glass of whiskey. We sat silently side by side, the tension growing till he started to speak. He spoke about the unexpected rain, the high inflation, the rising crime rate, the price of wheat. Everything but what was on his mind.

I placed my hand over his mouth.

'Soldier Rahim, we are both from this city. We both know how bad it is and how good it used to be.'

I moved closer to him and then very slowly, I placed my hand on his arm as if to brush off some lint. I can get him, I thought when he didn't move away.

I can get him easily.

I looked into his eyes and, before I could say anything else, he grabbed me with both arms and pushed me down on the rough floor. Flicking his long shirt up, he loosened the drawstring of his shalwar and, pulling savagely at my clothes, shoved himself sharply inside me. I cried out and it was then he realized.

'You are a virgin?'

'Was,' I replied, turning my head away.

Soldier Rahim fell back.

I had him.

⚖

That night, after Soldier Rahim left for his own moth-bitten bed, I couldn't sleep. I started once again on the abridged version of *Macbeth* you had given me. I struggled with the dense words, although my reading was getting better. The script began to turn into dancing ants and I must have drifted off at some point, for I dreamt of witches and mists, of daggers and bloodstained cloaks. I woke up gasping in the dark. Groping for the light switch, I saw something dangling above me. On the ceiling, a spider spun her web slowly, carelessly, dangerously unprotected. It was instinctive. I killed it before I knew what I was doing.

I always did hate impulsiveness.

The squished spider remained glued on the ceiling, directly in my line of vision, keeping me awake. I blamed it on *Macbeth*. This Shakespeare of yours could bring out the worst in people.

Should I have wiped the ceiling clean? Perhaps. But I found it easier to find my bedding elsewhere.

I knocked on your door.

⚖

I entered, without warning. You looked up in alarm.

'What the hell, Nazo? Haven't you heard of waiting for an answer?'

You held a cigarette in one hand and a glass full of some amber-coloured liquid in the other. 'Do you mind?'

I stood rooted, unable to tear my eyes away.

'Get out,' you said, your voice turning bitter. You took a big swig of the foul-smelling drink.

I hung my head. Not out of shame but out of defeat. How could I draw you away from these things? It would take less than this for the General's men to drag you out by your hair onto the streets and lash you raw, should it get out. But thankfully, being your private secretary meant nothing could get past me.

Unless, of course, you wanted it to.

'Please don't do this to yourself,' I whispered.

'Just get the fuck out of here, Nazo,' your voice slurred.

Always a good sign...

I approached you quietly, stealthily, hoping to take those two poisonous things away from you.

'Your feet,' I said, stopping suddenly. You must have stumbled on broken glass, for a thin trickle of blood trailed behind as you got up to stop me.

'Get out,' you said, this time with even less vigour.

I looked around. Shattered glass lay everywhere. Accident or deliberate? Knowing you, it was probably some sort of redemption attempt. On a closer look, little criss-cross marks lined your feet and ankles. You were cutting yourself.

'Stay still,' I ordered and surprisingly, you listened.

I took off my hijab and started cleaning your feet. I felt your hand stroke my hair. It was like a blessing. Almost maternal. Yet there was something else. Something almost primal that I could not ignore. The heat ... the heat in the room was damning. I tugged at your pyjama. You did not resist.

The softness of your flesh was as haunting as the hardness of your heart. I pushed my mouth into the wetness of your thighs. It felt like flying.

You rolled back your head and by the time I left, you were snoring gently.

Did you think I would forget?

Perhaps you wish I had.

Prosecutor: Your Honour, this cunning deceitful woman manipulated every relationship Madam Shah ever had. Look at this telegram she sent to Rani Shah's mother Begum Shah. It's genuine, Counsel. Begum Shah has confirmed that Miss Khan approached her to stop the wedding. Rani Shah was a politician, not some pop star or Bollywood actress whose career would end after marriage. What reason could Miss Khan possibly have for interfering in Madam Shah's private life?

Judge: Miss Khan, I urge you to answer the question.

Defendant: All I can say, Your Honour, is that politics is an obsession, an occupation, a disease, an addiction, a fascination, an absurdity, a fate. It is not a hobby.

⚖

In the coming weeks, you were edgy, nervous and uneasy around me. It never occurred to me that you could be ashamed of our intimacy. In fact, I doubted you even remembered, clouded as you were in the haze of alcohol. I thought it was because you had other more damning things on your mind. Pressure was building up from all quarters for you to marry. It seemed impossible enough that a woman would contest elections, but an unmarried woman – a joke.

'Find a man,' Major Q advised. 'Even if he is just a show-horse.'

I could see you thinking, considering, deliberating. My darling, Rani, I could see you succumbing. I wanted so much to tell you just then to hold on. I wanted to say: just a little longer. Not long before they *have* to listen to you.

But you were in no mood to hear me out. You seemed to get agitated at the sight of me. Distrustful, jumpy. I wasn't sure if it was because you had opened up to me the other night, or if you just wanted to put me back in my place. Remind me that I was nothing more than hired help.

It didn't help that every other person was asking you why it didn't work out with the Reed. Every now and then, someone would mention Mr Riaz and your face would cloud over thinking about the Reed. I wasn't sure if it was the memories or the persecution that was bothering you. But Rani, when your knee jerks, your foot is not meant to fly up and kick your face. Is it?

The maulanas were on your case. Every day a new slander on your character, a new insult, a new rumour. If you even stood next to a man, they had you sleeping with him. If you were photographed talking to one, you were deemed his mistress. If you were caught looking at one, he was proclaimed your dirty secret. Even the women around you were not spared. They dug up old photos of you and Yasmin in New York and proclaimed you lovers. Strangely, we were never linked.

People will believe anything but the truth.

The night our showdown happened, some close friends of your late father had come to see you.

'Get married, child,' one advised. 'Shut their mouths once and forever.'

His wife leaned forward and said, 'Here they don't take single women seriously.'

'A woman alone is easy meat,' another old loyalist added.

'A man's years are measured by his wealth but a woman,' his wife added, 'no matter how rich or powerful, once she is past thirty, no one wants her. After all, don't you want children, my dear?'

The final straw came when the old man stood up and said, 'What were you thinking when you refused to marry that nice boy you were linked with in Manhattan?'

'Such a nice husband Riaz would have made. And from such a good background too. Lovely couple you would have made. Beautiful children you'd have had.'

'Yes, indeed,' they all chorused.

Reed's words echoed in my ears, and I looked across to see if you were thinking the same. But your face was blank. Your fingers curled tight around a cigarette, furious white smoke billowing from your nostrils. A fire raged inside you and when I came close, it nearly burnt me.

'God has created a partner for each one of us,' the old man's wife was saying. 'If you find the perfect man...'

'Stay away from him,' I interrupted.

They all turned to look at me.

'It was meant to be a joke,' I said, but the room grew silent. 'An angel must be passing,' I said nervously. No one smiled.

All eyes were on me, including yours.

'Who is this girl?' the bearded old man asked.

'What business is it of yours whom Rani marries?' his wife glared. 'Such impudence from a servant girl.'

I looked the woman in the eye. 'I am Rani Madam's secretary, auntie, not just some servant girl. And for your kind information, Rani Madam is here to run the country, not some man's house.'

'How dare you insult me!' the woman stood up.

'Rani Madam?' I turned to you. 'Please tell them that what you are doing is far more important. Your life is dedicated to politics. You...'

'Enough.'

'But...'

'Get out!'

The old couple hurried out even though you were looking directly at me.

'Rani Madam, I...'

'Leave.'

'But...'

'No, Nazo. Not a word more. I've had enough of your meddling. Just who the hell do you think you are? If you hadn't come snooping into my life, I'd be happily married to Riaz right now.'

'He was not right for you.'

'*You* are not right for me.'

'Rani, please...'

You aimed an ashtray at me and missed. A mirror shattered behind me.

'It's "Madam" to you,' your voice was dry as ice.

I had to lean against the wall. My legs felt weak. My voice was small, pleading, pathetic, even to my own ears, as I said, 'Do I mean nothing to you?'

You spun around. 'Who are you, Nazo? My relative? My friend? My sister? You are nothing but hired help. Understand? I owe you nothing. *I* will make the decisions of my life. Not *you.*'

I looked straight into your eyes and asked, 'My loyalty means nothing to you?'

'Loyalty?' you began to laugh hysterically. 'That's the thing, Nazo. I trusted you. But you took advantage of my vulnerability. You're about as loyal as a snake, you bitch.'

'I did it for you.'

'Oh please. Just look at you, Nazo. Look at you! You're pathetic. Standing there in front of me with a newspaper tucked under your arm, diary in hand. I've more than made up for the fall you took for me. You came to me with nothing. Your entire family had been murdered. You were a bloody refugee for fuck's sake, and look at you now. My clothes, my shoes, hell you probably even wear my underwear. God knows what else of mine you've helped yourself to...'

'I am not a thief.'

'Of course you're not.'

You were suddenly calm. And then you said something that stung me sharper than a slap.

'You're a nobody.'

Prosecutor: Wonderful! What a fantastic storyteller you
    are, Nazo Khan. Have you ever tried your hand at
    fiction? No? Well, they say paper is free in jail,
    and as for time, you will have plenty. I beg your
    pardon, Your Honour, I digress. But you see Miss
    Khan seems to have conveniently left out little
    bits of truth which are imperative to the course
    of justice. The words 'unreliable narrator' would be
    so apt were she a character in the novel. Alas, all
    this is real. Madam Shah is gone, never to return.

Counsel: Is there a question in this?

Prosecutor: Yes, I would like to know how much Miss Khan
    was paid for switching camps.

Counsel: What nonsense!

Prosecutor: Yes, Counsel, perhaps it is. For I don't think
    she did it for money. I think she did it for pride.

⚖

Still a child at fourteen, I had hidden beneath the bed, watching
my family being slaughtered before my very eyes. I had seen my
father's head struck off his neck, seen it roll on the floor and land
inches from where I lay. I never thought I'd feel the same pain again.

This came close.

But I believe things happen for a reason. After I left your
house, I found I had nowhere to go, no one to go to, except ...
I toyed with the idea and then thought why not. There was only
one debt greater than that of a mother's milk; that of a woman's

virginity. Besides, what more did I have to lose, I told myself, as I knocked on Soldier Rahim's door.

He took me in. Let me stay in his room. And then in his bed. He made no promises, but he looked after me well. Even put in a good word with the Major and got me a job in the household. I made the parathas every morning. Thin, crisp, buttery and perfectly flaky flatbreads that nobody could fault. Soon I became indispensable.

Surely you would agree, that was the one thing I was good at.

In many ways, being in the Major's house was a blessing. Almost every evening there was a gathering of the top Army brass. I soon noticed that the growing discontent against the General was not just limited to the public. Internal conflicts were opening up. Grievances, complaints, neglect and corruption, they were part of the nightly discussions among the General's men at the Major's house. No one paid attention when I went in and out of the rooms, filling up their glasses with ice, serving snacks or collecting empty dishes, my face partly veiled, with only the hideous scar around my chin exposed. No one knew who I was and no one cared.

I was becoming good at being invisible. I learnt how to merge into the background, melting against the plants, or shrinking into an unlit corner when confidential information was being exchanged. No one noticed me. Or if they did, dismissed me as unimportant. There were, it seemed, many advantages of being a nobody.

Somebody like you would never know.

And then one day, I heard the unmentionable. I was collecting the dirty dishes when I saw Major Q lean conspiratorially towards another old colonel and whisper, 'Now don't tell this to anyone, but rumour has it that there is trouble in the Big Gun's mosque.'

Mosques and guns, that's all they were obsessed with, I thought, with a toss of my head.

The old colonel let out a low whistle. Taking a deep swig of his whiskey, he asked, 'But what of the small pistols? Can the Hangman silence them? What does the Big Brother say?'

'If the Big Gun stays,' a third man replied. 'The small ones will have to be squashed to make room.'

'I don't know about that,' Major Q rubbed his chest. 'I'm beginning to like the smoke from one particular small gun.'

'I've heard she's quite a tasty thing,' the other man laughed.

'What does she taste like? I wonder if she is as fiery in bed as she is in her speeches?' another old fogey leered. The room roared with obscene laughter.

A young soldier next to Major Q cleared his throat. 'Even the walls have ears, Major Sahib,' he said, looking at me.

Major Q frowned and motioned for me to leave. I quickly gathered the used glasses and pretended to hurry out. Outside the door, I stopped just short of closing it.

'And shut the door behind you,' I heard the soldier shout.

Quickly I pulled the door shut. Not a sound could be heard now. And then I noticed the glasses in my hand. I had always wanted to do this, I thought, as I pressed one against the door.

The sound was muffled but clear enough for me to make out one thing. Your life was in danger.

⚖

Whatever I heard, I kept to myself. Mainly because it did not make any sense. I knew it was a code for an attack, but when, where and how? For days I pondered over it. Talking to Soldier Rahim was useless, his lips more firmly sealed than the jammed handles of our rusty old window.

Everywhere I went, the words danced before me. Everything I heard, they echoed in the background. It came to a point that when I spoke, the words threatened to jump out. It was then that I became afraid. What if they got into the wrong hands? What if I repeated them to the Major? No, I must write it down on a piece of paper and bury the paper in a deep pit. My stomach was too shallow. It was as I was writing it down in my slow hesitant scrawl that it hit me. The Big Gun was the General and the small one was you. For the Big Gun to stay, the small one had to be squashed. And the Hangman ... it must be the dreaded Secret Service. So they were the real killers behind your father's death. I always knew the General was too dumb to plot it all on his own. And the Big Brother ... well, that was too easy to figure out. But the code, it was a date and the name of a weapon. What could that mean? And then it hit me. The meeting Major Q was trying to arrange between you and the General ... It was a front, a ploy to lure you into his den. The squash was a blast that would be meant for *you*, not him!

I rushed to your house. I had to warn you not to attend the meeting. Seeing my urgency, the old guards let me through the gates, but I hesitated at the doorstep. Did I really owe you this loyalty?

As I stood waiting, a car pulled up the driveway. The man driving it knocked down the potted plants on the steps as he skidded to a stop. One crushed sunflower came rolling up to my feet.

I lifted the broken stem and looked up to see a pair of white leather shoes emerge from the car. They stepped over the strewn flowers and proceeded up the steps to the doorway. By the time my eyes travelled all the way up the man's gold-trimmed white suit, all I could see was the back of his oil-slicked mop of hair, jet black and styled like a film star's.

It didn't take me long to sum him up. Why was it that you, who knew what was best for the Nation, did not know what was good for your own self? Your taste in men was appalling. And this man was no exception. Flamboyant, excessive, a womanizer and a flirt, Sardar Balgodi was a feudal lord, better known as the country's most infamous playboy. I shook my head in disbelief. Why? I asked myself. Why would someone repeatedly set themselves up for disaster? But then again, perhaps his flaws appealed to the perfectionist in you.

You never could resist fixing things.

⚖

I waited for a couple of hours in the servants' quarters, catching up on the house gossip. When Balgodi finally left your room, I slipped in. I found you sitting on the white loveseat in the living room, your gaze fixed to the floor. The curtains, I noticed, were drawn.

'So he is the latest?'

You did not look up, but I saw your forehead crease.

'Who the hell let you in?'

'Madam, I have something to say...'

'I don't wish to hear it.'

'Rani Madam, it's important.'

You looked up. Your gaze travelled the length of my body as

you took in my clothes, my cheap plastic watch, my black hijab styled exactly like your white one, and finally you saw on my arm a handbag which, unlike yours, carried nothing but some loose change for the bus.

You laughed.

At that time, I did not understand why you were laughing. The fool that I was, I smiled back.

Suddenly your face became serious. 'You are pathetic, Nazo.'

It was my turn to look at myself now. I saw my feet, chipped red nail polish on stubby toes, a dusty pair of chappals and huge angry corns. A few inches away, your feet rested on a velvet footstool, the skin ivory cool, your toenails painted a flawless crimson, the soles soft and clean.

'What do you want?' you asked, your voice curt and harsh.

'I just wanted to tell you that...' I stammered, tripping over my own words.

The very words that till this morning had threatened to gush out in front of the Major were being shy and reticent in front of you.

'I ... I ... wanted to tell you that...' and then I stopped.

I stared hard at the smooth skin of your feet, my vision blurred by the image of my own cracked heels. The more I stared at the softness of your heels, the more my insides hardened. Why did I owe you this loyalty, why did I serve you so faithfully? Would you do the same for me? Would you walk miles on a hot windless afternoon to warn me? Would you go hungry, waiting outside my door for hours just to meet me? No, you didn't care about me. To you, I was just an embarrassment, a drunken memory which needed to be erased. In your scheme of things, I did not matter. I was a nobody.

But in that moment, something inside me began to change.

Perhaps, I, too, realized that things didn't have to be this way.

'Well, out with it,' you lifted one smooth foot and crossed it over the other. 'I don't have all day.'

'I just wanted to tell you...'

'Tell me what? Don't get married? I hope you haven't come to give me any more of your useless advice. Listen, Nazo, I have had enough...'

'That your life is in danger,' I finally blurted out.

'What?' you leaned forward.

I turned away.

'Wait. Stop. Nazo!'

I kept walking.

'I said stop!' the panic in your voice when I didn't was unmistakable.

You ran after me and gripped me by my shoulders. Turning me around roughly, you said, 'Tell me everything you know. Where did you hear this? Who said it? How? When?'

I shrugged off your hands.

'You owe me this,' you said and grabbed my wrist.

I shook it free.

'Wait,' your voice was gentler now. 'Look, Nazo, I know you are working at the Major's. If you have heard something ... If the General is planning something...'

Fear was written all over your face.

You sat down. 'I can't go through his torture again. The rats ... the darkness ... I would rather flee. Look, you have to tell me,' your eyes darted from side to side, 'for the sake of your slaughtered family.'

The old loyalty took hold of me. My feet grew roots and I stood frozen.

A moment of weakness.

'What would you do if someone hit you?' I asked.

'Hit them back?'

'Then you already know what you have to do.'

I told you about the Major's plan, gave you the activation code and left.

How was I to know you would go through with it?

Counsel: But Madam Rani Shah took her back.

Prosecutor: As a maid.

Counsel: Nevertheless she was welcomed back.

Prosecutor: Exactly. Again and again Madam Shah dismissed her. Yet somehow, she managed each time to crawl back in.

Counsel: It's because my client is a true loyalist. Madam Shah always realized her worth and welcomed her back with open arms.

Prosecutor: Or under pressure. Miss Khan, I think you were blackmailing her.

⚖

It was a blast that rocked the city. Still the General survived. He was beginning to seem invincible. But at least it shook him out of his stupor. Elections were finally announced.

One minute we were reeling from the shock of the General's announcement and the next minute yours. You were going to marry. The papers were full of it. In fact, it wouldn't be wrong to say that news of your wedding overshadowed news of the elections. That too in a country that had been under Jihadist rule for decades.

No small feat, wouldn't you say?

News travels fast. Despite your reluctance, your mother arrived from Geneva. And then, the true fireworks began.

I was sent for.

Still hurting from the earlier spat, I made sure to wear nothing that had been owned by you or even resembled it. From my thin cotton suit to my cheap sandals, everything was brought from my own money. I felt rich.

'You look different, Nazo,' you said as I walked in.

Probably because you can't recognize any of your old things on me, I thought. Aloud I said, 'I must have lost weight.'

You went back to your papers.

'Mummy is coming and the new maid hasn't showed up. You know what to do.'

I stared at you. Was this your way of thanking me for saving your life?

'Bring me some tea,' you ordered as if I had never left.

I entered the kitchen, dazed and unsure.

'Oof, these rich people!' Refugee said. 'Servants come, servants go, all the same to them. What do they care? Sometimes I wonder if there is any justice at all in this world, what with the rich and their ways,' he wiped his brow and threw the sweat into the curry he was stirring.

'Perhaps we all look the same to them,' he laughed. 'What do you think?'

I wondered if I had got my old job back.

Your mother swept into the house with a bevy of suitcases and with a flurry of servants behind her. Begum Shah reminded me of the north wind knocking down everything in her path.

'What's this?' she demanded, her back straight as a rod, her hands fixed at her hips like the twin handles of an Egyptian jar.

For a second I thought she was talking to me.

'Oh...' I stammered, glancing around me. I moved quickly, tidying up the already neat room, fixing the already straight pictures on the wall, dusting things with the ends of my clean white hijab.

She marched towards me.

'Sorry, Madam...' I cowered as she approached, dread inching up my skin with every step. But she walked right past me.

'Just what is this mess?' she took off her dark glasses and shook them at you. It was then that I noticed her eyes. Both seemed to be the master of their own will. One was fixed on you while the other roamed freely.

Despite the comical eyes, there was nothing funny about her. She stood this close to you and I could feel you burn under the heat of her breath.

'Just what do you think you are doing?' she spat out the words, chewing every syllable. 'How can you announce your marriage without consulting me?'

You remained silent.

'Well?'

'You married Papa without telling anyone.'

She raised her hand. A sharp stinging slap landed on your face.

'How dare you? How dare you compare your father with that two-bit bourgeois? Really, Rani, your stupidity has exceeded all limits this time!'

She raised her hand again to strike you, and it was then that I broke my silence.

'Stupidity doesn't keep time, Madam Begum.'

'What?' she demanded.

'I said...'

'I heard what you bloody well said,' she blinked at me as if I was a pesky fly that had wandered in.

'I…'

'Shut up and get out! I need to speak to my daughter, in private.'

'No.'

'What?' she spun around to face me. 'You bloody fool. How dare you talk back? Get out!'

'No. I won't leave,' I stood my ground and said, 'Not if you treat our Rani Madam this way.'

'And just who the hell are you to tell me how I should treat my own daughter?' she said, raising her hand to strike me.

I stole a glance at your face and I thought I saw the hint of a smile. You were softening. Chuffed at this unexpected thaw, I announced, 'I am Nazo.'

She dropped her hand.

'Nazo!' she said, greeting me like an old friend.

You looked as astonished as I was.

'So *you* are Nazo,' she smiled, and I wondered if this was the calm before the storm. 'I remember you.' Her voice changed and instead of the growl, a sweet husky tone came out of her mouth. 'Why didn't you say so before?' I could see the corners of her mouth twitch upwards in a vicious smile as she turned her whole body towards me. 'Darling Nazo, how can I forget you? I am indebted to you. After all, you're the mole who told me about the previous suitor.'

I glanced across at you. Your face was frozen again, and you were staring at me in that unbelievable manner that can only be called betrayal.

⚖

Later that day, Begum Shah called me into the dining hall. You were sitting next to her, staring at some invisible spot in the distance.

'Nazo,' she said in a saccharine-sweet voice, 'I'm not at all happy with you.'

She tilted her face towards you, patted your head and put a firm hand around your shoulder. 'You have not looked after our Rani well.'

She leaned forward and pointing a finger at me, said, 'After all, we depend on loyal faithful servants like yourself for Rani's welfare. And you let us down. It was your duty to inform me about this relationship. The matter has reached talk of marriage and I was not even told of the courtship. *Ya Khudayi*! I am not at all happy about this.'

She shook her head for emphasis, her eyes wandering in different directions.

'The thing is, Begum Madam,' I hesitated, unsure which eye to make contact with, 'I no longer work here. I was dismissed.'

'What? Impossible! A nice girl like you?' She looked towards you and said in a voice as clear as a cloudless desert sky, 'Nazo is staying here. And that's final.'

Prosecutor: Like a cat, Miss Khan seems to go from door
   to door, never sticking to one house too long. And
   like a cat, she knows how to play the mice against
   each other.

Defendant: I thought you liked cats, Omar Sir?

⚖

The news of my departure didn't go down well in the Major's
household.

'Oye Nazo,' Driver Shafiq joked, 'you change households more
frequently than our politicians change parties.'

'She must have been a cat in her previous life,' the cook added.
'They change seven houses before they settle down.'

Only Soldier Rahim was quiet.

'So you are leaving?' he said later that night as I rolled up my
bedding.

'Just the household, not you,' I smiled.

He took me in his arms and hugged me so tight I could hardly
breathe. 'You will come back every night after work, won't you?'

I hesitated.

'I can't really work at Rani Madam's and stay at the Major's …
Not after their falling out.'

'Yes, you can,' he said and pressed his lips tight against mine.
That night he bit me, clawed at me, digging his hands roughly
into my flesh.

I let him. Told myself it was the price I had to pay for a roof
over my head when you turned me out.

'Nazo,' he kept whispering, as he made love to me that night with a ferociousness he had never shown before. I lay still beneath him, my eyes closed, my fists clenched. I was afraid of what was happening to my body, but I was more scared of what was happening to my mind. I found myself enjoying this queer violent side of Soldier Rahim. The more roughly he handled me, the sharper the fantasy became. Afterwards, when he lay snoring next to me, his face aglow with tiny beads of pearly sweat, I finally realized whose face I had been imagining. In the hot windless night, I felt my body grow cold. Because, Rani, it was you I saw.

The Begum sent for me early the next morning. I left Soldier Rahim sleeping.

You avoided me the next few days. Every time I saw you, you turned away, cigarette smoke billowing out of your mouth as if your very self was on fire. It burnt me to see you poisoning yourself with that filthy habit, but I was powerless. You wanted nothing to do with me. Then on the last day of her stay, the Begum invited your pompous boyfriend over for dinner. He was everything you were not. Flamboyant, crass, loud. He boasted his wealth, the expanse of his lands, the names of his ancestors. Shockingly, you listened.

'So, you are a miner?' I heard the Begum ask as I brought out the tea trolley.

The man did not even know when to take offence. He twirled his moustache and said, 'Minor? Oh no, no, I'm old enough to marry. I look young, but...'

'Coal miner,' the Begum thundered.

'Oh! Ah yes, yes, we have many mines. From here till there,' he stretched his arms wide. 'As far as the eye can see, the mines belong to our family. We mine everything from salt to coal to even,' he dropped his voice as if about to reveal a secret, 'even diamonds!'

The Begum shook her head.

'It is true, Begum Shah-ji. Just the other day, we found a big rock that a worker was trying to smuggle out. My uncle, who is like a hawk, caught him, and whipped the skin off him. He knew nobody would risk his hunter for an ordinary piece of coal, so he had it cleaned, and it gleamed like your daughter's skin. Shiny and beautiful. It was a diamond, I tell you. Ask anyone.'

I imagined the welts on the poor miner's body and felt my face grow hot. I looked at you and nearly threw up. You were staring adoringly into his eyes, as he said in his oily voice, 'No diamond is as beautiful as you, my dear Rani. I tell you that, my lovely.'

I heard the Begum clear her throat.

'So mining is your family profession?' she asked, as you continued shamefully to stare into his eyes.

'A miner is someone who mines the land, Begum Madam,' I said. 'Not someone who owns them.'

You looked sharply at me as the Begum smirked. The words had escaped before I could stop and now, I felt your burning stare sear me.

Balgodi frowned as he followed your gaze.

'It is not good to give these servant types so much liberty, Rani dear. All your Western education has made you forget that, here, the poor do not speak amidst the rich. It is considered out of order.'

You looked at the floor as the Begum smiled knowingly.

'Get rid of her,' he said. 'She has sprouted wings.'

The Begum stopped smiling and quickly jumped in. 'Oh, let it go, son,' she said, pushing her dark glasses up her nose. 'These are poor people. What do they know about manners and etiquettes.'

'But, Begum Shah-ji, give them a finger and they will grab your whole hand. Better not to let them take any liberties at all,' he said.

He was talking about me as if I was not in the room. Perhaps I *had* become invisible.

'Oh come now, let it go,' the Begum soothed. 'You know how it is with old servants. Sometimes they forget their place. Besides, good maids are so hard to find these days.'

I looked at you, but you avoided my eyes. Instead you lit a cigarette then put it out as Balgodi turned to look at you, his eyebrows arched. You did this decisively, one jab and one grind, not the series of genteel taps you preferred normally.

The Begum cleared her throat and said, 'That'll be all, Nazo.'

'Yes, Begum Madam,' I said, feeling as if a string had been pulled on some part of my body. I heard myself say, 'Thank you, Madam. Thank you, Sir.' Another pull and I picked up the tray to leave.

'Wait, Nazo,' I heard you call.

I turned, a faint smile of hope on my lips.

'There are some clothes on my bedroom floor. Take them. We can't have the servants of this house looking like trash. Especially not the old and faithful ones.'

You looked down at your diamond-studded hands and folded them into fists. I knew then, you wanted to hit me.

⚖

I walked into the kitchen, my arms stacked with used crockery. For a moment I stood there, the soot-covered walls closing in on me. Perhaps I shouted at the boy doing the dishes. Perhaps he shouted back. I can't remember. All I remember is the pounding in my head as if someone was landing blows on my scalp, one after the other.

'Move!' I said, pushing the kitchen boy away. I did the dishes with such vigour that a glass smashed in my hand as I was washing it. Refugee knew better than to scold me in that state.

Later when I had cleaned every corner of the kitchen, mopped the floor till my reflection could be seen in it, dusted every nook and polished every surface, Refugee announced it was time to turn in.

'Come now, Nazo,' he said, tugging at my elbow, 'there is nothing more left.'

I cracked my knuckles and said, 'There is one more thing I need to do.'

'What?' he asked, his voice a bare squeak.

'You'll find out soon,' I said with a slow smile.

'I hate it when she says that,' Refugee said, turning off the lights.

I waited till I heard you leave with Balgodi in his flashy red sports car, as vulgar as he was. And then I entered your room. The floor was strewn with discarded clothes, dirty underwear, even old unused pads. I started folding the sheets, picking up your shoes, hanging up your clothes. Your red silky underwear lay on the floor. Quietly I slipped it on. The silk swirled around, sensuous on my skin. I paused in front of the mirror. Staring at my reflection, I wished that just once, I could change places with you.

Be careful what you wish for.

Later that night, I took out the folder on Balgodi I had stolen from Major Q's house on my last day there. It contained information about Balgodi's exploits, his tax evasions, and even rumours of bonded labour at his mines. How could you marry a man who stood for everything you were against? I felt bile rise up my throat. I thought of leaving the folder with the freshly ironed laundry I had placed on your bed. But then I thought better of it. In the state you were in, it would only aggravate you. I had to find another way. I caressed your silky red underwear that I still had on. And that was when the idea came to me.

I told myself it was for your own good. We were not much apart in age, yet it felt as if you were a child. You had to be guided, warned, pulled back when you reached for something harmful, steadied when you stumbled.

And you had to be taught how to walk before you could run.

Counsel: Mr Omar, you are trying to mislead the court!

Prosecutor: Your Honour, my suspicions are not unfounded. Feeling defeated at Madam Rani Shah's decision to marry, Miss Khan tried to break up the marriage.

Counsel: Guesswork is not concrete evidence, Mr Omar.

Prosecutor: Court will see the point in a moment. Your Honour, please see this fax sent a few months before the wedding. It is addressed to Begum Shah, who did not receive it until she returned to Geneva. It reads, 'Danger. Daughter getting married'. What was dangerous about her daughter getting married?

Defendant: The man she was getting married to.

Prosecutor: Thank you, Miss Khan. You just confirmed my suspicion.

The Begum could not stop you from getting engaged to that moustachioed man, but she did manage to install me back in the house. Our relationship was strained. You seemed more determined than ever to make me see my place.

I was a reproach to you, and a necessity.

You misunderstand me, Rani. All I ever wanted was to protect you. I loved you, worshipped you. But you mistook my admiration for imitation. By dressing like you, I wasn't trying to compete with you. By warning you against the Reed, I was only trying to stop you marrying the wrong man. But you didn't see that. You just saw me as a gatekeeper, an interfering servant who'd crossed a line. You never saw my love, my dedication, my loyalty.

You never saw me for what I was.

But I knew that, like a child sometimes hits its own mother, you too had lashed out at me. Yet, like mother and child, our bond was unbreakable. For no matter what you did, my heart refused to turn against you. To say I hated my heart, right then, would not be a lie.

But love, like milk, can turn sour if left out in the open too long. My pride began to nag me. How long could I put up with such treatment?

For what happened next, could you really blame me?

The night Begum Shah was to leave, I went back to Rahim's house for the last time. You laid it down: if I was to return, I'd have to break it off with Soldier Rahim. It took me a second to choose.

He walked in just as I was packing the last of my things.

'What happened?' he asked softly.

I didn't answer. He slid his arms around my waist.

'You're not leaving me for good, are you?'

'I am.'

'What?' he stepped back.

'I am leaving you. Forever.'

'But … why?' he asked. 'What did I do?'

I took a deep breath and turned around.

'You lied to me. You are a married man. You are a father of three. You used me, Soldier Rahim. You have ruined me, left me with nothing,' the lies tumbled out like a torrent. I tried not to look into his eyes.

'Nazo,' he bowed his head. 'I thought you knew.'

'You thought!' I shut the lid on my little tin trunk with as much force as I could muster.

'Nazo, I...,' he stammered.

'How would I know? Did you ever sit me down and tell me you were married?'

'Nazo, I thought someone would have said something. I mean, everyone knows about my wife in the mountains.'

'Look, you are a married man and you should have told me that before you ... took my honour.'

'Nazo,' he said, grabbing me by the shoulders, 'I will marry you. A man is allowed four wives.'

'Yes, only four wives but innumerable lies. No, Soldier Rahim. Once a liar, always a liar.'

A sound erupted from his throat. A guttural sound that made me shiver. He raised his hand as if to strike me. Instinctively, I covered my face. When no blow struck, I peeped through my fingers and saw he was doubled over, trying to hide his tears.

The man really cared.

I stood where I was, wondering how it was that someone like him could love a person like me.

'Don't leave me, Nazo,' he pleaded. 'I love you.' He reached out to grab my hand, gripped it with all his might. And that is when I understood what it was all about. Love was just another name for possession.

'I can't let you go,' he said. 'I won't.'

I shook off his grip and stepped out. Before I shut the door, I turned back to look at him one more time.

'Get up, Soldier Rahim,' I said. 'Crying doesn't suit grown men.'

He looked crumpled, old and undone. A broken man.

It wasn't my fault.

⚖

Back at your house, the garden and walls were lit up with
miniature oil lamps, but the real fireworks were taking place
inside. I walked in to find you arguing with your mother. Begum
Shah was blowing her nose into a handkerchief, her wandering
eyes red and watery. Something told me it wasn't a cold that had
made her face swell up like a toad.

'I have no choice, Mother,' I heard you say. 'I have to do this.
For Papa's sake.'

'Rani! Your father would have never wanted you to marry an
uncouth tribal like that.'

'Papa wanted to see me in politics.'

'Oh Rani,' her voice dropped. 'Parents dream all sorts of things
for their children. Yes, your father wanted to change things, but
even he knew he couldn't install a woman on the heads of these
fools. They will never let a woman rule over them. Come back to
Manhattan, my darling. Leave this jungle of a place. You never
have to come back here.'

'No.'

A fresh bout of tears sprouted from the Begum's mismatched
eyes and she blew her nose even harder.

'Mother,' you said, your tone gentler this time, 'go back. You
don't need to worry about me.'

'Of course I do,' she said. 'I can't leave you to these dogs. They
will rip you to shreds.'

You let out a long exasperated breath. 'Mother, believe

me, Balgodi will take care of me. He's a powerful man. He has connections. People are…' Here you hesitated and looked around.

I stepped back into the shadows.

'People are afraid of him.'

The Begum's shoulders slumped.

'He will protect me.'

Suddenly the Begum looked small and shrunken. Her red nose seemed to encompass her entire face, her eyes shrivelled up like raisins, and I marvelled at how vulnerable she looked.

Perhaps she really did care.

'I hope you never know,' she said, gently letting go of your hand, 'what it is to walk away from your child.

She stood up.

'Goodbye, my little girl.'

You shivered as she walked out of the door.

A chill of the heart.

⚖

Twice Rahim came to see me and twice I refused to meet him. By now everyone knew that something was up. I didn't want him to think I left him because of you. He already hated you. I was afraid that Refugee or Driver Shafiq might tell him that I knew of his marriage. Deep inside, I knew it was only a matter of time before he figured it out. I felt like I was in an elevator cut loose at the top. Falling, falling, not knowing when it would stop. I could have put a stop to it, but no, I did not want to be caught. You see, telling a lie and being called a liar are two completely different things. One is an impulse, an instinct of survival, a reflex action. The other, plain wrong.

And I hated being wrong.

The bell rang again and I froze, wondering if it was him. It was. But before Rahim could approach me, there was a flurry of voices at the door. Balgodi's car entered the driveway. He stepped out in his usual pomp, his white clothes so starched and unfitting that they seemed to be wearing him rather than the other way around. He walked with his arms held out against his sides, like a wrestler entering a ring. A snap of his fingers and a couple of his servants came running up with a cigar and a matchbox. One lit it while the other stuck it in his mouth. He waved them away and they melted into the background. Balgodi strode up the driveway steps. No one spoke for a while.

'Is that the man...' Rahim asked.

'Who else.'

'Only Allah knows what makes people fall in love,' he said.

'You should know, Soldier.'

He looked at me and smiled kindly.

'I won't bother you any more, Nazo. I only wanted to tell you that I'm leaving. Going back to the village.'

I felt a tightening around my heart. Something was slowly squeezing, slowly stopping the flow of blood. I wanted right then to shut my ears, to stop him from leaving. Could it be that I had grown fond of him?

'Don't go,' the words escaped my lips before I could stop them. I saw the surprise I felt, reflected on Rahim's face.

'What's the matter, Nazo?' Refugee murmured from behind us. 'You are not falling for a married man, now, are you?'

Soldier Rahim's face flushed and he fingered the strap of his rifle.

'Perhaps,' I said, without taking my eyes off him. 'Perhaps I am.' Then turning to Refugee, I added, 'What's it to you, bastard?'

I took him to my quarters, away from the prying eyes of Refugee and the soft sniggering of the other servants.

The flow of blood in my heart began to even out as I put a saucepan on to boil.

'This is where it all started,' I said, as I pushed him down gently on the mat. The pan of milk brimmed over. Two cups lay in waiting.

My heart sped up, once again, pounding against the valves. No good ever came of these thing, I thought. Still, I consoled myself, I was the kind of woman who didn't even throw away old receipts. And this was a lover.

'Rahim,' I said, as I poured out the tea. 'I don't want you to go, but I can't be with you either.'

'But why, Nazo?' he gripped my hand. 'You are not her slave. You are allowed a life of your own.'

I felt a rush of blood to my head as I realized even he could see how much I cared for you. The only person who couldn't was *you*.

'I can't marry you,' I said, 'not yet. But perhaps one day...'

He reached out and took me in his arms. And I let him. He made love with a tenderness that was completely unlike the last time. Afterwards, it was I who reassured him that all I needed was time. He closed his eyes, silent tears seeping out of his eyelids. I reached out to wipe them, thinking, perhaps I too could have a home.

There was a knock on the door.

'Get dressed,' I said, tossing him his clothes as I rose hurriedly. 'It's time for Madam's afternoon tea.'

⚖

I was in the living room, setting up the tea trolley when it happened.

'What good will this do?' Balgodi said, coming up behind me. Before I could turn around, he had put his arms around my waist and was kissing my neck. The cups shattered to the floor, a deep stain spreading across the Persian carpet.

'You?' he said, as I got down on my knees. Untying my headscarf, I began wiping the rug with it.

'What the hell are you doing here dressed as Rani?'

I scrubbed harder, the thought of your angry face circling my eyes.

When I looked up, I saw him staring down at me. I tried to drape the hijab back across my chest, but the wet cloth only accentuated it.

'Ca … castoffs,' I stammered, as I picked up the broken pieces.

'Send in fresh tea,' he ordered, as I rushed out.

Outside in the hall, I could still feel his eyes on me.

Rahim was waiting for me when I returned to my little room.

'What happened to you?' he asked, getting up from the bed.

'The tea … I dropped it. On myself.'

He looked at me in that quiet way of his, then shook his head.

'That man is not right. I'd stay away from him if I were you.'

I looked up.

How could he know?

'Now change out of your wet clothes before you catch a chill. The weather is changing.'

If only feelings could change the way seasons do. But no. There is no change of colour, no drop in temperature, nothing at all in the air to warn you. And so it was that I was caught unaware when one day, watching your fiancé lean towards you, I felt something stir. Something deep inside me.

Prosecutor: Have you heard the saying about an animal who bites the hand that feeds it? I wonder if there is one for a servant who steals her mistress's husband.

Counsel: Objection! The world knows about Mr Balgodi's colourful personality. Mr Omar has got his facts wrong. It is he who tried to take advantage of Miss Khan. She is the victim here.

Prosecutor: But if she was being persecuted, as you say, why would she accept gifts from him?

Counsel: The fact that he was giving her gifts shows who was pursuing whom, my dear Mr Omar.

Loyalty is hard to find, Rani, but trust is easy to lose. Ever since I first heard of Balgodi's flirtations, I'd been wondering whether you'd forgive an unfaithful man.

But it never occurred to you if I would forgive an unfaithful woman...

It was one of those moments of unexpected clarity. One of those times when everything comes together. And so it was that one day, as I was cleaning your dressing room mirror, I paused. I peered closely at my reflection, touching my cheekbones, stretching the skin around my eyes, pouting my lips. But no matter which way I turned, I looked the same. Plain, ordinary, common and forgettable. And then I placed a hand over the scar by my chin. My face changed. I looked, I thought, almost pretty. I was the same height as you, of the same build, and my face had a similar bone structure. In a certain light, I realized, I could almost be mistaken for you.

A moment of truth.

In the coming days, I started to pay more attention to my looks. I bought a tube of whitening cream and started rubbing it in my skin at night. I also started using the scar-fading medicine, made out of shark bones, a Chinese herbalist had recommended. The scar didn't fade completely, neither did I become as fair as you. But it made me feel less like myself.

And when you live in the same house, tell me, is it unusual to bump into others? It wasn't my fault if certain people began to look at me in a new light. If at all, it was the fault of your castoffs. As they say, clothes make a man, or in this case, break a man.

It didn't surprise me that Balgodi had a roving eye, but that I enjoyed the attention was unexpected. I felt as if I had suddenly become powerful. I could walk in when you were deep in conversation and he would stop to look at me. At first you didn't mind. I dare say, you didn't even notice. And then one day, he brought you a gold bangle. I stared from my place by the door as he put it on your wrist. Later when you went up to bed and I came in to clear up, he grabbed my wrist and thrust something in my hand. A silver bracelet. I laughed and, the fool that he was, he thought he had me.

But he was wrong. I wasn't laughing because I was pleased with the trinket. I was laughing because it was so easy. I looked at him and thought, I could have him.

I could have him too.

That evening after dinner, when you went out in the garden for a stroll, for once he didn't follow you. He sat there, smoking in the air-conditioned dining room, choking the air with thin grey spirals. I leaned forward to clear the dirty dishes in front of him. He stared coldly ahead. But when I turned to go, he grabbed my arm and pulled me into his lap.

'What did you do with my gift?' he asked.

'Let me go, Sir.'

'Did you sell it?'

'Someone will see us,' I struggled half-heartedly.

'Let them.'

'What are you saying, Sir? My neck will be on the line.'

'You didn't like my gift?'

I smiled and bit the end of my hijab to cover my scar. 'Gold for the swan and silver for the duckling?'

He laughed and loosened his grip. I got up and ran to the door.

'Wait,' he said.

My hand was on the handle as he raised his arm.

'Catch,' he said.

As if I'd miss.

A thin golden chain swung from my hand. The chain he wore around his neck. A twenty-four-carat gold one.

I folded my palm around the glittery gift and smiled. You see, the ugly duckling *can* turn into a swan.

⚖

Perhaps it was the gold that made you do it. I was serving you your favourite meatball curry when suddenly you gripped my wrist. You brought it close to your face and stared at the delicate chain hanging from it. I had wound it twice around my thin wrist and pushed it up my sleeve, but you know what they say about gold dust and lust – two things one can't hide, *chhupay na chhupti*.

You didn't ask me where I got it. Instead, you got up abruptly, knocking back your chair. You marched into your room and from the noises, as you opened drawers and cupboards, I could tell you were hunting for your own gold chain. You must have found it, for you came out and resumed your meal as if nothing had been the matter. But I could see that the familiarity of the chain had disturbed you. You couldn't quite place where you had seen it before, yet suspecting someone of theft was not a thought that could be dismissed easily. Doubting them of cheating was even worse. The two thoughts must have collided in your head, for right after the meal you marched up to the telephone and dialled his number.

'We should set a date.' You gripped the receiver hard, green veins criss-crossing angrily on the back of your hands. 'For the wedding, Balgodi, what else?'

Prosecutor: It was a cold, premeditated act. An act of violence. Witnesses have testified that on the night of the wedding, Miss Khan pushed Madam Shah off the stage.

Counsel: But witnesses also say that it was Miss Khan who saved Madam from a dangerous fall by grabbing her arm just in time.

Prosecutor: Like everything else, it was an act. An act to gain trust. The truth is, her plan ran much deeper. Admit it, Miss Khan.

Defendant: I do.

⚖

And then the fateful, or should I say unfaithful, night came. The house was filled with flowers. Lit up like a castle. You came down, goddess-like, in your flowing white bridal gown. None of the frilly feminine stuff for you. You wore a graceful lace dress with a delicately embroidered white veil. Your groom marched in, wearing black tribal customs. The contrast between you two could not have been more stark.

Guests and dignitaries poured in. Drinks flowed, gifts followed.

And then, it was my turn to give you a wedding gift. After all, you had done so much for me, Rani. It was the least I could do to return the favour.

⚖

After the nikkah, dinner was served in the white marquee set up on the sprawling lawns of your home. You sat smugly on the stage, not quite the demure little bride but not the fearless revolutionary either. Your groom mingled with the guests, drinking scotch after scotch until the echo of his laughter dominated all other sounds. Why not? I thought, sending Refugee over with yet another tumbler of whiskey. After all, it was his wedding day.

Just before midnight, I went up to the stage with a plate of food for you.

'Please eat something, Rani Madam,' I said, holding it out to you. 'You must be starving.'

Deep in the midst of a conversation, you looked startled to see me by your side. 'Nazo,' you said, 'meet Pervez Sahib, one of our old Party loyalists. We have just managed to secure his release from the General's prison. Pervez Sahib has suffered a lot for the sake of democracy. Please take him inside.'

I looked at the man next to you. He must have been young at some point, but right now he looked as if he was born old. His lined face bore traces of torture where cigarette burns had been pressed upon his skin. The nerves around his temples stuck out and his eyes darted from side to side, as if any minute now the General's men would jump out of the bushes and drag him back.

'Poor man,' you whispered, tapping my shoulder. 'But for you, he'll do.'

Was it the weight of your words or the lightness of your touch? Suddenly I felt myself pushing against you. Perhaps it was the heavy dress or the exaggerated coiffure, but you lost your balance. You began to fall backwards. I grabbed your arm just as you were about to tumble off the stage, the plate in my hand splattering on the train of your white veil. Splashes of gravy smeared its edges and an oily stench filled the air.

'No!' you stared in horror at the spreading stain.

'Forgive me, Madam,' I said quickly.

Not a hint of regret.

You looked harshly at me.

'I'm sorry. I'll wash it out, no one will even know.'

'What do you mean?' you said, pushing me away. 'Do you expect me to sit here with my head uncovered on my wedding day?'

I offered you my hijab, but you looked horrified.

'Please, Rani Madam,' I said, 'let me wash it or the stain will set.'

Anger mapped your face, blue veins in your temple sticking out like tributaries.

Déjà vu.

'You can't do anything right, Nazo. You're bloody useless.'

'I know, Madam but nobody will notice your veil is not on. Not at this hour. Please let me,' I insisted, as you dabbed at it with a paper napkin. 'It's late and people are drinking. Only your close friends are left. No one will mind.'

'Yes, yes, Rani Madam, let the girl clean it,' Pervez Sahib added in his low shaky voice. 'The guests have mostly gone. And thankfully none of the journalists are left.' His eyes darted nervously, and he whispered, 'You never know whose side they are on.'

Reluctantly, you let go of the bridal veil.

'Five minutes,' you hissed.

'Five minutes is all it takes.'

⚖

Upstairs, I stood naked in front of your dressing room mirror. I picked up a dangling gold earring from your dresser and held it against my earlobe.

'Charming,' I said, the same way you did when someone cracked a joke not to your taste. I put the earrings back and picked up your bangles, watching them slide down my thin wrists all the way to my elbows. Your Chanel No. 5 looked too lonely to be left out, so I sprayed it at my reflection, then walked through the cloud, like I'd seen you do. The red lipstick beckoned next. I drew lines on my lips with my inexperienced hands only to look like a child's drawing where the colour had seeped over the edges. Lastly, I draped your wedding hijab over my head.

I looked in the mirror.

'Mirror, mirror on the wall. Who's the loyalist of them all?'

Footsteps sounded outside and I pulled the veil over my face.

Balgodi walked in clutching his bladder and rushed blindly to the toilet. So the tumbler had the desired effect, I thought with a slow spreading smile. He was staggering out of the loo when he noticed me. I sat on the bed and pulled the thin cloth further down my face. Beneath the veil, I wore nothing.

He came close and began lifting the veil, but the sight of my bare breasts stopped him. That was enough. There was no need to uncover the face.

'Let the wedding night begin,' he said.

Three thrusts and he slumped over me. The snores began almost immediately.

It was over in exactly five minutes.

You were humming when you came up.

I was scrubbing the gravy stains on your veil, now caked with dry white semen when you walked in.

'*Salaam*, Rani Madam.'

You must have forgotten all about it, for you rubbed your eyes when you saw me.

'Nazo, what are you doing here? Do you even know what time it is?'

'The thing about time, Madam, is that it can change anytime.'

'What nonsense,' you smiled. 'Now get out.'

'Yes, Rani Madam,' I said, invisible strings tripping my tongue and bowing my neck. 'Happy wedding night, Rani Madam.'

You shut the door in my face.

I waited outside till I heard a small stifled scream. Then I walked up to the mirror in the hall and, draping the wet veil around my head, I told myself it was for your own good. I warned you. But you went ahead and married a man who thought with his penis.

Your husband slept with me on your wedding night.

Yes, Rani, that's right. I had him first. Now, for the rest of your married life, you would be using my castoff.

See what he had reduced you to?

Counsel: Your Honour, prosecutor is leading the defendant. My client's words are being taken out of context.

Prosecutor: On the contrary, it shows that Miss Khan was plotting to attack Madam Shah. And she kept trying until she succeeded...

They say nothing in life is free. Everything comes at a price.

I say they are right.

The cost of revealing your husband's true face was higher than I had expected. That night, when I slid into bed next to Rahim, he knew something was different. He turned away from me and when I reached out to caress him, he pretended to be asleep. Somewhere hidden in his jagged breath, I thought, I heard a cry.

And that is how, when the time came, I knew the child could not be his.

The next day, I walked into the house with my heart pounding.

Had you, I wondered at this point, even noticed what had happened? Was the scream merely spotting a roach in the bathroom? I didn't know if I was deluding myself or just hoping for the best, but when you showed no reaction, I decided it was because you valued my loyalty more than this cheap voters stunt of a marriage. Balgodi, for you, was just a stepping stone to a seat in the Parliament. It's not like you loved the man.

Or so you thought...

In all the hoopla about your marriage, the General had ceased to be the threat he was. Indeed a bigger worry these days on my mind was your domesticity. So engulfed had you become in playing house that I feared you might just give up politics all together.

And it was this fear that led me to do what I did next.

The General, I thought, must be having the last laugh. Hardly had the excitement of your wedding died down that the news of your pregnancy spread like fire. Women, he must be thinking, good for running a home but not a country. For a politician, I was amazed at your lack of planning. Firstly, I couldn't believe you'd allow that scumbag to come close to you. Secondly, could you not have taken precautions? How potent must this man's sperm be, I thought every time I saw you bend down to vomit. Day after day, night after night, you doubled over, throwing up till your skin turned grey. A time came when, one hand clutching your stomach, the other clasped over your mouth, you dashed to the bathroom in the middle of a political rally. No more meetings, no more rallies, you ordered. All you wanted to do was rest.

She'll be knitting next, I said to Refugee, and indeed Balgodi's next gift to you was not a piece of jewellery but a ball of wool. He threw one at me too, but I threw it right back. What did he think I was, a kitten?

Meow. Curl. Scratch. If I was a cat, I'd scratch his face off, I thought, as I picked up the woolly strands you kept dropping on the carpet. You were dozing off in your green rocking chair, one hand on your belly, the other holding a pair of knitting needles. Gently, I pulled the needles from your grasp. The stitches came undone. I looked at the sleek grey metal sticks in my hand. Without the wool, they looked like small steel swords. I pointed one at your belly.

'Look what he has turned you into?' I whispered. 'A silly doting housewife.'

Pointing them accusingly at you, I thought, truly, Rani, you had trashed all my expectations. Whatever else, this content Mother Mary-like avatar of yours was something I'd never expected.

Just then you let out a gentle snore and a soft belch. I shivered. Something had to be done.

And as usual it fell on my shoulders.

I leaned closer.

Your unborn child was stubborn. Like you, not easily dislodged.

I should have known.

After the accident with the knitting needles, when you bled profusely having poked yourself in the belly while sleeping, you gave up knitting all together. You became even more lazy, just sitting around, doing nothing. Not even listening to the news or reading the papers. All of the General's latest exploits went unnoticed.

But as they say, necessity is the mother of invention. I tried ripe papaya, which Refugee told me you had to avoid strictly in your diet. But even that couldn't shift the bastard. One day, as you began your second trimester, I managed to set fire to the long trail of your hijab, hoping you would jump up and down and finally miscarry. But the unborn child was beginning to seem as invincible as the General himself.

Perhaps that's why their destinies turned out to be so similar.

Sometimes life doesn't go the way we want it to. Like a house of cards, we are forced to watch as it all comes crashing down. We stand back helpless, frozen in fear.

This was one such time. I could see you throw it all away, yet I was powerless to stop you. You neither listened nor cared. I wondered if this would blow over, but no. You were well into your second trimester and that damned baby was showing no signs of going anywhere but out into this world. I felt sorry for you. All your struggles, your sacrifices, your years in exile … all wasted. And for what? A selfish demanding baby who'd cling to you till your proud erect back became crooked as a sickle, suck you till your beautiful breasts dried up like shrivelled raisins, and challenge you till your will was broken. You were giving up your life, Rani. A life that was meant for us. You had forgotten your promise to us. You were no longer our saviour.

You needed a reminder.

Prosecutor: Your Honour, in the days leading up to the General's death, the kitchen boy swears he saw Miss Khan mixing something in Madam's food. The plan was to kill two birds with one stone.

Counsel: Mr Omar is letting his feelings for his friend, Madam Shah, get in the way of questioning.

Prosecutor: I thought you might say that, Counsel. I'll have you know that my words are backed by evidence. I'd like to call my next witness: kitchen boy, Mr Chachar.

Judge: Proceed.

Clerk: Please place your hand on the Holy Book and swear to tell the truth, the whole truth and only the truth.

Witness: I do.

Prosecutor: Now that you are done with the oath, tell me what you saw. Don't be scared, Chachar, just tell the truth. All right, why don't you just tell us how old you are?

Witness: Seventeen, Sir.

Prosecutor: Have you been working long at the Shah House?

Witness: Since I was thirteen, Sir.

Prosecutor: And you saw, just before the elections, Miss Khan mixing something in Madam Shah's food?

Witness: Yes.

Prosecutor: Did you tell the cook, Mr Refugee, about it?

Witness: Yes.

Prosecutor: And he ignored it?

Witness: Yes.

Prosecutor: Would you say it could be poison?

Witness: Yes.

Prosecutor: Thank you. Your witness, Counsel.

Counsel: Thank you, Mr Omar. Now Chachar, what happens
when someone is given poison? Do they die?

Witness: Yes, Sir.

Counsel: But Madam didn't.

Witness: Yes.

Counsel: So do you think it could have been something
else, like mint or aniseed, perhaps? For as far
as I remember, Madam Shah had terrible morning
sickness. Am I right?

Witness: Yes.

Counsel: So could it be that Miss Khan was mixing an
indigestion remedy?

Witness: Yes, Sir.

Counsel: So now you're saying she wasn't trying to kill
her but help her?

Witness: Yes, Sir.

Judge: Mr Chachar, can you say anything else besides yes?

Witness: Yes.

Counsel: Well there you have it.

Prosecutor: Objection, Your Honour, she could be adding
poison in small doses. Maybe it wasn't morning
sickness but slow death.

Counsel: Your Honour, I'm afraid my colleague's conspiracy theories are going from subliminal to ridiculous. The truth is, if my client wanted to kill Madam Shah, she would have done so long ago.

Confident that you couldn't possibly campaign and give birth at the same time, the General fixed the date of the elections at the exact time of your confinement. If anything, this should have made you snap out of your domesticated stupor. But it was not to be. You continued to laze around like a bloated mother hen, obsessed with the sight of your own belly. You were not even ashamed to go out in public, waddling like a duck, looking anything but the future leader of our Nation.

You were not the only one who'd lost interest in the General's hide-and-seek elections. It was your pregnancy that dominated the media more these days. In fact, even the uncertainty of the elections was drowned by it. Instead of 'Will he or won't he call the elections?', the question on people's lips was, 'Will she or won't she quit after motherhood?' It was hard enough for people to digest that a woman was vying for the top position, but a mother-to-be, out of the question.

Only those close to you knew that even if you did contest, your chances of being elected were slim. You were hardly able to move, Rani, let alone campaign. Unless, of course, it was to do some more shopping for the baby.

Truly, Rani, pregnancy had loosened the nuts and bolts in your brain. You were no longer capable of deciding your own good or bad. You spent hours reading mothering manuals, when you should have been lobbying. Even the women's cause didn't

light a spark in your eyes. You started asking me to turn away
activists and workers, not even bothering with false promises of
promoting the cause on winning a seat.

It was no longer a priority.

At first I was angry at your behaviour, Rani, but now I began
to pity you. After all, it wasn't your fault. Your body was going
through a change. It was bound to affect your mind. But then one
night I had a thought: I was still the same. I hadn't changed. So,
then, why was I just standing by watching you throw it all away.

I had to do something.

But what?

The answer to that came, of all people, from your husband.

Once again the women's group came knocking on your door and,
once again, you buried your head in the sand like the ostrich
you had become. I ushered them out, making excuses on your
behalf, their disappointed faces etched in my mind. What kind
of an example were you setting for them, I thought with a surge
of anger. That it's okay to give up everything you've struggled for
once you get married? That a woman's rightful place is at home,
breeding, cooking, housekeeping? I slammed my fist on the table.

Just then I felt a hand on my shoulder.

It was your husband. He looked startled when I turned around.

'You?' he hissed. 'How many times have I told you not to wear
her clothes. Don't you have any of your own?'

I could feel blood pounding in my head at the sight of him.
This man, who'd turned you into the grass-grazing cow you
had become.

'Surely you know that she can hardly get out of bed these days,' I said. 'She is expecting, you know. Expecting your child.'

Mistaking my anger for jealousy, he waved his hand dismissively and said, 'Bring my tea.'

I turned to go.

'And cut your hair short or something,' he murmured. 'You look just like her from the back.'

Of course, I thought.

That's it.

Since the day of your tainted wedding night, I had been wondering whether you knew. I didn't mean to humiliate you, Rani. I just wanted to protect you. I wondered now if your husband had noticed the difference when he finally made love to you. Probably he was too drunk to see that his prized bride had been replaced that night. Still, I couldn't help but wonder if *you* knew. If you did, you hid it well.

You always were so full of pride.

But the question was, if your own husband could mistake me for you ... then why couldn't someone else?

I called a meeting.

Yes, Rani, you heard me right. I, your illiterate servant girl, called a meeting of the Party bigwigs. While you were busy playing house, I was setting up shop. The flag of the Shahs was not going to fly at half-mast just because your attention was diverted. Not as long as I was alive.

And so, I began to plot.

But not against you, Rani. I did it for you.

I made appointments, drew up agendas, set up meetings. You laugh, Rani, but after all those years of rolling out meetings for you, I knew by now how to organize one for myself. Except I didn't say it was for me. Why would anyone listen to *me*?

And you were right, Pervez Sahib did do it for me. But not in the way you would have liked him to. You raise your eyebrows, Rani, but it was through Pervez Sahib that I operated. He was half deaf and half blind as it was and, in his zeal to please you, rarely questioned your orders. Yes, *your* orders. You may think you are as inimitable as your name suggests, but don't forget, Rani, God made each creature in pairs.

Counsel: Farfetched! Is my esteemed colleague seriously suggesting that Miss Khan impersonated Madam Shah? Am I the only one thinking that this is as fantastic as it is impossible?

Prosecutor: But that's just the point! Miss Khan can make the impossible seem possible.

Counsel: Mr Omar's imagination needs reining in, Your Honour. Members of Madam Rani Shah's party will be outraged at the suggestion. Does Mr Omar take them for fools? Or is he accusing them of lying as well?

How did I get away with it? *You are one to ask.* But if you insist, I will tell you.

It helped that you hardly ever answered your phone those days. Even if anyone had any doubts, they were unable to discuss them with you. Mostly I let the men talk while I sat quietly in a corner, pleading a headache, your trademark white hijab wrapped closely around my face. At other times, when I wanted to be involved in the discussions, I sat as myself, holding a large brick-like phone you called the cordless. 'Rani is listening through conference call,' I would say, making up a story about you being in a meeting with the American Ambassador or someone equally unquestionable. It was enough for them that their leader was present in spirit, if not in flesh. For you must have heard of the old Mughal strategy: kill the commander and the army's morale dies with him.

And the General, as you know, was a student of history.

But it didn't stop there. I wasn't just trying to keep up your Party's dying morale. I was out for victory. Whatever it took, however it took, *whoever* it took. I wanted you to win, Rani. I wanted it so badly that nothing seemed too big a price to pay.

Not even murder.

I made inquiries and when the time came, I went to see the Caretaker myself. I wore the white hijab and your huge black Chanel shades. I made sure to cover my face well and held myself straight, with one arm crossed over my chest like you. No names were exchanged. Only money changed hands for a sheaf of papers. It was the General's itinerary for his next round of meetings with the Americans.

It's true what they say, knowledge is power.

But power without purpose is useless.

By now I knew you would do nothing, even if I handed the leadership to you on a platter of gold. You just weren't in that state of mind right now. But I knew that your husband was not such a patient man. He had hoped that the marriage would yield more than just an idealist wife. If I'm not mistaken his eyes were on the end game. He wanted your power.

And power, like murder, is addictive.

Nothing wrong with that, I told myself one night, as I handed a confidential document over to him. At least he, too, wanted to see you elected. And if he got in the way later, he could always be dealt with.

I underestimated him.

But that's another story. For now, he played the dumb husband to perfection. I had to turn it right side up in his hands before explaining the power of the paper he held.

'The General's schedule,' I said, trying to keep the excitement out of my voice. 'And the passcode for the G1 plane.'

He stared at me, then at the paper. I could almost see the stream of questions running through his mind, like the ticker at the bottom of a news channel.

'I have confirmed information that the Big Brother is willing to sacrifice one of their own. If that's what it takes.'

Balgodi looked as if he would explode with disbelief. Scratching his head, he launched into a tirade of questions. 'How did you get this information? Why are you giving it to me and not to Rani? Are you trying to fool me? Implicate me? Is it really genuine? What do you want in return?'

'He killed my family,' I said, in reply to his bombardment. 'I want him dead.'

When it finally sank in, he reached for the telephone and dialled furtively.

'Aamir,' he said, 'a crate of our finest mangoes. Make sure it gets on the G1 military flight. Route 777, Operation Execute. I will send details of the passcode. And yes, the time has come to add the special ingredient. And one more thing, my boy. Make sure the mangoes are ripe. Check each one individually. *Arre*, don't ask why! Just think of it as a dying man's last wish.'

People say he loved mangoes.

⚖

That night after all the work was done, I crept into your room. You were lying on the bed, reading your favourite musty old novel. *Crime and Punishment*, the title read. I tried not to think about the contents.

'Rani Madam, shall I massage your feet?' I asked, wiping my hands on the edge of my hijab.

You raised your eyebrows but said nothing.

'They look swollen,' I said, reaching for the bottle of oil on the dresser.

'Okay. But heat the oil first.'

I began to rub the warm liquid into the soles of your feet. Your face relaxed, your eyelids drooped.

'Rani Madam,' I began. 'Won't you consider involving me in politics again? I really miss all the campaigning, the planning, the discussions … It's not that I don't like managing the house, but being in the office is something else. I was thinking...'

'Stop.'

You exhaled a long slow breath. Then peering at me over the book, you said in slow deliberate words, 'Nazo, I think you should settle down now. Find some nice boy and get married.'

My hands shook and a few drops of hot oil scalded my wrist. Pain seared through me.

I wondered if all my efforts would go in vain.

'The sooner the better,' you said. 'As they say, there is no time like the present.'

I placed your foot back down and thought, actually, there is no present like that of time.

Prosecutor: Miss Khan, where were you on the morning of 17 January 1992?

Defendant: Sir, do you remember what you ate for breakfast a week ago?

Prosecutor: Excuse me?

Defendant: Sir, what I'm saying is that if you can't remember what happened a week ago, how do you expect me to remember what I was doing on a particular morning years ago?

Prosecutor: Ah! Miss Khan, they don't call you clever for no reason. Please remember that it is you who's in the dock, not I. Let's leave the questions to me and answers to you.

Counsel: Objection, Your Honour! My client Miss Khan was trying to make a point. Mr Omar is being patronizing.

Judge: Overruled.

Prosecutor: Thank you, Your Honour. You see the reason why I think Miss Khan should remember the morning is because it was not like any other. It was the morning of the General's plane crash. It was the day she committed her first murder.

The crash, when it happened, was powerful enough to bring the entire Nation to a standstill. Of course it did not stop the General's colleagues from rushing to the Capital where the vacant hub of power lay. They flew off, even as the General lay roasting to death in the flames of the invincible G1 plane. No one knew how the US Intelligence had been infiltrated. How did anyone know the General would be flying on this plane and not his usual Eagle? There were no answers. All the clues were burnt. The only thing that remained intact were a few blackened mangoes ejected into the hills by the force of the explosion.

Villagers who found them said they tasted good enough to die for.

⚖

Like the sleeping beauty who wakes up to a kiss or the cygnet who transforms into a swan, you should, at this point, have reclaimed your rightful place too. This is where the story of your struggle should have found its happy ending. But instead, it was the beginning of the end for you.

The Jihadists ran for the hills, and while the entire Nation was rejoicing the General's death, you alone were mourning. I entered the house expecting you to be screaming with joy, instead I found you in tears. You sat alone, forlorn and tired, dressed in a widow's black, your hands stretched out in front of you, your palms facing the sky.

'Rani Madam?' I rushed over to you.

'Dead ... Dead.'

'Yes, he's dead! Isn't that fantastic? Nothing can stop you now.'

You slapped me hard across the cheek.

I had heard of people losing their mind to shock, and I wondered if this was one such time. After all, you had got your lifelong wish. The General was dead. Your path was clear.

'Rani Madam,' I said, pressing my palm against my cheek. 'It's all right. Everything will be all right now.'

You began to shake, your whole body shivering, your hands clenching and unclenching.

I dropped to my knees.

'Rani Madam,' I said, as gently as I could. I hadn't prayed in a long time, but I found myself on my knees. And I would have crossed all boundaries, too, had you not pointed to your stomach.

'Oh,' I said, realizing that you were mourning another death altogether. The death of someone who had not even entered the world.

Could God be so kind? I wondered, unable to believe that both barriers had been lifted at once. Could it really be true? Now, nothing could stop you. Except, of course, your own self. So many times you had been your own worst enemy. Still, I consoled myself, a known danger is better than an unknown one.

But how to make you realize? I wanted so much to make you see what a good hand fate had dealt you. But would you listen? No! You'd think I was trying to sabotage your happiness, keeping you away from the domestic bliss you seemed to crave so much these days. So many times, in these past few days, I had caught you talking to your dead father's photograph. 'I will be just like you,' I would hear you say. 'I'll have a house full of happy children and lead the Nation as well.' You fool! I wanted to shout. He was a man. He could have had ten wives and a hundred children, yet he'd be able to step out of the house each morning, go to work and not think once about them. A woman was different. She became bound to her child and stayed bound even after the umbilical cord was cut. And if she did manage to free herself, the world wouldn't let her forget that her place was back at home. Did you really not see how lucky you were as a woman to get this far?

My temples began to throb. Pain pulsed through my veins as I realized how dearly this could cost you. Till now, you'd been living off your father's legacy, but for how long? A daughter avenging her father's murderers can be inspiring. But a mother leaving her child to lead a country full of men was unimaginable. The public would have to open their mouths very wide and shut their eyes very tight to swallow this, Jihadists or no Jihadists. Come to think of it, even America had never had a woman president. So what of this backward land? And if by some miracle they did consider you their PM, how the hell would you go campaigning in your condition? You'd be nine months pregnant to the dot when the polls took place. You might even be in labour on the day of the election. How would you get sworn in? With an infant suckling at your breast? A fat, swollen, sleepless woman vowing to lead the country while she nursed her child. Seriously, Rani?

No, Rani *Jaan*, tears had blinded you. You could no longer see clearly.

But, thankfully, my eyes were still clear.

The baby was gone. I just had to make you realize what a good thing this was. You were free now. Truly free. Free of the General who wouldn't let you fly, free of the child who would bind you down. Finally, you were free to soar.

'Madam,' I began, but you hushed me with a wave of your hand. 'Rani Madam,' I carried on, 'it is God's will. Perhaps He has other plans for you. At least now you can focus on politics again…'

You pushed me away. I staggered but caught myself from falling.

'My child, my baby, my little baby…' you began to tremble.

How could I possibly bring up the General's death at this point? But still, I tried.

'Rani Madam,' I said softly, 'do you know what else happened today?'

'I don't care, Nazo,' you said, in an eerily hoarse voice. 'I don't care if the General blew to bits. All I care about is that my baby left me.' Your shoulders stooped and you seemed to be crumbling. Then just as suddenly you sat up and shouted, 'Balgodi! Oh, I didn't even think about him. Poor man, he will be so heartbroken.'

I didn't have the heart to tell you that he was busy raising toasts at the club.

Silent tears slid down your cheeks and it suddenly struck me, you really did love this child.

Perhaps even more than politics.

But could you, truly, not see how motherhood would take you away from your cause? From your own people? Weren't we your children too? Wasn't your life dedicated to us? But you were in no mood to listen. You sat there, weeping like a child whose favourite toy had broken.

It was unreal, sentimental, and overdone.

After a few minutes had passed, I could stand it no longer. I walked up to your rocking chair and held it still. Bringing my face as close to yours as I respectfully could, I whispered, 'Open your eyes, Rani Madam. You are no longer a mother-to-be, but you still have other duties to fulfil. You have a Nation to lead. Elections to win. Everything you have worked for is yours. There is nothing in your way any more. No one can stop you.'

Except you yourself.

You sat stone-still, eyes scrunched up like a pigeon wishing away a cat. Lips sealed, eyes covered and ears blocked, you reminded me of Gandhi's monkeys.

Hear no evil, see no evil, speak no evil.

And then I had a thought, perhaps it was I who'd been the monkey all along. Was I a fool not to have seen this sooner?

This is what it was really about.

The truth was before me. You wanted to have a child. You wanted to be a politician, a wife, a mother *and* a homemaker … You really thought you could have it all.

I felt a strange whirlpool like sensation in the pit of my stomach. I suppose a small amount of delusion was necessary to dream big, but with a greedy and corrupt husband like yours, you were in denial. Your heart would always be stuck in the child, and all sorts of domestic responsibilities would land upon your shoulders. You would be tired, depressed, neither here nor there. You would never have it all. Suddenly, your being elected as the first female prime minister of the country seemed much more plausible than you and Balgodi being a happy family.

I no longer envied you, Rani. I pitied you.

Slowly, I rose to my feet and made my way to the door. If this is what you wanted then this is what you would get. But my feet felt leaden. I remembered the saying: if you love someone let them go; if they come back they are yours; and if they don't, they never were. I placed my hand on the doorknob.

Truly, I tried to walk away.

But I couldn't. I loved you far too much for that. I knew that if the boys in khaki got wind of this, they would use it to delay the elections. Not that you seemed to care any more. Still, I tried.

'Rani Madam,' I said, turning around slowly. 'Have you told anyone yet?'

'Balgodi's phone is switched off.'

'I mean a doctor?'

'Phone lines are jammed. Must be the blast,' you said in a low defeated tone. 'Perhaps you should go to Dr Jami's clinic and fetch him.'

'But the bleeding has stopped, hasn't it?'

'Yes, Nazo, but there could be complications. And the baby, I mean the foetus. It came out ... in the toilet ... I mean I delivered...' you broke down again.

'Rani Madam, please. Get a hold of yourself. Listen to me, Rani Madam.'

Pressing your shoulders, I said, 'Madam, you must not tell anyone. Please! Not on the same day as the General's crash. The media will hound you. They will say you killed your own child to contest elections. They'll call you a witch, a *dyan*, a killer. The Jihadists will use it as propaganda. You have no idea how ruthless they can be. Wait a few days. Please.'

I could hear the slow creaking of the chair as it finally rocked to a stop. You wrapped your arms around yourself and shivered. The weight of my words seemed to have sunk in.

'Do you understand, Rani Madam?'

You looked so helpless, so small and wretched in that moment that I almost backed off. But I couldn't. At least one of us had to stay strong.

A low moan, a wild animal's cry of pain, escaped your mouth. 'Nazo,' you begged, 'just go away. Let me mourn my child. My baby, my poor...'

'They'll say you killed it.'

Your whole body shook as you cried.

'Rani Madam, you have to listen to me. You've got to be prepared for the worst.'

'What should I do?' you whispered between the tears.

'I know a woman who can help you. Very discreet.'

You stared unblinkingly at some faraway spot.

At least the sobbing had ceased.

'I will fetch her,' I said, without waiting for an answer. 'She doesn't live far from here. But before I go, where is the...'

I couldn't bring myself to say 'baby', and you couldn't bring yourself to say 'dead'.

In the end, I followed the trail of blood to the toilet. Inside, in the toilet bowl, I saw a tiny foetus no bigger than my palm. Fists curled, its head bigger than its entire body, floating in a pool of red.

It was a sight I would never forget.

The woman came. Nearly ninety, she moved slowly, and thankfully her eyes were too weak to recognize your face.

'In my business,' the old midwife murmured, 'we only recognize vaginas.'

I would have laughed, but she sent me off to bury the ... thing. I couldn't arrange a funeral or a burial in a graveyard, yet I knew I couldn't dispose of it any other way. The wild dogs and the stray cats would find it and, with my luck, leave it at your doorstep.

In the end, I buried it in the ground outside my room window. It was the only place that could not be overlooked by the rest of the house. It wasn't a shallow grave, yet, when I threw the first fistful of sand, I felt as if the thing's eyes flickered open. I laughed at my imagination. What would it say if it came alive, I wondered. Probably accuse me of having wished it to death. But this time, I swear I had nothing to do with it. You still don't believe me, do you? I suppose my story is a bit like the boy who cried wolf.

Except in your eyes, I was the wolf.

Counsel: My client had organized many things for Madam Shah, but murder was not one of them. She was not just a member of her staff but her friend, too.

Prosecutor: Well, as they say, Counsel, a foolish friend is worse than an enemy.

⚖

When I first found out, I thought I would lose my mind. And that is the worst thing that could happen to me. The mind is supreme, you see. Money, love, health, sex, it all happens in the mind. If you can control your mind, then you can do anything, I always say. But you never were interested in my views.

Mind games, you called them.

Since the incident, you had been sitting in the same rocking chair in which I had found you a few days earlier. You wore the same mourning black, the edges still caked with dried blood. It was as if you hadn't moved at all.

At first your inertia worried me. It was disconcerting to see you sitting like a Miss Havisham ... Yes, Rani, I did occasionally read the books you left lying around, however slowly. I have no great expectations of myself, but I do like to know what it was that absorbed you for hours on end. But I digress. What I was saying was that initially your motionless state, your lasting silences, made me uneasy, and my discomfort grew to a point where it became an affliction. Waves of nausea rode up my throat every time I saw you sitting so still. But gradually I began to understand that although you were sad, you were content in your grief. It was as if you had accepted your fate and were mulling over it. As if you had said everything there was to say, done all that you could do.

I only hoped you would come back to your senses in time for the elections. It would be horrible to see someone else reap the rewards of your hard work. Someone like your husband, I feared.

Last few days, the papers had been full of stories about him contesting on your behalf should the elections go ahead. And instead of refuting the rumours, he had been fuelling them with statements like, 'I will do my best to stand by my poor pregnant wife'. I wasn't sure if you were unaware or unaffected. In your statue-like state, hardly anything seemed to matter.

That day was no different. I brought you your tea, asked if you wanted to see the papers, make any calls, but you dismissed me with a wave of your hand. Once again I felt queasy. One minute I was putting down your tray, the next my head was spinning.

What goes around, comes around.

It was in the kitchen that Refugee found me retching my guts out. He placed a hand on my back and rubbed gently. 'Don't mind, Nazo,' he said, 'but you seem just like Rani Madam when she was expecting. Twelve times a day, I found her bent over, puking.'

I sat up straight. On the outside, I appeared impatient, brushing him aside as if I had some urgent work to do. Inside, I was trying to calculate how long it had been.

Only after I was sure, did I knock on your door.

'I'm pregnant,' I said, as soon as I entered.

A silence closed in on us. For a minute, I thought not even this could snap you out of your stupor. But I was wrong. Your left lip twitched, a small flicker of a smile. It was the first time since the twin deaths that you had displayed any emotion other than grief. I smiled back in relief.

It was then you got up and slapped me.

I didn't flinch.

You stared at me and then at your hand. Finally you spoke. 'So that is why you are here. To gloat.'

'It's your husband's child, Rani Madam.'

You struck me again. This time harder than before.

'I would have expected a better story from you, Nazo.'

I saw a glassiness in your eyes I took to be pain.

By now you had found out that Balgodi had a thing for other women, me being one of them. You blamed it on yourself. Having shut him out during the early days of the pregnancy, you told yourself it was his way of dealing with the neglect. I didn't have the heart to tell you that this had always been his way.

'Lies,' you whispered. Your eyes moistened as a single tear began its descent. And then, just as suddenly, your neck stiffened and your jaw tightened. 'So this is what it's about. This is why you didn't want me to tell anyone about the miscarriage. And what a fool I was to trust you again. After everything that happened. All this time, you were making a play for my husband.'

'I would never. Madam, please...'

You brought your face so close to mine that I was breathing your breath.

'Get out of my house.'

'Madam...'

'Now!'

'I was forced.'

You halted. Just for a second, but it was enough for me.

'You have to believe me, Rani Madam.'

'You lied to me before and you're lying to me again.'

'Lying is only easy the first time.'

You were trembling now, tiny bits of saliva gathering at the corners of your mouth.

I fell at your feet, gripped your ankles and begged, 'Madam, please, just listen to me. Just this once.'

You didn't move away.

I looked up and said, 'I know now how hard it is to keep up a lie, but the truth ... the truth is hard only the first time. It takes courage to speak the truth, but after that, it is easy to say it over and over again.'

I stood up and placed your hand on my belly.

'The child is his.'

You sank down to your knees. I don't know why, but seeing you crumple like a discarded tissue made me feel even worse. I didn't mean to bring you down, Rani. My intention was not to hurt you. All I wanted was for you to fight back. To see what a waste of time this pretend marriage of yours was. I wanted you to be whole again, but instead, you were breaking apart. I had to do something. I had to make you hate me again.

Anger, after all, is adrenaline.

You sent for me early the next day. I walked in, expecting to find you hunched and huddled, half curled into yourself, an injured cat licking her wounds. Instead, you were sitting up, peeling an apple.

'Fruit, Nazo?'

I looked at the slice you held out and felt a wave of bile ride up.

I gripped my stomach and lurched. You looked at my grey ashen face, my trembling hands, and smiled.

Instead of bile, I now felt anger rise up my throat. 'It may be funny for you, Madam,' I said, 'but what of this bastard in my stomach?'

You stopped smiling.

'Not funny now, is it, Madam? This *harami* growing inside me, this gift of your husband's.' I paused for effect, then said, 'If Soldier Rahim was to find out ... he'd never marry me.'

'But how would he find out,' you struggled to keep a straight face as you asked innocently, 'Didn't you break up with him?'

I bit my tongue. So you knew all along.

'Look, Nazo, it's no secret. Everyone's been talking about Rahim staying all night in your room. Why do you think I've been telling you to settle down?'

'Sorry, Madam, but I don't want to be just a wife,' I said, but the sarcasm was lost on you.

'Wife, whore, whatever you want to be, that's your problem. The question now is, what are we going to do with this child?' you pointed the knife at my belly. A shiver ran up my spine.

'Get rid of it, I suppose,' I said.

'Then why tell me?'

I had to give it to you. When you wanted, you could move like a chess pawn, determined to get to the other side and be the queen your name suggested.

'So,' there was a briskness to your voice as you said, 'you claim Balgodi slept with you and now you are carrying his child. And you had no knowledge of this when you told me to stay quiet about my miscarriage?'

'Swear on my life, Rani Madam.'

A slow smile began to spread across your face, and I felt the familiar dull ache pulling at my heart. This was no ordinary smile. This was the lull before the storm.

'Stay there.'

The words had barely left your mouth when you snapped into motion like a clockwork toy. First you went into the bathroom and took a long hot shower. When you reappeared, you were dressed in your trademark white hijab and a long green dress over white tights. It was as if you had washed off everything that had happened in the last thirty days. If your belly wasn't still soft and protruding I would have thought I had imagined it all.

'Bring me my diary.'

You walked up to the telephone, but your hand hovered over the receiver. You turned to look at me. 'If you cross me on this one, Nazo,' you said in a low hesitant voice, 'I swear I'll kill you.'

I braved a smile and held your gaze. For a second, I thought I saw the old camaraderie we had once shared. I saw your hand quiver, the nerves on the back stand up green. I saw your fingers twitching, felt the vibrations in your body, a heat emanating from your insides. And then I saw through you. I saw the wheels in your brain turning, the sentences forming, the numbers clicking, and then it was as if a curtain had dropped across the stage. There was only darkness. Complete and utter darkness.

When I opened my eyes again, I found myself lying on the floor.

Counsel: What of the fact that Miss Khan put her own political aspirations on hold to raise Madam Shah's children?

Prosecutor: Ha! Next my fellow counsel will say, she gave birth to them too.

The same old midwife was summoned. She declared me five months pregnant.

'What?' both you and I shouted in unison.

'How could anyone get this far without having any symptoms?' you looked suspiciously at me. Your face hardened. You turned away.

I told myself that this was my punishment for spoiling your wedding night. Though I was no believer in crime and consequence, I was touched by the fact that your heart was pure. For only those who believed got justice.

Just then you pulled out a crisp hundred from one of your books and handed it to the old woman. I noticed the title was *Crime and Punishment*. The letters seemed to be mocking me, again.

I wondered if this was a sign.

But this was no time to mull over your fat yellowing novels. I pushed the toothless crone aside and said to you, 'I can't have a child. I'm not even married.'

'Since when did that stop you, Nazo?'

I felt my face grow hot.

You had known all along.

But what you didn't know was that I did it for *you*. Did you really think I wanted that filthy playboy husband of yours? As the saying goes, you can show them God, but you can't make them believe. There was no point in trying to explain.

'Don't get rid of it,' you commanded.

You always were quick to see the loss and gains of a situation, and I was no exception. Just a situation that had to be dealt with.

'But why do you want me to keep it?' I asked, my voice rising. 'Why should I? I can't do this, Madam. Not even out of loyalty. Surely you know the life of an unwed mother in this society. If I live that is. With the General's Rape Law still in place, I'd be stoned to death before I even give birth.'

'I will bring up the child. As mine.'

I stood there, silent.

So this is what it was all about.

'Don't pretend to be surprised, Nazo. You're not that good an actress. We both know this was your plan all along.'

I felt as if I was walking on embers, my whole body about to catch fire. How could I convince you, Rani, that I had never planned this? I, who thought of motherhood as nothing but a shackle around a woman's ankle ... It occurred to me that if there was such a thing as karma, then this was payback time. Nature's curse for wishing your child ill.

But intention is not the same as action. Or is it?

Surely, Rani, I deserved a lesser punishment than this.

'Why not just hand me over to the Moral Police,' I asked quietly. 'I'll be out of your way for good.'

'Oh no, Nazo, my dear,' your voice became impossibly sweet. 'I couldn't possibly do that.'

I felt myself breathe again.

So you did care after all.

'Why?' I had to hear you say the words. 'Why would you do such a thing for me?'

You didn't meet my eyes as you said, 'Some things, Nazo, are best revealed when the time comes.'

Just like in the old days they sacrificed virgins and newborns to appease the gods, the twin deaths seemed to have unleashed some powerful force. A date for elections was finally set.

This time was different. People were unafraid. They ran out of their houses to greet you as we toured village after village in your open-top jeep, canvassing for votes. The General's death had changed everything. No longer was the fear of the Jihadists clamping their voices. They cheered as you drove past and, in return, you waved back. You stood for hours on your swollen feet. People marvelled at your stamina.

'Not bad for a pregnant woman,' I heard some men snigger. But you didn't care. The road to democracy was open and you were busy making your way up.

Your energy was unrivalled, your enthusiasm inextinguishable. You were yourself again. The elections were in the bag, of that I was sure.

Everywhere you went, people rushed out to greet you. I watched the crowds surround you, chanting your name, shouting slogans, pledging support, praying for your victory, and I thought this is it. This is where you belonged.

You were mistaken.

Everyday there were more and more visitors at your door. Old Jihadists changing allegiance, small politicians looking for a big ticket, activists with a list of the General's draconian laws against women they couldn't wait for you to repeal. Nobody went disappointed from your door. You assured them all that once you came to power, you would put everything right. As the political support around you grew, the possibility of a woman PM began to seem realistic.

I should have been thrilled.

But your popularity was not the only thing that was growing at an alarming speed. The wrong child grew and grew inside me until I felt my skin could stretch no more. I wore loose-fitting clothes, stayed away from the communal bathrooms and cut off all contact with Soldier Rahim. But I couldn't help missing him. Sometimes at night, I would stretch out my hand on the bare mattress beside me and feel the emptiness of the cold bedsheet creep up my skin. Perhaps you suspected treason, for in the coming days, you suggested I sleep in your room. On the floor of course, but nevertheless, to be in the same room as you, to breathe in the same air, to dream the same dreams – what more could I ask for?

Balgodi protested. Not liking the idea of me being in the same room as you, now that he had seen how useful I could be, he played the servant card. 'You can't have a servant sleep in the room!'

'You don't want any more scares, do you?' you pouted. 'The slightest of intimacy could cause me to miscarry. Like I almost did last time. I can't sleep with you and I can't sleep alone. What if I needed help at night?'

Like a petulant child, he persisted, 'You need me more than ever now, my darling. Let me be with you night and day.'

'No,' you said. 'With the elections so close, I need my rest. Besides, the doctor has said, too much excitement can cause the baby to stop moving. And you know, darling, how excited I get when you are close to me.'

Dumb as he was, I never expected him to give in this easy. But then again, I have been wrong about worse things.

'Anything for my unborn son's health!' he said, slobbering kisses all over your hand. No hint of the upcoming elections, I noticed, no guilt about the golden hen. Tears sprang from his eyes as he played the dumb husband to perfection. 'Give me a son! Give me an heir,' he cried.

Such melodrama, I thought. The man should have been an actor. He would have surely fetched the country her first Oscar. And you were no less. You batted your lashes at him and I watched as he succumbed. You handed him his pillow.

I moved in mine.

From then on, it was easy to get involved in your day-to-day activities. I wondered briefly if Balgodi had gone along with the charade because, like me, he too wanted to see you in power, albeit for different reasons. Watching you both, I sometimes wondered, who was making a fool out of whom.

Soon things took off and there was no more time to ponder about motives. Once again your passion for politics returned. Once again I became indispensable to you.

Once again our story began where it had left off.

Every now and then, we would summon the near-blind midwife to do a check-up, or should I say check-in, on me. She would coarsely feel my belly, poke her knobbly fingers up my vagina and wail, 'The child is too small! It's not growing properly. You must take her to the big hospital. Take her to the city!'

'This is the city, you old bat,' I would remind her, but she would crone on and on about how the British were doing wonders to develop the city.

'They've even put pukka roads in our little town,' she'd say, her cataract-ridden eyes widening with disbelief.

'The little town is now a sprawling city of ten million people,' I'd tell her, but she would laugh as if I had cracked a big joke.

'It's better this way,' you'd say, handing a hundred-rupee note to the senile old woman.

What were you thinking, Rani? I'd shudder at the thought of delivering in the old lady's trembling hands. She'll kill me and the child both, I would think. Many a time, I came close to voicing my fears but stopped midsentence, wondering if, indeed, that *was* the plan.

Prosecutor: I can see you hesitating. What is it? There is something you are not telling us. What are you holding back, Miss Khan?

Defendant: Some things must be held back. Should be held back, Omar Sir. With time, those unspoken words and secrets become like the air we inhale. Totally unnoticed but wholly necessary.

⚖

Time passed. The secret grew.

'Don't let me down,' you'd say every time you'd catch me undoing the bandages I tied around my stomach to hide the pregnancy.

I had come this far for you, Rani, I wasn't going to stop now. I wasn't going to abandon you like that two-cent husband of yours, who sat around drinking and seducing young maids in your own home.

All in the name of men's needs.

Needs, my right foot! It was about choice. And for once, you had made the right choice...

The day came. A day of choice. Of right and wrong. Of endings and beginnings. The day began like any other day. We left the house early in the morning in your open-top jeep and took the road to the rural outback. People lined both sides of the road, beckoning you, cheering you, urging you. 'Visit our village', they screamed. 'Come and see how we live'. 'We have no medicine'. 'We have no electricity'. 'No drinking water'. 'Give us medicine', more voices shouted.

You waved back, your voice booming through the bullhorn. 'The days of darkness are over. Light is here. I will complete what my father began. Vote for Shah and soon there will be food, shelter, work and education for every one of you. We are here to serve not to rule!'

A loud cheer went up at this reminder of your father's slogan.

'Serve not rule!' the crowds cheered as your jeep travelled slowly down the crowded highway. By the time we reached the first village, it was nearly lunchtime. As soon as we stepped out, a crowd of women gathered around us. They pawed at you, like animals, I thought. There faces were sunburnt, their skin coarse and their touch rough. But you didn't back away. Instead you reached out and shook their hands.

A filthy child in rags came up to you and tugged at your shirt. To my surprise, you picked her up and planted a kiss on her tear-stained cheeks.

'Do you go to school?' you asked gently.

The women looked at you, then at each other. A chorus of giggles erupted.

'There are no schools here, Rani Madam,' one of the tittering women replied.

You looked at once angry and amazed at this basic fact of life, and once again I was taken aback by how aloof your idealism had made you.

'Why? Why are there no schools here?' you demanded. Then you nodded knowingly and said, 'It's because the Jihadists don't want you to study. They don't want you to teach your children. They want you to remain poor and uneducated so they can manipulate you. But you know what? It's all about to change. I will build schools. I will provide education for your daughters. I will be the change.'

The women looked uncomfortable and the one who had spoken began chewing the end of her long veil. An old woman next to her said, 'Rani Madam, you are from the city. We village women are born to work in the fields, die in childbirth, and that is our fate.'

'Yes, yes,' the others echoed, 'it's written in our kismat. It is our fate.'

'Then change your kismat,' you said. 'Write your own fate.' You stood up, a staggering 5'6 inch giant amongst the stooping, scraggly women scattered by your feet. You looked at their thin, pinched, hungry faces and said, 'Iqbal said, Rise up so high that even God asks your will before deciding your fate. That's what you should aspire to. You can change your kismat, decide your own destiny, write your own fate!'

'Rani Madam,' I pulled you aside and whispered, 'these women can't even write their own name, how can they write their own fate?'

You gave me that look you did when I stated something wholly practical but incompatible with your textbook idealism.

Rolling your eyes, you said, 'I didn't mean literally, Nazo.' You turned to the women. 'You must learn to read and write. You must teach your children. They in turn must pass it on to their children. That's how change will come.'

As you spoke, I could see the dense fog in their eyes lifting. Although I was sure they'd never be allowed to step out of their miserable mud huts let alone be allowed to go to school, for a moment their eyes lit up with hope.

Sometimes a spark is enough to light a raging fire.

Later, as we walked back to the jeep, you said, 'Education, Nazo, education is the best weapon we have. I'll build hundreds of schools. I'll...'

And then you tripped.

Your shalwar cloth had snagged on a nail, making you fall on the hard ground. A sharp cry escaped your lips. The villagers rushed to your aid. They carried you to the nearest hut and put a warm cloth on your back.

'The baby will come soon now,' one of the women said.

'A fall can induce early labour,' another remarked.

They all nodded gravely. You tried to stand, but your ankle couldn't take the weight and you cried out in pain. The women mistook it for labour.

'Anytime now!' they chorused.

Perhaps this was the news the boys in the Capital were waiting for. Soon as they heard the rumours of your confinement, they moved the date of elections even closer. We had barely made it back to the city when we heard the elections were taking place the day after.

'There is no time to lose,' you said. 'There is work to be done,' you stood up abruptly, but your ankle gave way. You collapsed back down. Desperate, you called a doctor who although did not dispense any medicine, managed to inform the press that you were not in labour.

'A mere sprain,' he said and splat! It was splashed all over the papers.

'False alarm, fake labour.'

'Rani Madam not to give birth just yet.'

'Electioneers, here she comes!'

'Nothing can stop our lady of shah now!'

All sorts of jazzed up versions danced on the headlines the next day.

But the question now was, would the elections still go ahead?

Of course not. The minute it became apparent that you were not all that indisposed, the polls were called off. 'Till an indeterminable time,' the notice from the Election Commission read. In other words, there was no hurry. The Army could now look for another candidate to stand against you, at leisure. And till they found the guy who could take you on, democracy could wait.

As expected, you were furious.

⚖

But anger never did slow you down. If anything, it built you up. 'As if the General was not enough!' you fumed. 'Now his cronies want to play games! What are they playing at anyway? Do they really think they can delay democracy once again? Have they fucking learnt nothing from the General's ten-year rule? Do they really want to bring back the Jihadists? Those fuckers! Anyone but a woman! Those khaki bastards!' You raged and raved and then finally when you calmed down, you turned on me.

'The baby must come now. I can't wait any longer. If that's what it takes to make the polls happen, then that's what we will do.'

I stared horrified.

'What are you going to do? Rip it out of me?'

You laughed.

'Let no man born of a woman's womb slay Macbeth.'

'What?' I balked.

'Shakespeare, my dear.'

'Sheikh, who?' Surely you had gone mad to be thinking of Arabs right now! And then just as quickly, I realized you were banging on about your books again.

'What does that awful play have to do with this?' I asked,

wondering if all I had to do was to read some book to get out of this one.

'I mean Caesarean, Nazo. Have you never heard of it? It's an operation where the stomach is cut to pull out the baby.'

I swallowed.

'Is there no other option?'

'Oh don't worry, they will stitch you back up. There's hardly any risk at all. Besides you'd be unconscious the whole time.'

I thought fast. I couldn't take the risk. What if you left me there to die? What better way to get rid of me and claim the child as yours? Then who would be there to keep you from chucking it all in for a life beside the cradle.

A premonition, perhaps?

No. I couldn't let them take me to the theatre. But how could I convince you? I had to stop this. I'd never wake up, this much I knew. Once they put me out, you'd take the baby and leave me there to die. And the secret would die with me. Finish. *Khalass.* Game over and done. No. I had to think of a way to stop you.

'Just think,' I said. 'The surgeon might recognize me. Somebody could tell the press. Soon everyone would know.'

'There is such a thing as a bribe.'

'The boys in khaki could offer a bigger bribe. You'd be entering a lifetime of blackmail.'

At that point, you turned around and looked me in the eye. 'The same could be said for you. Why should I trust you?'

If we couldn't trust each other now, we never would.

Mustering up as much conviction as I could, I held your gaze and said, 'Your secret is safe with me.'

'How do I know?'

Where had I read that no one believes the simple truth, but everybody loves a lie.

'My child will have a better future with you,' I said. 'Why would I want to sabotage my child's future? Who wouldn't want their child to be part of the Shah dynasty? I don't want him or her to grow up to be a servant like me…'

You were quiet for a while. I began to wonder if you had thought this through.

'Caster oil,' you said finally.

I drank a whole bottle. We waited an hour. Nothing happened. Not even a single cramp.

And then in a span of six hours, you had me try everything, from raspberry tea to skipping rope. It was as if you wanted me to cough out this baby. Finally, I had to beg you to stop.

'We've tried every natural remedy there is!'

'There is one thing we haven't tried.'

'What?'

'Orgasm.'

Now I had heard everything.

'Where do you think I would find a man to sleep with me?'

'Well, you could always get Balgodi drunk,' you looked at me with such hatred that I had to lower my gaze.

So you did know.

'Or there is always Pervez Sahib.'

I felt a bubble of laughter rising up my throat. 'I thought you said orgasm.'

'Yes,' you conceded thoughtfully, 'his blind humping would hardly have the desired effect.'

Suddenly we were laughing as if the clocks had been turned

back and we were back in the cold and grey Uptown apartment. And then just as suddenly you were crying.

'Rani Madam, what happened?' I tried to hold you still, but you were heaving great big sobs as if some enormous gaping wound had opened up inside you.

'Please speak, Rani Madam. What is it?'

You pushed me away and shouted, 'Get away from me. I'm getting sick of you. Of Balgodi. Of the whole system.'

Before I knew it, you started toppling books off your shelf, ripping up papers, tearing Party posters, pamphlets, papers. And then, you flung down your father's picture.

'Oh I bet you never had to go through this,' you shouted as you stamped on the glass. 'Why did you do this to me? Do you even know what it means to be a woman in this fucking country? How could you do this to me!'

You brought your foot down with such force that shards of glass scattered everywhere.

'No!' I cried as a shard landed on your ankle, cutting into your skin. Blood seeped out. But that didn't stop you. Instead you kicked off your heels and started stamping until your soft white foot turned red.

'Stop,' I screamed. 'Stop it!'

'Take that, you bastard,' you screamed, kicking the broken frame.

'Stop hurting yourself,' I cried, but you were hysterical.

I felt a sharp pain rise inside, but this was no time to worry about myself.

'Please, stop hurting yourself,' I begged, but you went on tearing the room. Finally, you stopped in front of the dressing room mirror.

'I hate you,' you said to your reflection or perhaps to mine. Before I could ponder the thought, you lifted your jewellery box and threw it. The mirror cracked from side to side.

'Madam,' I wrapped my arms tight around you. I held you till you stopped struggling.

'It's okay, it's okay, it will all be okay in the end,' I kept whispering, my mouth inches away from your ear.

'In the end it will all be okay, Rani Madam. Please, trust me.'

I felt your body go limp. You were still crying but softly now.

'Hush, hush, I'm here with you.' I held you tighter, all the time repeating your name like a prayer.

Slowly, I walked you to the bed and began wiping the blood off your feet. I tore my hijab and wrapped it tightly around your ankle to stop the flow. Then I took off your bloodstained clothes and helped you into a clean white negligee. I lay you down, combed your hair and mopped your forehead with a cool cloth. Finally you were calm. At peace. I turned to leave.

It was then I heard you say, 'Stay.'

Very slowly, I turned back to face you.

'Don't go,' you said. 'Don't leave me.'

'I won't,' I said. I won't ever leave you.

Not till our dying day.

Prosecutor: I would now like to call my next witness, senior Party worker and politician, Mr R.S. Pervez.

Clerk: Please place your hand on the Holy Book and swear to tell the truth, the whole truth and only the truth.

Witness: I do.

Prosecutor: Mr Pervez, would you say you are a dedicated member of Madam Shah's party?

Witness: Yes, Mr Omar.

Prosecutor: Did Rani Madam have complete faith in you?

Witness: Yes.

Prosecutor: Did she ever confide in you that she mistrusted Miss Khan?

Witness: Yes. I mean no!

Prosecutor: May I remind you that you are under oath? You must answer truthfully. Did she or did she not try to keep Miss Khan out of Party politics following her appointment as the PM.

Witness: (Silence)

Prosecutor: Your Honour, Mr Pervez's silence confirms my fears about Miss Khan's character. I would not be surprised if Mr Pervez was threatened not to talk.

Witness: I... I...

Prosecutor: Witness dismissed.

⚖

It must have happened to you at some point. Time slows down. Everything appears in its full detail. You feel as if you can see the intricate patterns on a butterfly's wings; you remember the taste of your mother's cooking as if she was right there, feeding you with her own hands; and then when you look into the mirror, you see every line and crease and every trace that time has left on your skin. Yet, you feel nothing, as if you are a ghost, passing through the film set of your own life.

That was how I felt that day, as if I'd been turned upside down, emptied of all thought, all pain, all past. As if nothing else mattered but the present. I became trapped in the moment. As if the here and now was a bubble floating aimlessly in the sky. But like all bubbles, it too popped and I came crashing down to earth. The memory of our kiss became just that, a memory.

I know you must be shocked right now. I have broken the code. Spoken the unspoken. Told the truth untold. But the fact is, it happened. That night I sat next to you till dawn. I watched you breathe, the rise and fall of your chest, the barely-there parting of your lips as you snored gently. I watched over you. Like a mother, like a lover, like a dog guarding its master.

And then, just before daybreak, I leaned over and kissed your lips. It was then I knew, my deity was not made of stone.

Though I had been close to you before, never before had I dared to touch your mouth. Your eyes were closed and your breath even, but still you cannot deny it happened. I did not imagine it. And if the wrong child had not decided to make his entrance just then, it would have led to a lasting closeness.

⚖

The first rays of the sun were drawing patterns on the wall when I woke up. The curtains danced in the morning breeze as the muezzin's call to prayer filtered in.

'Sleep is better than prayer,' I murmured, rubbing my eyes. I stopped talking as a wave of pain rose up my belly. Then another and another, crashing against my insides like the choppy waves of the sea. I cried out as a sharp pain tore through me.

'Are you all right, Nazo?' you sat up in bed and looked over at me.

I nodded, trying hard to suppress the pain cutting through my belly.

'And the...'

'Yes, him too.'

'How can you be so sure it's a boy?'

'I don't know,' I smiled through the pain, 'I just feel it. Maybe it's my punishment.'

You propped yourself up on your elbows and looked at me with amusement. 'Since when did you start believing in karma?'

'Since I started caring,' I said, the pain subsiding as suddenly as it had begun.

'Caring?' you whispered.

'Yes, Rani Madam.'

You patted the space next to you and, wrapping up my bedding on the floor, I shuffled towards the bed. Your hand accidently grazed mine as I sat down. I remember, your touch was warm.

'Everything will be okay, Nazo.'

That was all I wanted to hear. I felt as if I had been rewarded my weight in gold. 'Believe me, Rani Madam,' the words tumbled out before I could stop. 'I always had your best at heart. Whatever I did, I did it for you. I only hope you can forgive me for...'

'I guess,' you said cutting me off, 'it's the intention that matters.'

I bit my lip. It was callous of me to bring up the wedding night right now. But I wanted so badly for things to be okay between us again.

'Nazo?' you asked softly. 'Don't let me down.'

'Rani Madam,' I said, the words feeling warm and velvety on my tongue. 'You can trust me with your life.'

As you did.

It was the right time. I could feel it. I came close. Today I was going to confess. Those three little words. Full of power. Full of passion. I reached out my hand. You took it. That was the sign I needed. I looked into your eyes and said, 'I...'

'Yes?' you squeezed my hand.

Suddenly I felt as if somebody had gotten hold of my insides and was twisting them into a tight knot.

'Stop, oh please stop.'

'Nazo,' you said, your face pale. 'Nazo, is it time?'

'Yes,' I whispered, through the sweat pouring into my eyes. 'Yes, it is time.'

'But ... there is no one here.' I could see the panic mounting in your eyes.

'Madam,' I said, trying hard to keep my breath steady. 'All I need ... is you.'

They say the time when a woman gives birth is when she is closest to God, and to death. I didn't know if I believed in God, but I did in death.

I wasn't taking any chances.

'Madam,' I said. 'you need to do exactly as I say.'

Your hands were cold as you nodded.

'Grab some towels from your bathroom closet, fill a bucket

with hot water and fetch the bottle of Dettol from the third shelf of your medicine cabinet.'

'Yes, yes,' you said, unmoving. 'Don't worry, Nazo. You'll get through this. Everything will be okay.'

'Just do it,' I shouted.

You snapped into action. I told you to tear the sheets, boil the water, sterilize the scissors. I told you to lay out the towels, soak up the blood and prepare for the afterbirth. I told you to hold the baby's head when it finally emerged. And when the time came, I told you to cut the cord. Only then did I close my eyes.

And so once again you brought me back from the dead, and what is it they say about people who save your life?

You become bound to them for life.

Whether you like it or not.

⚖

When I woke up a few hours later, the baby was resting on your breast. You had milk! Can a mother who miscarried still feed? I was astonished. Then I saw the little crescent shaped feeder you had placed in his mouth as you held him close. Instinctively, I snatched him away and placed him on my breast. But the little bastard turned his greedy sucking mouth away. Rejection. I laughed at the thought that men are born with the right. The little sucker. I couldn't help but smile at his crumpled little face, his tightly scrunched eyes, his fists folded as if clutching a piece of gold.

'They say it takes a while for the milk to let down,' you said, taking him gently back in your arms.

My son … *my child* … I nodded, my eyes already feeling heavy.

'But, Nazo, he is so small. What if he needs the hospital? He is premature after all…'

'Take him.'

'What? I mean, what about you?'

'I'll be okay. The world doesn't need to know about me. Take him to the hospital or call the hospital here. After all, you just gave birth, Madam. Let the world know. Isn't that the news they were waiting for? For you to be recovering from the pain of labour while they call the polls?'

You seemed stunned by my little speech. But only for a few minutes. Soon as the baby started crying, you snapped into action.

'All right then, let's go, little chap. We have calls to make. But first, I want you to meet your daddy.'

And I watched you go. Walk away with my child in your hands. And strangely, I felt no pain.

Witness: All this woman knows is to take, Omar Sir-ji. Take, take, take and then take some more. People like her do not know the meaning of gratitude.

Prosecutor: How do you mean, Mr Balgodi?

Witness: My wife was too generous with her praise. I used to tell her, don't spoil the servants, they will sprout wings. And you know how difficult it is to clip wings. I said to her, Rani dear, always pick faults in what they do. That way they will be too busy trying to correct their mistakes to think of new things. But my wife was too trusting. Look where the trust got her. Underground, Omar Sir-ji, underground!

Prosecutor: Can you give any examples, Mr Balgodi?

Witness: Yes, Omar Sir-ji. You know my poor Rani gave birth and went campaigning right away while that lazy Nazo shut herself in the room for a whole week. That too when Rani needed her the most. And even when she bothered to come out, she pretended to be sick and moped around the house watching one drama after another, on my television too! Once I caught her asking the maid to massage her feet, can you imagine?

Prosecutor: Thank you, Mr Balgodi. That'll be all.

Witness: Not all, Sir. She's a jealous bitch. She killed my ... my ... poor...

Defendant: Golden hen.

Witness: Look, look Omar Sir-ji, look at her cheek. We

clothed her, fed her, paid for her medicine, and
this ungrateful witch...

Prosecutor: Steady, Mr Balgodi. You may step down.

Witness: I will, but you better make sure this bitch is
hanged.

Counsel: Objection. Language, please.

Judge: Sustained.

Prosecutor: Your Honour, Mr Balgodi has a point. How is
it that a new mother can travel around the country
to campaign while Miss Khan who claims to be such a
loyalist stays back? Because it was a plot. Taking
advantage of Madam's absence, she chose to steal.
I have the testimony right here of a servant who
says he saw her tampering with the safe.

Counsel: Objection. Miss Khan had access to Party funds.
If she wanted to steal she could have embezzled
those. But not a penny has been mismanaged. The
accounts are free to access should the court care
to check.

Prosecutor: Well then, perhaps she was looking for
something in Madam Shah's papers? You know I'm
pretty sure that is usually known as spying.

⚖

They say good luck never announces its arrival. It springs upon
you unexpectedly, catches you unaware, then smiles at your
surprise. But in contrast, misfortune drops many hints of its
coming. And so it was that the day after you rushed the wrong
child to the hospital, the generals and the colonels in charge
announced a date for the elections.

'To be held in forty-one days,' the Electioneer informed us.

The headlines screamed injustice.

'A visibly frail Madam Rani Shah was seen leaving the hospital yesterday with her newborn wrapped in a blanket,' the TV blasted.

'How can a mother who has just given birth roam the country campaigning for votes?' the activists demanded.

'A Muslim woman must stay at home for forty days after birth. Will Rani Shah break this tradition too?' the outraged mullahs objected.

Foreign media showed repeated shots of you clutching the newborn, your face a ghostly white. And sure enough, you walked in just then, rubbing your temples and pretending to swoon.

'Oh Nazo,' you crooned. 'I feel so weak. I can't possibly campaign.'

We both burst out laughing.

'So what happens now?' I asked.

'We are boarding the Northern train, tomorrow. We will stop at every station, get off, campaign, distribute food and medical supplies, and get their pledges in return. Then off to the next village. And then the next. And next, till we reach the Capital.'

'But that journey will take days! Maybe weeks. It'll be exhausting and tiring and…'

'Exactly,' you said, with a slow spreading smile. 'Not something you'd expect a new mother to do, would you?'

In the heart of hearts, I knew you meant me.

What is that saying about saving a drowning man and sinking yourself? Well that is exactly how I felt as I held the whimpering little bundle in my hands while you prepared speeches for the campaign.

'Can I help?' I asked.

'The baby, Nazo,' you said waving me away, 'go look after the baby.'

'That boy will call you Mother at this rate,' Refugee would whisper jokingly each time you called for me, the baby inconsolable in your arms.

I felt conflicted as if I was being pulled in two different directions at the same time. This is what I wanted, didn't I? For you to be free to lead? But why then did I feel so left out? I felt like a dog on a short leash, chained to a fence while the master played fetch.

The other Party workers milled around you, discussing strategies and campaigns. I too wanted to be part of all this, I too wanted to make this change happen. But every time I put the baby down, he'd scream his lungs out. Only you or me could calm him down and, as your work was more important, the task fell on me. Eventually I thought it would be easier to tie him around my chest in a cloth sling than to put him down and listen to his shrill painful cries.

In the coming days, he slept on me, shat on me, suckled me, clinging like a drowning man to a piece of wood. I began to feel like a prisoner. I found myself thinking back to a childhood tale in which Sindbad couldn't shake an old man off his back. What did Sindbad do? I wondered one day when I had to take the baby into the bathroom with me to keep him quiet.

And that is when it hit me.

I can still remember the prickle of excitement I felt as I opened the medicine cabinet. I ran my fingers over the cool sticky exterior of the Calpol bottle. It had a picture of an innocent smiling baby, not of a skull and cross bones. Surely it couldn't be dangerous. As it is, you wouldn't leave it lying around if it was. I opened the cap with a rush and shoved a spoonful into the child's mouth. He promptly spat it out. Sugar. I thought. Running to the kitchen, I pulled out all sorts of sweeteners and mixed the medicine in them.

Drink, I encouraged him and the greedy boy that he was, he drank like it was his last day on earth. And after that, he slept. He slept the longest he ever had and even when he awoke, he was only half awake.

His face was serene, the calmest it had ever been. Surely that was a good thing, I thought as I entered a meeting. I began to mix it in all his feeds, and sometimes I even added it to his water. Now I, too, could be part of your entourage. I attended meetings with the baby sleeping peacefully in my lap or in his little Moses basket by your feet. You could get on with the business of election without guilt. And I could get on with my work. Once again all was well.

Until the day I found out what his silence would cost me.

I came in with the child at my shoulder. The little bastard was sleeping peacefully. You looked at him and your features softened.

'What a sweet child,' you said, taking him into your arms. 'You know, Nazo, the first few days, I was terrified of his shrill piercing cries, but now, just look at him.'

The boy promptly scrunched up his face and let out a loud snot-filled sneeze. I quickly took him from you.

'Here,' I said, handing you a tissue.

'Thank God, Nazo,' you said, wiping the front of your shirt, 'that you are here to look after my son.'

I knew that was the deal, but the words still came as a shock. There was no need for this pretence. At least not in private. I was his mother. But the way you were cooing at him, I could tell you wanted no reminding of the fact. Just then, Refugee called out that there was a courier at the door that needed signing. You rushed out, shouting that you'll handle it.

'No one is to touch this,' you said, waving the envelope in my face, when you came back in.

I watched you put it away carefully under lock and key and I knew something was up. Later, when you went out to a meeting, I took my hairpin and picked the lock. Sure enough, there lay the wrong child's birth certificate.

Alif Shah-Balgodi, it read.

Father's name: Billah Balgodi.

And then there it was: Mother's name: Rani Shah.

I leaned back against the cupboard and hugged the piece of paper tight across my chest.

What was I thinking? Of course this was bound to happen. Perhaps this had even been your plan all along. The pregnancy, the miscarriage, the surrogacy … all staged? Could it be that this was your intention all along? But why, Rani? Why did it have to be this way? I would have given you everything, Rani. All you had to do was ask. But you … you didn't even ask. You just took – what you liked, when you liked.

I looked at the piece of paper, my eyes blurring at this latest betrayal. One small tear rolled on to the paper.

You always did get what you wanted, Rani. You were daddy's spoiled little darling and I knew better than to stop you. This time, too, you would get what you wanted, but in the condition you want, that I can't promise.

Because some things in life can't be snatched.

From that day on, I doubled the Calpol dose. And that is how the child came to be known as the *wrong* child.

Prosecutor: Miss Khan, I know that you were close to the children, but to call them your own...!'

Counsel: Your Honour, Miss Khan loved the children so much that she calls herself their mother. Believes it to be the absolute truth.

Prosecutor: Actually, Your Honour, this only goes to show how unreliable her version of the truth is.

Like most things in life, I got over this one too. I shut myself in my little room till my bleeding body healed. Seven days later, I emerged renewed. I felt no pain, no bitterness. All I felt was shame at having doubted you. I told myself you did it for the Nation. After all, the Shah dynasty needed an heir. And what better way to get Balgodi off your back than to give him a readymade son. Perhaps now he'd let you concentrate on politics.

I threw myself into the cause. There was still so much that needed to be done. Exhausted and raw as I was from the childbirth, I did what I could. I rallied the women, canvassed for votes, but most of all I led chants of 'Long live Rani Shah' every time you appeared in public.

Yet, every now and then, I found myself sagging, sitting down by the child's cradle and talking to him in a rushed anxious stream. The poor drugged child would smile back, always happy, always content. At times such as these, I would look away, steeling my heart for he was not mine to love.

'What a sweet nature he has,' you'd say every time you'd take him away from me.

'He takes after me,' I'd joke and you'd turn your face away, as if I had made a bad joke. You never acknowledged me as his mother. It stung because despite everything I felt a pull towards this hapless little creature.

I tried not to love him. Truly, I tried hard. I told myself what mattered was your happiness. I revelled in the fact that you were back to your old self. You were smiling more, talking more. You kept saying you had it all: a sweet child, a great home and a wonderful career. You had it all.

But did you really?

Before we knew it, the day was upon us. Votes were cast. After a gruelling, nail-biting wait of twenty-four hours in which TV presenters entertained us with stale jokes between poll counts, as if nothing life-changing was about to happen and elections were a routine part of this tyrannical state, the results were announced.

Your party won hands down. There was celebration all around. Shots were fired. Sweets were distributed. Alms were given to the poor. Even I, who never bowed down before Him, found myself falling to my knees in gratitude. This was it. The darkness had lifted. It was time for light. The light *you* would bring to us, your people.

'Madam,' I rushed up to you as the anchor on screen announced the results, his voice cracking with amazement.

'We did it! We won,' I said.

'I've won,' you said, as shocked as a patient waking up from a coma. 'I've won the elections.'

I tried to ignore your use of the singular and said, 'Finally women will have a say. Rani Madam, do you realize what this means for us? We have a voice! No longer will we be treated as birthing cows...' But before I could say anything more, your husband burst into the room.

'You did it! You did it, my girl!'

He picked you up and swung you around. I watched from a corner as you both laughed. Not a single glance fell on me.

'Now hold that smile till I get back,' he planted a kiss on your forehead. 'Must dash, baby doll,' he said. 'I've got to go down to the mines and tell the rest of the family. Oh, my little Rani, you've done it. You've done the impossible.'

I watched in disgust as you reached out and kissed him, love spilling from your eyelashes as he repeated like a parrot, 'You've done it! You've done it, my girl!'

And then, just as he was about to step out, he pumped his fist and shouted, 'No one can stop us now. We'll rule this land. We'll rake it in with both hands! Must go tell my Baba this good news. Oh how happy my family will be!'

I watched your face crumple as he rushed out as quickly as he had come in.

Once again it was me who held you from breaking into pieces. 'You won, Rani Madam. In the end, that's what really matters. All's well that ends well,' I said. 'Isn't that what you always tell us?'

Instinctively your hand moved to your mouth and you said, 'And what if it doesn't end well?'

Then it's not the end.

Prosecutor: It doesn't end there. When she couldn't keep Madam from the elections, she tried to delay her taking office.

Counsel: Do you have an ounce of evidence to support the claim?

Prosecutor: I have an eyewitness.

⚖

A week later, I read in the papers the headline, 'The Tormentor Is Dead But His Apparatus Is Still Alive.'

How true, I thought. You had a landslide victory, yet the Parliament was not being formed. It was as if the caretaker government wanted to pretend the whole thing had never happened. You kept calling. They kept ignoring. In between, Balgodi would come in and demand to know when they would be handing over the keys to the treasury. As if that actually happened!

To top it all, his family would ring, asking for even more impossible favours: 'Please, daughter Rani, get my bill passed in the Parliament'; 'Look here, daughter-in-law, this contract must come to us'; 'You have to get us this tender!'; 'What happened about my bill?'; 'My loan should have been passed the day you were elected'; 'When will you get your cousin a government job?'; 'Have you looked at the loan request I sent you yet?' It didn't matter to them that you had not even taken office yet. Demands flooded in endlessly. And amidst all this, the baby fell ill. From morning to night, he would cry continuously. You'd place your palms on your ears and say, 'Take him away, Nazo. Take him far away.'

I'd look at the poor miserable tot's snotty red face and say nothing.

As they say, do a good deed and throw it into the sea.

And then one day, I found you hunched over your desk with your head in your hands. 'This cannot be happening,' you said. 'I have won elections fair and square. They've got to let me take office. How the fuck can a few men in khaki have such power over the government machinery?'

You were talking to yourself, yet I said, 'Don't worry, everything will be all right.'

I came forward and placed my hands on your shoulders. When you didn't react, I pressed down squeezing them gently. It was then you seemed to notice my presence. You shrugged off my hands and looked up blankly, erasing all memories of our earlier intimacy. In that moment, I felt like a stranger at home. It was as if no bond had ever formed between us.

At first I thought it was because of my leaky breasts, the smell of putrid blood and reeking sour milk that put you off, made you shrink away from me. But now it had been a few months, and I was beginning to realize that the matter was something else altogether.

'What is it?' I said.

You looked at me as if I had asked you to jump out of the window.

'You are unbelievable, Nazo,' you said.

I knew that tone of voice. You spoke like that when you were afraid.

'Shush,' I said. 'You'll wake the baby. *Your* baby...'

'Fuck the stupid baby,' you screamed. 'And fuck you. Fuck all of you. Take that rancid little bundle of yours and get out of my sight!'

For a second, I froze. I could imagine you speaking that way to me, but to the child...? I looked hard at you and then at my reflection in the mirror behind you. You sat there, regal in your lace-trimmed white hijab while I looked a shadow of my former self. My clothes were plain and dirty, stinking of sweat. Though we still looked similar, I now had large haunting dark circles under my eyes, my skin was papery thin, my breasts sagged and my stomach stuck out. I was a shadow of the person I'd once been.

You had asked so much of me, Rani, and now you were asking some more. Yet, I did what I had to, because it was my duty to serve you.

And serve you I did.

That night I phoned Soldier Rahim. At first he refused to talk to me, but when I threatened to write to his first wife about our affair, he relented. Still, I like to think it was my love and not my cunning that broke down his defence.

'Things are not good, Rahim.'

'Why? Your Madam has won the elections. Her husband is busy taking bribes left, right and centre. He's selling tenders, contracts and government jobs at sky-high commissions. They are raking it in even before taking office! So now, what else do you want?'

'But that is just Balgodi. You know Rani Madam is not like that. She wants to govern, not rule. She wants to serve, but the boys in the Capital are not giving her a chance. They won't even let her take oath.'

'They just want to show her who's boss. Once she gives in to their demands, they will step out of her way. That is as long as she doesn't interfere in their work, national defence and foreign policy and all, you know.'

No, I didn't know that foreign policy was the work of the Army. Aloud I said, 'But of course.'

'Yes, yes, then she should be fine. She should just be patient.'

'But Soldier Rahim, it's already been a month. When will they reveal their demands? Soon the window of the world will be on the country. In which Nation is an elected prime minister not allowed to take oath? Look, try to speak to Major Sahib. Tell him that Rani Madam is saying they can either do a deal in private or battle it out in front of the world media.'

'Nazo, I will try, but you know they don't care about international pressure. If Rani Madam pushes them too hard, they'll just start another skirmish across the border to take the public's eye off the ball.'

I conceded. That old trick always worked. Whenever there was a matter at home that needed attention, the Army distracted the people by starting a battle with the neighbouring land. I tried to put myself in the new General's place and thought, that would not only bring the public together in a sickening display of patriotism, but all grievances would be forgotten and forgiven on the home front too. Who'd care about a female PM raging to take office while the brave Army men were out there, fighting for the Nation?

'Well,' I said, pushing the scenario out of my mind, 'at least try and find out their demands. You know all the bodyguards. See if someone has heard anything. She's getting tired of just sitting around. Tell them, she just wants to be useful.'

Soldier Rahim seemed impressed by my change of tone and promised to help. I hung up feeling empty and hollow, wondering how much more the generals and colonels of this country would take from us before they let us do our work.

Even Shylock stopped at a pound of flesh.

♎

A few more torturous days later, I made up my mind to visit Rahim. Phone was too impersonal. Surely when he saw me and heard how badly you wanted to do something for the country, the patriotism in him would kick in.

Early that morning, I knocked on your door. I knocked again impatiently and, as soon as you opened the door, I handed you the baby.

'What's this?'

You looked at the little sleeping bundle in your arms as if you had no idea who he was. I turned to go.

'Wait!' you cried. 'Where are you going?'

'I have to go. It's important.'

'Who's going to look after this?' you asked, thrusting him back at me.

The baby started to cry at all the juggling and changing of arms.

'Hush, hush, baby. Look, Nazo, he's crying for you.'

I smoothed the baby's blanket and whispered, 'For someone who wanted to have a child so desperately, you seem very reluctant to take care of him.'

You looked sharply at me. But before you could say anything, a man's voice said, 'Do you know what we do with people in our villages whose tongues grow too long?'

I looked up to see Balgodi lying half naked in bed. His chest was bare and he was running his fingers through the thick hatch of hair that covered every inch of his skin. He looked like a wolf who had just had a big meal. Probably you.

He cleared his throat to get my attention.

'What do they do?' I asked, my voice bored and uninterested.

'They cut off their spiteful tongues.'

Click, click, click, he made snipping noises and I pretended to look scared.

'Forgive me, sir,' I said, thinking, the things I did to humour the rat. 'Please, sir. Don't cut off my tongue, Sir. I beg you please, sir.'

I snatched the baby back, pushed past you and laid his son next to him. 'Your son, Sir.' I backed away, still mumbling apologies, 'Forgive, forgive…'

Then without bothering to look up, I rushed out, lest you called me back in.

Once near Major Q's house, I hesitated at the gates. What if he had me arrested? Surely he would have suspected some foul play when I disappeared from his house so suddenly and reinstalled myself in your life. On the other hand, he may not even have noticed. Either way I was not taking any chances. I squatted down under the neem tree by the road and began a long wait. A thin grey feeling of exhaustion began to climb up my limbs and creep into my neck. My jaw relaxed, my posture slumped and my eye lids became heavy. A gentle breeze made the leaves dance. And I realized I hadn't rested properly since the birth.

I must have fallen asleep at some point, for when I woke up, a hundred mosquitoes were trying to drain the blood out of my body. I got up quickly, trying to swat them away. The buzzing creatures danced even more spiritedly as I waved my arms above my head to ward them off.

A van braked and a man with rolls of fat under his chin leaned out of the window. He spat out a stream of scarlet betel nut juice as he eyed me up and down. 'Oye woman,' he leered, winking at me, 'are you coming or what?'

'Huh?' I blinked, my head still heavy with sleep.

'I've got money ready,' he said, waving a green note about.

I spat at him.

'Fucking whore!' the man shouted, trying to swipe a blow from the window.

'Motherfucker!' I shouted, as he unlocked the car door to come after me. I ran.

With the balding fat man at my heels, I forgot all my doubts and rushed to the Major's house as fast as I could.

'Quick, open!' I began, rattling the gates.

A tall burly guard opened the eye slit in the metal door. 'Who is it?'

Just a six-inch view of authority was enough to make the balding man behind me disappear.

'Nazo. It's me, Nazo,' I replied, placing a hand on my heart to steady myself. What was the country coming to, I thought, as I tried to calm my breath. Women can't even step out of the house alone. And if they do, they are taken for whores.

'Nazo who?'

I peered closely to see if he was having a laugh. The man was as blank as an unused sheet of paper.

'Soldier Rahim's Nazo!'

'You can be Mohammad Ali's Nazo for all I care,' the guard replied, shoving a chubby finger up his nose. 'What do you want?'

'You must be new. Otherwise everyone here knows me.'

The man looked at my dusty clothes and sweaty face and seemed unimpressed.

'I'm here to meet Soldier Rahim. At least inform him.'

He told me to wait outside. I had to spend a good few hours staring at the man shove huge fingers into impossibly small nasal openings before Rahim came out.

'Any news?' I asked, as soon he came close.

'Nazo,' he said, holding me at arm's length and looking me up and down. And up again.

'Yes, yes I know I have changed.'

'Nazo,' he shook his head and drew in a long deep breath. 'I'm sorry you had to wait. Major Q was in a meeting and I was standing guard.'

'It's okay.'

'But it's hot. Must have felt like hell out there without any shade.'

I couldn't play the cat and mouse game any longer, so I said, 'Look, we both know I'm not here to chat about the weather.'

'Nazo, sit. Do you want a glass of water?'

'Just come to the point.'

'The point?' he shook his head. 'Oh Nazo, what have they done to you?'

'I am not a child, Rahim. No one has done anything to me. I know fully well what I'm doing and why. You'll see, my sacrifices will pay off one day.'

'That's what my mother used to say when my father would beat her. And do you know, when she died of broken ribs, he didn't even give her a proper burial.'

'Well then I better arrange my own burial before I go back to the Shah House,' I joked, but he was in no mood to laugh.

'Come, let me feed you something.' His eyes had a look of pity. I looked away.

'I am not here to eat, Rahim. I have to get back soon. The child...' I hesitated.

'Have you given that away too?'

The man knew how to reach inside and twist my gut with his words. I hadn't told him, but somehow he knew. He just knew.

'Soldier Rahim, just tell me what I need to know and I will leave. Okay?'

'Fine then,' he shouted. 'You are not the Nazo I knew. You are here on business so business it will be.'

'I would do the same for you, Soldier...'

'I'd never,' he didn't finish his sentence. Instead he looked into the distance.

'Well?' I asked impatiently.

He inhaled slowly. 'Their demands are high.'

'Rani is rich.'

'It's not about money.'

'Then?'

'It's about power.'

'She's willing to share.'

'Is she willing to share herself too?'

'What do you mean?' I was almost afraid to ask.

'They want her,' he said. 'For one night. One of the guards heard three generals discussing it and...'

'Stop.' I couldn't listen any more. Hadn't the bastards humiliated you enough already? Years of harassment and house arrest and now, this. And that too when you had won the battle fair and square. But then, I guess this was not about winning the battle at all. This was about winning the war.

I turned back slowly, wondering how on earth I would break this news to you.

In the end, I decided not to tell you after all.

I walked the five-mile road back to your house in the scorching afternoon sun, all the time wondering, why the hearts of men were so hard. By the time I reached Shah House, the last thing I wanted to do was stand in front of the stove. Yet the first thing I did was to brew you a steaming hot cup of tea. I poured it into a plain white cup with a hotel logo.

Outside your study, I removed the protective cloth I usually wrapped around the mug to keep it warm. Instead I pressed my hands against it. Pain seared through my fingers. But I smiled. A minute later, I wiped the surface clean of my fingerprints and wrapped the cloth around it again.

I entered without knocking. You smelled the brew before you saw it. Leaning back with your eyes closed, you inhaled the scent of cardamoms and cinnamon and nodded approvingly. Wordlessly, I handed you the cup.

'Ah, just what I needed.'

'I thought you might.'

'You don't have to, Nazo. Get Refugee to do all this.'

Oh but I do, I thought with a smile.

'What are you up to?' you asked, looking curiously at me.

If only you knew.

'Nothing,' I said and walked out. My hands raw and achy, my heart light and happy.

Prosecutor: I would like to call to the witness box Mr Bhooka who works the early shift at Hotel Hart.

Clerk: Place your hand on the Holy Book and swear to tell the truth, the whole truth and only the truth.

Prosecutor: Mr Bhooka, on the morning of 1 March, precisely a month after the elections, did you see Miss Khan at your hotel?

Witness: I think so.

Prosecutor: How can you remember what happened that night? A lot of time has passed.

Witness: I remember because she looked a lot like Madam Shah and, for a minute, I was taken aback thinking it was her. But as she was approaching the reception, she tripped in her high heels and her sunglasses fell off. That's when I realized it was just some woman dressed like her.

Prosecutor: I see. And what was she doing there? Don't be afraid. Please answer.

Witness: She ... she wanted to know which room the VIPs were in.

Prosecutor: And? What else did she ask you?

Witness: She asked for ice and soda water. We don't serve alcohol, Sir, swear on God. But if someone brings their own...

Prosecutor: Thank you, Mr Bhooka. You can step down now. Your Honour, why would Miss Khan be spotted in the company of senior officers, piling them with illegal alcohol when, after a decade of military

rule, democracy had finally been restored, and
that too by none other than her employer, Rani
Shah. The only reasonable explanation is that she
was playing a double game.

**Counsel: Correction. The witness said he didn't see Madam Shah
there. He never confirmed he saw Miss Khan.**

I spent the next few hours using Refugee's help to set up a meeting
with the new Army Chief, General Kamal and his cronies for that
very night. We booked a room in a hotel under the name of VIPs.

As day turned to dusk, my heart fluttered like that of a sparrow
stranded in the cold. What if it all went wrong? What if it backfired?
I'd be shot, killed or worse, raped and dumped in some gutter. As I
left Shah House, I wondered if I would ever see you again.

And so, Rani, once again, it was me on the altar, but you did not
even acknowledge my sacrifice. I took on your pain, your stress,
your sorrows and you, my dear, did not even know. Tonight,
it would be me who lay down before the trio. Me, who would
close her eyes and bear the humiliation. I imagined surrendering
myself to the new General, the Election Commissioner and the
Caretaker PM. I imagined the sheer look of hatred as they spat
on my face, kicked me with their boots, stripped me to the bone.
Perhaps, even shot me … The price of treason, after all, was death.

But if this is what it takes, so be it.

And in return, you would get a phone call bright and early the
next morning. 'The oath ceremony is taking place. Would you
care to join?'

In the end, it went far smoother than I had imagined. Men, I must say, are bigger fools than I give them credit for. How did I pull it off, you ask? Easy. Alcohol. Lots of it. As they say, a fool and his drink are soon parted. In this case, outsmarted.

And who would know about that better than you.

First, I set up a meeting for that very evening. I didn't want to give them too much time to think. Next I sent in three bottles of Balgodi's imported whiskey with a note that you were running late. I waited till their laughter became raucous and only then did I enter the room. I wore your trademark white hijab and large dark glasses that covered most of my face. I kept my head bowed, my arms crossed and my mouth shut.

'Gentlemen,' I said, mimicking your voice and dimming the lights.

They fell right for it.

I poured the whiskey and with a flick of my wrist, added a vial of sleeping powder into the tumblers.

It was all staged to perfection.

Timing was everything, I told myself.

After they had a few sips, I sat in the new General's lap, my hand accidentally overturning the table lamp as I did so. Darkness followed. He reached out to help me. I flicked open a small pocket knife and a glint of steel shone against the bald General's throat. He let out a gasp. 'Don't be afraid,' I leaned in seductively and, pointing the knife at him, ripped his shirt. The bastard shuddered with pleasure. I would have dug in an inch or two deeper, too, if at that moment, the baldie hadn't closed his beady little eyes. I watched him flop his arms in one last attempt as the tranquilizers worked their way up.

The other two followed suit. They swayed between disbelief

and disbalance as the drug took hold of them. One fell on his face reaching out to me and the other crashed into a wall.

In the morning they will remember nothing, I thought as I pushed one towards the bed, the other two into each other's arms. I tore off their clothes with my knife and smeared lipstick marks across their bodies.

For the final touch, I took out your bottle of Chanel No. 5 and sprinkled it subtly around the room. Carefully, I placed your sunglasses on the General's lap, and the hotel cup I had served you tea in earlier that day on the table. I checked again to make sure the lipstick mark on the cup's rim was the same shade as the one I had smeared on the men's clothes.

When the snores began, I stepped back and took a look at my handy work. Really, I thought, now I know how an artist feels when they create a masterpiece.

'Enjoy, ladies,' I said as I placed my hand on the doorknob.

⚖

Outside, I signalled to Refugee, who came out of the next room where I had stationed him.

'Got it?' I asked.

He nodded and pointed at his huge belly stuffed like a giant football, with silver, crystal and other hotel knick-knacks.

'But why do we have to steal?' he asked.

'So we can call the police.'

'The police! What if we get caught?'

I laughed and said, 'A good criminal always covers her tracks.'

'But you are not a criminal,' he said innocently.

'Exactly,' I replied. 'That is why it is necessary to call the police. They must know that I was never here.'

'Then who was?'

'Rani was.'

You laugh. Go ahead. Laugh all you want. But the last laugh is mine. Believe me, Rani, the boys would have wanted proof that it really happened. Besides I'm glad I saved you from the humiliation. And from the General's hairy old testicles.

Three days later, you walked up to the podium on the Caretaker PM's arm, completely unaware that he was mentally undressing you. You smiled when the Commissioner winked at you, and even let out a full-throated laugh when the new General commented on how ravishing you looked. How naïve you were, my dear.

Perhaps, in trying to shelter you from the prejudice around you, I had made you aloof. I had always been taught never to call a blind man blind or an old man old, but in your case, perhaps not calling a fool, a fool was making a mug out of them.

It was time for you to face the truth, Rani. At least a bit of it.

There was little celebration when you got home that day. Balgodi was shut up in his room and refused to come out.

'Get me a pack of cigarettes,' you said, after a fresh round of knocking on his door went unanswered.

It had been a long time since you asked me to fetch you a pack, and I hesitated at your door.

'Rani Madam,' I said, stepping in. 'You can't be smoking now,' I said. 'You're the Prime Minister. And...' I paused, 'a mother.' Though in all honesty, I couldn't even remember the last time you had seen the wrong child's face, much less held him. The child may as well have been a must-have accessory like that Louis Vuitton bag you flashed on occasions, then locked up in your cupboard, content in the knowledge that you possessed it.

'The cigarettes, Nazo.'

I hesitated, but your fingers tapping impatiently against the smooth Burma teak of your desk snapped my feet into action. When I returned with the cigarettes, Balgodi was still locked up in his room.

You lit one and took a long hard drag.

I thought it would be safe to ask, 'Is Balgodi Sahib not happy?'

'Oh, he's heard some rubbish rumours, that's all. Somebody's been filling his ears.' Then you preened sharply at me. 'You wouldn't have anything to do with it now, would you, Nazo?'

I might have everything to do with it.

Counsel: Miss Khan's presence in the hotel is debatable.

Prosecutor: But I have an eyewitness who says he saw her.

Counsel: Witnesses can be bought.

Prosecutor: What do you mean?

Counsel: Mr Omar, perhaps you are not aware, but that very night, there was a robbery at the hotel. The police searched the entire hotel the next morning, including the room where this so-called incident took place. Only four sets of fingerprints were found. None of them belonged to Miss Khan. Interestingly, though, Madam's sunglasses were found there, as was a teacup with her fingerprints and lipstick marks...

⚖

The next day, you called a meeting of the top government machinery. Generals and bureaucrats, judges and ambassadors, all sat around your father's long boardroom table.

'Gentlemen,' you began.

I watched closely to see if anyone would show disrespect by calling out 'Ladies', but for a change, the room full of men seemed respectful, even appreciative, of your authority.

'I have gathered you here today to ask you for your solidarity so that we may work together towards creating a better Nation.'

Balgodi, who had self-appointed himself as your political advisor, stifled a yawn.

'Our country is broken. It needs tenderness and dedication

to heal. We must come up with literacy policies, swift justice systems, anti-corruption laws, and move towards moderation. The whole world is watching us to see how we will emerge from ten years of Jihadist rule.'

Balgodi cleared his throat. You ignored him.

'Are you all with me? We have an enormous task ahead and I can't do it without your support.'

Balgodi scraped back his chair and left.

You carried on.

'I pledge that I will see neither night nor day. I will work relentlessly.' There was a round of reluctant applause as the men clapped half-heartedly. 'Now, here are a few proposals I have been working on.'

I too was clapping from my little corner by the cupboard when suddenly you called out my name.

'Nazo?'

'Me?'

'Yes, you Nazo.'

I snapped to attention.

'Some of the files are missing. Could you fetch the blueprints for the girls' school from my study?'

'Oh,' I said. What had I been expecting, I scolded myself, a call to arms?

I ran up the stairs two at a time and, as I passed your open bedroom door, I saw Balgodi lying on the bed with a bottle of whiskey in hand. He was drinking straight from the bottle. I paused. Surely he was gearing up to create a scene. Very gently, I pulled the door shut and slid the bolt from outside.

That should hold him.

When I came back into the boardroom, there was a passionate

discussion going on. The man next to you was speaking very loudly, and it dawned on me again that you were the only woman at the table.

'Madam,' he was saying, 'your plans are too idealistic. We'd be lucky if we can achieve a five per cent literacy rate in five years. A hundred per cent is next to impossible. In fact, it is madness.'

'Gentlemen,' you said in a firm tone, 'the world is changing. Literacy is the only way our country can enter into the new century.'

'If you ask me, we should focus on Islamic education only,' a grey-bearded maulana announced in a high nasal pitch.

Lucky that no one was asking him, I thought, but that didn't stop him.

'Create madrassas, teach them about Islam and Shariah,' he droned.

'I think my predecessor did enough of that,' you said dryly.

The maulana frowned. Then wagging his finger at you, he said, 'Don't forget, Rani, God does not like bold talk from a woman's mouth.'

'Now, Maulana Sahib. Don't get so serious,' Pervez Sahib quickly stepped in. 'We are just discussing options.'

'But, that is what I am also saying,' the maulana persisted. 'Islamic education is cheap and easily available. The figures will go up instantly. I'm saying for her benefit only. But she is coming up with lunacy, all this talk of English-Vinglish. What use is it to us? The name of God is all one needs to learn.'

'There is no harm in trying,' you said. 'At least let's discuss the options.' I could see a vein throbbing in your temples.

'The trouble is,' a bureaucrat said before the maulana could reply, 'the money we put into education doesn't trickle down.'

'Then we need a better accountability system,' you said.

The District Incharge shook his head. 'In my jurisdiction, the land owners and the feudals will never allow the villagers to go to schools. We'd be lucky if they allow the boys. Girls are out of the question. Ignorance is the best form of submission as far as they are concerned.'

'That is why I'm saying, give the funds to Islamic education. It is the best kind of education, only!' the maulana thumped his hand on the table.

You put up your hand to halt the discussion and laid out the plans.

'Gentlemen, I have been working on these strategies throughout my time in exile. I have been dreaming of a better Nation. And the day has come to share my vision.'

'This,' you gestured to the papers on the table, 'is the result of my labour. I have detailed policies, funding plans, literacy trackers, implementation strategies...'

The phone rang.

Damn, I'd forgotten about those new mobile phones.

You picked up.

'Get up right now,' his voice pounded through the receiver. 'You think you can lock me up? You bitch! Get up here right now or I'll break down the door. You fucking whore!'

You looked at me and I looked away.

You snapped shut your mobile.

'As I was saying...'

A loud banging could be heard coming from upstairs.

'Are you having some work done, Madam?' the maulana asked.

Before you could answer, your phone rang again. You switched off the ringer. The home phone began ringing.

'Well as I was saying,' you began, 'the next step would be...'
Somebody's mobile rang.

'Sorry,' a young embarrassed-looking officer said, 'but it's for you, Madam. It's Balgodi Sahib. He wants you to come to the bedroom, right now.'

A deep red rose up your neck and crept onto your face.

'Excuse me,' you said. 'I'll be right back.'

You got up from your chair and stood hesitantly for a while, looking longingly at your plans spread out on the table.

'Nazo, will serve you refreshments in the meantime.'

I stepped out of my place in the shadows.

⚖

When you came back, you seemed only half the person you were. In just half an hour, the man had stripped you of all your dignity. You moved stiffly and I could tell by the difficulty you had in walking where he had assaulted you. Your lips were swollen, your eyes red-rimmed, your hands shaking. The man had raped you.

Yet you continued with the meeting, albeit not as convincingly as before. The men too had an inkling that a woman had been put in her place. The meeting that had been called to implement your vision turned into a booty war as the men divided up portfolios while you sat back and watched. Every now and then you raised an objection in a small defeated voice, which was promptly overruled by the powerful voices surrounding you. If that wasn't enough, the baby began to howl loud enough for the noise to drift into the boardroom.

'Duty calls,' the maulana said, as if you weren't the head of state but one of his many hijabi wives.

You looked at him in surprise and then at the files in your hand.

'But I am doing my duty,' you said.

He looked horrified.

'What kind of a mother are you, Madam? Your child is crying and you are sitting here chatting?'

I could have slapped the man. I could have kicked him. And if I had the means, I would have killed him. But you just sat there stoically, inhaling long deep breaths. A sort of silence descended upon the room in which the baby's crying became even more accentuated. Finally you placed your hands on the chair's arms and raised yourself slowly by the elbows. I moved forward to pull the chair back and noticed with horror, three tiny spots of blood on the seat of your shirt. Quickly I draped my shawl around your shoulders to hide the shame. You seemed resigned and clutched the shawl tightly around yourself.

'Gentlemen,' you nodded.

'Madam,' they said, as they watched you leave with a slow heavy tread.

'Women!' the maulana said, as he helped himself into your chair. 'They think they can do a man's job.'

I swung around, but felt your hand restrain me.

'To win the war,' you said in a small defeated voice, 'sometimes you have to lose the battle.'

Prosecutor: There were many complaints against
    Madam Rani Shah's government, but what people
    didn't know was that it was Miss Khan running
    the show. While Madam Shah was busy with cultural
    activities and protocol during those early days,
    who was in charge? Miss Khan, who is a corrupt,
    unscrupulous woman. Bribes, petty politics and
    underhand dealings are associated with her person.

Counsel: But that can be said about many people around
    Madam Shah. In fact, she herself was not free
    of these accusations. And the fact that she felt
    comfortable enough to delegate her duties shows
    her trust in Miss Khan.

⚖

And now began a new era. Of corruption and terror. The little
monsters the General had unleashed during his reign had become
full-blown terrors. There was blood in the streets as ethnic rivals
battled it out in the city. Outside the house, your opponents
exploited these racial tensions while inside the Parliament, you
were held to account.

And what did you do about it? You, who should have stepped
up and held talks with the opposing groups, delegated it to the
men in your cabinet. Pervez Sahib held round table conferences
with the warring chiefs while you attended a fashion show. Cause:
the liberation of women.

'Women can be liberated in more ways than clothes,' I argued.

But you shot me down with a look. 'Be patient, Nazo', became your standard reply.

I learnt to hold back. What else could I do? Every time I tried to speak, you silenced me. If I tried to do something you told me to wait for the right time. When I wanted to accompany you to a meeting, you asked me to look after the baby.

'You are the only one I can trust, Nazo,' you'd say, handing me the screaming little bundle.

'I am his mother after all,' I would say, just to spite you.

You'd draw in one of your deep breaths, which seemed to have replaced your habit of smoking, and let out a long sigh, leaving me wondering what, if anything, you meant by it.

⚖

Things took a turn for the worst. The city turned into a war zone. As if the killings were not enough, another monstrous issue rose up. This one was going to take you under if you did not take a stand soon.

'PM's Husband In Talks With China.' 'Plans For A New Dam.' 'New Water Dam To Block Waterflow To Eastern Province.' 'PM Betraying Her Own Homeland.' 'PM Plans To Sell The Land.' 'Mr Balgodi Snapped With Chinese Envoy: Discussing Price Of Water?' The papers screamed betrayal.

'Have you seen this, Rani Madam?' I said, as I handed you your morning tea. 'Perhaps,' I hesitated, 'you should have a word with Balgodi Sahib.'

'So now *you* are going to tell me what to do?'

I stopped what I was doing and looked at you.

'Don't stare at me!'

'Your tea, Madam,' I said, having been chastised enough.

You flung the teacup at me. A few searing drops scalded my skin. I pressed my palm against the side of my face. But it did not soothe the burn.

'Take your witch's brew and get out.'

Something inside me snapped. I stepped up. 'You are being an ostrich, Madam.'

'Shut up, Nazo.'

But I couldn't stop now.

'He's betraying you. Burying your head won't make it go away.'

'I'll bury yours instead.' Before I knew it, you grabbed my hair and banged my head against the wall. I flinched, not from the pain but from the unexpectedness of it all.

Slumped against the wall, my hands covering my face, I thought, it was not the first time you had hit me, but it was the first time it had hurt. What had happened to you, Rani? Where was the bright young girl who wanted to make a change? Who was this helpless housewife in front of me? Hot tears welled up in my eyes, not from the violence but from the helplessness in yours. You seemed so powerless, so weak, shoving me aside instead of yanking out that useless man from your house. From your life.

'Madam?' I whispered, as blood trickled from a cut on my forehead and into my eyes.

You didn't reply.

'Madam, stop him. Stop him before he breaks you.'

'It's not so easy,' your voice came out a whisper, as you placed a hand over your belly. It was then I knew.

You were pregnant again.

⚖

Later that day, I 'accidentally' smashed your best crystal flutes. I simmered like the milk I was boiling in the kitchen. The thought of you having his child made my skin crawl. How stupid could you be, Rani. Hadn't you learned your lesson the first time? You didn't get it, Rani, you just didn't get it.

Grabbing a broom, I started sweeping the kitchen. I was picking up the broken pieces of glass when a shard pierced my skin. Blood seeped out. I watched the brown of my hand turn red. And that was when the idea first entered my head.

Holding the papers close to my chest, I approached your study. I stopped just outside it. You were on the phone, talking to someone. I tried to lean in closer without being seen. I thought I heard you say the name Omar. But before I could find out anything more, you called out, 'Who's there?'

I leaned back into the shadows. The plan would have to wait.

The next day, you got a call from the American Ambassador. I couldn't tell exactly what he said, but after you hung up, your face was pale.

'Get me Balgodi,' you said, your voice urgent.

I dialled his number and brought you the cordless.

You snatched it from me and shouted, 'Didn't I tell you not to meet with the Chinese?' There was a pause, then you screamed even louder into the phone.

'How could you be so callous? How could you? I ask you to do one thing and even that you can't do right. You just can't do anything right.'

I had never before heard you talk to your husband this way. Moreover, why was he putting up with it. Just the fact that he hadn't hung up on you meant that he was tolerating your temper. Was it the pregnancy? Could men really love their wives such when they were carrying a child? Or was it because he needed you for something else? Something that his usual whores and harlots could not give him…

Before I could ponder further, you turned around and flung an overflowing ashtray at me. 'This is still your job, isn't it?'

'Yes Madam,' I hurriedly cleared the ash off the carpet and made to leave.

'Wait.'

There was something in your voice, a kind of realization, a weighing of things. I dared not breathe. You looked long and hard at me as if you were trying to see inside me. It was a while before you spoke. And when you did, it changed my world.

Once more.

'Can you still type?'

And so we began all over again….

Later that day, you called me into your study, which had now become your home office. And a good thing, too, as you hardly seemed to leave the house these days.

You looked serious. I was intrigued.

'I have a plan.' Your voice was strong. 'I need your help.' There was a finality to your tone.

I watched as you jotted something down. You wanted to be taken seriously. And for that, you needed my help. Since the day the General had died, this was the first time I felt worthwhile, needed, dare I say, appreciated. You needed me, my acquiesce and obedience.

'Here's your appointment letter. You are hereby reinstated as my personal assistant.'

As on previous occasions in my life, I thought not in words but in little vignettes of memory. I had been here before. Out of the chaos and noise of this maddening city, the dirt and breath of politics, the indifference of the mob, I'd found a purpose again. This was my calling.

Finally you felt it too.

'Close your mouth or a mosquito will fly in.'

I realized then that I was gaping.

'Catch,' you threw the cordless at me.

'You can handle the NGOs and the press for starters. After that, get my diary in order. But most importantly, Nazo...'

'Yes?'

'Keep an eye on Balgodi.'

So there *was* something more to this than just my services. You were like a jigsaw puzzle, Rani. A jigsaw with the last piece missing. Anyone who attempted to piece you together got nothing but frustration. Why did you want me to keep an eye on him? Why not just have him shut up somewhere? Why must you play this game of happy families with a man who was nothing but trouble?

However, I did as I was told. A week later, I reported that Balgodi had been going ahead with meetings despite your warnings. Contrary to your reservations, he had entered into talks about the dam. The press were sniffing. A scandal was imminent.

You slammed me. 'I told you to keep an eye on him!'

'An eye, not a leash,' I replied.

You paused as if deciding how much of your thoughts to reveal.

Finally you said, 'I want to make sure he doesn't enter into talks with the Chinese again. This Blackgarden Dam issue has gotten out of hand. Really, what should have been so simple has become so complicated.'

I turned to go, but something stopped me.

'Rani Madam,' I hesitated, 'the people from the Environment Agency were saying entire villages would be wiped out if this was to go ahead.'

'Yes, Nazo, I do know that and I do care. You don't really believe all those lies that the Opposition is spreading about us? I would never let that happen.'

I was quiet.

'Fuck you, Nazo! Here I am sacrificing my entire being for the people of this country and you think I'd sell out to the highest bidder. I would sell my land? I would sell my people? I would sell my soul? I, who went through torture, exile and what not, to restore democracy?'

'Not you, Madam, never.' I hesitated. 'But your husband…'

'Listen, Nazo. I'm in this for the long haul. Even if he wanted to do something vile like this, I wouldn't let him. I want to win the elections again and again and again till I set this country in order.'

I felt a warmth engulf my entire body.

How could I have doubted you…

'Do you trust me, Nazo?'

I looked into your eyes and said, 'I do.'

Little did I know then, what those two words would cost me.

Prosecutor: Are you suggesting, Miss Khan, that Madam Shah told you to spy on her own husband? I'm sorry, but this is just too much to swallow for any sane person.

Counsel: Objection, Your Honour. Mr Omar is trying to walk my client into a trap.

Judge: Overruled.

Prosecutor: Thank you, Your Honour. However, Counsel's analogy is very apt. Walk into a trap ... how true. I'd like to talk about the Blackgarden Dam Project. I know for a fact that Madam Rani Shah was strictly opposed to it. She bore it as a cross upon her heart. But the project went ahead and not only was it erected, the rights were sold to foreigners who are planning to turn it into a hydroelectric plant for alternate energy, but not for us — for China! How did this change of heart happen? Perhaps Miss Khan could tell us?

⚖

When a dog goes mad, most people would shoot it. But not you. You weren't the kind to put animals down. You'd take on the trouble of nursing it till its dying day.

And when you invite trouble, it never comes alone.

That day there was a furious protest outside Shah House. Local and international media and activists picketed. 'Stop the Dam!' 'Don't sell our water!' 'Looters, robbers, stop stealing our water!' Voices rose and fell, anger lingered in the air.

Inside, we were like an old couple by the hearth. I sat typing
out your latest press release, jabbing the keys hard, one at a time.
You were smoking, papers littered all around you. The outside
seemed another country.

But the peace was broken.

A red splosh, as sudden as a gunshot, appeared at the window,
and I looked up to see a rotten tomato sliding down the glass. You
sat up startled, your papers falling to the floor.

The intimacy was gone.

My finger slipped and I mistyped. Angrily I tore out the paper
mumbling, 'See where marriage to Balgodi has got you.'

'You have no idea.'

I looked up from the eerie clownish smile of the typewriter
to see you staring serenely at me. It was unlike you to behave so
calmly in the face of a storm. Had you become complacent? Or
overconfident.

I watched you reach for yet another cigarette. It hung sideways
from your lips as you struck a match and lit it. You sucked in your
cheeks, taking a long slow drag. Your face took on the bony horror
of a skull and, for a second, I felt myself shiver. In the still heat of
the room, you looked grey, ashen, almost ghoulish. But then as you
slowly relaxed and your cheeks fleshed out, you transformed again.

No, I thought, people never change.

They just reveal themselves slowly.

Outside, the noise grew. The chants got louder and I could hear
the distant wails of the siren as police vans arrived to dismantle
the mob.

'Rani Madam,' I approached you cautiously. I had to know.
Just had to. Did you really not care about the mob or was this
all politics?

The slow buzzing of the intercom interrupted us and, before I could speak, you pressed the answer button. Balgodi's voice boomed into the room, asking you to join him in the library.

'Of course, darling,' you got up to leave.

Protests raged outside. I watched you walk away.

A trick of the eye.

The next day you announced the twelve-member delegation that would be heading to Saudia to cement new trade pacts. After the names had been discussed and the list concluded, you made a surprise announcement. 'And the delegation will be headed by Mr Balgodi.'

Your husband looked surprised and a little horrified at the thought of seven whole dry, sexless days in the kingdom. His face battled pleasure and anger as he decided upon a reaction.

'Darling, you know I can only trust you to get this job done right. The Saudis are loaded and need to be milked just right,' you whispered.

That settled it. Balgodi coughed joyously and beckoned me to put him on the first flight to the 'riches', as he referred to the holy cities.

The next few days passed peacefully and things began to come under control. But the minute Balgodi got back, the circus began again. There were arguments, accusation and, I suspect, violence.

One night I found you slumped against the bathroom sink, a small razor poised in your hands.

'Rani Madam?' I said.

You turned around slowly, a disgraced, deadened look in your eyes.

I looked away.

Why was it, I wondered in that moment, the more I came to know you, the less I understood you. Go far enough and something happens, a transformation, an effect of solitude and strangeness, of power and persuasion and you begin to turn into someone else. Like a chess player who plays the next move brilliantly but doesn't take into account the next three.

And chess is all about the end game.

'Get away,' you said.

No, I was not ready to let go of the old you. Not yet.

I snatched away the blade.

'All this self-harm will kill you.'

You grabbed my hand and pleaded, 'Give it back, Nazo.' Your eyes wide as a child's as you said, 'Everything that hurts me, makes me feel alive.'

Next night, it was the same old story. After a rocketing argument, Balgodi had stormed out of the house while you sat sobbing in your study. Around midnight, I knocked on your door. When there was no reply, I stepped inside. You sat slumped on the desk. I shook you gently. When you looked up, your eyes were drugged, your lids heavy, your tongue thick. You were lying in a pool of your own vomit.

A wave of nausea washed over me, along with an overwhelming feeling of love and pity. I felt like a mother watching her child bleed.

'Nazo,' you slurred, as I bent down to clean you up. I wiped your face with a warm towel, got you some aspirin and forced a few sips of coffee down your throat.

Somehow I managed to get you to the bedroom and put you in bed. Heaving under your weight, I said, 'You shouldn't be drinking in your state. It's bad for the baby.'

'It doesn't matter,' you said slowly. You rolled up your shirt and patted your belly. 'The bitch is a girl.'

'Rani Madam,' I said, genuinely shocked that you, who had spent your life proving to men that you were their equal if not better, should regret carrying a girl.

'Shame on you!' I spat out the words.

You let out a ridiculous little giggle.

'It's not me, you fool. It's him. He wants an heir.'

'You have an heir,' I said, forgetting for a second that the wrong child did not really count.

Perhaps you didn't hear me or perhaps you chose to ignore it, for you continued to smile goofily.

'A girl can be an heir, Rani Madam. Look at you.'

'Yes,' you laughed. 'Look at me.'

'Your father chose *you* to carry his name, not his son.'

Your upturned mouth took a downward turn and your eyes began to glisten at the mention of his name.

Quickly I added, 'And as it is, these days neither boys nor girls look after their parents.'

You smiled.

Encouraged I added, 'Girls can do anything men can do and better.'

'You're such a feminist, Nazo.'

'What's that?' I asked.

'Someone who believes in equality for women.'

'Isn't that what our fight is about, Rani Madam?' I asked.

You must have seen the disgust on my face for you looked sheepishly up at me and said in a little-girl voice, 'How do you do it, Nazo? How can you resist a drink?'

'I don't like giving in to a bottle,' I said, remembering the one time when I had passed out after drinking left-over wine from a party at your Uptown flat. I had woken up dazed. I had no idea what or how I had ended up on the cold bathroom floor, lying face down in my own vomit. Rest of the day was spent in shock at how alcohol could take over a person's very self, snatching control, taking charge, dictating one's words and actions. I had no memory of what I had done or said. No, not for me such a cruel unyielding taskmaster. Why people willingly let something take over them, I would never know. My addictions were different...

I snapped out of my thoughts as your head bumped against the bedside table. You were trying to fish out a flask of whiskey from the drawer.

'Come on now,' I said, 'Hand it over, you've had enough.'

'No,' you shouted, 'mine!'

'You are behaving like a child.'

You fell back against the pillows as I snatched the flask from you. A sudden rage ran through me. I was on fire, furious at how you took your privilege for granted. Instilling your idealism in me and then mocking me, baiting me, egging me on. You had no idea of what you meant to your people. I pushed you hard. I held down your arms and straddled you. For a second, you were pinned under me, the look of a deer in headlights on your face.

The next thing I knew, my mouth was brushing against yours.

I hadn't meant for this to happen, but happen it did. I had vowed to myself that I would never come close to you when you were drunk. But the pull was too strong. I became the goddess on the flying tiger, a painting I had seen on the back of a water tanker. Together we were soaring.

The more we tussled, the more tangled we became.

Perhaps it was inevitable…

At first you resisted, but then you seemed to relax. If I didn't know you better I would have thought you were enjoying the roughness.

Or perhaps I did know you better…

I pressed your wrists into the mattress and you struggled, turning your head this way and that. Yes, I was right. You were enjoying this.

'Stay still,' I said, pressing your wrists harder.

But I hadn't realized how strong you were. You shifted your weight and, before I knew it, you had gripped my shoulders with both hands. Then you turned me sideways and, like a small child, lay lengthwise against me, fitting yourself into my back and calves. Your chin rested at the nape of my neck, your knees snuggled in mine. Your breath slowed, evened. I felt the warmth of your melting body against mine.

When I tried to speak, you pressed your palm over my mouth. Pulling me in, you wrapped your arms and legs around my stomach and thighs, squeezing the breath out of me, imprinting yourself on my body. Spooning me like a sheltering mother.

But I wanted more than this innocent caress. I wanted something explicit, dominant and sensual. I lifted your hand and brought it close to my mouth.

You tried to untangle yourself and pull back, but it was too late. I pulled you closer. Almost roughly, I gripped your wrist, thrusting my back into your stomach.

We lay curved, like a double-edged sickle, pulling, pushing, neither of us giving in or giving out.

What did this mean, I thought as I sucked your fingers, while your arm wrapped itself around my neck. Had there always been this element of violence between us? Was it passion or repulsion? I didn't know. All I knew was that I wanted to savour this closeness for as long as I could.

And then I felt as if my air supply was being cut off. Darkness began to descend on my lids. Truly, I would have died that night, had I not found the strength for one final push.

I broke away.

But not for long. You lunged at me and confined me with your whole body, suffocating me with your sweet sickly perfume till the pulsing of your blood numbed my mind.

I had your whole attention.

'I am Rani Shah. I'm the Leader. Do you understand?'

You yanked my head back. One more pull and you would have snapped my neck in half.

'You alone are Rani Shah,' I said, my voice a hoarse little whisper.

Resting your elbows on the mattress, you slowly raised your head back. You looked like a cobra rising from its sleep. So cruel, so majestic, so unattainable.

I had never seen this side of you.

I remembered to breathe only when you pressed my head into your chest. You held me close. Closer than the dark. You smoothed my forehead with your palms, all the time drawing me in as if trying to merge our bodies together. It hurt so much that I began to see white spots in the space before me. I struggled to raise my head, but you kept me headlocked, smiling that deep self-assured smile which made you seem indestructible.

It felt almost maternal.

⚖

I did not rest that night. Instead I died, a dreamless sleep.

I came to life, blinking against the early morning sunlight filtering through the curtain partings. My hands and feet felt as if they had been bound with ropes. Every muscle ached, yet I felt renewed.

I watched the sun come up and light your body golden. When the muezzin's call for prayer began echoing through the sky, I pulled a sheet over you and touched your cheek. I sat at your feet, admiring your God-like charisma. Even in sleep, you seemed perfect.

And then you sneezed. Little drops of snot flew out of your nostril and you turned your head, absently wiping your nose with the back of your hand. Your eyelids firmly shut, saliva gathering at the corner of your mouth. You licked your lips and I smiled at this sudden vulnerability. You seemed so pathetically human. Gone was the indestructible, infallible, politician. You seemed … almost ordinary.

But your humanness assured me too. After all, even prophets were allowed one mistake. I bent down and kissed your forehead. Behind me, I heard the door shut softly. A click and the sound of footsteps disappearing down the hall, their echo sharp in the fading silence.

Had someone been watching us?

⚖

In the morning, you woke up as if nothing had happened. You kissed Balgodi on the forehead and sat down to breakfast. When I served you tea, you did not look up.

'Rani Madam, shall I get the day's schedule?' I asked.

No response.

Balgodi looked up, his expression blank and heartless.

You reached for the teapot and he lowered his paper to look at you. His gaze, unblinking and cold, reminded me of a hunter lining up his prey through the eye of a trigger.

'Madam, please remember to sign my re-appointment letter, today. Pervez Sahib needs it for the accounts.'

His eyes narrowed.

'Madam?' I asked again.

You didn't look at me as you chewed your toast.

The hunter was taking aim.

It was a full minute before you spoke.

'I'll remember.'

I noticed you were careful to avoid the hunter's eyes.

'Thank you, Rani Madam. I won't let you down.'

The gun was lowered. The hunter leaned back, as if the animal had just revealed a weakness, a limp or a wound.

'Nazo,' you said in a low voice, 'have you sent off that press statement yet?'

'I had some more urgent work to take care of first,' I said, as I picked up your empty mug, touching your hand as if by accident.

When I looked up, I saw your husband staring hard at me.

Ready, aim, shoot.

As I suspected, your husband had no foresight. He was a man who reacted only to what was in front of him, not bothering to see beyond the obvious. That morning, too, he couldn't resist cashing in on the situation. As I cleared up the dishes, he told you that he wanted to buy horses.

'I want to set up a stud farm.'

You continued chewing like a bloated cow.

'I need money to buy horses,' he demanded.

Like a guilty parent giving in to a petulant child, you sighed and said, 'Nazo will take care of the logistics.'

I bit my tongue, hard. I tasted salt as blood seeped into my mouth. But it hurt more that I had been discarded yet again like a used tissue. I was a dirty secret that must be hidden, bought, bribed.

I brought you your cheque book and turning to your husband, you asked, 'How much?'

And just like that, you put a price on it.

Prosecutor: No one is denying that Miss Khan was useful. But not always in the right way.

Counsel: Prosecutor is being derogatory.

Prosecutor: On the contrary, I have evidence that she pressured Madam. Your Honour, here is Opposition Leader Mr Nawabzada's testimony in which he recalls how Miss Khan tried to influence Madam Shah's decision to hold off the dam. He remembers this clearly because it was the only time they agreed upon something.

Counsel: Do you believe everything you hear, Mr Omar? Could this statement not be politically motivated? As an experienced staffer of the Party, Miss Khan would be very resourceful in Madam's absence. Surely Opposition doesn't want that...

Prosecutor: Counsel, Mr Nawabzada had staff with him who can confirm the conversation.

Counsel: Ah, in that case, has Mr Omar ever heard of the expression 'devil's advocate'?

⚖

'The time has come for you to be useful.'

I looked up from my work to see you standing in the doorway.

'The Opposition Leader will be here soon. There might be a few officials with him too.'

'Shall I organize tea?' I asked.

'There is more to being a PA than serving tea, Nazo.'

I knew that, but I didn't know that you did too. Aloud I said, 'Yes, Rani Madam.'

You walked up to your desk and, picking up a paperweight, you turned to me. 'This meeting will be a little different, Nazo. I want you to take part in it.'

Perhaps you mistook the surprise on my face for concern. In the next breath, you said, 'Of course I will tell you exactly what to say. You needn't worry.'

Before I could protest, you said, 'Now here is the plan. When the issue of the dam comes up, I want you to disrupt the meeting. Ask questions, give out facts, quote figures … anything you can think of to support it.'

The buzzer rang. Refugee's singsong voice came through. 'The guard says, Opposition Sahib is here with his bald head and protruding stomach, scratching his belly and demanding to see you immediately…'

You cut him off with the flick of a button.

'Shall I make him wait?' I asked eagerly.

You looked approvingly at me and said, 'You learn quickly.'

After an appropriate wait of about half an hour, I got up from my desk and, with a stretch and a yawn, announced that Madam was now free.

There was some static as the Opposition Leader raged and raved about how his important time had been wasted. Finally he burst through the door with his entourage. Red-faced and breathing through his mouth, he lunged towards a chair and started heaving heavily.

'Please be seated,' you said, with a sarcastic smile.

He looked at you with great annoyance.

'We are not here to talk small.'

'Small talk,' you suggested helpfully.

'Don't act smart, Madam. We are here to tell you that as long as I am alive, the dam will not be built. Only over my dead body!'

You seemed like you'd easily walk over his dead body, so I said, 'Sir, the dam will provide employment for millions. At present, only one male in five families is earning in the area of Ghot Machira. The area where the displacement will take place is already dead. You see the fishermen have long since lost their livelihood to trawlers.'

'Oh, but Nawabzada Sahib is right, Nazo,' you said patronizingly. 'We cannot ignore the fact that the people who have been living there for generations will be displaced. It's a sensitive matter.'

I blinked. What were you playing at now? Why prep me with all the reasons the dam should be built then argue against it?

You cleared your throat and I returned to the script.

'But, Rani Madam, these people are starving. For centuries, economic migrations have taken place for man. It's the cycle of life. Is it not time for them to move on to greater opportunities? Don't they deserve a chance?'

'It is not just the people we are worried about,' you argued. 'What about the fish? It will be a great ecological disaster, Nazo.'

I softened. You always were kind at heart. Even the fish were not lost on you. But aloud I continued as directed, 'When there are people to worry about, how can you be thinking of something as small as fish.'

'Nazo, it is a complicated matter.'

'No, Rani Madam, it is very simple. The dam is good for the economy and economy is what makes the country run. I can't think of one good reason for it not to be built.'

'My first thought is for the people who live there. Don't you agree, Nawabzada Sahib?'

Both you and the Opposition Leader were on the same page now as you argued against my point.

In the middle of all this, the man suddenly realized that he was agreeing vehemently with you. He wiped his sweaty bald head and then, pocketing the handkerchief in his waistcoat, he turned to you.

'Rani Madam, I have to say that I was not aware of your true intentions. You seem very knowledgeable about the dangers of building the dam. In fact, some of the points you mentioned, we were not even aware of.'

'Nawabzada Sahib, I am glad that you have finally realized that we are both working for the good of the country. I can assure you that like you, I have no intentions of letting this project go ahead. But you must understand that I am under great pressure. You know that I have bosses too.'

He nodded sympathetically and looked up at a photograph of the oath ceremony on the wall. From behind the glass, the new Army Chief beamed down on us.

'Yes,' he mumbled. 'The bosses…'

The meeting came and went. I was none the wiser than when we started, but happy that a decision had been taken. You had planted me as a villain, pro-Army and corrupt, but I was happy to make the sacrifice. Content in the knowledge that you, too, didn't want to see this ugly monstrosity built.

After we saw Nawabzada safely out the door, beaming as he announced to his supporters that he had convinced you of his view, I brewed a celebratory cup of hot chai.

I knocked on the door and entered without waiting as had become my habit. You were smiling into the phone as I heard you say, 'Yes, Sir, the paperwork is ready. The dam is ready to go ahead.'

My hands shook. I placed the teacup carefully by the papers and waited. When you hung up, I said, 'But, Rani Madam, you just agreed the dam will be a complete disaster.'

'The Nawabzada has left now, Nazo. No need to act.'

'But the fish…'

'Can go to hell.'

'And the fishermen?'

'Can leave.'

I took a step back.

Don't believe everything you hear.

Why was I shocked at this new avatar of yours? Hadn't you just said you, too, had bosses above you? And perhaps if you gave in on the dam, they would give in on the schools. I decided to leave it to you.

And so I left. But not before I knocked over your tea, accidentally of course, on the papers you were looking at so intently.

Prosecutor: Are you aware that a few days after the Opposition Leader's visit, a letter of blackmail was found on Rani Madam's desk. Miss Khan was sent for right away. It doesn't take much imagination to piece that one together.

Counsel: On the contrary, my client was called in to be consulted. As mentioned before, Miss Khan's opinion was highly valued by Madam Rani.

Prosecutor: Miss Khan, I'd like to hear from you.

Defendant: As you know, Omar Sir, there are three sides to every story. Yours, mine and hers...

⚖

Things would have carried on in the same vein had it not been for the letter. Barely a few days had passed since the meeting with the opposition, when an annoying journalist wrote a particularly scathing article about the project. Uproar followed, not that you cared. I was arranging a pacifying meeting with the anti-dam lobby when you sent for me. I entered to see you looking ashen, almost ghostly. For a minute, I thought it was the backlash that had you in this state, but no, I was wrong.

You got up when you saw me. Your forehead was scrunched in anger and your fists balled tightly. 'I never expected you to stoop this low, Nazo.'

When I didn't reply, you lowered your tone. 'Look, is this about the dam? Because I can assure you it is out of my hands.'

I leaned in. 'Madam, what are you talking about?'

'The letter. Don't say you have nothing to do with it. I know you well. I suppose it was too much to hope that a poor, hungry, low-class woman like you can dream of something beyond the stomach.'

I felt as if you were slapping me with every word that you uttered.

'Here I was trusting you and the backstabber that you are...'

'Stop it,' I said, my voice a near growl. 'I don't know which letter you are talking about.' I held up my hand to stop you from talking. 'No, Madam, you can either trust me and we can find out who is really behind this letter, or you can go on insulting me and stay in the dark forever.'

You took a deep breath and turned your face away.

'Look, Nazo, I'll be honest with you. If it wasn't for the photographs, I wouldn't have suspected you.'

'Photographs?'

You nodded. 'Here, now you tell me, what am I suppose to think?'

You handed me an envelope, watching me closely as I opened it. I never got to the letter. The photo of two intertwined female bodies made my hands sweat. The faces had been blacked out, but there was no mistaking who they were.

'What does he want?'

'He or *she* doesn't say. The letter just says they'll let me know their demands when the time comes.'

A drop of sweat trickled its way down my forehead, resting on my temple. You leaned in close and flicked it off like a fly.

'Listen, Nazo,' you stood so close that I could smell the cardamom on your breath.

'If this ever gets out, I will kill you.'

Sometimes words do speak louder than actions.

Prosecutor: Madam Shah was a visionary who could foresee change, economic growth, revolution, development. She knew that new alliances were needed. Old friends could no longer be trusted.

Counsel: I object, Your Honour! Prosecutor is insulting my client. His finger was pointing at Miss Khan when he said those last words.

Prosecutor: Actually, Counsel, I was talking about countries. But as they say, the guilty always feel accused. What I meant was that Madam Shah knew that our country needed to form new alliances, that America alone could not be relied upon.

Counsel: Of what relevance is that to my client?

Prosecutor: Very relevant. Miss Khan did not want this to happen. It is common knowledge that the US is afraid of China's growing influence and wanted to curtail our country's friendship with China. Now, perhaps she was working for the CIA or perhaps not, but for some reason or the other, she wanted the old status quo. These faxes and emails to the US consulate are proof.

Counsel: Your Honour, why would Miss Khan use her own email ID or staff number if her intentions were questionable? My client was simply following orders.

Prosecutor: Oh, but it didn't stop at correspondence. She was intent on bodily harm. Miss Khan, isn't it true that you assaulted a Chinese diplomat? If I recall

correctly Madam Shah was very upset by your sudden
act of violence.

Defendant: At least, Omar Sir, it wasn't premeditated...

⚖

That afternoon, you had an unexpected visitor. A man with
thin yellow skin and grey slits for eyes stormed into the house
despite the guards' protests. He started speaking rapidly in what
seemed like English, but I couldn't be sure. He shook his head,
gestured with his hands and stamped his foot. For such a small
man, I thought, he certainly had a lot of energy. Before we could
stop him, he sprinted past Refugee and me and made his way up
to your study. I don't know how he knew where you were, but
he knocked at the very room you were in. When you opened
the door, he fired off a string of insults. In the end, he asked for
Balgodi. Your complexion, I noticed, turned a ghostly shade
of pale.

'Guards!' you ordered and the men came running up. 'Calm
him.'

Immediately, the security held him by the arms. But he shook
off their grip with three swift karate moves.

'Don't touch,' he said.

'Please,' you said. 'Please calm down. We can talk about this.'

'I am Diplomat,' the small man asserted.

'Mr Kim, I know who you are. Please...'

'No, Madam. You have no idea who I am or what I can do.'

'You!' I shouted. How dare he talk to you like that. 'I don't
care who you are,' I said. 'You need to show some respect to our
Madam. Understand?'

'Your Madam, crook,' he said, and that was when I landed him a left-hand jab. The man was shocked at being struck by a woman in a hijab, but you looked even more shaken.

'Nazo!' you shouted as the man swayed left, then right, before falling flat on his yellow face. You stood mortified. 'Between you and Balgodi, I don't know what I'll do!'

The next thing I knew, you were rubbing your temples and cursing as you dialled your trusted old Party member Pervez Sahib's number. 'Please, Pervez Sahib, come quickly and help me clean up this mess with the Chinese ambassador's attaché.'

China had not, in those days, shown its hand and I couldn't help but wonder what the fuss was all about.

'It's just the Chinese,' I said, walking into your study without knocking.

'Please, Nazo,' you waved me away as you swallowed an aspirin.

'But, Rani Madam, it's not like we punched the American ambassador. In fact, won't the Americans be happy to hear of this run-in?'

'Ever heard the saying,' you said as you picked up the phone, 'your enemy's enemy is your best friend?'

So that, my friend, is how the game was played.

⚖

The next few days were spent in keeping the Chinese at bay and the Americans happy. Where in all this was the time to look after your own countrymen?

It had become routine now for the newspapers to rage about you and your misdoings. Those who knew politics knew that you had little say in the house of Parliament and those who knew you personally, knew that you had even less say in your own house. I was one such person who knew both the home truths. But I also knew that you were trying very hard.

'Democracy farce.' 'Rani as corrupt as the general.' 'Our sacrifices were in vain.' 'Elected government as corrupt as the dictator.' 'A let down to women all over.'

Shout a lie loud enough and it silences the truth.

All those years of hard Jihadist rule had toughened the journalists. They had, in my opinion, become used to abusing those in power. Having power meant misusing it, or so they tried to make the Nation believe. Habits after all were difficult to break.

What the press didn't know was that you were trying very hard to balance it out. A hospital here, a shelter there, and perhaps in return for all the corruption and bullying you were trying to get a repeal on the Rape Law. Although I had to say the pregnancy seemed to have dulled your mind. You seemed to have turned a blind eye to many of the things you would have raged about earlier. But I knew you well. You would never willingly do wrong to your Nation. Not unless, and I sat up suddenly as it occurred to me that, perhaps you yourself did not know what was going on. After all, why would they tell someone who wasn't a player?

And just as I thought, not everything was as it seemed. You were too trusting. And it was my experience that if you trusted someone blindly, they became blind to your trust.

Prosecutor: Just like a king's eyes and ears are his courtiers, a PM, too, cannot govern without complete trust in her staff. And it's this trust, Your Honour, which is in question today.

⚖

Barely had we settled things with the Chinese that another commotion erupted.

'Rani Madam,' I said, walking into the room, armed with newspapers blaring headlines that called you a liar and a cheat. 'Have you seen the papers?'

'Fetch my ciggies, Nazo.'

Oh no, I thought. Here we go again. The ostrich, the burial, the denial...

'Now.'

'I will. But first, please answer me. Madam, you gave me your word. You promised not to give in. You said that you won't sell out to the Chinese.'

'I didn't.'

I could hear the sincerity in your voice, yet something was not right. You refused to meet my eye.

Suddenly the noise of glass breaking outside made you look up. In your eyes, I saw fear.

Shrill screams, loud thumping, raging footsteps, and the next thing we knew – the commotion outside had waded inside, knocking down the hundred-year-old wooden door in the courtyard.

Refugee came running in, his breath ragged and eyes wide.

'Rani Madam! Oh God, O' Prophet, Jesus Christ!'

'They are all here,' I murmured.

Ignoring me, he fell to his knees. 'Tragedy has struck. *Gazab ho gaya!* Oh no! Oh no!'

You stood patiently, tapping your fingers on the desk, waiting for his theatricals to end.

'Speak already,' I cut him off with a little shove.

'The Opposition Leader has brought a large crowd to our door. He says if Balgodi Sahib does not come out, he'll let the mobs loose on us. They have bats, stones, sticks – some even have guns!'

'What?' you looked at me. 'Why wasn't I informed of this? Surely he'd been planning this for a while.'

'Rani Madam, that's what I came to tell you.' In reality, I had no intention of informing you about Balgodi. I narrowed my eyes at Refugee. He hurried out.

'Madam, the papers are accusing Balgodi Sahib of selling out. It's all over the news.'

You switched on the TV.

'The police has issued an arrest warrant against Mr Billah Balgodi,' the newsreader announced on the screen. 'It is said that a case has been filed against the PM's husband. The complaint has been registered on behalf of the residents of the dam-affected district by a lawyer who does not wish to be named for security reasons.'

On television, the Opposition Leader praised him, 'This lawyer has done what we all could not do. Registered a police complaint against a powerful man despite threats. This act of bravery must be applauded.'

You flicked channels and came across the Opposition Leader nodding his bald head and addressing a think tank. 'But of course, selling the Nation's resources is unconstitutional. This lawyer has raised an important point. It must be stopped. The court is right to halt the proceedings and to issue a warrant for Mr Balgodi's arrest.'

You switched it off.

'Nazo?'

I looked up, expecting you to fall apart.

But you seemed calm. Calmer than I expected. Almost pleased, if I'm not mistaken.

'Don't say anything to anyone till I say so. Do you understand?'

Before I could ask you anything more, there was a knock on the study door. I was annoyed at the interruption, but you rushed to answer it. Your left eye twitched as you greeted the tall, burqa-clad figure in the doorway.

'You can go now, Nazo,' you said, giving me a little push. 'Go, hold off the press. Remember, no comments.'

I stood rooted, curiosity digging my heels deep.

'Go on, off you go.'

I stepped out, but did not leave. Instead I knelt down and peered through the keyhole.

'Did you bring it?' I heard you say.

A pair of hands, the shade of exquisite ivory, emerged from the folds of the black burqa. The skin was smooth, the nails clean and cut neatly. But something seemed out of place. Perhaps it was the sheer size of the hands. Surely they were too big to be a woman's. I tried to peer at the veiled face, but even the eyes were concealed behind a pair of thick sunglasses. The person thrust forward a brown file, and if it wasn't for the large white knuckles and the hairy wrists, I would never have guessed what you were up to.

Money changed hands. Though the notes were wrapped in yesterday's newspaper, I could tell what was inside it. I watched the wordless exchange then hid behind the curtains as the figure approached the door, a pair of large Nikes on his feet giving him away, most likely as the undisclosed lawyer who halted the dam's sale.

As soon as the figure came out of the study, I slid out after her. By now I knew, I wouldn't get any answers from you.

You just had to know.

'Nazo,' you called after me just as I descended the staircase. I pretended not to hear and was about to catch up with the figure, but you shouted my name loudly. I stopped, aware that your call was more to alert the figure than to beckon me. The figure hurried its step, exiting through the back door to avoid the crowds, and lunged into a waiting car. I watched from the window as the car sped down the street. There was, I noticed, no number plate.

Balgodi was arrested. We watched open-mouthed as the police handcuffed him in his own house. As expected, he kicked up a fuss, shouted threats and swore loud enough to wake up the neighbourhood. The police went about doing their job almost apologetically, their heads bowed, certain that when he was released they would all lose their jobs. In the end, when nothing worked, he looked at you like a petulant child being dragged away to boarding school while the parents watched.

'Rani,' he pleaded. 'Tell them to stop.'

And to my surprise, you didn't. You stood there, stoically clutching your belly, playing the great sacrificing leader who puts the Nation before family. *Waah*, Rani! You could act when you wanted to.

Or perhaps, it suddenly occurred to me, you weren't acting.

Instantly I felt happier.

'Let them do their job, dear husband,' you said tragically, a few crocodile tears glinting at the corner of your eyelids. 'We cannot take the law in our own hands. If you are innocent, of which I am certain, you will soon be free.'

The police nodded appreciatively and the media was grateful for a sound bite they could now replay all day. Personally I thought, a few days in jail would do the bastard good.

Counsel: Would you call filing an FIR against Madam Shah's husband a breach of trust, Mr Omar?

Prosecutor: You should ask Mr Balgodi that, not me. It is no secret that he blames his arrest on Miss Khan's lobbying. If I recall correctly, in his press statement upon release he more or less said so.

Defendant: I would gladly take credit for this, but, Omar Sir, you and I both know that it wasn't me.

Counsel: Miss Khan, are you suggesting that the human rights lawyer behind the arrest was the prosecutor, Mr Omar, himself?

⚖

With Balgodi in jail, a new era began in your political career. Once again you were the golden girl who put the law ahead of her own family. Even the maulanas, who had berated you earlier for throwing your lord and master in jail, breathed a sigh of relief. Everyone seemed pleasantly shocked at the sudden end to Balgodi's corruption.

But like happiness, peace doesn't last long.

Now that the dam issue had come to a halt, another crisis erupted. The head clergyman of the First Central Church filed a case against you. During the flash floods the previous week, the entire Christian village of Monti Basant had been wiped out. The clergyman accused you of genocide. He issued press statements against you, saying that you were trying to wipe out the Christian population. He argued it was to build a vote bank of Sunni

Muslims whom you had offered to resettle in a nearby village. All this after Balgodi had sold their 'Masih' land to a multinational company. 'Modern colonizers,' the clergyman called them.

But it didn't end there. I couldn't help but relish when Balgodi sent word from jail. Once again he stuck his little foot in his big mouth with, 'Why can't the minority understand that foreign investment is good for us? The Christians should make room for progress instead of standing in its way.'

The message got in the hands of the press, accidentally of course, and started a crossfire.

'So kill us off?' the Christian leaders raged. 'Is that your solution?' they demanded. The priest of the Second Central Church filed a lawsuit against the company. Others started to follow. The head of the Christians' Association in the Capital wrote a scathing letter to the press. The Minority leaders accused you of murder. The Opposition took the opportunity to jump up and organize a march, right outside your residence.

'It is a well known fact, ladies and gentlemen,' Nawabzada ranted outside the gates. 'The Balgodi family are mine owners who have long since exploited poor miners. Not satisfied with our sweat and toil, they now want our blood too. Will you let them get away with it?'

'No!' a chorus rose up from the crowd.

'Down with Balgodi. Down with his wife.'

'Death onto them.'

'Who pays these people?' I said, watching the drama below from your study window.

Outside, the Opposition Leader wiped his round bald head and continued to thunder like a black cloud. 'The Shahs and Balgodis have caused these floods. They alone are responsible.

Their carelessness, their selfishness, their discrimination has caused the death of two hundred Christian villagers! Rani Shah is no leader. She can't even control her own husband. A wife does what her husband wants her to!'

'Death onto them!' the crowds cheered. 'Down with Rani Shah!'

Enough.

I drew the curtains shut with a flourish. 'Nawabzada is one to be giving marital advice. And besides, just how can you be held responsible?' I asked. 'Aren't floods an act of God?'

'Apparently not,' you said, without looking up. 'The journalists are saying the flash floods were caused by man-made faults.'

'What rubbish,' I said. 'Next they will say, *you* lured the devil away from angelhood.'

You looked up from your files and stared thoughtfully at a spot on the wall. 'I fear, Nazo, they may be right. To show the need for a new dam, the Army did not use the old dam as it should have been used.'

'You mean they deliberately let innocent people die to prove a point?'

'It's about money, Nazo. If they can prove the dam is a must, they will get millions of dollars from the World Bank. And that money will go straight into their pockets.'

'But Madam, you can't let that happen!'

'Oh, Nazo, stop looking at me like I'm a magician who'll whip out a wand and reform their corrupt selfish attitudes. My powers are limited.'

'But your brain isn't.'

'Excuse me?'

'Look how you managed to get rid of Balgodi.'

You raised your head slowly and turned your whole self to look at me.

'Your plan,' I said. 'You know, to get rid of him?'

You stood up, your eyes on me.

'I did not plot to get anyone behind bars. Least of all my own husband.'

For a moment, we both stared at each other.

And then I bowed my head and said, 'Of course, Madam.' Inside I thought, what are you up to now, Rani? Why this sudden performance? I wondered if perhaps you *wanted* the dam to be built. Could it be that one of the pockets to get filled was yours?

⚖

A few weeks later, the newspaper splashed pictures of Star Abbey, your huge palatial house that had been purchased in Scotland, secretly and recently. A few weeks ago, I would never have even doubted that Balgodi alone was behind this. I would not even have suspected your involvement, but now with him behind bars, I wasn't so sure.

⚖

That night, I found you in your usual state of distress, slumped on your desk, with a glass of whiskey and an overflowing ashtray as your only company.

'The boy wants to say goodnight,' I said, bringing the wrong child in.

You waved at him without looking up. By now the Calpol had made him permanently groggy. He always seemed slightly dazed and half asleep. I called Refugee to take him away and he toddled out, his head flopping to one side in perpetual drowsiness.

You didn't seem to care.

Just as well, I thought, turning my attention back to you. You had bigger things to worry about. Like how to get out of the latest scandal your husband had embroiled you in. I shuddered to think that if he could influence you so from inside a prison, what would he do when he got out?

'Madam, don't worry,' I said, more out of loyalty than conviction. 'It is probably another of the Opposition Leader's schemes to make you look corrupt. Since you turned your husband in, the public has been in your favour. He must be trying to manipulate public opinion by splashing all this nonsense in the papers.'

You held up your glass and swirled the amber liquid inside. 'It's not so simple, Nazo. The media and the clergy are blaming me, as if I'm single-handedly responsible for everything that went wrong.'

'Surely, Madam, they've enough sense to...'

'See for yourself.'

You put down the glass and turned on the TV.

Sure enough on a talk show a well-known political analyst was saying, 'To get funds from the World Bank for a new dam, the government deliberately put lives at risk. The waters were intentionally misdirected, the floodgates opened when they should have been shut. The PM alone is responsible for this. It's impossible that she had no knowledge of what was happening under her nose!'

You switched the channel.

'Rani's Star Abbey! A palatial home bought with innocent taxpayers' money! Built on the deathbeds of those who were swept away in the floods! Who is to blame if not our corrupt leaders?'

You switched again to find a fiery old ex-Party worker demanding the government's resignation. 'Fresh elections should be held. We must get rid of this corrupt regime.'

You turned off the TV and looked at me.

'What have I done, Nazo?'

'You've done the right thing. The honest thing.'

The fool that I was, I thought you were talking about turning him in.

You laughed a hollow little laugh. 'I knew about Star Abbey.'

'You did?' For a second, I wondered if I had misheard you.

'I … I wanted to safeguard my daughter's future. He … he said it was for her … her wedding dowry…'

Wedding dowry, daughter's future … was I hearing you right? You, a woman who had taken on the generals and the Jihadists, was planning her unborn daughter's wedding!

'Rani Madam, how can you even talk about such a disgusting thing like dowry?' No. I didn't believe you. This wasn't you. This was Balgodi talking. He was playing with your mind. He was far more clever than we gave him credit for.

You leaned forward and placed your hands under your chin.

'You think if Balgodi was here, they would have dared come after me like this?'

'Don't even think about it, Madam.'

You rubbed your swollen belly and handed me a newspaper. On the front page, there was a picture of your jailbird husband looking serious and contemplative.

'This would never have happened if I had been there to protect my wife. I was her eyes and ears. Putting me in jail was the Opposition's plan. Once I am out, I will shut that Nawabzada up so tight, he'll forget where his mouth is.'

I looked up from the paper to see you reaching for the phone. 'No,' I whispered, but it was too late to stop you. Your hand was already on the dial.

Prosecutor: The Moghul kings used to dress up as peasants to roam their kingdom at night. But modern day politicians have no choice but to depend on intelligence from their subordinates. Miss Khan was a trusted soldier who gave into greed. She misled her leader, her country. As a PA, was it not her duty to keep Madam Shah aware of the situation?

Counsel: My client has never neglected her work.

Prosecutor: That year, hundreds of soldiers lost their lives in a fake war. A war that was planned behind Madam Shah's back, an event that shattered her image in the public eye. As PA, was it not your duty, Miss Khan, to inform her of public opinion?

Counsel: Can Mr Omar provide any evidence that proves Miss Khan had not done her duty? Please see, Your Honour, Exhibit D, a record of newspaper clippings and daily faxes which Miss Khan meticulously recorded and presented to Madam Shah every morning. But as the saying goes, one can take a horse to water, not force it to drink.

A new crisis erupted. The country found itself at war.

A mountain peak that was uninhabitable, a barren piece of land no good to anyone, was being fought over with the arch-enemy.

'Now why would anyone post their army to protect a peak that's not useful to anyone?' I said, as I read out the day's appointments, a meeting with the Army General being top of the agenda.

'Land is land,' you replied, without looking up from your notes. 'We cannot give up even an inch, smaller as we are in size than the enemy.'

I shook my head.

'No, Rani Madam, a Nation is made by its hands not by its lands.'

'Well said,' you smiled. 'But still, it is a glacier. A source of water...'

'But, Madam, these water wars will take our Nation down. Is it really worth the blood of our young men? Look at all the Army casualties, and for what? Peak or no peak, our taps are still dry. We still have to pay water tankers for filthy salt water twice a week, we...'

I heard the sound of clapping behind me.

'*Waah! Waah!* Nazo-ji! Very good, *kya baat hai*. Where did you learn to spout such wisdom?'

I took a step back.

Balgodi came forward. 'Surprised to see me? Didn't you tell her about my release, Rani?'

He placed his hand on your shoulder, his eyes still on me. 'You don't seem happy to see me, Nazo. What to do, not even the strongest jail can keep me in for long.'

I swallowed hard, thinking, that was all I needed – for Balgodi to suspect me as the woman who'd filed the case against him.

Twirling the ends of his moustache, he strolled towards me and said, 'Perhaps we've given you too much freedom.'

I winced as he pinched my cheek.

'Clip her wings, Rani. She is flying too high.'

I stepped back, a sick fear rising up my throat.

'Now get out,' he hissed.

In my haste to leave, I left my appointment diary behind. Outside, I stood at the door, about to knock, when I heard him say to you, 'I hope you have learnt your lesson. You are nothing without me, understand, nothing? A woman without a man is like a fish out of water. What did you think, Rani? That you could leave me to rot in jail while you played leader-leader? The Army and Secret Service will chew you up and you would not even know. It is because of me that you are still in that chair, you understand? And what did you do for me? Send me to jail! You ungrateful woman.'

'It ... it helped the image of the Party...'

'Fuck the image of the Party! People here have short memories. Your big sacrifice has already been wiped out by the floods and the discovery of our palace. The public just needs flesh to bite on, you understand? Don't you see, they are there to be exploited. It's their fate, their need! Just like a whore needs to be fucked...'

I burst into the room.

'Yes?' he barked.

I stared at you. You were sitting there, calmly. No tears, no remorse, not even a clenched fist.

'I ... I ... Refugee's asking what to cook for lunch.'

'Cook all my favourite dishes, what else, you stupid woman! I've been having watery lentils for weeks. Meat, I want good meat.'

His mobile rang just then and he waved me away.

I closed the door softly and stood outside. Any minute now, I thought to myself, you'd stand up and put the bastard back in his place.

'There, that's sorted,' I heard him say, as he clicked his phone shut. 'The new Army Chief has agreed to a meeting. Here, at 4 pm today. Now remember, Rani. Let him do the talking. It was hard enough negotiating this one. Do you even realize how much this skirmish over the peak is causing the defence budget? It all comes out of the central treasury, you know. Less money for us.'

'Oh well,' he continued his monologue, 'at least the public will be distracted. A battle with the neighbouring country always makes them forget about domestic issues. Just you wait and see, a few more days and nobody will even remember the floods or the palace. And don't you dare pay any attention to that goofball Pervez Sahib or that witch Nazo. They are all out to get you...'

I waited outside hoping to hear a reply. But none came. Not even one tiny protest at this manipulation, this rampant corruption, these baseless accusations.

I began to wonder, Rani, whose side were you really on?

Prosecutor: Just look at this testimony of an old widow who lost her son to war. When she knocked on Madam's door for justice, Miss Khan had her thrown out. I'm sure that Madam Rani Shah would have reacted differently. But what would a childless woman like Miss Khan know of a mother's pain.

Defendant: I'm not childless, Omar Sir. I just chose not to be a mother.

⚖

The blue sky was streaked with orange. I yawned and stretched. Outside, the sun was just rising from its slumber. It had been a restless night and the muezzin's high-pitched call from the nearby mosque added to my agitation. I scowled at the nervous buzzing of a mosquito as it flitted lazily around me. I slapped it dead.

Hearing me stir, Refugee called out from outside, 'Get up, Nazo Madam. Say hello to God too sometimes.'

'Get lost,' I shouted, as I picked up a cigarette and lit it.

Refugee poked his head around my door.

'*Tauba tauba*,' he touched his earlobes. 'God forbid, Nazo, since when have you picked up this nasty habit?'

For a moment, I thought he meant missing my prayers. It was only when he began to cough and told me to put the vile thing away that I realized he meant cigarettes.

Truth be told, even I had no idea when I had started to smoke. I thought back to a saying I had heard once about owners becoming like their pets. But it was the other way around in my case.

265

'Well?' he said, leaning against the doorway, his huge belly protruding in front of him like a giant balloon.

'Times change,' I said. 'Just look at yourself. Such a starved, skinny Afghan refugee you were in New York and what a fat monster you've become, now.'

'*Oye*,' Refugee shouted, throwing a dishcloth at me.

Before I could respond, a loud banging was heard from outside. It was as if someone was rattling the iron gates with all their might. We both ran outside to see the guards trying to hold back an old woman who kept throwing herself at the door. She was beating her chest and wailing as only a mother could. 'Murderer, killer, she took away my son. My only son! Dead! Come out, you witch.'

I looked up towards the drawn curtains of your bedroom window. Not even a stir.

One of the bearded guards, who'd left his prayers at the commotion, grabbed her by the shoulders.

'Take control of yourself,' he said, shaking her by the shoulders.

'They killed my son! Sent him to that fake war. Butchers! Murderers! Killers!'

'Be quiet!' the guard shouted.

I rushed to her.

'Leave her!' I ordered.

'Be patient, Amma.' I turned to the old woman. 'Have faith in God. Your son died for his land,' I said. 'He's a martyr.'

The old woman looked at me with such hatred that I had to lower my gaze. She flung her long chaddar at me and said, 'Cover yourself, girl.'

I looked down to see that I had rushed out in my night clothes, my head uncovered, my braless breasts visible through the thin cloth.

'Shameless, all of you,' she said and turned to go.

I let out a slow breath and bent down to pick up the piece of cloth at my feet.

At that very moment, she turned around suddenly and threw a rock at me. It went flying over my head and smashed the French window behind. A loud crash and then complete silence.

You slept on, as only the conscienceless can do.

I brought you the morning post. More letters from widows and mothers who'd lost their sons in the useless conflict.

'Do you really have no say in this?'

'No,' you replied.

'Rani Madam, you are the prime minister. How can a country go to war without your consent? How do you expect me to swallow such farce?'

'Then don't.'

You rose up from the chair as if to leave. Then just as suddenly, you sat back down.

'I'm powerless.'

I couldn't help but laugh.

'If you are not powerful in the PM's chair then what use is it?'

To my surprise, you too broke into a laugh.

'It must be the country's worst kept secret. But the PM is just a puppet. You know who really rules the country, Nazo? The Army. And whatever is left is divided between the Secret Service and politicians. The three forces are tussling with each other for power. But the real players are the Military.'

'And you let them be?'

You smiled patiently as if addressing a naughty child. 'Ah,

Nazo, sometimes you have to lose a little to win a lot. It's all about give and take. When you grow up, you'll understand.'

Well then, I thought, I had better start growing.

Prosecutor: The real war was just beginning, Your Honour. Miss Khan was testing the waters with this. The real corruption began afterwards.

⚖

They say the more a caterpillar struggles in its cocoon the more beautiful a butterfly it emerges. You had been struggling for a while, but there were no signs of the end. Things were becoming worse by the day, yet you could do nothing. You had fought so much, lost so much. When would the metamorphosis complete?

The war had cost you dearly. You had lost all credibility. There was talk of a no-confidence motion. You cabinet's corruption had gotten out of hand. Yet you watched from the sidelines. The time had come to give you a good push. You were so close, yet so far. Once again jubilation turned into despair and I found you hunched on your desk with your head in your hands.

'Rani Madam?' I burst in, holding a confidential fax from your foreign counterpart. 'Look at this! The neighbouring PM wants to put a stop to it. He wants a ceasefire.'

I expected you to jump out of your chair, but you remained rooted to the spot.

'Did you hear what I said?'

'The Army Chief has said no,' you said flatly.

'To hell with the him,' I shouted. 'Put your foot down. Tell them you won't let your people be crucified like this.'

'You know I can't. They'll get rid of me and put someone who listens to them in charge.'

'But if you don't stop this war, the people of this country will do the same to you.'

The silence was earsplitting.

But silence is the strongest argument.

Slowly I began to realize that this was your manner. You came close to achieving something, then gave up just before you got it. Perhaps you were afraid. Afraid of your potential, your own power. You made things happen, yet became stagnant at the realization that you could. You craved power, yet you didn't know what to do with it once you possessed it. Were you a coward or just naïve? Sometimes I wondered, Rani, whether you'd become so obsessed with restoring your father's legacy that you had no idea how the system actually worked. You with all your foreign education, you really thought that the country could be run with goodwill alone.

What a joke.

Just like a car needed petrol to run, a politician needed power. And power can never be handed over. It has to be snatched.

'Madam, you have to do something,' I said, my voice shrill and urgent. But you were lost in some sleepless stupor. You were already miles away, looking at a tiny black and white print of your unborn's latest ultrasound, your features twisted in some maternal epiphany. The PM's fax lay untouched on your desk.

No, Rani, you could not do it. I had given you every chance. Had sold myself to smooth your path, but you were a coward. You were afraid of your own power. Power meant choice and you were unable to make one. Enough. You had to go.

You did not deserve it.

But then who did?

I looked into the mirror and knew, the answer was me.

Counsel: Like I mentioned, Your Honour, Miss Khan was a dedicated employee and her only ambition was to serve.

Prosecutor: Is Counsel saying that Miss Khan never took advantage of her position in Madam Shah's household to accumulate bribes and wield unauthorized power over others?

Counsel: A preposterous accusation.

Prosecutor: Well then, perhaps these bank statements of numerous deposits in her account might jog her memory. Surely a servant girl could not be drawing a salary such as this?

Like the smoking, it began so seamlessly that I myself did not notice how or when it all started. Perhaps it was when that industrialist called to arrange a meeting with you and I slammed the phone down, still smarting from your inertia on not stopping the useless war. Twenty minutes later, I found a briefcase on my desk filled with bundles of thousand rupee notes and a piece of paper that said, 'Please grant us an audience with Madam for five minutes. If she gives the building contract to us, there will be more of this coming your way.'

I folded the note and, carrying the case under my arm, marched up to your bedroom. I was hoping you would ring the corrupt industrialist and return the money before Balgodi saw it. I knocked, but you weren't in. I was about to bin the note and return the money myself when a thought occurred to me. I found myself walking up to your dresser. I ran a hand over your creams and then looked at my reflection. I had the same pale complexion as you, but whereas yours was creamy and glowed, mine was shot with pimples and dry patches from years of hard water and cheap soap. We were both orphans, but you were the heiress to a political dynasty and I a servant's daughter destined to be a servant. Holding all that money in my hands, I thought, why did it have to be this way? Why couldn't a servant's daughter become a prime minister and a PM's child, her assistant?

A crackling noise and I looked down to see I had crushed your jar of face cream. Blood seeped out of my palm and mingled with the thick white of the cream. It was a strange sensation of soft, velvety pleasure mixed with a sharp pain. I rubbed my palms together, but the two wouldn't blend. The red and the white ran parallel. Like us, I found myself thinking. We were both women, we both had blood the same colour running through us, keeping us alive, egging us on. But we could not be more different. You could touch heights that I would never be allowed to go near. What separated us? Glass ceilings which like promises were made to be broken.

It was time for a change.

⚖

Back in the office, I emptied the money into the bin. 'I'm taking out the trash,' I shouted to Refugee, as I closed the study door. But instead, I headed to the servant quarters.

Later, when I had hidden the bin bag under my mattress, I found the industrialist's note. I memorized the number and then did what I always did with unwanted paper. I chewed slowly, like a desert camel, in no hurry to get anywhere. It was all about the journey you see.

The destination was secondary.

The following afternoon, I cancelled all your meetings with contractors and made sure that only the man who had sent me the briefcase got to see you. Naturally, the contract was his. The next day, I waited in anticipation for the next installment, but nothing came. I knew what I had to do. I sat on his file till in desperation, he called to ask why the paperwork had been delayed.

'You tell me, Sir,' I said, and before long, another briefcase arrived at my desk.

And that was how it all began.

At first the bribes were small and the jobs too. I'd tell people you weren't in when you were, not to keep you from something, but to see how badly they wanted to meet you. Of all things, I loved to make people wait for an audience with you. It made me feel like you were the queen, your authority was respected, you alone held sway over their destinies. I wanted so much for them to realize how important you were. And it worked. As it is with most things in life, when you pay for something, you appreciate it more. So, I put a price on it. First it was for meetings, then it was for papers that needed your signature, orders that needed verification, contracts, bills ... I held onto all sorts of things, causing unnecessary delays. As the tasks grew, so did the bribes.

It was then I realized, I wasn't alone.

⚖

It turned out that I was not the only one playing this game. I already knew of Balgodi's corruption, but I had no idea there were others. There were so many middlemen between you and the Nation that even a cynic like me was taken aback. There were hundreds of other departments where projects could be stalled, tenders halted, files stuck. All these people were in it for a cut and by the time a case reached you, the person would be at the end of his tether. I wondered if you too asked for a cut, but then dismissed the thought. What did you need money for?

Sometimes the closer you look the less you see.

I suppose that was the only explanation for your aloofness, Rani. Else how could you not see the rampant corruption and the injustice taking place right under your nose?

Lucky for you, I was there to restore some checks and balances. I came up with a system. For every five bribes I took, I gave three back to a women's cause. I guess you could call me Robin Hood Nazo.

You think I lie, but I have no desire to make myself feel important. That's for people who doubt themselves. I tell it straight. Did you know, if it wasn't for me, a sixty-year-old retired teacher with four daughters, two of them mentally challenged, would have remained homeless. Not because she couldn't afford one, but because she invested all her savings into a government housing scheme only to be refused possession. She couldn't pay any more bribes, you see.

When she came to me, she had bills and paperwork saying she had moved in.

She took me to her shack outside the multistorey building and said, 'Tell me. She too is a woman and a mother. How can your Madam let this happen? Her officers lie, ask for bribes, harass my girls! We powerless women live under the open sky, roofless, despite paying them every cent we had for a house. And they show us as living here when the house is padlocked. No one comes to see the reality. They go by the fake papers.'

'I have come,' I said.

She looked at me with her hazy cataract-ridden eyes. I'm not sure if it was disbelief or disillusionment I saw reflected, but I wish I had been there to see her face when I sent ten of the city's best goons to throw out the corrupt government contractor from the building. By now I knew it was useless talking to you. You'd sing your old song about courts and procedures. And the government chain of command would take years for the thing to be corrected legally. I had to make a choice and unlike you, Rani, I chose to act.

I suppose, sometimes, might is right.

Prosecutor: The deposits on Miss Khan's balance sheet could match the earnings of a stock broker. A very successful one at that. But what is disturbing is that there are an equal number of withdrawals.

Counsel: The statements could be fake.

Prosecutor: Don't try to mislead the court. The bank verified it. The question is where was she moving these funds? To a terrorist organization perhaps? Or maybe she had been plotting the assassination years ahead...

It was a hot afternoon, and I walked back to my room to find an even steamier scene unfolding inside.

'What the fuck are you doing?' I caught Refugee fooling around on my mattress. The young tea boy, Chanchar, pinned under him, face down.

'You couldn't find any other place for ... for,' I smacked my head for lack of a word.

'Relax,' Refugee said, putting his vest back on, while the boy squirmed out from underneath. 'As it is your mattress is rock hard. Who can have any fun on this lumpy piece of turd.'

If only he knew why.

'Well, then, take your soft pudgy ass and your thin bamboo-stick lover and get out.'

'Don't be angry, Nazo,' Refugee laughed and added, 'You too have once loved.'

Despite the joke, his words hurt.

'Don't you two have any chickens to slaughter, goats to kill, eggs to whip?' I pushed them out and bolted the room from inside.

Immediately I stripped the sheets and with all my strength flipped the mattress. I stuck my hand in and felt around the cotton stuffing. Nothing.

For a moment, I berated myself for leaving the door unlocked. How could I have been so careless? What if they had robbed me?

And then I felt it. The thin crisp sensation of bank notes. Quickly, I pulled each bundle out and stuffed it all into a bin bag.

It was time to open a bank account.

Depositing money in a bank turned out to be harder than borrowing it. Eventually it was Refugee who introduced me to the bank and helped me open an account.

In return, I had to help him out.

'Why do you only help women, Nazo?' Refugee argued and showed me the photo of a man who had filed a case against the admissions committee of a prestigious college.

'Because nobody else does.'

But Refugee was persistent. Much as I was reluctant, I took on the matter.

This man, unlike most creatures of his gender, wanted to educate his daughter. The cynic in me believed that it was because he had no sons, but Refugee, who I suspected was getting a cut, convinced me otherwise.

'Give him a shadow of doubt,' he pleaded, 'a mere sliver.'

After some prodding, I found that the man had taken a loan

to get his daughter into the National Engineering College. But by the time he got the loan passed, he'd had to bribe so many people that the entire loan amount went into the bribery. His daughter, Refugee told me, was one of the only thirteen girls to pass the entrance exam but had to sit out the year. And the next year, too, she had to defer as the father did not have sufficient funds. She was promised a government bursary the following year. But when the year came, they found her seat had been sold to someone else. The girl was crushed. The father defeated. The man had defied society, kept his daughter unmarried so she could study, and now he was being punished.

I was impressed. His daughter too was a struggler, knocking on all doors, unlike some women, I thought, who born into power take their privilege for granted. I liked strugglers. My favourite being the upturned beetle who continues to kick its legs in the air. You see, I liked the idea of deciding its destiny. The power to crush the beetle or to turn it upright. And so I took it on.

But you forget, playing God is the prerogative of men...

Azizullah was her father's name. He paid Refugee the cut, but I waited a few months before I saw him. I wanted to see if he would give up.

Refugee, too, had lost contact with him when suddenly one day I read about him in the paper. I rang up the journalist who'd written his story, and got his number. The journalist was incredulous. 'Rani Madam herself wants to see a small man like him?' he asked.

I sighed. Why do we believe the most horrid stories without a blink of the eye and if someone tries to do good, what do you get? Suspicion and sarcasm.

The following day, I tried to reach Azizullah. When I finally

got through, I said, 'This is your lucky day. Rani Madam wants
to see you.'

He hung up on me.

'Why are you joking, sister?' he said in a resigned voice when
I called back. 'Why would the PM meet us? As it is they have
thrown my case out of the courts because I did not have money
to bribe a hearing. Leave us alone now. Please, I have no more
bribes to offer.'

Like I said, suspicion and sarcasm...

⚖

It took many more calls before I convinced him. When the day
came, I cancelled your meeting with a rich businessman wanting
to open yet another cooking oil factory and gave Azizullah the
slot. My efforts did not go to waste.

You remembered him from the papers and immediately made
calls on his behalf. See, Rani? I knew it. Deep inside, you still
cared. Your heart was in the right place. And that's what really
mattered.

'Get me the principal,' you said on the phone.

Azizullah sat resigned in front of you. Listless hands in his lap,
head hung low, hopelessness stooping his shoulders and curving
his spine, unable to believe his luck could change.

He shook his frail head and mumbled, 'Perhaps I should just
get her married.'

I saw a familiar flash of rage, two purple spots appeared and
disappeared from your face. You said nothing, but when the
principal came on the line, you did not greet him. Instead you
asked, 'How many years to your retirement, Mr Principal?'

Subtle yet deadly.

I imagined the balding principal squirming in his chair as he absorbed the full impact of your words. Frantic pleading, like mice running helter-skelter, came from the earpiece. You held it away till it was over.

'Now shut up and listen,' you said. 'The girl's name is Rehmat Fatima. It is not a favour I am asking. Give her her right. If she has cleared the entrance, been granted a bursary, how dare you stop her admission? On what grounds? Oh don't give me excuses. Not in my administration, you are not getting away with this.'

The next day, the papers led with the news of Rehmat Fatima Azizullah's admission and your success. You restored the girl's admission and, in the process, your own formidable reputation.

And me? I remained in the shadows, happy to have set things straight.

⚖

But as always where there is light, there is darkness. A few days later, I got a tearful call from the girl to say she had once again been dropped from the college.

'Why?' I asked, shocked that anyone could overturn the PM's decision.

'The college principal said it had been pre-allocated to a boy. My admission was a mistake. He said PM Madam herself overturned it yesterday…'

'What nonsense,' I shouted. 'Rani Madam was not even in the city yesterday. Let me find out the real story.'

I rang her father.

'Is this how you repay Rani Madam? She put herself on the line to help you and you flung it back in her face. You small people are all the same. Tell me, how much did you sell it for?'

The man was quiet for a while, then said, 'Miss Khan, you are right to tell me off, but we small people have nothing save for our honour and when that is threatened...'

I was taken aback. 'Who threatened you?'

'At first they tried nicely. Said girls were a waste of a degree as they just got married after college, while a boy would go on to earn and feed a family. The principal's PA begged me to give it up and when I didn't, I started getting threats from unknown people. They said if I let her study, they would dishonour her, kidnap...' he broke down.

So the Jihadists were back at it. Aloud I said, 'Don't worry. I will take care of them. We'll soon have her back in that college.'

'It is too much for an old man like me, Nazo-ji. I just wanted my daughter to become independent, but perhaps it's true, women are better off married. An unmarried daughter is a liability. I don't want her to study any more.'

'Your daughter will go to college,' I said firmly, 'but it might have to be a lesser known one. Perhaps a small private one.'

'Thank you, but we have had enough.'

'You can't give up.'

'Why not? Who are you to stop my daughter's marriage?'

Not again, I thought.

'Get your daughter on the line.'

The man passed the phone to his daughter with great reluctance.

'I don't care where I study, Miss Khan,' she said, as soon as she came on the line. 'But please, I just want to become someone. I don't mind going private, but I can't burden my father with the expense.'

'You don't have to worry about that. Just study hard and show

them that a woman can do something useful besides breeding.
Don't let me down.'

Inevitably, my eyes rested on a photo of you.

⚖

It turned out the Jihadists weren't behind this after all, but
someone much closer to home. It didn't take much investigation
to find out that the student the seat had been allocated to was
Balgodi's lazy nephew. You'd think a villain would get tired of
being so predictable, but not your husband.

There were fireworks of a different kind that night and I only
hoped Balgodi wouldn't find out about my role in it all. After all,
I'd kept his dirty secrets buried for so long.

I arranged for the starlet Dolly to visit him at his office. What
followed is not hard to guess, except what he did not know was
that it was all prearranged.

I started a rumour of their flirtation and sent you a copy of
the cheque he made out to the actress for her services. When he
got home that night, you demanded an explanation. Of course
he had none, so he stammered and stuttered, disbelief dripping
from his face.

'What actress? What money?' The man couldn't think on his
feet. Not even to save his life.

I stepped in.

'Madam, the truth is,' I stared menacingly at him, 'Balgodi
Sahib is setting up a cultural fund in your name and Dolly Madam
was hired as a consultant. He tried to hold her off, but she kept
throwing herself at him. The whole office is witness.'

He looked at me in surprise and then began nodding his head
like a clockwork toy.

'Yes, yes, oh yes.'

You looked long and hard at me before turning your back at him, your belly just beginning to swell.

⚖

Later that night, I found him in the lounge, alone. I approached him with a glass of whiskey.

'Sir,' I said.

'I thought a dog's curved tail could never be straightened, Nazo,' he grinned, taking the glass from my hands, his fingers lingering on mine longer than necessary.

'I'm not a dog.'

'Right, my mistake. You're a bitch.'

'They keep the mice away, Sir.'

I looked down as he twirled his ratlike whiskers and smiled. 'Thanks for helping me tonight.'

'My pleasure, Sir.'

'So what do you want from me?' he grinned.

'The girl whose seat you snatched...'

'What? What girl? What seat?'

'The engineering student whose seat Rani Madam herself restored.'

'That girl chose to get married. Sensible thing to do.'

'Yes, but you see, Sir, the media has been asking me who got the seat. For some reason, they think a corrupt politician has something to do with it.'

Balgodi nearly choked on his drink.

'What did you tell them?'

'I didn't give them any names, Sir, but...'

'But what?'

'But I told them that you would compensate the college's injustice by providing a lavish dowry for the poor girl. After all, she willingly gave up the seat to a boy after all the trouble Rani Madam went through. You know what I mean, Sir?'

He leaned back and looked me up and down.

'Impressive.'

'I learn from the best, Sir.'

'Hmm, dowry. Now that's a good idea. A good solid tradition. And as I always say, a girl's place is at home, behind the stove.'

'Yes, Sir. I have the cheque ready, Sir. You just sign it.'

He held out his hand regally, then let out a yelp.

'Ten lakhs!'

'The cost of sealing one's lips is high, Sir. Besides, it's a one-off.'

'And how do I know I can trust you?' he narrowed his eyes at me.

I smiled and said, 'Let's just call it honour amongst thieves.'

Prosecutor: Unfortunately, it didn't stop at the bribes.
Official secrets were leaked. The nuclear programme
being one such confidential document that got into
the wrong hands.

Counsel: My client denies any knowledge of it.

Prosecutor: Then why do we have a copy of a fax regarding
the handover of Dr Kabir to the Iranians which was
sent to the Army Headquarters from Shah House
using Miss Khan's swipe card and password?

Counsel: Circumstantial evidence. Anyone could have used
it to implicate Miss Khan, even Madam Shah herself.

Prosecutor: They could have, but how do you explain
that the very same day she visited an Army major.
Coincidence, Miss Khan? Or is there a backstory to
this as well?

⚖

I was riding high. But just like the high tide pulls you in deep
without you noticing, I, too, found the sand slipping beneath my
feet one day. It all began with a simple phone call. From Iran. I
should have known, there is nothing simple about Iran.

'Hello, Rani Shah's PA speaking.'

'My dear lady,' the voice on the other end was heavily
accented, 'I am a representative of the president, his Highness, the
Honourable Ahmed Mojahideen, Security Head of the Republic of
Iran. I am calling today because we wish to maintain confidential
talks with Prime Minister Rani Shah. I repeat, confidential.'

Now I had no way of knowing if this man really was calling from Iran. After all, why wouldn't their Ambassador here contact us directly if it was so? Unless of course, the matter was so confidential that even he didn't know about it. In which case, it was dubious, unofficial and risky – something I wouldn't recommend for you to get mixed up in.

I decided to play it safe.

'Madam is busy for the next three months.' I put the phone down, satisfied that I had played my part right.

Sure enough the phone rang again, immediately. The angry trilling echoed through the empty room. I settled into a chair and crossed my legs. The phone rang again as I was examining the back of my hands. My cuticles needed attention, I thought as the phone continued to ring. The shrill trilling seemed to get angrier as the noise reverberated through the hall. Tring, tring, trinnnnng! And then, before I could decide whether to clip my nails or file them, the door opened and in you walked.

'Are you deaf?' You picked up the phone and glared at me.

'Hello,' you shouted into the mouthpiece. 'What? Yes of course!' your tone changed and you smiled. 'Your Highness. Yes, yes. I'm honoured, Sir. Of course, Sir.'

You motioned for me to get the diary.

'Very well, Sir. I shall pass you on to my assistant now. Of course, I have instructed her to find the first available time. And, Sir, may I just add, I am glad you came directly to me instead of going to the Army or Secret Service. It is necessary not to discriminate against the PM of the country on the basis of her gender. Oh yes, I know how highly you regard women in Iran.'

⚖

They say curiosity killed the cat.

I say the nukes did. Yes, what I'm about to say now will hurt you, but then the truth often does. You are the one, Rani, who told me about Pearl Harbour, about Hiroshima and Nagasaki. You are the one who told me that revenge can destroy a human being.

Killing one bad person gives rise to ten more…

Do you remember your own words? No, because you are the one who showed me that words are just clunky hollow meaningless sounds, tossed about like crumbs to hungry mouths when an audience is needed and snatched back when no one is looking. Where were all the women's schools you were going to build? Where were the repeals to the Rape Law? You were so busy hanging on to your seat that it had come down to a sickening power game between you and the Army. You had lost sight of your goals. You could no longer see the bigger picture. You had lost track, Rani.

But you forgot, I was keeping score.

You played your cards just right. You brought in the scientist responsible for creating the country's nuclear programme. You questioned him, accused him of selling national secrets, till he went red in the face denying it.

It was then you said, 'I believe you.'

The poor man looked so relieved, he seemed to deflate like a punctured balloon. But then you got up and started to pace the room. You reminded me of a hungry tigress stalking her prey. 'I believe you, Mr Kabir, but no one else will,' you finally said.

The man fell to his knees.

'Please, Madam, you have to help me. The Army and the Secret Service, they will arrest me and my whole family. The Jihadists are already on my back. But I promise you, whatever information has been leaked to them, it's not through me.'

'Only the courts can decide that, I'm afraid. I have no option but to hand you over to the Police.'

'Please, Madam, your father brought me in. He was my mentor. I swear upon your father's grave that I'm innocent.'

'Yes, I know, and that's why I wanted to speak to you myself before the matter went public.'

'Please, don't let this happen. It will become a scandal. I'll be ruined. My name, my reputation, all my hard work...'

'It is your life I'm worried about, Dr Kabir,' you said, placing a hand on his shoulder.

The scientist looked up, as if suddenly realizing that the water was way over his head. The matter was no longer limited to a few journalists asking him uncomfortable questions or people calling him a traitor. It was a case of losing his life to the hangman's noose. Sweat broke out on his forehead and his hands started to tremble.

You placed your hand on the sobbing man's shoulder. 'There is one way.'

'Please, I'll do anything.'

'If you confess...'

'But I haven't done anything!'

'I know, and that's why I will issue you a pardon and send you into exile. No. No, listen to me first. Not just any exile. I can send you to Iran where you can live in comfort. Your whole family will be provided for. And most importantly, you will not have to be ashamed. You will be welcomed there. In fact, you will be honoured. A position in the government will be granted to you.'

The man seemed relieved, but then suddenly he asked, 'But why Iran?'

'Do you know any other country that does not bow down to the West?'

His shoulders drooped.

'Look,' you said, your voice gentle. 'It's not just a matter of you being tried in a court of law, my friend. The matter has reached the CIA. And you know that the Army are American puppets. They will put political pressure on me. They will try to evoke the extradition treaty. And once you are handed to the Americans, it's out of my hands. But if you are already out of the country, in a safe haven like Iran, no one can reach you.'

'I'll do as you say,' his body went limp and he seemed resigned to his fate.

'Of course there is something I must ask you in return for the risk I am taking on your behalf.'

You leaned closer and whispered something in his ear.

'Secret programme', 'expertise', 'nuclear weapons' – a few snatches of your conversation drifted my way. I watched from the shadows as the man covered his face with his hands. His whole body shook and a primal sound escaped his throat. He cried the way a grown man never should. I shuddered. There was something familiar about it.

And then I remembered a similar scene from twenty years ago. My father lay facedown on the ground and the General stood over him. 'Bow,' he said, as he pointed a sword to his head. I remembered watching my father being decapitated for resisting. I remembered his flesh splattering out on the floor, the blood reaching my toes. I remembered my feet turning red.

This time there was no blood, but your hands were still red. Rani, you had to be stopped.

⚖

That night, there was celebration at your house. You gave me the keys to the champagne cupboard. 'Use the new flutes, the crystal ones. And, Nazo, this time please try not to drop them.'

'Any special occasion?' I retorted, hoping you'd notice the sarcasm in my voice. Was I the only one who thought giving the bomb to Iran was madness?

You smiled and uncrossed your legs. 'Let's just say that the Army is not the top dog around here any more. The carpet has been pulled from under their feet and they don't even know.'

'Not yet, at least.'

Your forehead wrinkled with worry but only for a second. Soon you put on a smile and said, 'Well, by the time they do, Dr Kabir's confession will be on national television.' Then you got up and walked up to your father's photo. 'The taste of revenge is sweet.'

I looked up and for the first time, I saw you for what you really were. Just an ordinary woman. A broken one at that, hanging on by a thread.

You didn't need to do this, Rani. You didn't need to fall this low. What difference was there between you and the evil General if this is what power did to you?

Still talking to the dead man's photo, you said, 'I can't wait to see the look on the Army's face when they find their precious bomb has been swiped from under their noses!'

I felt my face grow hot and hands go cold.

'But at what cost, Madam. Did you ever stop to think of that?'

You turned to look at me, the smile frozen eerily on your face. And then you said, 'Some things cost more than others, Nazo. But they only sell if they are up for sale.'

I took a step back.

It's one thing to know the cost of something Rani, another to understand it's value.

That night, I sat on my mattress and pulled out all the money I had. I laid each note flat on the floor and before I knew it, I had a carpet of notes.

I had all this money, I thought. All this money! And what use was it to me? Could I save that scientist's life? Could I clear his name? No. I was just a cog in the machinery, a pawn in a game of chess. I had thought that if I had some money, some contacts, perhaps some power to my name, I could get your attention. I could get you to see my point of view. I used to think that you'd take me seriously. Listen to me. Understand me.

But I was wrong. You were determined more than ever to ignore me. My advice was overlooked, my presence deemed unnecessary. You made me feel like a nobody. Every time I brought up the Women's Rights Bill, you told me, 'Later'. Whenever I mentioned the stalled schools, you said there was no hurry. The rape injunction was low priority and widows' pensions, unmentionable. Lesser things demanded your attention.

But it was my own fault. I was gambling too low. If I really wanted to change the state of affairs I had to raise the stakes. It was time to take on something bigger.

It was time, my dear, to take you on.

Prosecutor: You can't deny, Miss Khan, that cracks had begun to appear in your relationship with Madam Shah.

Defendant: She was my mentor.

Prosecutor: Really? I think that at this point you seemed to have found a new benefactor.

Counsel: Objection.

Judge: Overruled.

Prosecutor: Your Honour, all evidence points to the fact that Miss Khan was working as a double agent. The only nation to benefit from the whole nuclear fiasco and the fall out with Iran was the United States. And Miss Khan is the only member of Madam's staff who was seen meeting with an ex-Army major who is known to have ties with Uncle Sam.

If anyone had asked me a few years ago if I would ever work for the Army, I would have called them crazy. But today that was exactly what I was about to do.

I took a deep breath and rang Major Q's bell.

'Soldier Rahim is not at home,' the guard said, as soon as he saw me.

'Actually, I'm here to see Major Sahib.'

He looked suspiciously at me then, shoving his fingers up his nostrils, told me to wait outside. Few hours and many boogers later, the guard finally agreed to let me in.

Instead of going up to the house, I went around the back and stood outside the French windows to Major's study.

'Nazo? Rani's PA? What is she doing here?' I heard the Major ask his assistant.

I stepped inside without knocking.

'Just five minutes, Major Sahib. Five minutes alone and I promise you'll thank me for the information I have for you.'

'Information?' the Major said, looking as shocked to see me as I was to see him. His peppery hair had turned silver. His moustache was droopy and his left hand shook. Clearly the Army was not doing well under democracy.

'I'm here to give you some important information,' I began, but as expected, he didn't believe me. Fortunately, I was not one to back down easy.

'Major Sahib, do you really think I would risk my life to come here if it wasn't important?'

'All right,' he said, dismissing his assistant.

'Well?' Major Q asked, puffing away at his cigar.

Now that I had his complete attention, I decided to play chase.

'Not like this.'

'Then how?

'It comes at a price. After all, what I'm about to tell you may cost me my life. Shouldn't there be some security…?'

Joining his fingertips together, he placed them under his chin and said, 'As they say, my dear, the best things in life are free.'

'Well, Major Sahib, then this is not the best thing. You only tell me, what is good about the country's nuclear technology being leaked?'

'What rubbish,' Major said.

I had expected a more dramatic reaction, but the old man just twirled his moustache and puffed some more.

'Don't waste my time, dear,' he said.

'I'm serious.'

'Seriously deluded,' he laughed.

'But it's true, Major Sahib. I have classified information that the secret has been leaked.'

'Impossible. The Army has the knowledge sealed. It is not only difficult, it is impossible for anyone to infiltrate.'

'Except, of course, the man himself...'

Now I got the reaction I had hoped for. The Major stood up abruptly, knocking back his chair, the cigar hanging limp from the corner of his mouth.

'I don't believe it. There is only one person who has this information and he ... he would never...' the look of disbelief on his face turned to terror.

This was my moment. I closed in for the kill.

'History is my witness, Major Sahib. You must remember that Shahjahan had the hands of the craftsmen who created the Taj Mahal chopped off so they could not create a replica. Those men, too, must have assured the Emperor that the knowledge was safe in their hearts, but then again the heart is a strange thing, Major Sahib. It raises us to great heights, then plummets us down faster than we can say, "Stop".'

The Major reached out and held me by the arm. 'Stop your riddles, Nazo. What has Rani got on us?'

Gently, I pried loose his grip and then, folding his hands into my own, I placed them on my heart.

'Swear upon your life, Major Sahib, she's got the creator

himself on his knees. The creator of the nuclear programme, that is,' I added, as he looked up. 'Dr Kabir has the knowledge in his brain. Till that is functioning, he can create as many nukes as he wants.'

The old Major shivered. 'What are you saying, girl?'

'What you are hearing, Sir. She's handing him over to the Iranians. To help them develop the dirty bomb. Top secret. Only three people know about this. Her, me and now you, Sir. Not even Dr Kabir knows who his end user will be.'

The Major started pacing the room. 'And if you are wrong about this?' he asked.

'The question is not if, but, *how*? How will you stop this disaster from happening?'

The Major stopped pacing. Rubbing his chin, he murmured, 'If only the Iranians had contacted us first.'

'You must have heard the saying, Major Sahib: if the mountain won't come to Mohammed, then Mohammed will go to the mountain. It's still not too late to get in touch with the Iranians. I understand that the Ambassador doesn't even know about it. Yet.'

The old Major pumped his fist in the air like an excited child. 'That's it! An internal whistle-blowing. Brilliant!'

And just like a child, a second later his mood darkened and he asked, 'What's in it for you, Nazo?'

'Sahib, even an illiterate like me knows that if the technology gets in the wrong hands, it could mean the end of the world.'

The Major seemed to find it amusing and nodded patiently. 'Yes, of course. End of the world and all.'

And then as if I'd made a great joke, he started laughing.

For a second, I wondered if I had made a mistake, but his mad laughter stopped soon enough and he composed himself.

'Nazo dear, I mean, what cut are you looking at for keeping us in on this?'

'A power cut,' I replied.

'Excuse me?' the old Major looked taken aback by my answer.

'You'll know when the time comes,' I said. 'For now I'm doing my duty.'

I turned to leave, then paused near the door. 'But there are a couple of girls' schools whose constructions have been halted. Some ex-Jihadists in the Army are opposing it, I hear. Perhaps you can get the work restarted?'

'Of course, my dear. The schools should be fully operational in six months' time.'

'Thank you, Major Sahib,' I said. 'I'll take your leave now.'

'Nazo,' the Major called after me, 'you are smart for a woman, you know. You should be working for us.'

I stopped in the doorway and said, 'You mean, *with* us.'

⚖

They say if you want to learn the arts, study the Masters. But in this land, if you want to learn the subtle art of bribery, look to the Army. I was living proof, for the cut I got for blowing your Iran nuke deal was enough to provide a future for hundreds of little girls.

And this was just the beginning.

Dr Kabir's release had been no small feat. With the whistle-blowing, the US stepped in. Amnesty got involved. The UN sat up. The man got away safely, but nobody saw it as a triumph of good over evil. People saw it as a power play. And once people in the market heard that the Army had dealt through me, there was no doubt left that I was the woman to go to. The bribes I was offered were enough to fill the stuffing in my mattress. But now it was no longer about money. It was about power, the power to do the work that really needed to be done, but which you, in your PM's chair, were powerless to do. I became the moat around your castle. The drawbridge they had to use to get through to you. But I had always said, I didn't want to be your gatekeeper.

I wanted, instead, to be a kingmaker.

In the coming days, I expected you to be furious, but once again you retreated into a domestic stupor, waddling around with your stupid belly bloated like a village belle. Gone was that hot edge of revenge, which after the blow from the Army, I expected you'd turn towards me. Instead, someone else came after me.

Someone I had greatly underestimated.

Prosecutor: She used her influence dangerously. She let people who bribed her have an audience with the PM, and those who couldn't afford to were left out in the cold. Miss Khan behaved like a bouncer!

Counsel: Mr Omar, perhaps you are not aware, but it is the job of a secretary to sift the important from the unimportant. Madam Rani Shah could not possibly meet everyone who knocked on her door. Miss Khan merely helped her prioritize.

Prosecutor: But she treated Madam Shah's diary like a power trip. She wanted control. And we all know what a dangerous desire that is.

It was then the threats started.

Word spread fast in the market and before I knew it, I had him on my back. I was counting my commissions to send to a women's shelter one day, when Balgodi showed up. He slammed his fist on my desk. 'What do you think you are playing at?'

I would have thought I'd be scared at being found out, but it felt surreal, as if I was staring down at myself from the ceiling, or acting in a play. A small nervous laugh escaped my throat. Balgodi took it as defiance.

It didn't help.

Balgodi brought his face close to mine and said, 'You are playing with fire, Nazo. This isn't child's play.'

'I'm not scared,' I whispered, 'of a few singes.'

He caught me by surprise as he threw back his head and laughed. Then just as suddenly, he grabbed my arm and pinned me against the wall.

'Do you know why they call me the Commissioner? Not because I commission, but because *I* take it! I take the cut. You get that? *I* take it. It's mine. All of Rani's bribes come my way. My way!'

He squeezed my throat till my eyes began to cloud, then released me as quickly as he had attacked me.

'Looks like no one taught you to share,' I whispered, coughing and wheezing for breath.

Big mistake. Balgodi turned back and grabbed my jaw.

'If you know what's best for you, Nazo...'

'Don't worry,' I whispered through the pain, 'I won't take away *all* your toys.'

Balgodi's face took on a menacing, look and this time even I thought I had gone too far.

'You bitch,' he seethed. 'You really don't know when to stop, do you?'

I nodded and braced myself for the assault.

But he let go of me. I opened my eyes just as he slammed me back into the wall and pinched my nipples hard. I tried to scream, but he slammed my jaw shut.

'What was that about taking away my toys?'

Tears came in my eye, but damn if I was going to give in.

'You forget, Nazo. *You* are the toy.'

A hound that tastes blood never drinks anything else again...

It wasn't blood I craved but something stronger. The episode with Balgodi had shaken me. But I was like your James Bond martinis. Being shaken made me even better.

Balgodi didn't know it, but the fact that he felt threatened by me felt like a compliment. I began to feel slightly God-like. I could make things happen. It was so easy. Life was so easy. Giving life was hard, but taking it … easy.

Balgodi was keeping a close eye on me, but you on the other hand seemed aloof and distanced. If you suspected that I had a hand in alerting the Army about Dr Kabir's handover, you never said anything. I wondered if at some level you knew what you were about to do was wrong. It was like a repeat of the wedding night, but there was little time to think as at the height of the political crisis, you developed pre-eclampsia. You had no choice but to let me take on more of your work. During the few weeks when you were advised complete bed rest, you gave me free rein of your appointment diary. It was as if you didn't care what happened to the country or the government. Now was my chance to make a change. Lobby for new laws, exercise justice and also rake in the bribes. Balance the good with the bad.

But I had to be careful. Balgodi was on my tail.

Prosecutor: She forgot Rani Madam had other well-wishers. Mrs Yasmin Haroon is one such person. If she were here, she would testify to Miss Khan's deceitful nature.

Counsel: Then why isn't she here?

Prosecutor: Frustratingly, her passport was stolen at the last minute. She is unable to travel.

Counsel: Ha, I bet Mr Omar would blame that on my client too.

Prosecutor: I wouldn't put it past her because you see, Mrs Haroon would have revealed Miss Khan's true face in no time.

⚖

I was going full speed ahead. The schools project was on a roll. New schools were being initiated every month. At this rate, there would be a literary centre in every village across the country in just under a year. There was the matter of finding teachers, allocating lands, changing attitudes to girl's education and of course a steady flow of funds, but I had it all in hand. Not long before this nobody became somebody, I found myself thinking.

But then something happened to put a halt to all my plans. A ghost from the past, a reminder of the person you once were, made a comeback.

⚖

'Mrs Yasmin Haroon from New York is here,' Refugee announced
one day as you were dictating a letter to me from bed.

You looked at me, but I was just as surprised as you were.

'I didn't call her,' I added quickly.

You laughed. 'I couldn't be happier if you did.'

'Rani!' Yasmin cried, as she burst into the room. 'What's this?'
The smile was replaced with a worried frown. 'Why are you in
bed? Are you ill?'

'Yasmin,' you said, sitting up with some difficulty. 'I'm so
happy to see you, my friend.' You reached out and hugged your
friend. 'Just tired, nothing to worry. I'm expecting again.'

'Congrats!' Yasmin pulled you into a tight embrace.

I watched from the corner, twisting the ends of my hijab wistfully.

'Well, you've done it, Rani! You really have, Madame Prime
Minister,' Yasmin said, with an exaggerated bow.

'Hard work pays off,' you laughed back.

Your laugh, I noticed, was hollow and fake, as powerless and
shallow as you.

'Look at you!' Yasmin held you by the shoulders. 'You are a
leader, a mother, wife, women's right champion, a tour de force!'

You did not even blink at the obscene amount of undeserved
praise being heaped on you.

'It's been a hard journey,' you said quietly. 'But I told you,
nothing can stop me. You should have stayed with us, Yasmin. I
wouldn't have to depend on strangers then.'

You glanced sideways at me.

Point taken, I blinked back.

'Ah, the kindness of strangers...' Yasmin laughed.

'Can be dangerous,' you mumbled.

'What?' Yasmin asked.

'Nothing. Tell me, have you come alone?' you asked.

'Yes, my husband had some business in Dubai, so I thought I'd take a flight back home and see my old buddy. The children are with my in-laws.'

'I'm so glad,' you said warmly.

'So am I. It's hard to believe so much time has passed.'

'Yes,' you said, and in the same breath added, 'Nazo, tell Refugee to arrange for tea.'

'So where is this son of yours, the future PM?' Yasmin asked as I was leaving.

'Bring in the child,' you called after me.

A few minutes later, I entered with the wrong child in tow.

'Say salaam,' I said.

The child looked terrified and started crying. Yasmin seemed to sense that there was something wrong.

'Come here, darling,' she said.

He hid behind me.

'He's a little shy,' you said, and Yasmin stared at you with wide unblinking, lizard eyes.

I looked at you, too, but your face registered nothing. No emotion at all.

In this wordless exchange, I suddenly realized that you were the only person who did not notice his deformity. I wondered if it was because you didn't want to or you didn't have to.

I remember wondering at that moment whether you loved the child at all. Maybe he was just a means to an end.

'Have you shown him to a doctor?' Yasmin asked.

'Why?' you sounded genuinely alarmed. 'There is nothing wrong with him. He's just a shy little boy. Keeps to himself. Peaceful and quiet, just like good children should be.'

Your look was soft as you stared at him and I felt guilty for doubting you. Perhaps through some deep maternal instinct, you wanted to protect him from a terrible diagnosis. Shelter him.

'Anyway, I can't stand loud, howling children. So distracting.'

Suddenly your look became hard and this time, I found myself doubting my own judgement. The earlier softness in your eyes was not for the wrong child. It was for the child you never had. You hated the fact that your child died while mine lived.

'Take him away now,' you ordered as if he was some toy that had to be cleared away after playtime was over. You looked impatient, angry, and then it struck me. How could I have been so blind? How did all those Calpol bottles appear in the cabinet in the first place? And every time one finished, it was replaced by a new one! Someone was planting them there. Someone wanted to make me pay for my sins...

My knees felt week. I needed to sit down.

'Nazo, can you not hear me?' you said. 'Please take the child away. It's time for his milk, I should think.'

I took his hand and pulled. 'Let's go.'

'Wait,' Yasmin said. 'Come here.'

The child shrank back.

'Come here, little one,' she tried again. The child hid deeper into my legs, covering his face with his palms.

She walked up to him and gently pried away his hands. She placed a kiss on his forehead and handed him a present.

The child promptly tore open the wrapping, and out popped a Jack in the Box, his clownish smile eerily ominous. We all screamed in surprise. And as I cleared away the paper, the child stepped forward.

'Mama,' he said, and we both looked up at him.

Prosecutor: I would like to present the court with some further evidence. Please see the child's diagnostic report at age two. The child had an unusual amount of Paracetamol in his body. Evidence suggests he was deliberately made dependent on painkillers.

Counsel: That doesn't prove Miss Khan was a bad secretary or assistant. If at all, it proves Madam Shah was a bad mother.

⚖

Now I was convinced. It was not just our appearance that was similar, truly our destinies were intertwined. If you were inactive, I too must be made politically impotent.

Or so it seemed...

Perhaps it was Yasmin's concerns or your own insecurities, but you suddenly decided that I was needed more at home than in the office. You were in hospital birthing your first child, or should I say second, when you called and gave me strict instructions to leave everything and look after the wrong child. While the child was visiting you at the hospital, on Yasmin's insistence, one of the doctors decided to check him and diagnosed him as slow. Whether it was the diagnosis or the guilt, you took it to heart.

'Leave everything, Nazo,' you instructed in a panicky phone call. 'Just look after the child.'

A part of me wondered if this was because you cared or

because you didn't want anyone to know that you didn't. The fear of being found out is all encompassing.

Trust me, I know.

⚖

That night I went into the wrong child's room and stood over his bed. He looked so small and helpless, his neck cradled against his shoulder, a thin trickle of drool on his chin. I caressed his sleeping forehead and something moved inside me. I felt like a candle, its wax melting quickly and precariously. I pulled my hand away.

No, I could not do this. I told myself, I was not meant for this. I was meant to be some other person. I was needed elsewhere. I had the schools to think about, Jihadist laws to get repealed, rape cases to fight against. I did not have time for all this maternal bullshit. No, not for me, these matters of the heart.

I ran out of the room.

Outside, the light was on in your study. I went inside.

It was empty, the phones silent, the in-tray sparse. Your diary was blank, barren and forlorn. With you in the hospital, few people came to the office. The tenders were approved by Pervez Sahib and the other deals went through the President. The bribes had come to a slow grinding halt. As had the schools' project.

I could hear the relentless thumping of my heart as it slowed. I ran a finger over the desk, making tracks in the dust, and felt a strangeness inside. At the end of the day, I thought, this was all I had.

This was all you had.

And now even this was denied to me.

You had given the power of attorney to Balgodi and he now

had total control over your affairs. Did I say affairs? Well that was one thing he had plenty of.

As they say, while the cat is away the mice will play.

And it was on one such day, when he was rollicking with his harlots, that we got our horns tangled. And how...

The emptiness I felt at being cut off from politics was once again eating me up inside. I couldn't let myself get close to the wrong child, for I knew you could claim him again, anytime. He never was mine to keep, I told myself. Instead I focused on the schools' project. But without a steady flow of funds, it was proving difficult to keep the momentum going. I needed another way to feed the projects I had started. Now that the bribes had slowed and my Party powers frozen, there was little to do but wait. Nobody was interested in backing the schools. The activists were too scared, the local governments uninterested and Balgodi wholly against it. I had to find a new way to make things happen. And that was when I discovered the most powerful organ of the body. And it wasn't the brain.

Outside, it had been raining for six hours straight when the phones started trilling. An important bridge, newly built by one of your contractors, had collapsed. The press wanted answers. I paced the hallway. You were drugged and asleep in the last stages of your pregnancy at a nursing home. Pervez Sahib was locked away in the lavatory with some indigestion remedy and the other Party seniors were on a foreign delegation visit. There was no one I could consult. It wasn't the press handling that was weighing me down, but the fact that *I* had arranged your meeting with this contractor. I consoled myself with the fact that the bribe he had given had paid for the construction of a girls' school in the most backward areas of the country. If only I could explain it to you before the press splashed it on the front page. Still, I doubt you'd understand.

I tried you once again on the phone. No answer. Just then I heard laughter coming from Balgodi's room. The idiot was enjoying himself when seventeen people were dead. That murderer!

I charged into his study. The room was full of smoke. There were bottles of whiskey all around and a near naked girl was dancing seductively in front of him.

I threw her a towel and motioned for her to leave. She looked at Balgodi, but I cut in, 'Leave or I'll call the police. You can phone him from jail to get you out. Now go!'

'What the hell, Nazo?' he slurred.

'The President has called an urgent meeting.'

He looked up at me bleary eyed. 'Now?'

'No, next year.'

'Make coffee. And keep the sarcasm for your groom.'

'What?' I said acidly. 'So you are not going to marry me any more?'

Balgodi dismissed the dancing girl and turned his attention to me.

'So, you were saying something about marriage?' he grabbed my wrist and pulled me onto his lap. 'Haven't we already celebrated our wedding night, though?'

I felt my face grow hot. How could he remember? He couldn't possibly! He was so drunk ... perhaps you had told him? No, you wouldn't. You couldn't.

'Come. Bring that tight little body of yours closer to mine.'

'Why should I give it to you?' I played coy, though inside, my throat was tightening with fear.

'Either you do what I say, or I tell the President that the bridge contractor was one of your bribes. Your choice.'

So he wasn't that drunk after all.

'Tell me one thing,' I said, pushing him off, 'why do you play so dumb when you know everything that goes on?'

'Didn't I tell you, Nazo darling? You're playing with fire.' He grabbed my wrist and began to twist it. 'You are the toy. And I am the fire.'

How did he know all this? I thought as I struggled to break free of his grip, pain searing through me. Inside, I was trembling, but hell be me if I'd let him know.

Balgodi pushed my head into his crotch. I screamed.

'Rape Laws are changing,' I said, pushing against his hand. 'You'll go to jail.'

He laughed as if I'd cracked a joke. 'I don't see four witnesses. Do you?' he said, pulling my hair so hard I thought my scalp would rip.

I closed my eyes and got down on my knees. I unzipped his trousers, and only after the act was over did I look up. Never before had my mouth tasted so foul.

God had given me the ability to forget, if not forgive, easily. I waited a few minutes till his head lolled back, then I got up and went into the attached bathroom. I contemplated washing my mouth out with bleach, but then settled for a lesser chemical. I must have gargled a hundred times, for when I finally looked up from the sink my mouth was an angry patch of red.

I stepped out of the toilet and peered at him. He seemed to be settling into a deep sleep.

'Nazo,' he said sleepily, 'is it better with a woman?'

He winked and closed his eyes.

So he knew about you and me...

⚖

I stood where I was, my hand frozen on the doorknob. He knew. He knew how I felt about you and still he forced me. Was this my punishment, I thought, disgust filling my mouth like vomit. Like it must have been of the women before me. Words and images came back to me of Mahi, the sixteen-year-old girl who had been raped by her male cousin to 'fix' her. The NGOs had been knocking on your door, protesting against this 'corrective rape'. 'It is becoming common practice,' they had said. 'It has to be stopped.' I had met with the activists to discuss this while you waddled around in your pregnant best, promising justice when, and if, you got time away from your knitting.

I followed up on your hollow promises. I set up appointments with the legislative committee, negotiated with the press. I did the legwork while you collected the accolades but not the criticism. At the first sight of resistance, you backed out. You were afraid the maulanas would crush you if you took a stance.

'They will say, I'm trying to promote homosexuality, Nazo. Please understand, they will accuse me of being anti-Islamic. I can't take this on, simply can't.'

I knew now the real reason why you had backed down.

I turned to leave but caught side of Balgodi's sleeping face. His nasal hair curled as he snored. His cheeks puffy like a toad, his lips in a snarl. He looked spiteful.

I knew then, this had to end.

I pulled open drawers and cupboards, looked through shelves, behind pictures, under the bed, till finally the first rays of the sun began to seep through the chinks in the curtains. Somewhere outside, a car horn blared and a crow cawed. Any minute now Balgodi would wake up. I could feel the icy cold fear creeping up the back of my neck. My hands began to shake. Stop, I told myself. If I'm going to find it, then I'll have to think like the bastard. I was tempted to kick him in the ribs, but I used all my self-control to keep my muscles still. And that was when it hit me. Where would I keep something I didn't want you to find? Somewhere you'd never want to look.

Quickly I stepped over Balgodi's limp body and rushed to your bedroom. There in your cupboard, under a pile of unworn formal clothes, lay your gold-edged wedding album. I found the envelope between its pages.

A photo of me. I was not alone. You were with me. Your arms were pinned down. I looked as if I was about to devour you. My head reeled. Someone had been watching us. And not just anyone. Your own husband.

So I was right. It wasn't love that held you back but blackmail. *Perhaps, love is a form of blackmail.*

I leaned back against the wall and closed my eyes. Was there no one true to you? Such extortion. And that too by your own spouse. How low could a man fall? An envelope full of photographs, of me and you in an intimate embrace, our bodies pressed tight against each other, coiled like a comma, me and you parting reluctantly … I tucked one into my bra and pressed it close to my breast. I tore the rest with a steely heart and swallowed each piece. I knew by now that there was no better shredder than the kind God had fitted inside our mouths. I was just wondering how you could stand a man so sly when I suddenly realized, it was because you had to. There was no way he'd let you go. You were his golden hen. Only in death would you be rid of him. But knowing him, he wouldn't even let you die in peace. No, he wouldn't slay his golden hen ... But as long as I was alive, Rani, I would protect you from him. Even if it meant stripping you of your power. You and I were a team. And in a team, it didn't matter who held the reins.

Before I could ponder further, hidden behind Balgodi's cigars, I saw a roll of negatives sticking out. I struck a match and thought, silly man should've known better than to keep the two together.

Prosecutor: She began to think she was invincible. And as they say, pride comes before a fall.

Counsel: Don't you feel the same could be said about Madam Shah herself?

If there was one thing I learned while you were in the hospital it was this: everything is about sex, except sex. Sex is about power. And it was this power I wanted to take back from your dickless husband. I wanted to break him, humiliate him, bring him to his knees. I began to study him closely. His weakness, I knew, were horses, women and money. I considered putting all three in a room and making a video, which I would then leak. I would make the happiest day of his life the saddest.

But before I could put my plan in action, you came back from the hospital. The sight of you changed everything. I knew now that hurting Balgodi meant hurting you.

Loyalty was your greatest strength, and your greatest weakness.

It had been a tough labour, the doctors chorusing their surprise on the unusually tough second birth after a simple home delivery the first time around. I wondered if you kept your front or squealed out and confessed at the first jab of pain. From what I heard, you held it together for a long while, but the stubborn baby refused to come out.

Perhaps she knew what was in store for her.

In the end, you opted for a caesarean, the pain being too much for you. You were discharged a week later. Once back, you tried to catch up on work, feeling exhausted amidst the new baby's wails. You put up a stoic demeanour, but the baby cried day and night. She clung to you, her small fists clutching your shirt with all her tiny might. Like a leech, I thought.

I watched you carefully. I wanted to see if there was any gratefulness or recognition. Hadn't I been right about motherhood? Hadn't I warned you? It sucks you in, Rani. At least at this stage in your career, you could afford to take a break, but would you be where you are now if you had children before contesting? Oh Rani, aren't you glad I did what I did the first time around?

But no, there was no remorse in your eyes. You seemed all right, even happy at times to be spending time with a howling baby instead of solving the nation's problems. At times, Rani, your fallibility shocked me.

Each time I looked at you, your housewifely behaviour, your motherly instincts and stereotypical femininity, not only disappointed me but terrified me. I needed to look away. Forget that I had once thought you were our messiah. You were just another foolish woman. Everything about you was average. Average mother, average wife, average politician. You didn't want to do great things. A little bit of this and a little bit of that. Do you think Jinnah cared about his family when he was creating Pakistan? Do you think Gandhi fussed over his children's homework when he was resisting the British? Or how about Abraham Lincoln or even your favourite, John F Kennedy? Forget the men, Rani, do you think Mrs Thatcher got the title of Iron Lady by waddling around pregnant in public?

Respect has to be earned, Rani. Leaders are made not born. You either cared enough to be someone or you *didn't*.

⚖

Fuelled by my anger, I began to take on even more under-the-table work. Yes, I did abuse my position. But I only took on work, Rani, which you should have.

You began where I ended.

I worked night into day to push my schools' project. People thought it was your drive, but I didn't care. I just wanted it to happen. I now knew my real power. It was all up here, in my brain. I feared no one and in turn everyone feared me. During the day I went about my work, but at night I tossed and turned, telling myself it didn't matter who got the glory as long as the job got done. But a tiny thought still lurked inside. A voice mocked: a gatekeeper's daughter will remain a gatekeeper. Political dynasties in this country were like royal ones abroad, I found myself thinking. A woman could rule only if she was blue blooded and perhaps that was one of the reasons the people of this land had accepted you. Daughter of the Shah, they called you. But me, I was a daughter of the soil, and like dust, I was worth nothing.

Still I kept on trying. You always said, I was a stubborn one.

And soon enough, the day came when people began to bypass you. They seemed to realize who the real force was. NGOs approached me, aid workers came to me, the poor and destitute knocked on the kitchen door sure that their cause would be heard and their bellies filled.

'We had such high hopes for Rani Shah, but she has done next to nothing for our cause,' they would lament.

I would nod and think to myself, that's why I should be in her place. And one day, I said it aloud, surprising even myself. 'The elections will be held soon. I am thinking of contesting.'

The replies were even more surprising as people began to agree with me. 'Well, you will certainly have our vote,' they nodded. 'You understand us. You are one of us.'

It was not just the needy who came to see me. The ones with too much money also came to me. Money is a habit, and as you know, once you get used to making it, it's hard to stop. You have to make more, at any cost.

'Please help us, Miss Nazo,' the rich would say. 'Balgodi Sahib takes our money and there isn't any guarantee that he'll get the work done. Whereas with you, there is satisfaction every which way.'

At first I would bristle at their snide remarks, but soon I got used to them. They just couldn't separate the woman from her sex, these rich fat men, but then, that wasn't my problem.

My cupboards had overflowed and I had to open yet another savings account. If only Soldier Rahim could see me now! I had smiled at the thought as I walked out of the bank.

I see you are smiling too. But your smile is a sad one. You think I sold out.

But, Rani, it wasn't about greed. I wasn't materialistic. I was practical. Money was the only thing that could make me powerful. A powerless woman is a useless woman.

You should know.

Prosecutor: Miss Khan was a foot soldier who thought
herself king. At first it began by taking credit
here and there for small efforts, which were
obviously carried out on Madam's orders, like the
schools' project. But slowly she began to believe
her own lies. She was like the spider who gets
tangled in its own silken threads. She could not
tell the difference between reality and her own
fabrication. Many people have said that she began
to refer to herself in the third person like Madam.
She dressed like her and tried to speak like her.

Counsel: But, Mr Omar, surely Madam would have noticed
such behaviour.

Prosecutor: Madam Shah dismissed the imitation as flattery.
Big mistake.

Counsel: My client was inspired by Madam. No harm in
that.

Prosecutor: No harm? Miss Khan began to campaign for a
ticket to the intra-Party elections!

Counsel: Nothing wrong with having a bit of ambition.

Prosecutor: It was about power, Counsel. Read the kitchen
boy's testimony where he saw Miss Khan threaten
the cook with a knife when he stood in her way.
What does that tell you about her ambitions? She
was, is, ruthless.

⚖

'Delegate,' you would say, every time a decision came your way.

You can delegate responsibility but not authority, Rani. You simply didn't care any more.

It was the same that day, when the women's group came to see you. You had been up all night with the new baby, as had your husband, but for different reasons.

At my insistence, the watchman buzzed you, ignoring the strict do-not-disturb instructions.

'Rani Madam is fast asleep,' Balgodi shouted, after cursing the watchman for waking him. 'As it is we have bigger problems to solve than listen to these women wail. Get rid of them and don't dare disturb us now.'

'Madam is sleeping fast,' the watchman said, shooting me a murderous look.

'But we have come all this way to meet her.'

'And we have written her many letters! Called her so many times. Surely she can give us five minutes of her time.'

'Come back tomorrow,' he said, trying to hustle them out.

'It's true, a woman's worst enemy is another woman,' one of them shouted.

I shuddered. You were turning your own against you.

'We had come with such high hopes,' they protested.

'Go, go!' he shouted.

The disappointed women turned to leave. I knew tomorrow would be the same story so I ran after them.

'Wait,' I said. 'Please accept Rani Madam's apologies. This watchman is new to Shah House. The idiot doesn't know what he is saying. The fact that the guards outside let you in shows your name was on the list. Actually Madam is in a very important early morning meeting. She has ordered me to help you.'

The women looked doubtful so I added, 'To do with national security.'

They nodded thoughtfully.

'Your cause is important to her.'

They smiled.

I took them to the grease kitchen, a place I doubted you even knew existed in your house. By the time Refugee had served us all tea, I had heard their entire story. After my family's murder, I'd begun to feel that my heart had become stone hard and nothing more could penetrate it, but hearing their story, I felt a stirring.

What the women told me was nothing new, it had been in the papers as had several similar cases before it, but listening to it made it real, up-close and immediate. Mai Mumtaz, a young girl from the interior had been gang-raped as punishment for a crime her brother had committed. And worse, this was not some barbaric impulsive act but a premeditated cold-blooded one. The Jihadist Tribunal of Elders, still functional in the remote parts of the country like in Mai Mumtaz's village, had, after much debate, deemed it the best possible justice. And when Mai had, after this horrific act, refused to lay down and die, the provincial government had turned silent, pleading ignorance. And the central government too had played it safe, saying they could not interfere in the Jihadist Tribunal's matter, lest they rise up in revolt and lead another revolution. Police and Judiciary all turned a blind eye. Instead of supporting her cause, they put it down to tradition.

The seriousness of men, I thought. None of these people in authority seemed to realize just how much courage it took for the girl to report her rape. Jumping into a river would have been easier. Living this nightmare every day was harder. But for all practical matters, she might as well have been dead. The world thought her disgraced and even her own family didn't want her. Physically injured and mentally tortured, she had nowhere to go.

My glance fell on a quote from her father saying that if she had any honour she would kill herself.

'Instead of telling the world the story of her disgrace, she should drown herself in the river and spare us the shame. At least in death she would have some dignity.'

It didn't stop there. The activists showed me more press clippings. So much slander, so much abuse, as if she had invited the men to an orgy. Were women really so helpless in our country?

In the hospital pictures of the battered girl, she seemed only half human. I looked away. You slept comfortably in your four-poster while this girl struggled for her life in a narrow hospital bed. She was paying with her life for the laws you should have repealed long ago. A salty bile rose up my throat.

It was time for a change, Rani Shah. A much needed change. I picked up your appointment diary and crossed out your meeting with the arms investor. Next I took out the inauguration of a new clothing boutique. Carefully in small dark letters, I wrote on top of the list: Justice for Mai.

In the coming days, I had three more meetings with the women's group. I sat with the women for hours, working out the appeal procedures and reassuring them that you would get them justice. You were, after all, a woman and a new mother. Who else would feel another woman's pain better? Surely you wanted a better world for your daughter. Wasn't that why you came into politics?

But I was wrong.

'It's not easy to change these laws,' you argued the next morning when I brought up your morning tea. 'They are hundreds of years old, beyond jurisdiction.'

'But, Rani Madam, if you don't take this on, then who will? Do you expect a man to change them? No, this change...'

'Save the speech, Nazo,' you cut me off. 'These things happen on a daily basis. It's a man's world out there. How many people can I take on?'

'But if you don't get her justice...'

'Look, these are the Jihadists you are talking about. It's like stirring a hornet's nest. Do you really want to create an uprising?'

'If you don't take them on, who will? And you know they will start getting stronger again if you leave them be. You've got to take a stand, Rani Madam.'

Before you could reply, the baby started crying. You took a deep breath and said, 'This is a useless conversation, Nazo. Things are not as black and white as they seem to you. No, please. I'm really tired. I need to feed the baby and to be honest, my milk dries up with your speeches.'

I watched as you held the baby to your breast, a maternal glaze taking over your eyes. It was as if a door was closing, a shutter was falling. This was your time with your child.

I was dismissed.

Outside, I grappled with the reality that this was it. You were not about to take on the Jihadists. Far from it. It was up to me to get Mai Mumtaz justice, which meant things were about to get tense.

Finally.

⚖

'I warned you. You can't change these things,' Refugee said to me when I came back down.

'She wants more milk to drink. She's feeding,' I informed him.

'She's turned into a cow, that one. Swear upon God, what happens to these women when they become mothers? *Hai Allah,* just imagine, this is the same woman who was fighting for democracy in New York some years ago.'

'Yes,' I nodded, 'she's the same woman. Maybe it's us who saw her differently back then.'

Refugee paused to look at me. 'Now leave it be, Nazo,' he said. 'Don't look so sad. Here, have some *garma-garam* chai.'

'Thanks,' I sat down at the kitchen table, Mai's ordeal still haunting my mind.

Refugee scratched his belly, then letting out a huge belch said, 'Probably the Jihadists got the hots for the girl and planted a fake crime on the brother.' He laughed as he put more sugar in his tea. 'They've been doing this for generations where I come from. Every time they get horny, they organize a mass rape in the name of honour.'

The tea wasn't very hot, but I felt as if my mouth had been scalded. 'Fuck these Jihadists,' I said. 'This is the last time they will treat a woman like an animal.'

'Hah,' Refugee snorted. 'Even goats get more respect in the Jihadist regions. At least they give milk. Women, good for nothing but giving birth to more mouths.'

I stood up and banged my fist on the table. 'Fuck you, Refugee.'

'I … I was just thinking from the Jihadists' point of view,' he added hastily as I reached for a sharp knife. 'I would never think so lowly of a woman.'

'Such men should be castrated, don't you think?'

I pointed it at his privates.

'Nazo sister, you are scaring me!'

'If it wasn't for us women, you wouldn't be here, you bastard.'

I slammed the knife on the table, splitting an apple into two perfect halves. I looked up to see Refugee cowering on the ground, his head between his knees, his hands touching his earlobes.

I put down the knife and laughed.

In the end, Refugee was right. The NGOs got their aid and attention, thanks to my collection of bribes, but neither the courts, the press, nor you, were useful when it came to getting her justice. The General's Rape Law remained unchanged and the Jihadists thrived, snug in the knowledge that they hadn't been reprimanded by a woman's government for a vile act against her own kind. I couldn't just stand there and do nothing. Could you really blame me, Rani?

So that is how I came to plan, what I called, the revenge.

Prosecutor: They say Madam Rani Shah didn't forgive easily, but Miss Khan neither forgave nor forgot. As for holding a grudge, she wouldn't let go even if she was sinking with the weight of it.

Defendant: Forgiving people is not my job, Omar Sir.

Prosecutor: Then whose is it?

Defendant: God's.

Prosecutor: So is delivering justice, Miss Khan.

Defendant: In that case, why am I in a court?

⚖

It took more than half of the money in my mattress to dig up the dirt on the Chief Jihadist Elder. It turned out that he was not as pure as he claimed after all.

'Let him cast the first stone who himself is free of sin,' I said, as I went ahead and plotted the public stripping of the man who had sentenced Mai Mumtaz to this fate.

I wasn't surprised when I found out the Elder had a thing for boys. But I have to admit that even I was shocked when I found the victims were as young as five. Once my mole got hold of the abused boys, a sack of wheat each was enough to get them talking. Photos were splashed in the newspapers, confessions telecast, activists involved, until the Elder's credibility was mixed in mud – his name a big black blob. His entire family was shunned. He was removed from the Jihadist Tribunal of Elders. But it wasn't till he was disgraced from the village itself and had to leave his ancestral lands that I breathed a sigh of relief.

But not for long…

⚖

'I bet now he regrets his decision,' I said, showing you the newspapers next morning.

'See,' you replied as you changed the baby's nappy. 'These things have a way of sorting themselves out. There are NGOs and activists to do this kind of work. All we can do is support them through aid. Find out which agency this was and give them an anonymous donation, won't you.'

You were still in la la land, playing happy families. Nevertheless, I tried.

'Rani Madam, it wasn't an agency, it was…'

'Please, Nazo, not now. I need to feed her.'

I nodded. It was useless telling you anyway. You would never believe that I had brought a Jihadist Elder to his knees. I, Nazo Khan, a simple girl from the ashes. No Shah in my name. No power in my game. Yet, Rani, I had done what you with all your privilege couldn't do.

I had done justice.

Prosecutor: Knowledge is power. Power to do good or power to do evil. In the right hands, it can do wonders … but in the wrong ones, it destroys. Miss Khan had the power of knowledge. Unfortunately, she misused this power. She was flying too high.

Counsel: I will say that again, Mr Omar: being ambitious is not a crime.

Prosecutor: No, it isn't. But sometimes we touch such heights, we lose our grip on reality.

Counsel: Your Honour, I feel my colleague needs a break. He is being too philosophical.

Prosecutor: For what is to follow next, Your Honour, I think we all need a break.

If dealing with the Army had been a feather in my cap, bringing down the Jihadist Elder was a whole flock. Soon I was not only negotiating with the Army and the Secret Service but with other political parties as well. So it was no surprise when one day Refugee, who was now my part-time PA, came to tell me that a breakaway faction from the Jihadist party wanted to see me. At first I was a little hesitant about fraternizing with the enemy, but then I felt thrilled that they were reaching out to a woman. I was flattered. Times were changing, I thought. The Jihadists were asking a woman for help!

'About time,' I said, 'the bastards understood who's in charge.'

'Another opportunity to expand the business,' Refugee chimed in.

I was flattered not deluded. 'No,' I shook my head firmly. 'No dealings with the Jihadists. Not unless they pledge their support on the Rape Law repeal.'

'Have you heard of shooting the messenger? I'm not delivering that message! They'll be outraged at your front. Besides they'll never give in.'

'They'll come around,' I said with a slow smile.

But how, I would never have guessed.

The day the Jihadists came for me, I was at the NGO centre with Refugee and the wrong child. I recalled someone mentioning that the systems had been malfunctioning all day. Neither the buzzers nor the telephones were working. Even the mobile phones were without signal. That alone should have been a warning to me, but I was riding high on the fact that a new school had just been inaugurated in a remote area of the country. I ignored the fact that the guards were off duty or that none of the regular staff could be seen milling about. And so it was that when the shouts began, I stepped into the foyer without thinking.

'What's going on?' I asked, seeing the reception area completely deserted.

'We have heard a lot about you, Nazo-ji,' a man's voice sounded. I turned around to see a stranger standing behind me. I finally picked up the scent of danger. Two others appeared out of nowhere and I took a step back. I didn't like their unshaven faces or their sweat-drenched clothes. They wore large rolling turbans and their voices had the gravelly accent of people from the mountains. They seemed like the kind of men the security would never let in without asking. They seemed like hardcore Jihadists.

Instinctively I knew something was wrong. I pressed the alarm.

The men seemed unperturbed. 'We have heard a lot about your skills,' the first man said, with a lewd grin.

The second man coughed, 'Exceptional skills.'

I realized what they were talking about and turned away. I was used to bawdy humour, but this was too much. After all they had come to me. I didn't go to them. The nerve.

'Get out,' I said, wondering why it was taking the guards so long to show up.

The one in front grabbed me by the elbow and jerked me around to face him.

'It is good to share, Nazo-ji. Why save it all for the boys on top. Let it trickle down to the ground as well.'

'Yes, Nazo-ji,' the other one said, pushing me roughly against the wall.

'Let me go or I'll scream.' But before I could say another word, the first guy pulled out a gun and pushed it into my ribs.

'Scream and I'll shoot you.'

Believe me, when one sees death in the face, it is not easy to think of anything. I did as I was told.

'Now come quietly with us or we'll shoot you and that little rat of yours.'

I turned around to see the wrong child standing mutely in the doorway.

'Go inside, go to Refugee,' I said.

Immediately, I felt a sharp pain in the small of my back as the man poked me with the gun's nozzle. 'I said no talking.'

'Go!' I shouted.

He twisted my wrist so hard that I thought I'd never be able to lift it again.

'Come quietly or there will be more pain.'

'Okay,' I whispered, pain blinding me as black spots danced in front of my eyes.

Refugee walked in just as the men were pushing me out.

'Not a word,' the men whispered. 'Scream and we'll shoot all three of you.'

Refugee froze.

'Nazo,' he said, his voice tense, 'where are you going? And who are these men?'

'Answer him,' they whispered.

I looked at the men. 'Everything is okay,' I said, my voice a shrill squeak. 'Can you look after the child?'

'Let's go,' the men gave me a shove.

'Nazo!' he called out after me.

We got into a car waiting outside. The gates, I noticed, were unmanned, the cameras and buzzers ripped out. I prayed feverishly that you were all right.

'Where are you taking me?' I asked. In reply, they struck me on the head. Darkness descended all around.

⚖

When I woke up, I was in a bed with musty sheets and my wrists and ankles hurt. I tried to wriggle my hands but realized I couldn't . My hands and legs were stretched out and tied at the bed ends. My clothes were missing. I was naked save for a dirty sheet thrown carelessly across my stomach and breasts.

A man came in and laughed at me.

'They said you looked like Rani Shah. But I think you're better than the real thing.'

'Let me go,' I shouted.

'You are the one who sent the message about the Rape Law. You want to change it, *hain*?'

The men laughed savagely and closed in around me.

'Let's give you your own case to campaign, huh?' one of them sneered.

'Come on, woman,' another spat on his palm and rubbed me.

'Dry as the Indus river,' he laughed.

A third appeared and took his clothes off. Soon all three were upon me. Calling me names, hitting me, kicking me. I thought they would tear me into pieces.

'You think you can disgrace our Elders?' They slapped my face and yelled, 'You dare break the Jihadists? Take that, you whore!'

'You filthy woman! We will make an example out of you.'

They lit cigarettes and pushed the lighted ends into my skin.

'When we are done with you, no one will dare raise a finger at the Jihadists.'

'Rani,' I cried, 'save me!'

But the more I called out your name, the more they laughed and enjoyed themselves.

'When Rani finds out, she'll skin you alive,' I shouted.

They scalded me with burning hot water.

'Clean-up time, you dirty woman.'

'I will send you to jail. Rani will have you hanged.'

But they only laughed harder.

'Her hands are tied,' one of them said crudely. 'She's more fucked than you are.'

'Stop!' I screamed as they turned me over.

'I'll tell Balgodi! He will find you!'

One of them poised a knife against my throat.

'Stop. Don't touch me. I'm telling you, Balgodi will skin you. Don't touch me. I'm his special woman…'

'Who do you think told us about your tight little body, you bitch?' they laughed like hungry hyenas gathering their prey.

'Can't keep the spoils to himself.'

'No, no, it can't be…'

They dug my face into the mattress and placed the tip of the knife on the small of my back. 'You'll have a good case,' one of them shouted.

I screamed as the pain tore through me.

Before I lost consciousness, I heard their laughter surround me. Like vultures circling the dead. Except I wasn't dead.

Not yet.

⚖

Afterwards, they threw my battered body out of a moving car on the road in front of Shah House. I had nothing to cover myself with. I cowered in the dark, clutching at leaves and dirt. I remember the stray dogs and their yellow eyes. The look of pity.

Somehow I crawled to the outside kitchen. Refugee mistook me for a beggar.

'It's me,' I whispered, my body shivering and raw.

He dropped the pan in his hand.

I watched the oil sizzle on the ground before it traced a path to my bare toes. I didn't flinch.

⚖

Later, when Refugee had wrapped a blanket around my shoulders and put me in a tub of hot water, I asked for you. You didn't come to see me until the next day. And when you did, you averted my gaze. You never were good at looking pain in the eye.

'I want to press charges,' I said.

You placed your palm on my hand.

'Do you know who they were?'

'I know who sent them.'

You cleared your throat. 'Nazo, the thing is...'

'I want justice.'

'Justice?' you laughed a hollow little laugh. 'Justice says a woman has to provide four witnesses to the rape. Can you provide them, Nazo?'

'Then change the law.'

You were silent.

'You have majority in the Parliament. Use your power.'

'Ha,' you snorted. 'You know well how powerless I am.'

I was sick of you playing the victim. I lay battered and bruised, shattered to the bones, my spirit crushed, my body humiliated, and still it was somehow all about you.

'Bullshit,' I said. 'Change the law. At least try. If not for me, then for other women who go through this.'

'Look, you've been through a lot. This is not the time to...'

'Look at me, Rani Madam,' I flung away the sheet covering my bruises. 'We both know what this law is about. It applies to economic transactions not horrible physical blood-tearing rape! Who in the world would stand by and watch a woman being raped and then go to court about it? Answer me, Madam. This law is to keep us down.'

'Nazo, for goodness sake! Haven't you learned anything from

all this? Look what bloody happened to you when you raised your voice against it. I have children, Nazo. I can't afford to get mixed up with the Jihadists.'

I got up and slapped you.

'Then you don't deserve to be our PM.'

You pressed your hand against your cheek and stared disbelievingly at me.

I slapped you again.

You remained silent, your guilt screaming louder than any words could have.

I grabbed your hair and pulled you close.

'You don't even have the courage to save yourself. How can you save anyone else?'

It was a few minutes before you recovered.

'Nazo,' you pushed me away. 'You're in shock,' you shook off my bruised hand, making me wince with pain. 'I'm only trying to help you. Going to court and telling people all about how you were raped by three men is not going to help you. You'll become a laughing stock. Besides, you brought this upon yourself. The whole city has been talking about your exploits. You can't just pick and choose who you bed. You...'

'Madam,' I said, my voice barely a whisper. 'How did you know there were three of them?'

Prosecutor: I won't ask you what happened when you were assaulted, but I would like you to tell the court what happened next. For I feel something important changed in your life. This was a difficult time for you. You became resentful of the system, laws and lawmakers. Would it be right to say you blamed Madam Shah somehow?

Defendant: It is hard to tell exactly when you fall in love with someone, Omar Sir. But the moment you fall out of love is a definitive one. This was one such time.

You avoided me after that day. Refugee brought me an envelope full of money and a letter of recommendation for the doctors to admit me to a private hospital. You always were good at polite little bribes. Both lay unopened. I did not thank you, nor did I blame you. I simply stopped talking.

Soldier Rahim came to see me.

'Come away with me, Nazo. We'll start a new life, far away from here.'

But something inside me had been broken. If the price of hubris was heavy, then the price of betrayal was even heavier. I felt shattered. Irreparable. For the first time in my life, when I looked at you, I felt nothing. No hatred. No love. Just numbness.

Where can I go, Soldier Rahim, I thought. Everywhere I go, it will follow me. If only I could leave this body.

Soldier Rahim, shocked by the hopelessness in my eyes, said nothing further.

The wrong child came to see me. He pawed at me with his little hands and consoled me in his incomprehensible speech, but I felt nothing. Not even annoyance. I felt as if I was frozen. After a while, you asked everyone to leave me alone. I was given no tasks to do. Not even light ones. All day I sat looking at walls, wondering when they would close in on me. I watched you go to work, come back, eat, sleep, play with your daughter, as if everything was the same as before.

Only I knew that nothing would ever be the same.

⚖

'Nazo,' you came to see me a few weeks later. 'Dr Farooqi thinks you are suffering from a nervous breakdown. You need help. He...' you looked away. 'He suggested E.S.T. It involves electric shocks. It will hurt, but it will help you get better.'

I just stared at you, the same numbness making my eyelids heavy even as you went on talking.

'Nazo, it might turn into something worse like a mental illness. Look, I know we have had our differences in the past, but I can't let you waste away like this. Nazo, at least try...'

I drifted into a deep cavernous black sleep.

Prosecutor: Miss Khan, you were admitted to a mental asylum. Am I right?

Counsel: My client was only there for a few days, and that, too, due to a terrible shock. It is no reflection on her current state of mind.

Prosecutor: I'm not so sure about that, Counsel. Your Honour, please see Exhibit E, a report from Dr Farooqi about Miss Khan's diagnosis of schizophrenia. It is not a result of a shock, but an underlying illness which surfaces due to a shock. It shows that Miss Khan had always been mentally unstable.

Counsel: Defamatory!

Prosecutor: But I have medical evidence. Your Honour, I would like to call upon Dr Farooqi to come to the witness box.

Judge: Permission granted.

Prosecutor: Thank you, Your Honour. Dr Farooqi, please tell us some of the symptoms of schizophrenia.

Witness: Obsession, paranoia, extreme idolization.

Prosecutor: And what happens when such people fall in love?

Witness: They usually become fixated on the person. They are obsessive, stalkers...

Prosecutor: Excuse me, but what if they hate someone? I mean, are such patients dangerous? For example, if

> they start believing that someone is their enemy,
> can they go so far as to kill them?

Witness: I believe so. Yes.

Perhaps I would have spent the rest of my life sitting in a dark unlit corner if it hadn't been for the unexpected visitor.

I'm unsure how much time had passed. It could be months since that terrible night or it could have been a few hours. But one day, I was sitting in the dark when there was a knock on the door. I opened it to see no one outside. As soon as I shut it, the knocking began again. I swung the door open to, once again, see no one there. I began to feel scared. I didn't believe in ghosts or spirits, but the invisible knocking was beginning to unnerve me. So when the knocking came a third time, I picked up a vase, threw open the door and swung the vase blindly before me. Nothing but the swishing sound of air cutting air.

And that is when I felt something touching my feet. Stifling a scream, I looked down to see a cockroach climbing up my bare foot. The vase dropped from my hand, narrowly missing the repulsive creature. I crouched down to take a closer look and sucked in my breath. The resemblance was undeniable. The same cross-eyed features, the same ruthless scowl and the same buzzing antennae that gave him a frown of concentration, always scheming, always planning. And most of all, that look of brutal self-righteousness.

There was no doubt about it. The cockroach in front of me was undoubtedly the General's reincarnation.

The past had come back to haunt me.

Quickly, I put an upturned glass over him. Let him suffocate,

I thought. But then what if he came back as something bigger, something mightier? Where had I heard that if someone died an unnatural death, they keep coming back till death claims them naturally.

'It's your karma,' I said to him, 'that you have come back as the lowliest form of life.'

'Talking to yourself again?' Refugee said, as he brought me tea. 'Are you feeling hungry today or still on hunger strike?'

I stared at him speechless, willing him to come forward and accidentally squish the cockroach General.

'Step on it,' I prayed silently.

But he walked right out without a second glance. When I turned to look down again, the creature had escaped.

That was the first time I realized that there is such a thing as accountability.

Perhaps you do get what you deserve.

By lunchtime he was back. I reluctantly left my dark hole to come to the main house. But he was already there. I saw his little feelers waving blindly before he climbed up the leg of the dining table and sat himself behind your soup bowl. I held my breath. Would you notice him? You were so distracted by the news on TV that you weren't even looking at what you were putting in your mouth let alone what was crawling about on the tablecloth.

Still, I held my breath. What would happen if you saw him? Would you see through the disguise? Would you be repelled enough to crush him? I wondered if you'd step on him. Or perhaps you'd scoop him up with a piece of paper and throw him out of the window.

You always did make me do your dirty work. Or at least, you tried...

'Nazo?'

I looked up, startled at the sound of my name.

'What are you doing here? Are you all right?'

I continued to stare mutely, unable to bring the words out.

'Stop staring at me. For God's sake, speak! Really, Nazo, I do think you should go see Dr Farooqi at the Psychiatric Centre. Believe me, they won't lock you away in an asylum. He'll just give you some pills to relax your nerves. I'll see to it that you are taken care of.'

That's exactly what I was afraid of.

That night when I got to bed, the cockroach General was already on the pillow, waiting for me. He scurried up to me, climbed onto my hand and up my arm and before I knew it, he was sitting on the tip of my nose. I felt my eyes centre in to look at him. He nuzzled his feelers against my skin, tickling my nostrils. I sneezed. Achoooo! A loud sound, a swoosh of breath and spit, and he went flying across the room.

Tentatively, I moved closer. When he didn't stir for another few seconds, I wondered if I had killed him.

Once again.

The next day, I awoke to a black dawn. There was a dust storm brewing, the musty scent of wet earth lingered in the air. The darkness before the rain, I thought.

It seemed a long time since I had stepped out into the kitchen, my world now limited to my room and your suite. I took a few hesitant steps down to the grease kitchen.

I found it the same.

How surprising it was that I had changed yet everything around me was still the same.

'Ah, Nazo, come, come,' Refugee rushed to greet me as if seeing a long lost friend, and perhaps he was.

He settled me on a chair as if I was some fragile piece of china, easily breakable.

'Get her tea,' he shouted to Chanchar. 'Ah, my poor Nazo,' he turned to me. 'Hai! What have they done to you.'

I tried to smile, but the muscles around my face felt stiff.

'Quick,' he shouted to the tea boy. 'Tea, now!'

Chanchar placed the cup down with trembling hands. I noticed he avoided my gaze.

'You can't bury the truth,' Refugee said, as he stirred sugar into my tea. 'You will see one day that justice will prevail. They will catch those culprits.'

How could I tell him that I too was a culprit? Perhaps this was my punishment for plotting another human's death. However nasty he may have been.

Refugee's words kept circling my thoughts, darkening my mind like black clouds blocking out the sun. There was only one person who could help me.

It took great courage to telephone him. My hands shook as I dialled the number, my palms sweaty as I waited for him to pick up.

'Can you come?' I whispered, my voice sounding foreign even to my own ears.

Barely an hour later, there was a gentle knock on the door. Once again I found myself at his mercy. I fell into Soldier Rahim's arms as soon as I unlocked the latch.

'Save me,' I said, tears flooding my eyes. 'Only you can save me.'

'Nazo,' he said, rubbing my back. 'Oh, Nazo, what has happened to you? What have they done to you now?'

'He's following me,' I whispered. My eyes darted around the room as if any minute now he would pop out.

'Who's following you, Nazo? There is nobody here.'

'He's following me. Always following me.'

'Who?'

'The General.'

'The General? But he's dead, Nazo.'

'He's back.'

'Oh, Nazo.'

'Look!' I pointed to the cockroach nestled comfortably in the folds of my hijab.

Before I could say another word, Soldier Rahim flicked it off and stamped on it with his boots.

My screams were so loud that Rahim had to clamp his hand on my mouth.

'Nazo, please!' he said.

'You killed it,' I said, as soon as he lifted his hand off my mouth. 'You killed the General.'

'That was the General?' Soldier Rahim looked at the crushed creature and let out a laugh that was louder than all my screams.

⚖

Why didn't he believe me, I wondered that night in bed. Why did he think I had gone mad? Could anyone really deny the resemblance? Surely you would have believed me.

If only you had seen him, Rani.

The next day, I decided with great conviction to tell you the truth. But instead of believing me, you had me bundled up in the car and sent to the clinic for the first of the electric shocks.

Defendant: Receiving a shock and giving a shock, both are terrible things, Omar Sir.

Counsel: Mr Omar, my client has answered your question. Is there any further questioning to be done?

Prosecutor: No. No further questioning. Witness dismissed.

Counsel: Very well, then. I would now like to ask the Prosecutor Mr Omar to step into the witness box. For, after all, by virtue of being a good friend to Madam Rani Shah, in the months leading up to the assassination, he too had been spotted at Shah House. Kindly take oath, Mr Omar.

The cure was not much different from the crime itself. Once again my hands and feet were bound, my mouth gagged and my body tortured. This time with wires. Currents ran through my body at regular intervals. I felt as if I was being struck by lightning. Repeatedly.

At the end of it, my mind felt as if it would explode. I felt, when I came back home, only half the woman I had once been. But I vowed never to tell you this, lest it gave you just the reason you needed to send me back to the torturer's clinic.

That night, I slept a dark deep sleep, waking up the next evening. I felt groggy and disoriented, as if I had been on a long journey and had only just returned. My hands were clammy and my mouth felt as if it had been stuffed with cotton wool.

I was just debating whether you had done this to abrade me or help me when there was knock on the back door. Convinced that the General was back, I swung open the door, my eyes on the floor. And what did I see? Not a black scrawny creature but ivory, sculpted to perfection. I saw before me, the most exquisite pair of feet I had ever seen. Oval nails, perfectly trimmed and embedded in pearly white skin, lighter only by yours. The beautiful feet before me were clad in slim tan leather slippers. I raised my eyes slowly, taking in the crisp white trousers, a pale shirt with a Mao collar, wide chest, a strong burly neck, clean-shaven jaw around pink fleshy lips, an aquiline nose and hazel eyes that stared deep into mine.

'Hello,' the man said, in a deep husky voice.

Something about his accent was reminiscent of yours.

'New Yorker?' I asked.

'Yes,' came the surprised reply.

I smiled.

'You seem to know the accent well,' he said. 'Are you also from there...?'

Was he being polite or just dumb, I wondered. Could he not see from my attire that I was a servant? I decided on aloof.

I must have been staring at him, for he coughed, looked embarrassed, then said, 'Sorry, I just meant that not many people can gauge my accent from just a greeting.'

'I've been with Rani Madam for a long time, sir. I do know this accent well.'

He held out his hand. 'Well, any friend of Rani's is a friend of mine.'

Yes, I thought, he was definitely stupid.

I reached out to take his hand and that was when I hesitated. There was something oddly familiar about those hands. Perhaps it was the sheer size of them. They didn't seem to fit in with the rest of his refined, dare I say effeminate, body. His hands were large and burly, like that of a butcher.

Or of a killer.

'My name is Omar,' he cleared his throat. 'Good to meet you.'

I looked at his hands again and a shiver ran up my spine. I remembered now where I had seen such large hands before. The burqa hadn't done a good job of concealing them.

Slowly I held out my own limp, sweat-soaked palm.

He shook it. His grip was as strong as I anticipated it to be.

'Hello?' his voice seemed to come from far away. 'Miss?'

I snapped out of my thoughts. 'Sorry, sir ... I.'

'No worries,' he said, flashing me that gorgeous smile. 'Is Rani home?'

Is Rani home? This guy was good at putting on the 'dumb' act. 'No, she's gone to the market to do groceries,' I said. 'Part of a PM's job.'

He let out a loud laugh. Two dimples deepened his cheeks and I felt myself flushing. The man was beautiful.

'You're very funny, Miss...?'

'The main entrance is there,' I told him, looking away. 'You've come around the back. Didn't the guards direct you to the watchman? He mans Rani Madam's home-office.'

'Oh,' he said. 'The last time I came here was through the back way ... Anyhow, this place is a maze. Shall I go back to the entrance?'

'Please come with me. I will take you around to the home-office. Madam might be running a little late with her appointments, but there is a very nice waiting area and reception there.'

Omar started to laugh.

Was he laughing at me? I rubbed my temples, my head still sore from the treatment.

'Actually I've known Rani since we were at college together. All this feels a bit formal. But I guess she is the PM now. One must follow protocol. I just hope she's pleased to see me.'

'So how did you get in, if she's not expecting you?' I asked, confused. The guards were not supposed to let in anyone without permission. Fear began to grip my throat.

'Foreign press!' he held up a card and dispersed all my dark thoughts. 'I'm a human rights lawyer, but these days I'm working on an investigative report for a news channel. I'm here to do some research. I find this press pass gets me through all sorts of doors and walls.'

He grinned again and I felt myself melting at the sight of those crater-like dimples.

'I wanted to surprise Rani.'

'Oh, I see,' I bumbled, unable to focus beyond those dimples, his perfect teeth and toothpaste smile clouding my vision. 'In that case, I'm sure Rani Madam won't mind if I take you straight through.'

Perhaps it was the medication I was on or perhaps it was his dimples, but forgetting protocol, I led Omar straight to you.

Or should I say I led you straight to him.

⚖

We crossed the inner courtyard and entered the main house. Your study was the first door on the left, and I could hear voices.

'Rani Madam,' I barged in. You were in a meeting with your Party workers.

'Nazo?' you looked surprised to see me. 'How are you feeling now?'

I sighed. 'I'm fine: Your good friend, Omar from New York, is here.'

'What?' you looked flustered.

'Omar, your fr…'

'Yes, but what is he doing here?' you asked in a shrill shriek of a voice.

The others turned to look at you.

Balgodi, too, looked up from his corner where he was puffing away at his cigar and flipping through a magazine, probably *Playboy*, I thought.

'Surprising you,' I said triumphantly.

'Who is this Omar?' Balgodi frowned. 'How do you know him?'

You shot me a look as if somehow it was my fault that his curiosity had been aroused.

'If you don't want the surprise, shall I ask him to take it back?' I asked, puzzled at your nervousness.

Now it was your turn to frown. 'No, no. I'm coming. Just ask him to … I … Oh, just seat him in the lounge.'

Then before Balgodi could quiz you further, you stepped out of the room, leaving me to answer his barrage of questions with my dazed look and fuzzy tongue.

⚖

Later when you rang the bell for Refugee to bring in the tea, I took the tray from him.

He gave me a sly look and said, 'Tread carefully, Madam Nazo. *Husn waalon se Allah bachaaey.* Believe you me, the prettier the boys, the harder their hearts…'

'What?' I asked, sure that I had misheard him.

'It's hardly been a day since your treatment, Nazo.' He winked and added, 'Don't go falling for a pretty face now.'

Damn it, I thought. How is it that in every household the cook knows before everyone else what's going on.

'You needn't worry,' I said.

And it was true. It was nothing less than curiosity that was making me restless about Omar. There was something oddly familiar and at the same time disturbing about him. Yet I was sure that I had never met him before in my life. Oh well, I thought, as I walked in with the tea, at least he got my mind off the cockroach General.

I found you both embracing.

You pulled back awkwardly as I entered.

'Omar, it's been so long!' you said, a bit too loudly, I thought. 'It is so good to see you. I was just thinking the other day, it's been too long. I must ring Omar, I told myself. My dear friend, Omar!'

'Good to see you too,' he said, playing along.

'So what brings you here, so suddenly?' You were smiling away, as if you were happy to see him, but I could hear the slight note of anxiety in your voice. I was tempted to pull the mask off your face, but unfortunately for me, it was glued to your skin.

'Ah, here comes Nazo with the tea. Is Refugee sick?'

I ignored the sarcasm in your voice.

Omar got up to help me. He leaned forward and took the tray from me, our hands touching ever so briefly.

'Please, Omar, sit,' you said.

'You don't have to be so formal, Rani,' he said, placing the tray gently on the table in front of you.

'As if I would let you go without any tea. In fact, you are staying right here as my guest.' Then before he could reply, you said, 'Shall I pour?'

'No,' I cried, and you both looked up at me.

'I mean,' I looked around, wondering why I had screamed like that. 'I mean, I will serve it. Thank you. Thank you for the opportunity.'

Omar laughed and you rolled your eyes.

'I take it you've met Nazo,' you said, making a gesture with your hand as if to indicate I was not all there. I felt an angry heat well up inside. My glance fell on the fruit knife in the tray. Perhaps you caught me staring at its sharp blade, for you quickly added, 'She is indispensable to me. The little ones, especially, are so close to her.'

I guess you knew your limits.

But you didn't know yours…

You looked sideways and caught me staring at Omar. You narrowed your eyes.

'And you know, Omar, poor Nazo has vowed never to get married. That's how devoted she is to my son.'

This was news to me.

'Well, I remember you taking a similar vow about not getting married and devoting yourself to the country,' Omar said. 'But I guess people change with time.'

Ha, I thought, finally, someone who could stand up to you.

'Perhaps,' he looked warmly at me, 'Nazo will change her mind too.'

Perhaps I would.

That night, after a long time, I felt something stir inside me. A kind of warm curiosity about this handsome stranger. But I let it simmer. After what had happened to me, I had vowed I would never ever let a man come near me. But something about Omar's gentle charm was drawing me towards him. Not a sexual attraction, but a different kind of pull. I wanted to look at him and believe there was beauty amidst all the ugliness life had thrown at me.

I wasn't sure if it was the medicines, the electric shocks or just a feeling of familiarity that was making me feel this way. But before I could ponder further, Refugee buzzed to say dinner was ready.

'I'll get Madam and the guest,' I buzzed back. I crossed into the main house and was climbing up the stairs when I heard a loud crash. When I got closer, I heard voices coming from your room. Another argument, I thought.

I gauged your husband was throwing one of his tantrums. Sure enough when I got to the door, I heard him say, 'But why does he have to stay here?'

'Because he's my friend from college days.'

'Whoever heard of a girl and a boy being just friends.'

'Oh, Balgodi, I don't have time for this nonsense. Look he's a well-known human rights lawyer. Has clout in the foreign media. He can be really useful to us. Perhaps he can restore your image in the public eye.'

'What's wrong with my image?' I heard Balgodi shout.

'I mean the misconceptions people have about you,' you said soothingly.

'Huh,' Balgodi retorted.

Just then the baby began to cry.

'Now look what you've done,' I could hear you cajoling the baby. 'And besides, Omar needs to stay here for a few days to complete a book he is working on. There's a chapter in it on the first woman PM ever in our region.'

'Don't forget you could have never done it without me,' I heard Balgodi say.

'Oh yes, husband dearest,' I could hear the sarcasm concealed in your voice as you proceeded to explain how Omar's stay and subsequent book was vital to Party re-election.

I smiled. Every time you want a lie to become the truth, all you have to do is tell it to the press.

True lies…

Just then, I felt a hand on my shoulder.

'Waiting for something, Nazo?'

I turned around to see Omar standing behind me.

'Oh, Omar Sir, yes, Sir,' I nodded, annoyed at having to miss the rest of the argument but at the same time pleased to see him. 'I was just coming up to say, dinner is served.'

'Well then, let's go.'

I hesitated.

'Shall we?' he stood at the top of the staircase with his arm held out.

Was he crazy? Did he really expect me to link arms with him and walk down the stairs?

'Sir,' I said, smoothing down the creases on my crumpled shirt, 'you go on. I have to wait for Madam.'

'All right,' he said, whistling down the steps, two at a time, 'suit yourself.'

If only I could.

Omar's presence in the house was like heralding in spring after a long lonely winter. Although I was still curious about his past, especially where you were concerned, I was now more intrigued about his future. What were his plans? Why was he really here? He always got a dewy look in his eyes when he looked at you, and you seemed to be spending more energy avoiding him than trying to explain your point of view to him, which is what you normally did with members of the foreign press. Who was he really? Why was he here? Something told me I would soon find out. All I had to do was to keep my eyes open and my mouth shut.

Something was about to happen, I could tell. I had a nose for these things, Refugee often said. That day, too, there was a meeting of the top Party brass going on in your study, and I stood outside trying to listen in.

My ear was pressed against your study door when I heard Omar's gravelly voice behind me. 'Nazo?' I jumped. Never before had someone snuck up on me like that without my knowing. Maybe he really was a CIA agent, like Refugee suspected. I turned around slowly. Omar's handsome face gazed down at me. He was standing close.

Too close.

'You shouldn't be here.'

'You shouldn't be here either,' I said.

'You're not easily intimidated, are you?'

His English was much too good for my comprehension, but I tried to keep up.

'No, I'm not, but ask me anything and I'll know the answer.'

He laughed a husky little laugh and said, 'Okay, I will.'

'Go on,' I challenged.

'Will you have dinner with me?'

My mind went blank.

'What happened? Thought you had the answer to everything.'

'Sir,' I said, looking down at his handsome feet. 'I can serve you dinner, but … I can't have it with you.'

'Why?'

'Because…'

I looked up at him. Did he really not understand? Was he that naïve or just incorrigible?

'Yes?'

'Because … that's the way it is.'

'Why?'

'Because things don't change around here.'

'Why?'

'Because if one tries to change things, they are stopped. Violently, harshly.'

Thoughts and images of the rape flashed through my mind and I stepped back. Once again, I could hear the voices in my head, feel the burns on my skin, and then the roach's feelers began tickling my bare feet. I saw in my mind the dead man's teeth.

'Excuse me, Sir,' I said, backing away abruptly as waves of nausea rushed up my throat. 'I have to go.'

'Nazo, wait.'

I thought he'd grab my arm, but he was a gentleman.

'Please,' he said, his arms firmly by his side.

I looked at his earnest expression and shook my head. No. Not for me, these matters of the heart. For my heart knew what my mind only thought it knew. And my mind told me to stay away.

I didn't expect Omar Sir to persist and, unfortunately for me, he didn't. This was one time when I was annoyed at being right.

With the medication, I began to feel better, and after a few days, the violent thoughts no longer disturbed me. Strangely, now it was me who began to find excuses to talk to him. Brought him his tea, knocked on his door at meal times instead of using the intercom to inform him, made sure to stop him after dinner to ask what he wanted for breakfast. All this he answered with the utmost politeness, but he never once asked me out again.

It was unlike men. Yes, the more I thought about it, the more I was convinced he was doing this on purpose. It was a strategy and it was working. I wanted him to pursue me. If for nothing else, then just for the fun of it. I watched him, shyly, daydreamed about him and made up stories in my head about his background. And for this, I was grateful. For a little while, and a little while only, life once again seemed purposeful.

That is, until I found myself once again outside the gates of Paradise. You betrayed me, Rani Shah, just when I thought I could trust you again.

Judge: Are you sure you want to do this, Mr Omar? As prosecutor, you don't have to. You can be exempt.

Prosecutor: Thank you, Your Honour. But if my colleague feels I'm needed in the witness box, then I must respect his wish.

Judge: Proceed.

Counsel: Mr Omar, you have questioned my client's psychosis, accused her of paranoia and obsession, but did you ever see Miss Khan show any resentment or aggression towards Madam Shah?

Prosecutor as Witness (PW): She is very good at concealing her emotions.

Counsel: I mean, were there any instances when Miss Khan was treated harshly by Madam Shah and she complained? As employees, I'm sure we all have those moments when we can't stand our bosses.

PW: Yes, there were moments when Rani Shah treated her harshly.

Counsel: Was there violence?

PW: At times...

Counsel: And did Miss Khan retaliate?

PW: I have to admit, I never saw her lose her temper.

Counsel: Well then, how can you accuse her of being a psychotic obsessive killer? You have to hate someone a lot to even contemplate hurting them.

PW: Perhaps she just hadn't reached her tipping point, then.

Counsel: Is there a reason why you say that? Did she
     receive a shock of some kind? Some sort of pedestal-
     shaking news, a betrayal perhaps?

PW: I think so … yes.

Counsel: Please elaborate.

PW: I'm afraid I can't.

Counsel: In that case, do you not think that if at all
     there was some misunderstanding, the person who
     caused it would be an accessory to murder? Do you
     know who could have deliberately created tension
     between her and Madam Rani Shah?

⚖

It was back.

I'm not sure what it was that triggered it, but something
made that familiar cold fear return. It was at once unknown and
recognizable, a strange trepidation, a dread that inched up my skin.
It had no name.

I woke up in the middle of the night, afraid that someone had
broken into my room. Someone was there, watching me. With
trembling fingers, I flicked on the bedside lamp.

On the foot of my bed, I found Refugee rummaging through a
briefcase I kept hidden under my bed.

'Refugee?' I asked, my voice drugged with sleep.

'Oh, Nazo, I didn't mean to wake you. I was looking for money.'

For a second, I thought it was a bad dream. My friend was
robbing me and not even a hint of apology in his voice.

'But … what…'

How could I point out politely that stealing was wrong.
Stealing from friends, even worse.

Refugee paused, frowned, then started to laugh. 'Oh, ho! You always think the worst of me, my *jaan*. It's for the schools' project. I didn't want to worry you, but, Nazo, the Jihadists have burned down three of your girls' schools and are threatening to shut down the others. It's on the news. The school guardians have been ringing one after the other asking for security funds. I was hoping you had some stash stowed away, but there is nothing here. If we don't do something soon, Nazo, all your hard work will go to waste.'

'Rani will help,' I said.

Refugee snorted, 'Madam's government is nothing but a bystander.'

Shame tore through me. Why did I, after all this, still feel as if it was my fault?

I felt under my pillow and pulled out the cheque book. 'Here. This is the last of it.'

Refugee reached out to take it. 'You have to get back in the game soon, Nazo,' he said, with a look that was not all too sincere. 'You have to get better fast or all this will shut down.'

My head fell back against the pillow. I felt tired. Exhausted. Yet the journey had just begun. Friends, I thought as I drifted into an uneasy sleep.

Friends make the worst enemies.

The next morning, I woke up with a violent shudder. There, sitting on my blanket, staring right at me with a hundred watchful eyes, was the General.

It was all I could do to keep myself from screaming. I rang Soldier Rahim, but he didn't pick up. There was no one else I could trust. Except you. Despite the fear of electric shocks, I knew I had to tell you. For I alone was not responsible for his death.

Was I?

'Madam,' I rushed into your bedroom just as you were getting out of bed. 'Rani Madam, I saw him.'

'Saw whom?'

'The General. He's come back again.'

'Oh, Nazo,' you rubbed your temples. 'Please don't start that again. Not now. I really don't have the time. Or the energy.'

'But, Madam, you said you would believe me. Yesterday when I said there was something I needed to tell you, you said I could come to you. You said I could confide in you, especially anything to do with the General.'

'I thought it was something important like a coup being planned or something. How was I to know you've started imagining things again? Look, Nazo, last week one of the servants told me that you insisted the dead General had come back as an insect to avenge his murder because you were involved in his killing! Instead of all this nonsense which might end us both in jail, you could have just asked him for some strong pesticide.'

'But it's true.'

'I'm warning you...'

'But, Madam, just look at it. He's staring right at us. There's got to be a reason he's come back. Please just look into its revolting eyes.'

'Nazo,' you said gently, 'that's just a fly.'

'But surely you can see the resemblance. The way it flutters its wings, the way it is staring right at me as if to say, you killed me.'

You rolled up your newspaper and before I could finish my sentence, you swatted it. The squashed fly lay dead at your feet.

'You killed it! You killed the General!'

Perhaps it was the right thing to do to a hysterical person, but it still stung when you slapped me.

'You have become delusional, Nazo. Stop this behaviour or I'll have you locked up in a mental asylum.'

'How would you like it, Madam,' I asked, holding my cheek, 'if no one believed you when you said you are their PM?'

For a second, I thought I saw a light in your eyes. A sudden realization, as if you had finally understood what I was trying to say. But the next minute it was gone.

'Enough, Nazo. Go change the boy's nappy. And if you don't stop this nonsense, I won't let you near the children. The only reason I'm tolerating your crazy behaviour is because the boy is attached to you. But if you don't stop, I'll forget that you are his mother. Understand?'

I didn't, but I nodded yes.

That evening, as I was clearing up the dinner dishes, Omar came in to ask for a cup of green tea.

'I'll bring it to you,' I said. 'Refugee has turned in for the night.'

'I'll make it myself, no problem.'

'No, no, please, Sir! I'll do it.'

'Okay,' he said, a bit taken aback.

'Five minutes,' I said, when he continued to stand there. 'I'll make it as soon as I've fed the cats.'

I opened the kitchen door and threw the leftovers to a pack of waiting cats. They scrambled towards it, scavenging and wailing, fighting each other viciously. A fly buzzed over their heads, and before I knew it, my heart had welled up. I found myself crying at the sight.

'Nazo,' Omar came up behind me, 'are you all right?'

'Yes,' I said, hurriedly wiping away the tears.

His voice sounded apologetic, as if it was the task of making tea that had reduced me to such a state. 'Look, forget about it,' he insisted.

'No, no trouble,' I said, smiling now. 'Please go in. I'll bring it.'

A little while later, I took him his tea. He was sitting in the last of the evening light, looking through some photos.

'Thanks,' he said, his fingers lingering longer than necessary on mine as he took the cup.

'I've seen you feed the pigeons in the mornings and the cats at night time. Do you have a soft spot for animals?'

'Only for strays,' I replied.

He seemed unsure if I was serious or joking.

'Come sit here,' he patted the sofa next to him. I sat down wearily. I was tired of fighting him.

I looked at the photographs of your latest rally in his hand and couldn't resist asking, 'Do you have any old pictures of you and Rani Madam? From your college days?'

'Why?' He seemed surprised.

'I want to know what she was like before...'

He nodded.

'Yes, I know what you mean. She was a different person before her father's death. She never wanted to go into politics, you know.'

'She didn't?' It seemed unimaginable that you should want to do anything else.

'Oh no. She wanted to be in the Foreign Service and travel the world. It was because of the sudden death, the murder of her father, that she was pushed into politics. She had no choice, the poor thing. She was the eldest and Shah Sahib trusted her with the responsibility.'

'She could have walked away if she really wanted to,' I said, my heart still unconvinced.

'It's not so easy, Nazo. The Party's expectations were on her shoulders. And then a promise to her dying father ... it was too complicated. Believe me, I tried. We all tried to persuade her to stay. If she had, perhaps we would have been together now.'

I looked up, shocked at this admission. But it was too dark to see Omar's features clearly. In the fading evening light, he looked a mere silhouette. He seemed content though, lost in the sound of his own voice, seeing something beyond his closed eyelids that I couldn't.

'Did you,' I hesitated, 'did you want to marry her?'

He laughed. I felt my hopes rise.

'Well, I was too young to think about marriage. But I certainly wanted to spend time with her, travel with her, and perhaps in a few years' time, our relationship would have become more serious.'

'So why didn't you?'

'Rani is more traditional than you think. I realized much later and with great surprise, that the idea of living together didn't appeal to her. She always wanted marriage, kids, a stable home, a large family ... That's why we were all so shocked to hear about her decision to give it all up and go into politics.'

I nodded, something slowly making sense.

'She was so spirited then and full of great ideas for equality and democracy. But now,' he shook his head. 'Now she seems to have gotten comfortable with the idea of power.'

'Absolute power,' I said.

Suddenly the room was flooded with a bright orange light. You stood in the doorway, your finger on the light switch.

'There you are.'

We both looked up at your daunting figure looming in the doorway, unsure whom you were addressing.

'Omar, I've been looking all over the house for you. I...' you paused. 'Nazo, don't you have any work to do?'

I wasn't sure if you were teasing me or serious.

'I'm sure there are dishes to be washed or laundry to be done. Whatever tasks you do, just get on with it. Now.'

I knew then this wasn't a joke. I got up slowly.

I suppose it was true, time was a thief. Was this the same woman who had made me sit next to her, let me lie on the same bed as her? It's not that I felt used. Instead, I felt a great sadness inside, like I was free falling into a dark pit. It was so unlike you, Rani, to insult me like this in front of a guest. You wanted me to fall in his eyes. I could see that. But could you not see that by doing so, you were lowering your own self? Why were you doing this? Clearly you were jealous. But what then of all your talk about your mad, divine devotion to your husband and children and home ... You were the one, Rani, who didn't know where your loyalties lay.

An unexpected sound broke from my throat. I rushed out of the room and stood outside the door trying to hold back the tears.

'Rani,' I heard Omar say, 'what's happened to you? You've started behaving like that feudal lord husband of yours.'

'Don't worry too much about her, Omar. She is just a nuisance. A zero in my scheme of things.'

'Even zero has some value, Rani.' His tone was sharp.

'Yes,' you laughed. 'But only if it stands behind a number. On its own, it's nothing. A nobody.'

I knew then you weren't discussing numerical values. I was the zero in your eyes. And if I hadn't heard what Omar said next, perhaps I would have continued to believe in my nothingness.

I was about to leave when I heard him say, 'Amazing thing, this zero. Put it behind a digit and the number increases in value. Let it come in front of a digit and its value falls. In a way, don't you think, Rani, it's a kingmaker?'

Queenmaker in this case.

Prosecutor: Your Honour, we know that Miss Khan suffers from schizophrenia. Her account of things can't be trusted.

Counsel: Objection! The opinion of one practitioner cannot be established as a diagnosis. Court requires testimony of three psychiatrists to agree.

Judge: Sustained. Do you have any other questions, Mr Omar?

Prosecutor: Yes, Your Honour. Miss Khan, what I'm about to ask you will be difficult for you to answer. I know that. But we both know that you must. There was an incident at Shah House, which upset you. What I want to know is if that is what triggered this horrible tragedy?

Defendant: Sometimes the predator becomes the prey.

Prosecutor: A simple yes or no would do, Miss Khan.

Defendant: Omar Sir, all I can say is that sometimes you don't realize that the person you are using is actually using you. It was the same with me.

Later that night, Omar came to see me. He burst into my room without knocking, his cheeks flushed and eyes wild.

'Tell me, you don't mind?' he demanded.

'Mind what?' I sat huddled against the wall.

'Mind being talked to in that nasty condescending tone.'

'What are you talking about?'

'You don't know?' he asked, kneeling down beside me on the floor.

'No.'

'Fine then. Let me say it very clearly. I'm talking about Rani. The person she has become. It … it upsets me when she treats you so badly. She wasn't like that, you know. Both of us. We wanted to do so much. I, through my writing and legal aid, and Rani, through her politics. And now look at us. All our idealism has gone down the drain. I'm working for a cheap channel, but more to fund my human rights campaign than anything else, and God knows what Rani is trying to fund.'

'Probably Balgodi's pockets.'

Omar burst out laughing, then seeing the look on my face, he stopped. 'Sorry, I thought you were joking.'

I smiled, then frowned, unsure what I meant, if anything at all.

'Nazo,' Omar said, patting my hand. 'Listen, I know it's none of my business, but it just irks me when I see people taking advantage of others…'

So it wasn't about me…

'I want you to know that I appreciate what you do for her. You look out for her, take good care of her kids, her home and from what I've heard, you were a darn good PA too. People say you were her wing man on the schools' project. It must have been a lot of hard work to lobby the funds instead of using the State budget.'

If only he knew.

I tried to smile, but instead a tear slid down my cheek.

'If truth be told, Nazo, she is where she is because of you,' he said.

'Don't sprinkle salt on my wounds, Sir.'

'You don't know your own value, Nazo,' he smiled and

squeezed my hand. 'As they say, behind every successful woman is another woman.'

'Don't you mean behind every successful man there is a woman?'

Omar hesitated. He seemed to be deliberating how much to reveal. 'I ... I should go now, Nazo.'

'Omar Sir, wait,' I grabbed his hand and pulled him back beside me.

'I killed someone.'

'What?'

'I killed the General and now he keeps coming back to haunt me. Today he came as a fly. Tomorrow ... who knows what shape or form he will take tomorrow?'

'Nazo, there is nothing to be afraid of. Believe me, no one is coming after you.'

Why did I think he would be any different? I turned away my face.

'Listen to me, Nazo. It wasn't you.'

I looked up.

'But it was me. I gave Balgodi the secret code, I...'

'That's what you think.'

He had my full attention. 'What do you mean?' I almost didn't want to know.

'Do you really think it is so easy to kill a man as powerful as the General?'

It wasn't making sense. What was he saying? I shook my head hard.

'What I mean is, that Balgodi doesn't have the brains to hatch such elaborate plans. There is only one mastermind behind all this,' he grinned as I looked up, 'and it's not you.'

'Excuse me?'

'You are just a front, Nazo. A scapegoat.'

I had a sudden urge to press my palms against my ears. But I continued to listen as if my mind and body had both been paralyzed.

'What do you mean, Omar Sir?'

'I mean you've been used. Led to believe that all your sacrifices were for a woman who'd restore order, avenge your parents' death, lead the Nation out of darkness. Lies. All lies. The truth is that Rani is not who she claims to be.'

'No,' I whispered. 'You don't know anything, Omar Sir. The real truth is that her hands are tied. She can't do anything for us because they won't let her.'

'They who?'

'The men.'

'But she has a clear majority in the Parliament.'

'You don't know half the humiliation she's been through. She tried, she wanted to, but she couldn't, don't you see...'

'That's what you think, Nazo, because she made you think that. The truth is, she loves Balgodi. She did what she did willingly for him. He painted rosy pictures of marital bliss in the palatial gardens of Star Abbey and she went along with it. I knew love was blind, but in her case, it's dumb, deaf and stupid.'

'Why are you lying, Omar Sir? I thought you were her friend! The truth is Madam hates Balgodi.'

'That's what I thought too,' his voice sounded bitter.

It was then I realized, he too loved you.

'He's the father of her children,' he said. 'She'll stand by him no matter what the cost.'

'It's not true.'

His face hardened. 'So you think that she cares about you? The Nation? Me?' Omar was laughing now, but his laugh felt unexpected and hostile, like someone trespassing.

I was no longer curious. Instead I felt as if he was an intruder, crossing into my little world and destroying it.

'You think this is funny?' I took a step forward and hissed, 'Who do you think you are, huh? You come here, challenging everything I have ever believed in. You are asking me to believe that the woman I respect, trust and love is not who she claims to be. You can't do that, you understand?'

Omar wasn't laughing any more.

'Choosing money over power is a mistake that everyone makes, Nazo. But choosing love over power is a mistake that only women make.'

'The power of love is greater than the love of power, Omar Sir.'

'Not if it's wasted on the wrong person, Nazo.'

Coward, I thought. All men are cowards. Scenes and images I wanted to forget flashed in my head. My wrists began to hurt from phantom abrasions, my mouth felt sore. I leaned against the wall and closed my eyes.

All men deserved to die.

When I opened my eyes again, Omar was still standing there.

'If you won't leave,' I said, 'I will.'

He grabbed my arm just as I was about to open the door and swung me around to face him.

'Look at me,' he commanded. The gentleman was gone and I saw him for what he was – just another man out to break a woman. The memories came flooding back and before I knew it, I was sliding to the floor.

'Go away,' I heard myself shout. 'Don't touch me.'

'Nazo.'

I buried my head in my knees. 'Please go away,' I cried. 'Leave me alone.'

'This isn't the time to hide, Nazo. It's time to open your eyes.'

His voice was slow and deadly serious. But it wasn't violent. I forced myself to open my eyes.

'Look, I didn't want to show you this,' he hesitated. 'But I can't let you take the blame for something you didn't do. I know you love her. But she only loves herself.'

He shoved a folder at me. 'When they showed me the evidence against Rani, I refused to believe it. I told them I would investigate myself. That's why I came ... Here, take a look at these documents. These are the photos, letters, faxes and emails I found during my research.'

No. I did not want to see this. I had to get away.

'Nazo, stay,' he pressed my hand. 'The time has come for you to know.'

'I don't want to.'

'You have to.'

It was like witnessing a roadkill. I did not want to look. I wanted to shut my eyes and turn my head away, but it was as if something had taken hold of me and was making me watch the blood, the gore, the anguish and helplessness of it all.

I could not tear myself away from the sight. The sheaf of papers before me were more sickening than the beheaded body of my father, his battered brains spread patiently beside him. It was terrifying.

And just as intriguing.

I touched the bank statements. They were under your name.

Five wire transfers from the US. An enormous deposit from a bank in Beijing. Several more incoming payments from a member of Opposition. Two or three deposits by a Kashmiri organization and a transfer of several millions to the Muslim Brotherhood Support, and finally, an arms receipt from the bloodiest terror group … the Jihadists.

I looked away.

'Why should I believe you?' I asked, tears blinding me. 'It could be Balgodi using her.'

'Does he tell her what to say and when, also? Take a look at these.'

Transcriptions of telephone calls discussing the export of nuclear technology not just to Iran but also to North Korea and Syria. But the most shocking of it all was a paper tucked at the back, dating to 1992. I touched a fax from the CIA.

You had known about the General's death all along.

In fact, you had planned it. You had instructed them to hand over the General's itinerary to me. I felt like a puppet who'd only just realized its strings were being pulled by someone else.

'Like you, I too thought Balgodi was using her. I offered to take her away from all this, Nazo. I came here for her. Dug up all this evidence, yet … in the end…'

'She betrayed us.' I closed my eyes.

So this is how Mohammed must have felt that day in the Kaaba surrounded by the stone idols, the realization only just beginning to dawn upon him that the statues were lifeless and powerless, their godliness just an illusion.

Like him, I too wanted to destroy everything around me. I wanted to smash my phony idol. Avenge this betrayal.

But unlike him, I knew I couldn't. I was after all a woman.

Only a woman. A thing to be seen and felt but not heard, unless of course, she were to voice assent.

I knew now why people didn't speak out. Sometimes silence is easier.

I picked up the fax with the General's death warrant and ripped it.

'No!' Omar shouted.

It was too late. I swallowed the paper in one gulp.

'You fool!' he shouted. 'You destroyed the evidence!'

We were all the same underneath.

Covering my ears, I said, 'I don't believe you. Rani would never,' my voice broke. 'She's trying to protect him, can't you see? She loves him…'

Omar slapped his thigh, jolting me into paying attention. His voice seemed resigned as he tried one last time. 'Look, the reason I showed you all this is because you are close to her. You can help her. We can help her together. Are you with me?'

The answer was simple.

I looked into his eyes and said, 'No.'

The biggest mistake people make when they tell you not to trust someone is that they think you will trust them instead.

You see, I hadn't yet forgotten the time when Omar came to see you wearing that burqa. I was sure now that it was him. I knew that he had helped you get rid of Balgodi once before, when you could see no way out. I knew it was he who had filed the case against him. I knew you two went back a long way. What I didn't know was why he wanted to expose you now.

What I did know was that we all have many faces underneath the one we wear. That yours would be so terrifying, I could never have guessed.

You had played me, Rani, but you forgot, the price of betrayal is high. If you were a player, so was I.

You began this game, but I would be the one to end it.

Prosecutor: I read somewhere that when you begin the journey of revenge, start by digging two graves: one for your enemy and one for yourself. An eye for an eye, a limb for a limb – revenge can drive the best of us to utter destruction. But don't you think, Miss Khan, sometimes revenge is necessary?

Defendant: I think an eye for an eye will make the whole world blind.

Judge: Order, order. No laughing in court.

After that night, Omar's charms failed to lift my spirits. For me he was just a dreadful reminder of your betrayal. I still could not believe that you had known about the General's death, but had let me suffer the guilt during my breakdown. But I suppose anger was fuel and everyday I felt a little bit better, revenge egging me on to recovery.

I went regularly for the electric shocks, took all my medication on time and threw myself into the cause.

Perhaps I was in denial.

I spent the next few days trying to avoid him, but he caught me standing by the window one day.

'What are you looking at?'

I looked over my shoulder to see Omar standing behind me.

381

'I'm looking at the cuckoo bird.'

'Really, where?'

'See there.'

I nudged him towards the glass.

'That bird, the dark ugly one with the orange beak that looks like a scar.'

Omar's gaze inadvertently travelled towards my own scar.

'Over there,' I pointed to the window.

He looked away embarrassed.

'Can you see her?' Tapping the glass, I said, 'We call her koel.'

'Of course. The muse of many an Urdu poet.'

I nodded. 'She's known for her sweet voice. Not her looks, obviously.'

Omar smiled and said, 'She's also known for her ability to mimic.'

My turn to look away.

'Look, Nazo,' he pointed excitedly, 'it looks like she's building a nest in that tree.'

'No, Omar Sir, the koel never builds her own nest. She always stays in the nest of others. And do you know, when she has eggs, she hides them in a crow's nest. The crow brings them up, thinking they are its own.'

'But I have heard something else.'

'What?' I looked up slowly. His eyes were the colour of autumn leaves.

'Tell me, Nazo. Is it true that the bird throws out the eggs if she thinks someone else has touched them?'

I nodded slowly. 'Sometimes it is necessary.'

'Look, Nazo,' he hesitated, 'I'm sorry about the other night. I feel somehow as if I've broken your favourite toy. Pushed your idol off the pedestal and smashed it into a million pieces. Please forgive me.'

'My love for Rani Madam is not so weak.'

He nodded. 'We both just want the best for her. Well, it was nice getting to know you.'

I stepped back. 'You're ... leaving?'

'My work here is done.'

I looked up at him and then down at my toes. Something was sinking inside me. I didn't know what it was I was feeling – love, sorrow, excitement or rejection.

'Do you *have* to go?'

He smiled. 'Why? You want to come with me?'

I looked at the koel bird, her furtive glances, her neck bobbing up and down, as she tried to find a secure spot for her eggs in someone else's nest.

'I have to wait,' I said, 'until the eggs hatch.'

I was looking after the wrong child the day Omar finally left. He came to say goodbye and saw me feeding the boy with a baby's bottle, his long legs dangling off my lap and touching the floor.

'What's wrong with him?' he asked.

Once again, I saw him through the eyes of a stranger and I felt chilled to the bone. I grabbed the child to my chest and held him close. Perhaps it was the very first time, for he pulled away, surprised.

Omar seemed to understand. He took a step back.

'I see,' he said.

And he did. He seemed to have understood everything without a single exchange of words.

I was terrified. His power of perception shocked me. I should have known then, this Omar of yours was no ordinary person.

Prosecutor: Ah, but revenge is a strange emotion. Someone
  like me, however angry, would try to make a person
  understand their mistake rather than punish them.
  But someone like you might eliminate the root cause
  of the problem. I believe the word is murder. Horrible
  as it sounds, Your Honour, Miss Khan, in her rage,
  wanted to kill not just Rani but the entire Shah
  clan. She wanted to make sure the dynasty did not
  carry on. It is not a new idea. Many revolutionaries
  have adopted this method to end royal and political
  dynasties. But in this case, she killed our hope as
  well...

Omar's departure left a vacuum in me. I felt like a big gaping
ravine had opened up, and I once again found myself thinking of
things past.

'It's no use, thinking of things that are over and done with,'
Refugee would tell me. But my mind felt as if a great abyss was
sucking it in. The three bearded faces would come to me in my
dreams and I would wake up, gasping for air and wondering what
I had done to deserve this. I stopped going for the electric shocks,
forgot about my medicines. Even stopped going to the meetings.

And as if things weren't bad enough, *he* reappeared.

The General was back. Perhaps being blown to bits once and
squashed to a pulp the next time had increased his karma. This

time, he came back as a toy. And not just any toy but a hysterical laughing Jack-in-the-Box, the children's favourite toy. That laugh, I'd think every time the annoying toy popped out of its box, how can you not recognize that shrill piercing evil laugh. It sent a shiver through my bones every time I looked into its mad eyes, its tongue hanging out, its lips stretched into a moronic grin.

'I'm back,' it seemed to be saying. 'You'll never get rid of me. You can't bury the past. Murder catches up with you…'

'Oof,' I screamed one day as I was changing the wrong child's nappy. He was four and still refused to use the toilet. I had been playing a game of snakes and ladder with Refugee, and I was finally winning when the child called out, 'Chhi, chhi!'

Reluctantly I left the game, knowing that Refugee would turn a winning game into a losing battle by the time I got back.

'Chhi, chhi!' the wrong child was screaming as I came in. He sat there squalling in his own filth, his eyes closed and fists clenched. He bared his teeth like a dog when he saw me, drooling as he did so. For a minute, I felt an icy grip around my heart and I longed to reach out and pull him to me, to clean his face and plant a kiss. What had I done to this little creature? It wasn't his fault that he had been born to a woman who could not become his mother, and to a mother who could not be an ordinary woman.

I touched his face and pushed his hair out of his eyes. And there it was, the same dark eyes, the slight squint, the helpless gaze that was sure to melt my heart if I let it.

No, I could not risk it. If I gave in now, I would crumble.

I steadied myself.

'Off,' I said, as I pushed him away from myself.

'Mama,' he mumbled, and I tore my eyes away from his hapless, goofy grin.

'Mama,' he said angrily now, trying to pull me towards him.

'Don't,' I said, swallowing a dry painful lump.

'Mama, mama!'

'I am not your mother.'

He started screaming, flailing his arms and trying to put them around me.

'No, please.'

He lunged at me and I felt something wet splat against me.

'Oh no,' I said, as I saw a brown liquid stain the floor.

I picked him up and put him on the changing mat by the window.

'My God, I can hardly lift you now. You have got to stop this, child,' I said. 'You are old enough to use the toilet.'

I forced down a wave of nausea as I folded the foul-smelling cloth.

Just then he grabbed my hair and pulled. 'Mama!'

'Why are you making my life miserable?' I shouted. 'I am just a servant.'

'Mama,' he cried.

I looked around.

'Shhh! I am not your Mama.'

The child screamed.

Just then the toy Jack-in-the-Box jumped out and startled me.

'Shit!' I cried, as the nappy flew out of my hand and splattered on the carpet. 'That doll! That terrible doll,' I picked it up and slammed it against the wall. 'As if I didn't have enough work to do already!'

On an impulse, I opened the window and threw the laughing toy out. I stood there for a while, feeling the sea breeze caress my closed eyelids, filling me with a sense of freedom as I realized I was rid of the torturer, once again.

How was I to know that the wrong child would jump out after it?

⚖

The funeral was small. We stood in shocked silence, soaking in the unexpected rain. When they lifted his little body up for the burial, I ran after them.

'Stop,' the maulana said. 'Women are not allowed in the graveyard.'

I looked at you, but you looked away. I watched as they took my son away and, strangely, it was the first time I felt like his mother. A shrill primal cry rose from my throat.

'My son,' I cried, 'my child.'

'Be strong,' you said.

I pawed at his coffin. 'My son.'

'Nazo, please.'

'My son, my child.'

A few journalists looked at me curiously.

'That's enough, Nazo.'

My fingers slid across the open coffin. I touched his stiff little fingers. Cold. So bitterly cold. His small hand hung limp and lifeless, poking out of the white shroud. A cry emerged from the pit of my stomach.

'Come back,' I cried. 'Come back, my son.'

'He was *my* son not yours.'

I began to wail, a sharp piercing sound filled with longing.

'Stop,' you said.

Cut off. Ejected. I felt, once again, erased.

In the days that followed, I sank into a strange contemplative silence. Many days passed and I stayed inside my head. I spoke to no one and no one spoke to me. I went about my daily chores as if nothing had changed, yet feeling a strange numbing ache inside. I had read somewhere that when people had their arms or legs amputated, they continued to feel the pain where no limb existed. I knew now exactly how they felt.

Each time I came across any of his clothes or things, I felt as if something was slowly squeezing itself around my heart. One time, I came across his milk bottles and I felt I couldn't breathe.

But you went on with your daily life. People marvelled at how, despite being a mother in mourning, you showed such professionalism. Only I knew that you were heartless.

Do unto others as you'd have them do unto you. I used to think that was the most laughable of sayings I had ever heard. But suddenly it all began to make sense.

Not much time had passed when the Filipino nanny you'd hired to look after your daughter reported that she didn't respond much to anything. Fearing the same fate as the wrong child, you had her checked by the city's best paediatrician. With great regret, he reported that your daughter was deaf and mute.

You were shattered, less by her diagnosis and more by Balgodi's reaction.

'Well, thank God, she's just a girl,' he said, waving you away. 'We'll worry about who will marry her when the time comes. It's not like she has to go out and earn. In fact, it may even be a good thing – a woman who doesn't answer back,' he laughed.

Seeing the pain on your face, he got up and patted your shoulder. 'Okay, now don't look so worried. These things happen. It is God's will.'

You placed your head on his chest. After a few minutes, he gripped you tightly by the shoulders and held you back to face him.

'Now I want you to listen carefully to me, Rani,' his voice was low but menacing. 'From now on, you must keep her at home. Don't send her to school or to any birthday parties, not even to the park. I don't want the whole world to know you've given me another dumb child. They'll think it's God's curse or worse, there is something wrong with your eggs.'

You pulled away. Your eyes unblinking like that of a lizard.

'Now then, Rani darling,' he said, softening his tone and running his finger along the curve of your waist, 'when are you going to give me a real heir?'

⚖

That night, I found you snuggled in your daughter's little bed, your feet curled around her and your arm placed protectively across her chest. I found my throat tightening. Is this what I had been protecting you from? This very raw emotion of a mother's love that no one could deny. The very feeling I thought would make you weaker was making you stronger.

I watched the moon paint you both silver and then tiptoed to the small blue cupboard in the corner. Opening it, I gathered all of the wrong child's belongings and wrapped them in a cloth bundle. Later I buried everything in the back garden alongside the unnamed grave of your foetus.

I planted marigold seeds in the soil there. Afterwards I kept toiling the mud around it till my raw hands became chafed. It was only then that I felt some of the burden lighten.

In the morning, I asked you to send me for E.S.T. treatment. I wanted to start feeling again.

Prosecutor: There is a difference between ambition and obsession. Miss Khan is someone who gets what she wants at all costs. It wasn't luck or fate but cold-blooded calculations that got her to the place where she found herself contesting as a Party member, vying for a place in Madam Shah's own party!

Counsel: Miss Khan had every right to pursue her political career. In fact, Madam Shah encouraged her to do so.

Prosecutor: When a dog bites its owner, Your Honour, most people would put it to sleep, but not our Madam Shah. Poor Madam Shah kept trusting her blindly. In the end, she paid for it with her own life.

Counsel: Speculation!

Prosecutor: Exhibit F: Party nomination papers. It is no secret, Your Honour, that Miss Khan contested from Madam Shah's party as a forerunner in the re-election. What is not well known, however, is that she did not have the support of Madam herself.

Counsel: I would like to ask the Prosecutor, how would it be possible for my client to attain a ticket without the Party Chairperson's consent? My colleague's tales are turning from riddles to ridiculous.

Prosecutor: It is possible, Your Honour. Miss Khan launched a secret campaign while Madam was deep in grief over the death of her only son. Taking advantage of the distraction, Miss Khan ended up creating divisions within the party. Being childless herself

> and having no sympathy for a grieving mother, the
> heartless woman that Miss Khan is, she saw her
> chance and moved in for the kill. She lobbied till
> the acting Party Chief, unaware of the differences
> between Madam and her, issued her a ticket.

Counsel: Your Honour, my client's desire to contest shows
ambition not suspicion.

Prosecutor: But, Your Honour, this was no ordinary ambition.
This was a very dangerous act of dislodging the
leader. Her eye, you see, was on the endgame.

⚖

The government was dismissed. The court levied charges of
corruption, the Opposition accused you of incompetence, and
the public rose against you because of the high inflation. You
accepted your fate quietly, submissively, nicely.

Mice are nice, Rani.

Once again it was me who brought you back to your senses.

The electric shocks, repulsive though they were, were
beginning to shake me out of my stupor. And that is when it
occurred to me. Perhaps you too needed a shock…

I raised a motion for a Party ticket. As your secretary, I argued,
I knew the workings of the party better than anyone else. I wanted
to contest.

It was only after the Party granted me a ticket, not bothering
to ask you for your opinion in your silent uncaring state, that you
snapped out of your grief. You came back to work.

You ignored me. And I ignored you. I told myself that you
needed me. I suppose I was in denial, behaving like an addict who
consoles himself that the drug is addicted to him rather than the
other way around.

In private, I continued to grieve for the child I had never felt anything for when he was alive, and you continued to grieve for the child in front of you, one who was totally unaware of the affection you showered on her.

How I envied that child.

Defendant: The endgame? The game had not even begun,
    Omar Sir. I did what I had to do because nobody
    else would have. You see, nobody knew her the way
    I did. People were afraid of Rani Madam's cold
    demeanour, but only I knew that to create warmth,
    it is necessary to light a fire.

⚖

Elections came and elections went. The Party lost badly. The
Opposition swept to power. But the new government was even
more corrupt. People revolted. Not even a year had passed when
the assembly was dissolved and fresh elections were called for.

This was your chance to resurrect yourself and you knew it.
But what did you do? Instead of political planning, you were
family planning.

You, who'd never believed in God, travelled to a neighbouring
country to get the blessings of a hocus-pocus holy man. The more
I knew you, Rani, the less I understood you.

'Why are you doing this?' I asked when I found out.

'None of your business, Nazo.'

'It is my business.'

'You are not my PA any more.'

'I'm your political opponent now.'

'We are in the same party, you stupid fool.'

'Politics within the party. You have competition now, Madam.
The party is divided about your ability to lead. They want a
new chair.'

You placed your elbows on the desk and held your head in your hands.

'Nazo, what do you really want?'

'I want to know why you are vying for power when at the end of the day, all you are is a housewife who wants to breed. Do you know what they call you behind your back? They call you the Perpetually Pregnant Prime Minister. That's what you've made of your father's political party.'

You gripped the edge of the desk and your knuckles turned white. I wondered if I had gone too far.

But I was wrong. You swallowed the lump in your throat and rolled your hands into tight fists. When you looked up, your eyes were red rimmed from holding back the tears.

'Why can't I be both, Nazo? Why won't you let me? Thatcher did it. Indira Gandhi did it.'

I have to admit I was surprised. I didn't expect you to fight back. How could I explain to you that neither Thatcher nor Indira were married to cruel and corrupt drunkards. Or should I say, *devoted* to.

It was time to pull out the trump card.

'Madam,' I said. 'In the coming elections, I will run against you.'

You called my threat a bluff. But when you held the 5 × 7 photo in your hands, the reality of my words sunk in.

'You want me to withdraw?'

'On the contrary, I want you to contest. But only if you will take your job seriously. If you won't lead, I will.'

'Nazo,' you said, your voice softening. 'Did we really care so much for each other? Was there ever such intimacy between us?'

You caught me off guard. I looked away and you snatched the photo from my hands.

'An honest mistake,' you said, ripping it in two.

I knew the situation was past threats. If you didn't understand the seriousness of the matter now, you never would. Still I tried.

'You can't keep going like this, Rani Madam. You'll lose everything you have worked for. You have to choose.'

'I'm a woman first, a politician second. It is my right to have a family, like it or not.'

'Then take a backseat. There are others to lead the party.'

'Ha,' you laughed. 'The Nation won't accept them. The public wants me because I am my father's legacy.'

'And I am yours. Let me take over.'

'You?'

I could see disgust and surprise alternating on your face.

'Yes.'

I knew what I had to do next would not be easy for you, but it was the only way to shake you out of your inertia.

I produced the fax. Once Omar had shown me the original, it was easy to trace a copy of the General's death warrant.

Your face paled. 'I would have expected this from Balgodi, Nazo. But never from you.'

'What can I say, Madam. You don't know me well.'

'Oh, I know you very well, you knifing bitch. I knew all along what you were after.'

I shrugged my shoulders. 'Power is a strange thing. It gets to the best of us.'

You threw your head back and laughed. 'Even if I made you the Party Chair, the public would never accept you. You keep forgetting, Nazo, you are a nobody. No family background, no vision, no brains. Just a stupid tagalong. I never should have taken pity on you.'

You leaned in close, your eyes narrowed, your voice deepened. 'You have seen my friendship so far, Nazo. Now you will see my enmity. Not long before I'm back in the PM's chair and then...'

The plan had worked.

I could hear the fight in your voice. You were back in form. What could I do, Rani? Despite all your betrayals, my heart still urged to shout, 'Long live Rani Shah!'

I guess the power of love is *stronger than the love of power.*

Prosecutor: If Rani Shah had been able to complete her campaign, had her life not been cut short, she would have been re-elected. Perhaps that's why she was eliminated.

Counsel: She was not a martial law dictator that the only way to get rid of her was to kill her, Mr Omar.

Judge: Order, order. No laughing in the court.

Counsel: I beg your pardon, Your Honour, but I do feel Mr Omar is being dramatic.

Prosecutor: Ah, but you forget, Counsel, that a dead PM is often the best election campaign a party can have.

⚖

You called it blackmail, but when a parent threatens a child to get him to study, is that blackmail? No, Rani, it's called doing it for the child's own good. I could only hope that one day you would realize this. But for now, it had snapped you out of your torpor and you poured all your energy into lobbying. Though you made sure to leave me out.

I didn't mind, for, as you once said, in your scheme of things, I was a zero. My job was to stand behind you and edge you on – to victory.

⚖

You were leading the pre-poll counts by a sweeping margin. You didn't need to campaign this hard, but it was as if a spirit had possessed you. I didn't even need to bring up the photos. In fact, I had burned and buried the negatives long ago. I had known that the mere threat of a scandal big enough to stain your Mother Teresa image was all that was needed to jumpstart you.

But this time, you seemed not just to be going with the flow but directing it. It was as if your old fighting spirit had returned. Once again you were the leader who'd lead the Nation out of darkness. It was as if you had awoken from a long deep sleep. You were the Rani from New York, the one who would do anything for her people. The saviour. The prophet. The leader in you had returned.

It made me think, something was not quite right.

When Omar came back to see you, I was convinced that things were not as they seemed. One day you even caught us sitting on your sofa and talking as equals, but you did nothing to stop us.

You neither acknowledged me nor ignored me. I constantly wondered if this was forgiveness or acceptance. After all, now I too was a contesting member of the party. Although I gave up the idea of standing against you, for a more preoccupying thought on my mind these days was that of the death threats.

As your campaign gained momentum, so did the threats. Word had it that the Jihadists were out to get you. 'All we want is restrain,' they said in a video statement. 'A woman's place is at home. We are only trying to show her the right path.'

'And what if she continues to contest?' the anchor asked them.

'Then we will do what should be done with disobedient women.'

I felt a chill in the still afternoon heat when I heard those words. But I shrugged it off. You were Rani Shah. You were invincible. Or at least you should be. The show had to go on.

There was an audience waiting...

And so we went on with our campaigns – you with your PMship and me with my humble local candidacy – presenting a united front. It was for the best.

Was it?

Whatever emotions raged inside us, we both came together when we campaigned for the party, your father's pride, your legacy and our reason to unite.

It was, you see, all about the bigger picture.

We knew there was danger, but the day the first bomb went off, we were both taken by surprise. It wasn't fear that haunted us but something bigger. A feeling of impotency, of hopelessness, a stale sense of melancholy that haunted us.

We all have to die someday. But you seemed to be hoping otherwise. Love does that to people, I had heard. It makes them want to live forever. It makes them afraid of death, of the inevitable. For three days and four nights, you woke up soaked in cold sweat, clutching your daughter as if you'd never see her again.

On the fourth day, you called me into your office.

'I'm going away for a few days.'

That's right, I thought. Run away at the first sign of danger.

'When I come back...'

I will quit politics and raise a dozen children. Just as the General and his Jihadists wanted.

'Nazo, did you even hear what I said?'

'Yes, Rani Madam,' I pulled myself out of my thoughts and nodded.

'You didn't hear a word.' You heaved a dramatic sigh, then said, 'I asked you to get this list of things ready by the time I come back. Please go over it now. As you are obviously distracted.'

I looked down, expecting nappies and cooking batons, but instead I saw a list of campaign materials. To say I was surprised would not be a lie.

'Rani Madam, what's all this?'

'Sorry to disappoint you, Nazo, but I'm going ahead with the rallies.'

'You are?'

I stared blankly, unable to comprehend this courageous side of you. I would have thought you'd bundle up shop after the incident and stay out. But you surprised me, Rani. Every time I thought you fell a bit more, chipped a bit deeper, peeled a little harsher, you emerged even finer. Perhaps my eyes hadn't mistaken a stone for an idol, after all. I still wasn't sure where I stood with the evidence Omar had showed me, and this just proved to me that you really were who you were meant to be. It was then that the precariousness of the situation struck me.

'But…' I took a deep breath.

'Yes?' you lifted a perfectly-arched eyebrow.

Perhaps you mistook my concern for your security as my own insecurity, for your face hardened in defiance.

'Look,' you said, 'my mind is made up. I'm going ahead.'

'But you can't,' I argued. 'You can't go to the rally. It's not safe.'

You let out a laugh. 'That's very sweet of you, Nazo. But the thing is, people are expecting me. You see, I'm Leader Shah's daughter, the true heir. People want me.'

'So do the Jihadists. There's an open threat to your life. They'll never let you…'

'I will do what I like.'

'But, Rani, it's not safe…'

You drew in a sharp breath. My words seemed to be sinking in and I could see you were thinking about it. Finally you spoke. 'I'm not a coward. Besides, hiding won't make me safer, Nazo. If death is my fate then it will find me. And if I'm meant to live…'

'We only get one life, Rani.'

'I might as well use it.'

Your mobile rang. We both looked up, startled by the high-pitched ringing. There was, I noticed, no number on the caller ID.

You pressed it to your ears.

'Rani Shah speaking.'

The voice at the other end was threatening. You clicked on the speaker and whispered, 'Page the tracing team.'

I hurried to the pager just as the voice said, 'Stay home. A woman's place is at home. Shame on that bastard husband of yours who sends you out to work. Open your eyes to Allah's word. Stay home.'

'Are you threatening me?' you shouted.

You had to challenge him.

'I'm warning you,' the voice growled.

A soft click and he hung up.

'Losers, cowards! Who would have thought these big bearded men would be so afraid of women! Bastards. All of them bastards.'

You lit a cigarette and took a long hard drag.

'Nazo! Get my campaign schedule ready. Now!'

'But, Rani Madam, you can't ignore their warning.'

'I see warnings every day, Nazo. If I started taking them all seriously...'

And suddenly you started laughing. Your laughter cut the tension in the room like a knife slicing butter. 'Catch,' you said, tossing the empty cigarette pack at me.

I missed it. Like all the other things I had missed before this.

Judge: Mr Omar, why are you so convinced that Miss Khan murdered Madam Shah?

Prosecutor: Because, Your Honour, I know this woman is lying!

Judge: How can you be so sure? Mr Omar, the court orders you to tell us any information you are withholding, no matter how damaging to the deceased...

⚖

Later that evening, as you were briefing me on the campaign, Omar burst into the room.

'Rani, oh thank God you haven't left.'

'I haven't, yet.'

'Rani, your life is in danger.'

'My life,' you laughed. 'My life was never mine to keep, Omar.'

'Rani, you can do so much. Don't play into the hands of these mad men. They are trying to coax you out so they can ... so they can...'

'Kill me?'

Omar looked into your eyes and said, 'You are needed, Rani. Much needed.'

I thought I saw an exchange, some sort of private look, and I knew then where I had seen it before.

'Nazo,' you gestured me to leave.

I was hardly out of the door when you said, 'Don't worry,

Omar, my dear. I've cancelled the rallies we had planned. But what they don't know is that I have organized new ones.'

⚖

When Omar stepped out of the room, I was waiting for him.

'So here you are again.'

He stopped at the sound of my voice, but he didn't turn around.

'It's good to see you, Omar Sir. Always nice to see you in your own clothes.'

'Sorry?' he turned to face me.

'I never did understand what you were doing in a burqa that day? I mean why the elaborate disguise?'

Omar stared blankly at me, so I continued, 'You know when you helped Rani Madam put Balgodi behind bars. Remember?'

But the revelation did little to shock him. Omar smiled and said, 'I underestimated you, Nazo. You seem to know everything.'

'Not everything,' I replied, despite the sarcasm in his tone. 'Some things I would never have learnt about your help.'

The muscles around his jaw tensed, though his smile stayed in place.

I was beginning to enjoy this. 'But,' I continued, 'never mind our little secret, tell me about yours and Rani's. Don't worry, I'm only asking about the veil. Was it her idea?'

The smile got deeper, wider and even more strained. 'You surprise me, Nazo,' he said. 'For someone who seems to know so much, you say very little.'

'I'm not a tattletale.'

The smile disappeared. Omar looked grimly at me. 'Thing is, Nazo, you forget that I'm a lawyer too.'

'So?'

'If I had filed the case as myself or even as a man, Balgodi would have tracked me down. And killed me.'

'Or,' I paused, but only for a second, 'he would have suspected you of being her lover.'

'Nazo!'

'Omar.'

My voice was calm even as his face turned a deep red.

'I know it's her you were scared for. I know it's Rani Madam you didn't want him to hurt. I know, Omar Sir. I know because I would have done the same. Look, Omar Sir, I can see that we both love the same woman. What I don't understand is why you collected all that evidence against her. You don't betray someone you love like this. You used me too. Trying to turn me against her. You wanted me to go public with it, didn't you? You pretended you cared for me. But it's Rani you wanted and when she didn't leave Balgodi for you, you tried to destroy her – through me!'

'Enough!' He turned to leave, his eyes wide and his face flushed.

'No. You can't just leave. You have to tell me, Omar!' I tried to keep him from going, but he shrugged me away.

'Just drop the act,' he turned back slowly, his face still red, his forehead creased. 'I know, Nazo, I know what you have been upto. We all know that someone has been leaking important information about her whereabouts...'

'And you think it's me?'

'Who else hates Rani so much?'

'You.'

For a moment, he looked as if he would hit me, but then he took a step back.

'You think I hate her? I? The one person who has laid down everything for her?'

That was supposed to be my line, I remember thinking.

He stared silently at me when I didn't reply. When he finally spoke, his voice was weary. 'If at all, Nazo, it's my fault, for thinking you'd understand. I never should have trusted you with it. It was a moment of weakness. I hated to see you suffer. But I realize now, I shouldn't have told you.'

'So then why did you?' my voice was cold, my tone harsh and accusatory.

But Omar seemed impervious to it. He came close, so close that I was breathing his breath. And then he said, 'For every good reason there is to lie, Nazo, there is a better reason to tell the truth.'

Prosecutor: Your Honour, I read somewhere that what we do for ourselves dies with us, but what we do for others lives on forever. It makes us immortal. We had many expectations from Madam Rani Shah as the PM. And so we became obsessed with what she hadn't done and forgot what she did do. Would you agree, Miss Khan?

Defendant: In her absence is her presence, Omar Sir. If only you could see what was right before you...

Prosecutor: Please, stop your riddles, Miss Khan. For God's sake, stop it. It's hard enough for me to accept that Rani is gone. Your Honour, there is something I wish to tell the court. You see the reason I am so sure Miss Khan killed Rani is because it was I who told Nazo about...

Defendant: Your Honour! I have something to say first!

Judge: There is no need to scream, Miss Khan.

Defendant: Sorry. It's because I have something very important to say.

Judge: Yes, Miss Khan?

Defendant: I just remembered that on the day of the murder, Rani Madam received a threatening phone call, and I had placed a request for it to be traced. Perhaps if the number has been obtained...

Judge: The court orders Telecommunications to provide details of the trace.

And then came the day when you chose to rally in the Capital, the playground of death.

'Do you know how many politicians have died in that city?' Balgodi asked, as you were getting ready.

'Yes,' you answered, looking at him through the mirror, 'three.'

'Oh,' he said, as if hoping to be provided with a less accurate figure.

'And counting,' I said.

Balgodi seemed to shiver as he walked up to you and said, 'Perhaps you should go on your own.'

You turned around sharply.

'You are coming with me,' you said, placing a firm hand on his wrist.

'Oh no *ji* no! The Jihadists have probably laid a death trap for us there. I don't think you should go either.'

'I'm going, Balgodi, whether you come with me or not. People are waiting for us.'

He stepped back just as I stepped forward.

'I will come with you, Madam.'

You smiled.

And my fate was sealed.

Despite multiple threats by the Jihadists, you ventured out. You put on your bravest face and kissed your daughter goodbye. 'Mummy has work to do,' you told the little creature whose world sound couldn't penetrate. I remember her tiny hands waving, her fingers outstretched as if trying to catch some magical residue you might leave behind. I remember you looking back at the little girl, your gaze lingering a second too long. I remember you stalling, hesitating, running back for one last hug before proceeding for the security briefing. I remember the look of panic on your face as the doors sealed behind you.

At the security briefing, they said it was perfectly safe. Your vehicle was bulletproof, or so they said. Barriers were in place, they assured us, although later when we got there, we saw only flimsy plastic partitions that people kicked down easily. They told us cell phone signals had been jammed so no device could be detonated, but at the rally, we saw people talking on mobiles all around us.

'This is the tightest security cordon ever,' the Army officer in charge informed us at the briefing.

'No,' I said, 'the tightest was when the General's plane crashed.'

'Don't joke,' the Army officer said.

'Not at all,' I replied. 'I never joke about death.'

It was at that moment that Omar came back from wherever it was that he had disappeared to.

'Hello, Omar Sir,' I called out. 'From the way you disappear, one would think you were Mullah Omar of the Jihadists!'

Ignoring my remark, he went straight past me and up to you.

'It's not safe,' he said, looking deep into your eyes. If the urgency in his voice weren't so earnest, you two would have looked like lovers about to elope. 'You can't go, Rani. A journalist friend has intercepted direct Secret Service reports. Look, they clearly state that the Jihadist threat is real. Bin Laden has declared a woman's government unIslamic. His supporters think killing you would grant them a one-way ticket to heaven. Rani, do not go to that rally unless you have a death wish.'

Any sane person would have at that moment turned back, but

not you. You threw your head back and laughed. 'Papa used to say, don't stop living for the fear of death.'

'Rani, your father preferred to die than bow down to the General. You can't do that.'

'He was a man of principle.'

'And you are the mother of a child who needs you.'

That's right, I thought to myself. Throw in the motherhood card! Now I would *have* to step in to prevent this from turning into a third-rate soap opera.

'Rani Madam,' I said, 'perhaps you should take Omar Sir's warning seriously. The rally can be reorganised.'

'You stay out of this, Nazo,' Omar said. Holding you by the shoulders, he shook you. 'Rani, listen to me, there is danger.'

'I'm going.'

He stepped back. His voice had a defeated tenor to it as he said, 'All right. If you've made up your mind, I won't stop you. But before you go, there is something you should know.'

'Yes?'

He hesitated.

'Tell me, Omar.'

He looked at the Army officer who coughed and excused himself.

He looked at me and I looked right back at him.

'I've heard rumours that there are people plotting to kill you. People close to you.'

I moved closer.

'Even if they regret it now, there is nothing they can do to stop it. Rani, it is risky.'

For a change, you stood your ground. 'Even crossing the road is risky,' you said.

'You don't have to take this risk. You're a mother, a wife ... a woman.'

You looked straight at him and said, 'Omar, even superwoman has to take a risk sometimes.'

And then you did something I had never seen you do in my entire life. You winked.

⚖

The three of us stood outside as the convoy of cars rolled out. A sleek black SUV stopped at your side. We watched as you climbed into the huge black car and disappeared. I felt as if a giant eagle had swallowed you up. But then you rolled down the tinted window and poked out your head.

'What's the matter, Omar? Don't want to cover this event?'

Omar looked away.

'Sorry, Rani. You're on your own on this one,' he flung his hands in the air and shook his head. 'You never did listen to me.' He looked away and I thought I saw a solitary tear slide down his cheek. 'Goodbye, Rani.'

I watched as he walked away without a single glance backwards. You turned your attention to me.

'What about you, Nazo? It doesn't get any more political than this.'

I looked at Omar's receding figure and then at you. You were smiling. I took a deep breath and climbed in after you. Immediately the sharp smell of leather made my head reel. It was true. You smell fear before you feel it. I knew now why the General had insisted that the American ambassador fly with him.

Keep your friends close but your enemies even closer.

Not that it stopped him from getting killed.

'This is it,' you said, breaking into my thoughts. 'It's the final countdown.'

How was I to know that, for once, you were telling the truth?

Clerk: Sir, the trace report is here.

Judge: Well?

Clerk: The sim card is unregistered, but...

Judge: Yes?

Clerk: It was bought using the Prosecutor Mr Omar's credit card.

⚖

Hundreds awaited you at the Capital's political rally. I could see the free food stalls and free buses that had been used to lure them in. I wondered if you noticed them too.

But your focus was singular. As soon as we arrived, you got out of the car, pushing away all Party delegates with a wave of your palm. You walked up to the podium.

At first there was complete silence, then a low rising. The crowd seemed to be closing in on you. Slowly. Steadily. Seamlessly. You tapped the mike. People stopped but did not back down.

'My fellow countrymen,' your voice boomed out, but there was a low tremor to it, making your words sound hollow. 'My brothers and my sisters,' you tried again. 'I, Rani Shah, salute you!'

People listened but did not cheer. I saw an old woman with deep furrows in her forehead staring straight at you. The sorrow, the rejection, the sheer indifference on her face was enough to make my skin crawl.

You placed your hand over the mike and looked at me.

'Is this even on?'

I climbed up and tapped the mike. We were losing them. They were starting to chatter amongst themselves. I shook the mike. A boom of static and a loud screech, like nails on a blackboard, made the crowd look up. I held on.

'*Salaam* people,' I basked in the attention. 'Look up! You don't have to go to the government with your pleas any more. The government itself has come to you. Come forward and meet your leader.'

A man with a chequered turban and holes in his vest shouted back, 'Listen, listen, listen to these liars.' I noticed the plate of free food in his hand.

Another man stood up. 'Today these leaders have come to us for votes, because they need us. Tomorrow they'll forget us, again. We won't see them till the next five years.'

You snatched the mike from me. 'I have served you like my father before me, faithfully and sincerely.'

'Liar, liar, liar Shah!' a few media people joined in. 'Where are the changes you promised? Where is the literacy? Where is the repeal to Rape Law? Liar, Liar, Liar Shah, Rani Shah, Liar Shah!'

You were losing patience, I could see. You fumbled and fussed over the mike. Once again I stepped in where you fell short. Snatching the mike from you, I shouted, 'Silence! Rani Shah is here to serve, just like her father before her. Long live the Shahs!'

'We've had enough!' someone shouted back. 'We won't be fooled any more. Times have changed.'

I cupped my palms around the mike and said, 'Time doesn't change, my friend. It only passes.'

I motioned for the loud speakers to be turned on full strength and started a counter slogan of 'Long live the Shahs'. For a few seconds, the restless buzzing subsided. Taking advantage of the lull, you stepped forward and took the mike from me.

'Listen to me, my countrymen,' you said, your voice clear and powerful this time around. 'You can't see God, but you believe in Him. I can't show you proof, but I ask you to have faith in me. Like you did in my father before me. My father gave you a roof over your head, cloth over your body and bread in your belly. Look how he transformed a ghetto into a model township, and look how the General turned it into a no-go gangster area. If you don't want me I will go away. Allah knows how much I have sacrificed already to be here with you. My home, my son, my father ... but if you support me, I promise to fight for your rights ... It will take time. Change doesn't happen overnight. I can't turn around the General's law instantly, but I can assure you, I won't give up. Tell me, are you with me?'

The zest, the fervour, the vigour as you led the chant of 'Long live Leader Shah' was unsurpassable. The crowds rose up in appreciation. Never had I heard a more passionate speech, never had I seen a woman sweep a crowd off its feet without baring a single bit of flesh. Instead, it was as if you had stripped off all facades of gender and class. You stood there with your soul bared. The crowds stared in rapture.

You had them. You had them in your palm, Rani, because today, you were speaking from the heart.

'I will get you justice. I will get you food. I will provide shelter. I will see that your children get the schools they deserve and your daughters are not punished for being born a woman.'

'Jiye Shah, long live Rani Shah!' people began to cheer.

'I will give my life for you. I am not afraid.'

'Jiye Rani Shah.'

The crowds chanted as if possessed.

'Long live the Shahs!'

I stood still as if under some sort of spell. Was this real or had I travelled back in time? As I listened, I closed my eyes and imagined myself falling through the black whorls of time. It was 1983 and you were speaking at a rally in Downtown Manhattan. You were once again young and innocent, untouched by greed and corruption, free from the pull of family, unaddicted to power. You were waving to the small crowd that had gathered there to hear you. When they started clapping, you turned to me and said, 'Not long now, Nazo.'

The noise was getting louder and when I opened my eyes, I saw that the crowds had moved in close. Dangerously close. There was a rising, a kind of stirring, and suddenly the crowds tussled towards you. They wanted a piece of you. What had I missed? What could you have possibly said to get them charging with such vigour? All I knew was that we needed to get you back in the car. Together, the guards and I helped you get to the car. We pushed you in and locked the doors. The car began to rock from side to side as people pushed against it.

'What happened?' I somehow got into the car and asked, my voice so high pitched that it sounded unrecognizable to my ears.

'I told them a story.'

'A story?'

You nodded, calm and serene, despite the crowds pressing against the windows.

'Must have been some story.'

'It was the story of our country.'

'Rani Madam, just what did you say to them?' I asked, as some people shouted your name with great fervour while others threw rocks with such force that I felt the bulletproof glass would shatter.

'I told them the story of a country whose founder was an Ismaili, its president Shia, its prime minister Sunni, its army Punjabi, its bureaucrats Muhajirs, its scientists Ahmedi, its peasants Hindu, its workers Christian, its teachers lazy, its doctors greedy, its labourers hungry, its politicians corrupt, its biryani Sindhi, its naan Afghani and its youth, still hopeful.'

'Madam?' I stared incredulously.

'Nazo, where are we heading? Why are we lying to each other constantly? Why can't we all just be what we want to be? I don't want differences to mean distance any more. I want us to accept each other. I want them to embrace each other.'

Like I have embraced you.

Aloud I said, 'Be careful.'

'I am past caring. I want them to react. I want them to think about my words.'

I could see the old you. The one who knew exactly what she wanted.

'If this country is going to sort itself out, it needs to face its reality. You can't solve a problem if you don't think there is a problem.'

You were so open and exposed, yet you seemed fearless. I, on the other hand, could feel my hands trembling, my palms wet with cold sweat.

'You took a risk,' I said. 'It could be the last speech you give.'

'What can I say, Nazo? Every story begins with an end.'

Prosecutor: At exactly 5.13 p.m., she was shot... You were the last person to see her alive, Miss Khan. What were her last words?

Defendant: Don't stop living for the fear of death.

Prosecutor: And what did you say in reply, Miss Khan?

Defendant: Don't die for the fear of living.

And then, there it was. The moment when you opened the sun roof and waved to your supporters. A gunshot, followed by a blast. Blood everywhere. I reached out to protect you, but when I raised my hand, blood dripped down my wrist. A dull ache rose up my abdomen and I realized ... it was I who had been shot. I looked up to see you smiling benignly at me. In your hand, a small steel contraption with smoke rising out of its nozzle.

Forgive me, Nazo, but for me to live, you had to die.

Prosecutor: Let me remind you, Miss Khan, that you are under oath. I will ask you one final time: did you kill Rani Shah?

Defendant: Nobody killed her.

Judge: Miss Khan, please answer the question. Did you kill Madam Rani Shah?

Defendant: What does it matter who killed whom, Your Honour? Death comes to all of us. We all have to go back to our Maker one day. And we all go empty handed.

Prosecutor: Your Honour, once again Miss Khan is dodging the question with the cunning of a chess player!

Defendant: A game of chess, yes, that's what it was, Omar Sir.

Prosecutor: Game's over, now.

Defendant: And now the king and the pawn must both go back in the same box. At least in death, we are all equal.

⚖

The blood shone a bright red. I touched the wound and thought, if I had known then, what I know now, would I have let you do it?

Not that I could have stopped you, Rani. You always said that the world was divided into two kinds of people: those who knew what to do and those who waited to be told. You always did what you wanted. Dare no one could have told you otherwise.

Still, I wish I had tried. Perhaps then, in those last few moments after the blast, when you wiped the blood from my eyes, I would have looked up at you and said, 'Don't blame yourself, it wasn't your fault. Go and live your life. Be the mother, the wife, the woman, you always wanted to be.'

But that would be a lie. Like you once said, in fear we recognize each other. And you had recognized me. So many times, with reason or without, I had pretended to be you, Rani.

Now, it was my turn.

THE VERDICT

Bailiff: The honourable human rights lawyer Mr Omar has presented many fine arguments against Miss Nazneen Khan's case. Although his words evoke passion, unfortunately the scale of justice only tips towards hard evidence. As such, he is unable to provide any concrete proof that suggests Miss Khan's presence in the car that day was for any reason other than being Madam Rani Shah's trusted employee and confidante. Therefore, the court releases Miss Khan without charge.

Prosecutor: What? That's injustice!

Judge: Order in the court. Mr Omar is reminded to observe court conduct.

Prosecutor: But this is insane! All evidence points at her. I know she killed Rani! She's a murderer.

Judge: I'm warning you, Mr Omar. Now, Miss Khan, you are free to go. However, the court advises you to refrain from any political participation and rallying in the near future.

Defendant: Of course, Your Honour. I have already decided to leave politics and return to normal life … for the time being at least. Thank you, My Lord, for believing in me.

⚖

'The judge sold out.' 'No justice in this land.' 'Everything is fixed.' The court buzzed with shocked murmurs and then, all of a sudden, there was complete silence. People watched as the accused took off her glasses and adjusted her white hijab. A flick of the wrist, a nod of the head, and a new hum rose through the speculating crowd. Whispers rode high as people marvelled at the striking resemblance between the poor servant girl in the dock and the dead politician.

When the cameras approached, the woman quickly bowed her head and turned away from the flashing lights. The court was adjourned and the crowd trickled out, the press following close behind, amidst loud grumbles of a bribed verdict.

'The whole trial was staged!'

'A waste of time.'

'The judge was bought.'

'The case was a farce!'

'Justice has sold out in the Nation.'

The muttering faded as people poured out onto the streets. Soon the court was empty. Footsteps echoed as the defendant stepped down and the lawyer hung up his cloak.

'Omar,' a voice called out and the prosecutor stopped in his tracks.

'I never knew you loved me so much.'

The lawyer turned around slowly. When he looked up, his face was pale, almost as if he had seen a ghost.

'Or that you were such a good lawyer.'

The prosecutor seemed to waver, but only for a second. He gripped the edge of the table. 'Rani?' he whispered.

She held up her hand.

'Three weeks from now, we will begin again where we left off, far away from here. I will be waiting for you and for my daughter.

You will bring her to me, won't you?' she reached out to touch his shoulder. 'I'm counting on you, Omar.'

And before he could utter the words, she was gone. Only the faint echo of a whispered name remained.

'Rani,' he said, more to himself than to the receding figure. 'Rani, was that really you?'

The woman kept on walking, her footsteps fading fast.

Not even a backward glance. Omar let out a long slow breath. For once he was glad he had lost an argument.

The lights dimmed and the shadows grew long. Silence gathered in the airless courtroom. The lawyer stood where he was.

'Poor Nazo,' he finally said.

'What's so poor about her?' a cleaner sweeping behind him asked.

Omar shook his head and said nothing. He waited till the sweeper had finished cleaning and then he too got up to leave.

Before turning off the lights, he turned to the vacant bench and said, 'Your Honour, once upon a time there was a handmaiden who wished to be the queen. Only she did not know that in this land, rulers are born, not chosen.'

Love me or hate me, both are in my favour.
If you love me, I will live in your heart forever.
And if you hate me, I will always be on your mind.

The grave has become a shrine. More so, because overnight an epitaph has appeared on the tombstone. It is written in red, and in daylight, it looks like blood on stone. Some say it's a quote from a famous playwright. Shakespeare perhaps. And why not? People say you loved books.

But then, *people will say anything…*

Acknowledgements

This book began as a fun 'past time', when I joined a writing circle, soon after my daughter was born. I was living in London at the time and on a visit to the Tate Modern one day, while my little girl slept peacefully in her pram, I came across a photography exhibition titled 'Missing People'. These were people who had disappeared or were presumed missing, possibly dead. Most were victims of their circumstances, but there were a few who had chosen to remain hidden from the world. One such person was the Palestinian terrorist/liberator Leila Khalid, who had undergone several plastic surgeries to hide her identity and carry out her operations. It was from there that the seeds of the novel were sown in my head. At the same time, I had been interested in gender-based research on female politicians in South Asia and how they negotiate power in a patriarchal society. I was interested in the idea of choice feminism and whether in the case of Muslim women leaders it hampers or empowers them. Combining academic research with a fictional (wild) imagination, the result was *Nobody Killed Her*.

Along the way there have been many benefactors who have helped this book stand on its feet. From it's very first reader Diya, whose encouragement was key, to the legal eagles who deemed it unpublishable (and in doing so made me revise it to a better story), to the unyielding alchemist, Kanishka Gupta who revived it, to the beautiful Minakshi Thakur whose faith in the book was unmatched. A heartfelt thanks to Marti Leimbach for her incredible kindness and writerly support, and to Dr Degraeve for letting me write at work. A big shout out to all my friends for their babysitting help, emotional support and last-minute proofreading: Zeenia, Naheed, Perviz, Najia, S.R., Nadia Alyafai, Shaila, Jyoti, Manish, Aida and Violetta – and to all those who have touched my heart with their kindness. A very special thank you to my children Danyal and Selina Maya who are my lifelines and without whom I would be incomplete, and my superhero and biggest critic, Shahzeb Jillani, and to Ami and Abbu for love always!